CORRUPTION
OF BLOOD

Also by the author

Justice Denied
Material Witness
Reversible Error
Immoral Certainty
Depraved Indifference
The Piano Teacher
No Lesser Plea
Badge of the Assassin

ROBERT K. TANENBAUM
CORRUPTION OF BLOOD

A DUTTON BOOK

C 1

DUTTON
Published by the Penguin Group
Penguin Books USA Inc., 375 Hudson Street,
New York, New York 10014, U.S.A.
Penguin Books Ltd, 27 Wrights Lane,
London W8 5TZ, England
Penguin Books Australia Ltd, Ringwood,
Victoria, Australia
Penguin Books Canada Ltd, 10 Alcorn Avenue,
Toronto, Ontario, Canada M4V 3B2
Penguin Books (N.Z.) Ltd, 182–190 Wairau Road,
Auckland 10, New Zealand

Penguin Books Ltd, Registered Offices:
Harmondsworth, Middlesex, England

First published by Dutton, an imprint of Dutton Signet,
a division of Penguin Books USA Inc.
Distributed in Canada by McClelland & Stewart Inc.

First Printing, November, 1995
10 9 8 7 6 5 4 3 2 1

 REGISTERED TRADEMARK—MARCA REGISTRADA

LIBRARY OF CONGRESS CATALOGING-IN-PUBLICATION DATA

Tanenbaum, Robert.
    Corruption of blood / Robert K. Tanenbaum.
      p. cm.
    ISBN 0-525-93870-2
    1. Kennedy, John F (John Fitzgerald), 1917–1963—Fiction.
I. Title.
PS3570.A52C67   1995
813'.54—dc20   95-12803
                                         CIP

Printed in the United States of America
Set in Plantin Regular
Designed by Leonard Telesca

PUBLISHER'S NOTE
This is a work of fiction. Names, characters, places, and incidents either are the products of the author's imagination or are used fictitiously, and any resemblance to actual persons, living or dead, events, or locales is entirely coincidental.

This book is printed on acid-free paper. ∞

To those blessings in my life:
Patti, Rachael, Roger, and Billy

Acknowledgments

With utmost respect and admiration for Michael Gruber, my partner, collaborator, and confidant who is primarily responsible for the excellence of this manuscript and whose brilliance, expertise, and professionalism make this manuscript what it is; many kudos to "fast" Eddie Stackler, my editor, who is on track to be the next Henry Robbins who believed from the very beginning.

AUTHOR'S NOTE

Since it is a matter of record that the author was at one time counsel to the House of Representatives' Select Committee on Assassinations, and charged with investigating the assassination of President Kennedy, the reader may wish to know whether the present volume tells, at last, the real story.

As is inevitable with a work of this type, the answer must be ambiguous. On the one hand, much of the documentary evidence mentioned here actually exists, or did exist at one time. The author observed it with his own eyes. Also, of course, some of the characters mentioned are historical personages, either identified by name or thinly disguised, although they may not have done or said the things attributed to them herein. The reconstruction of the assassination itself, as given here, accords with the facts as known to the author and available in the public record, although not necessarily with the conclusions of the Select Committee.

On the other hand, obviously, no one named Butch Karp was ever involved in the work of the House Select Committee in 1976. Despite superficial similarities, the author and Butch Karp are different people, or rather, the author is a real person, while Mr. Karp is not. As to the *real* story of the assassination of John Kennedy, the author remains unsure, as are we all, as, in all probability, we shall ever be. The assassination has receded into mythology, and has become—like the tales of the Old West and the lives of secular saints like Washington and Lincoln—fair game for the fabulist, the moralist, and the entertainer.

Thus, in the present work, the shadows thrown by various culprits, which we perceived vaguely through a fog of deception nearly twenty years ago, have been resolved into sharp focus, by artifice. In short, what you are about to read is, merely and entirely, a work of fiction, based on a real event, like the Warren Report . . . *in my opinion, of course*!

The Congress shall have Power to declare the Punishment of Treason, but no Attainder of Treason shall work Corruption of Blood, or Forfeiture except during the Life of the Person attainted.

—United States Constitution, Article 3, Section 3

CORRUPTION
OF BLOOD

ONE

Nearly all Americans above a certain age can recall where they were the moment they learned of the assassination of John F. Kennedy. A much smaller number can recall where they were when they discovered who really did it.

One of these few was sitting in a dripping raincoat in a reading room on the fifth floor of the Lauinger Memorial Library at Georgetown University, in Washington D.C., on a rainy April day in the year 1977. On the wooden table before him was the sort of hinged cardboard box, the size and shape of a large book, that attorneys use to keep together all the material connected with some legal combat: a literal "case." Within it were several dozen typed pages, including a letter from a United States senator, several memoranda from the files of the Central Intelligence Agency and the Federal Bureau of Investigation, a thick packet of handwritten notes on lined yellow paper, two bankbooks, a small ledger, some photographs and clippings, a tape cassette, and a reel of 8-mm home movie film. There was also a sealed olive jar full of alcohol in which floated a chunk of human flesh.

The man shivered and stood to remove his sopping raincoat. A young woman, four seats down at the long table, glanced up at him from her thesis research (American Policy in Honduras, 1922–39) and then, a moment later, gave him a longer look, for the reading she was doing was tedious and he was not an ordinary-looking man.

He was very tall, for one thing, a bit over six-feet-five. His body, in its damp and rumpled dark suit, was broad-shouldered and rangy. He walked over to a display case and seemed to stare unseeing at a selection

of colonial maps, and she could see that he walked with a slight limp. His face, profiled, was moderately beaked and high cheekboned, the eyes having a slight oriental cast, and the sallow skin of his face and the lank dark hair, soaked and plastered tight against his skull, contributed to the general impression of the East—some Tatar or gypsy blood perhaps, she thought. You got to see all kinds in the Georgetown library.

She thought idly about who he might be. Not a bureaucrat. A bureaucrat would not have been caught in the rain. All bureaucrats in Washington carried those little spring-loaded folding umbrellas. Not military either. The hair was too long, and he was not old enough to have been retained on active duty with that limp; mid-thirties, she reckoned. Too obvious for a spy, with that size. A diplomat, perhaps, maybe from the Other Side. That was romantic enough. But an Eastern diplomat would have been dry; they went everywhere in cars with dark tinted windows. A professor, then? A professor might have forgotten his umbrella. . . .

Suddenly, he turned and stared directly into her face. She immediately dropped her eyes to her monograph and tried to get back into the reading. When she looked again, sideways, surreptitiously, he was still staring at her, unsmiling. He had peculiar eyes, long, slightly slanted, and very pale hazel, almost yellow. She felt them etching away at the side of her head. After a few uncomfortable minutes, she gathered her papers together and left. No, not a professor at all, she concluded.

She was correct. The man was a lawyer, surely the most common profession in Washington, but one that had not occurred to the young woman in her idle guessing, because he was not a Washington lawyer. He was a homicide prosecutor named Roger Karp, and he had come from the New York District Attorney's Office some seven months ago to serve as counsel to the House Select Committee on Assassinations, specifically to run the investigation of the murder of John F. Kennedy. This investigation was complete, as far as Karp was concerned. A few minutes ago he had quit. He certainly would have been fired if anyone knew what he was doing with the stuff in the box. Legally, it belonged to the United States government, and he was breaking the law by holding on to it.

Karp sat back in his chair and watched the back of the retreating graduate student. He rubbed his face vigorously, as if to massage from it the malign expression that had spooked the woman, vaguely regretting having used on a perfectly harmless citizen the tactical-nuclear stare that

had wrung confessions out of desperadoes in the Tombs, back in the city.

He had been paranoid, of course, but paranoia had become his natural state. He could not remember a time when he had not been beset by people trying to screw him personally or at least trying to stop him from doing his job. It had been bad enough at the DA, and magnitudes worse since his arrival in the capital.

He opened the box and spread the contents across the table, resisting an impulse to look furtively over his shoulder. He had taken the subway (as he still called it, although everyone else used the pretentious "metro") from the Federal Center stop near his office to M Street, and then had walked to Georgetown. Karp was a devotee of public transportation and he had never acknowledged that there were wide swaths of D.C. that had no subway stops at all. The storm had broken while he was riding on the shiny, toylike train, and he had been soaked during the absurdly long walk to the university.

He picked up the stack of yellow legal pads held together by rubber bands—his notes of the last seven months—and began a familiar activity: paging through the scribbled notes and making private marks here and there, recasting the information onto fresh sheets of paper, turning a mass of associated evidence into a story that he could tell to a jury. That he would never tell this particular story to an actual jury was at this point irrelevant. He wanted to make the complex material accessible and convincing to . . . whomever. God, maybe. It was both an irrational and a sacred act, like washing a corpse.

He worked quickly, because the material was familiar and he had kept good notes. He marked the various documents and other evidence with large circled letters, which he then keyed to the appropriate sections of his expository text. He also wrote a brief provenance for each item. It wasn't a legally acceptable chain of evidence, but it would have to do.

As he concentrated, his tongue crept out between his lips, a boyish trait. Any number of these survived in him, a remarkable fact given the atmosphere of grotesque cynicism in which he plied his trade. His friends called him Butch, a ridiculous name for a huge, dignified, grown man, but one that, oddly enough, suited him. In any case, he refused to answer to any other, as he had since the age of four.

Karp wrote very quickly, boyishly, of course, in a large round hand, the same school penmanship he had learned in the New York City public schools, in an era when they still functioned as educational institutions. He still got his hair cut in a barbershop run by an elderly Italian in a white smock; his inability to find one of these in the razor-cut, blow-dry

capital of the world was evidenced by the current length of his hair, which crept below his collar for the first time in his life. Karp had skipped the sixties.

He retained most of the Boy Scout virtues. He was courteous, loyal, brave, clean, and thrifty, passing on reverent. Many of the types, on both sides of the law, with whom he dealt in the New York criminal courts, took this as evidence that he was also a sucker, a mistake few made more than once.

Karp had, in fact, the best homicide prosecution record in the recent history of the New York DA's Office. He had tried over a hundred cases, losing not one. He was arguably the best person in the country to investigate the assassination of John F. Kennedy, assuming that anyone in charge really wanted to find out what happened in Dallas. As it turned out, they did not.

Putting down his pen, he riffled through a stack of legal bond, looking for a reference. A square yellow slip of paper dropped out onto the table. Karp picked it up and studied it. It was a telephone message slip dated seven months and three days earlier. The overture to this farce.

Karp shuffled through his message slips after lunch, arranging them in order of importance. Most of them were bureaucracy at work, it being a fine habit of bureaucrats to call during lunch hour, passing the buck, but not having to actually come to any closure on the issue at hand. Karp, as the chief of the homicide bureau, got a lot of these calls.

In turn, he would spend the odd lunch hour in his own office, eating a greasy sandwich and returning the calls to vacant offices, leaving his own messages. One slip popped out at him because it had an area code in front of the number. A Bert Crane called While You Were Out. Karp pulled the phone book out of a bottom drawer and found that the code was for Philadelphia.

Oh, *that* Bert Crane. In the narrow world of prosecuting attorneys, Crane was something of a star—or had been. Karp seemed to recall that he had resigned as district attorney in Philadelphia some years back and was now a prominent member of the criminal bar. His reputation was based largely on a case against the assassins of an insurgent union leader, in which he had convicted not only the killers but the racketeering Teamster boss who had hired them.

He's going to offer me a job, thought Karp. This happened at least once a month, mostly from white-shoe law firms in the city who wanted a name prosecutor to handle the criminal stuff that occasionally came their way, as when the drunken heir runs the Ferrari over the old lady. Occasionally, Karp would get a serious offer from a big-time criminal lawyer, the kind who write books about their own genius. Like Lucifer with Christ, they stood him on a mountaintop and showed him the treasures of the earth. Karp had always turned them down, for reasons he could not quite articulate.

It was, after all, past time for him to leave the DA's. He had been there twelve and a half years, ever since law school; it had been his only real job. It was more or less expected that after a period of seasoning in the DA, lawyers with ambition would go private, or switch over to the federal side, or, after a little longer, become judges. He looked around his office. It was a small spare room with a frosted-glass-windowed door that gave on the bureau's outer office, where the clerks and secretaries sat. It contained a battered wooden desk, a leather chair behind the desk and two in front for visitors, and behind these a long, scratched oak table with a miscellany of chairs around it, for conferences.

These furnishings were part of the original equipment of the criminal courts building, which had been constructed in 1930. The leather of the chairs was cracked, and gushed white stuffing. To the right of the desk were two large windows looking out on a short street and the New York State office building across it. If you stood at the window and leaned out you could see the trees of a tiny park, beyond which was Chinatown. It was the office's best, or rather its only good feature.

Karp was no sort of status hound, but he understood that the tattiness of his personal surroundings and the even worse conditions with which his staff had to contend were petty symbols of the contempt for Karp and all his works that steamed perpetually in the heart of Karp's boss, the district attorney, Sanford Bloom.

Bloom had not the guts to fire Karp outright, but neither Karp nor anyone who worked for him would ever get a new office or new furniture. The paint would rot off their walls. Their promotions would be delayed and their personnel records screwed up.

Everyone in the DA's office knew this. As a result, only the

intrepid came to work for Karp in the homicide bureau, and what should have been the cream of the DA's prosecutorial staff grew milky with the years.

People didn't stay long, and those who did were mostly the hacks, or those too uncouth for private firms. Fanatics like Karp, who lived only to try cases and put asses in jail, were fewer and fewer as the years passed.

Karp didn't want to be a judge. He wanted to be twenty-four and working, as he had then, for the finest prosecutorial office in the known universe. He sighed and looked at the little yellow slip, and dialed the long-distance number.

He gave his name to the woman who answered and she put him through to Crane instantly. Crane's voice was deep and confident, and "cultured" in the style of classical music announcers on FM radio.

Crane got quickly to the point. "Joe Lerner gave me your name. As you probably know, I've been appointed chief counsel to the House Select Committee on Assassinations."

Karp didn't know. He had almost no interest in political news and restricted his newspaper reading to the crime reports and the sports pages. Nor did he watch much television. But he had a vague recollection that Congress was reopening the investigations into the murders of both Kennedy and Martin Luther King. And he knew who Joe Lerner was.

"How is Joe?" Karp asked.

"Fine. He's working for me now."

"No kidding? Doing what?"

"I'll have two assistant chief counsels. Joe is going to be running the Martin Luther King side of it. He recommended you highly."

"That's a surprise," said Karp, genuinely surprised.

"Oh?"

"Yeah, Joe and I had a little bit of a falling-out just before he split from the office. He was my rabbi when I was breaking in and I guess he assumed I'd keep following his lead."

"This was about some case?"

"No, it was a political thing. Joe thinks I lack political judgment."

A pause. "Well, he thinks you're a hell of a prosecutor, anyway. The best is what he said, actually."

"Next to you, of course. And him."

Crane had a booming laugh. "Of course! Look, maybe the best thing would be if you could run down here to Philadelphia and we could discuss it face-to-face. I'd like to meet you and I'm sure Joe would like to see you again. I know you've got a tight schedule, but could you make it, say, Thursday, day after tomorrow? We could have lunch and talk."

The man's diffidence was starting to annoy Karp. Just once, he wished one of these guys would call him up and say, "Hundred and ninety grand a year for defending scumbags, plus you kiss my ass. Yes or no?"

"And what would we be talking about, Mr. Crane?" Karp asked.

"Please—it's Bert. Well, of course, about you joining our team. Joe suggested that you might be interested in new pastures. Something with more scope for your abilities."

"You mean as Joe's assistant?"

Crane chuckled. "No, no, of course not. I want you for the Kennedy half. In charge of it."

"Oh," said Karp, and then couldn't think of a bright rejoinder.

"You're interested?"

"That's a good word," Karp admitted.

"Fine. I'll expect you in my office Thursday, eleven-thirty." Crane passed on some details about how to get to his office and then closed the conversation.

Karp made the rest of his calls and then futzed around for the remainder of the afternoon, irritated that he was unable to maintain his usual focus. His job consisted largely of supervising the work of thirty other prosecutors, which meant that he had to be passably familiar with several hundred homicide cases at once.

There was a man talking to him who suddenly stopped. Karp realized with a start that the man was waiting for a reply. He was a junior prosecutor and he had just asked Karp for some direction on a case.

Karp felt an embarrassed sweat blossom on his face.

"Sorry, I was somewhere else. Hit me with that again."

The young man said, "This is *Wismer*. Defendant beat his estranged wife to death with a blunt instrument. The case . . . the charge is murder two. . . ."

The kid was nervous. Karp recalled that this was probably his first murder case solo, and could be his first homicide trial. It did

not occur to Karp that the kid was nervous because he was presenting an issue to a demigod. Awe made Karp uncomfortable, and so he simply refused to recognize that it existed.

Collins, his name was, Karp recalled. A neat, strong-looking black kid from upstate somewhere, and an athlete, like nearly all the people Karp hired. He had a pencil mustache he kept fiddling with. From time to time he glanced at his watch.

Karp reached into his mental files. "Yeah, *Wismer*, guy's got a sheet as a petty thief and dealer, seen leaving the wife's apartment, picked out of a lineup. What's the problem?"

"Somebody called the cops, wouldn't give the name. A woman. Said there was a boyfriend, and he did the crime. The boyfriend's a man named Warren Hobart. Also not a taxpayer: did time on a 120.10 a couple of years ago plus the usual drug shit."

"Don't tell me—he looks just like Wismer."

Collins smiled. "Well, they're both medium-sized, skinny, medium-dark black guys. Surprise."

"So, put them in a lineup and see which one the witness likes best."

"Um, that's the problem. The cops think it's bullshit. They got the guy, Wismer. Case is cleared."

Karp's brow clouded at this, and he asked, "What's the rest of *Wismer*? We have any physical evidence?"

"We have a print on the murder weapon."

"Which was?"

"A juice machine."

"A what?"

"Yeah, right. It was one of those old-fashioned kind of orange-juice squeezers—all steel, weighed a ton. Must've just grabbed it there in the kitchen and whapped her a couple upside the head. Crushed in her temple bone."

"Okay, on the cops—who caught the case again?"

"Angeletti, Zone Six Homicide."

"Yeah, Vince Angeletti. Look, here's the thing: the cops got a lot to do, especially uptown there, and the last thing they want to do is to piss on their own cleared cases. But with the situation as it is right now you couldn't convict Wismer of criminal mischief, much less murder two. You got to get them to check out this character Hobart. Don't ask them, tell them. If you get any more shit from Angeletti, let me know and I'll fuck with his head. His

lieutenant is a good buddy of mine. You got to remind these guys once in a while who's in charge of a criminal prosecution. When you got Hobart, do the lineup again, and make sure whoever's on D is there to see it. If your witness waffles, I think we're fucked. Or we could get lucky and find a bunch of bloody clothes in Hobart's closet. He's got that assault conviction."

"But we have Wismer's prints. . . ."

"Come on!" Karp said impatiently. "The guy lived there. You want to put him away for twenty-five because he squeezed some orange juice last April?"

Collins looked down at the thick file folder on his lap, weeks of work gone glimmering. "But," he said despairingly, "Wismer *did* it."

"Yeah, I agree. He probably *did* do it. But probably isn't good enough. Domestics are hard to prove circumstantially anyway. The killer was intimate with the victim and they shared a space—fibers, hairs, prints don't mean much. You need an eyewitness to the crime itself, or a confession, which is how we clear ninety percent of domestics. Without that . . ." Karp shrugged and added, "I like it when they keep the bloody knife, or bury the stiff in the basement."

Collins was looking stunned. "So . . . what? He *walks* on this?"

"Not necessarily. If your witness gives him a good ID in the lineup with the boyfriend, or if the boyfriend has a cast-iron alibi and Wismer's loose for the time of, then you got something to work with."

"You mean plead him?"

"Offer man one, settle for man two. Ask for twelve, they'll offer six, you'll close on eight. He'll do maybe four and a half."

Collins's smile was rueful. "You've done this before."

"How can you tell?" said Karp, returning the smile. "So. I think that's how it's gonna play. On the other hand, you know how I run the office; it's your case, your call. You want a trial slot on this?"

"I think I'll pass this time," said Collins, looking relieved and at the same time faintly ashamed of being relieved. He looked at his watch again and leaped to his feet. "Jesus! I'm due in calendar court four minutes ago. Thanks a lot, sir!"

"No problem," said Karp, "and don't worry about Wismer. You stay around long enough, you'll catch him on his next wife."

Collins laughed racing out.

Sir? When the hell did they start calling him that? Karp sighed and rubbed his face. He looked with distaste at the pile of case folders waiting his review in the wire basket on his desk. They came in at an average of three a day, each one representing a New Yorker who had dealt with one of life's little problems by terminating the existence of a fellow citizen. Most of them were pathetic shards from the rubble of life in the lower depths, like *Wismer.*

He knew he had cheered up Collins. He did that for his staff half a dozen times a day. Collins was a pretty good guy, in fact, better than some of the newer people he'd had to take in just to keep up with the killing. Collins would probably get it after a while, get the sense of what was possible in a system essentially corrupt, a system designed to fail most of the time. A lot of them wouldn't, ever. And, of course, Collins would probably leave shortly after he knew what he was doing, and Karp would have to pump up another kid.

And the pumping, what he did for Collins and the others, drained him, which was to be expected, but the problem was, nobody was pumping *him* up. Zero strokes for old Butch these days. The only thing that kept him going was doing trials himself, but running a bureau with thirty lawyers in it didn't give him much time for trials, not the way he liked to do them.

He thought about his conversation with Crane. There were some strokes in that. "The best," for example. He might even have meant it. The notion of working for somebody who liked and respected him had a certain appeal. Since the death of the legendary Francis Phillip Garrahy, the district attorney who had made New York a mecca for every serious criminal prosecutor in the country, and the accession of Sanford L. Bloom, Karp had not had the pleasure. It had been eight years, all uphill.

Karp picked up the phone and punched the intercom button. Connie Trask, the bureau secretary, came on.

"Connie, what do I have Thursday?"

"Nine, you have staff with the DA, moved back from Monday. Ten-thirty, you have a meet with Sullivan at felony, his place. Lunch is open. Then, one to three, meeting of bureau chiefs on affirmative action, three to four, meeting on paperwork reduction, four to five you have marked off for grand jury. After five you're

free as a bird, except it's your day to pick up the kid at day care."

"Okay, cancel the whole day. Get Roland to cover me on the grand jury, and reschedule Sullivan. The rest, get somebody to pick up any paper they hand out."

"Right. Taking a mental health day?"

"No, I'm going to Philadelphia."

"A day in Philly! Lucky you! Is this business? You want me to cut a travel voucher?"

"No, it's personal."

"What should I say if *he* calls. Which he will if you cut that staff meeting."

"Tell the district attorney I'm visiting our national shrines in order to renew my commitment to our precious civil liberties," said Karp. "He'll understand."

At 5:15, Karp was immersed in a case, writing notes for one of his people, when the intercom buzzed, and Connie Trask said, "I'm going. Want anything?"

"No, go ahead."

"Don't forget the kid."

"Oh, shit!" cried Karp, looking at his watch to confirm that yet again he had left his daughter waiting at the day care on Lispenard Street. He shoved some reading into an old red pasteboard folder and cleared the building in three minutes.

Six minutes after that, he was at the day care, a cheerily decorated Tribeca storefront, at Lispenard off Broadway. Karp went in and found his daughter playing with a small ocher girl (they were the last two kids in the place) and Lillian Dillard, the proprietor. Dillard, known to all as Lillie-Dillie, was an unflappable ex-hippie who wore her graying hair in a long plait that hung to her tailbone, and favored fashion statements that included tentlike smocks made of Indian bedspreads and lots of clanking silver. She had somehow, in the midst of her serious participation in the sixties, obtained a degree from NYU in early-childhood education, and she ran her operation with love and a slightly wacky efficiency. Her most valuable trait in Karp's eyes was that she allowed forgetful dads to pick up their kids a half hour after the agreed time without coming in for a load of horseshit.

Lucy Karp caught sight of her father and, as usual, shrieked,

"Daddy, Daddy, Daddy," flung herself into his arms, and otherwise behaved as if he had just returned safely from four years on the Western Front. Karp did not mind this one bit.

He hugged her and inhaled that ineffable smell that rises from the skin of well-tended young children: eau de kid, the world's most expensive fragrance. He put the three-year-old down, found the lunch box and the drawing to show Mommy, said good-bye to Lillie-Dillie, and they headed off, hand in hand, north on Broadway. As usual, they stopped as Dave's for a couple of chocolate egg creams, which they sipped at the marble outside counter.

"So, how was your day?" asked Karp.

"Okay. Jimmy Murphy threw up."

"That was the high point, huh?"

"And . . . and . . . Patrick Allessandro hit me with a big block, right here." She indicated a patch of flawless skin beneath a lock of black hair. "I *hate* Patrick Allessandro."

"It looks all right. Does it need a kiss?"

"No. Lillie-Dillie already kissed it. Daddy! Why does that lady have purple hair?"

Karp looked over at where Lucy was pointing.

"That's actually a man with purple hair, baby. And I guess he thinks it looks pretty." Karp did not admonish his daughter that it was impolite to point, and that loudly noting the personal peculiarities of passersby in New York was a good way to get yourself killed. Time enough for that.

They finished their drinks and walked a few more blocks to the industrial loft building where they lived. Since he had started to drop off and pick up Lucy twice a week, Karp had gained a better appreciation of what a miracle it was to have superb day care halfway between where he worked and where he lived, all of it within convenient walking distance.

The downside was the five-flight climb to the loft itself. Karp had an artificial left knee, the result of a basketball accident in his sophomore year at Cal Berkeley, the agony of which he had nobly ignored for years, until it finally crapped out. He would never have chosen to live in a walk-up, and had not chosen this one either, but rather its owner, who flatly refused to live anywhere else.

The two of them clumped up the dusty stairs together, singing "A Hundred Bottles of Beer," a ritual which required also that Karp become confused about how many bottles of beer were left

on the wall, with Lucy correcting him, and then arguing about it, and giggling, until Karp started tickling her on the last flight of stairs, and then, snatching her up and throwing her over his shoulder, running up the last flight, to arrive breathless and laughing at their red door.

Marlene, the wife, was not home. Karp and family lived in a single room, thirty-three feet wide and a hundred long, a former electroplating factory loft. It was divided like a movie set by plasterboard walls into suitable areas: master bedroom (a sleeping loft) with closet space beneath, a bathroom, a kitchen-and-dining area, a living room, a nursery, a gymnasium, and a study, all facing on to a long corridor that ran end to end. Karp went to the closets under the sleeping loft and changed into chinos and a black T-shirt. Lucy ran to watch "Sesame Street" on the TV in the living "room."

Karp efficiently set the table for three, opened the freezer and removed one of the many Tupperware containers waiting there, and ran hot water over it for ten minutes. A large wet reddish brick, loosened by the heat, dropped out into the pot Karp had prepared, and he placed this on a low heat. He didn't know what it was, but it would probably be good. Marlene staged a giant cookfest once a week, on Saturday, making some huge treat from scratch—lasagna, chicken cacciatore, spaghetti and meatballs, ravioli, beef stew with wine. They feasted on it fresh and then she froze the rest in boxes, and they ate from these the rest of the week—that or takeout. Karp couldn't cook and Marlene wouldn't, during the workweek.

Karp sat with his daughter, learning letters and numbers, while the loft filled with the odor of dinner. It was spaghetti and meatballs, a winner. After dinner, Karp cleared up and chivied Lucy into the bath. Marlene had saved one of the thousand-gallon black rubber electroplating tanks from the former factory, scrubbing it out and adding a heater and a filter to make a huge hot tub.

Lucy cavorted in the warm water with a variety of floating toys. Her mother had drown-proofed her at eight months, and she swam like a little eel. Karp knelt on the concrete tank stand and washed his child's hair, to some men, Karp included, life's most sensuous delight not connected to actual sex.

After that, into the yellow nightie printed with rosebuds, and

some sitcom TV. At eight, *Goodnight Moon* was read and the duck-shaped night-light switched on. Karp sat by her bedside for half an hour, watching her fall asleep.

He fell asleep himself shortly thereafter, stretched out on the tatty red velour sofa, reading cases. He was awakened by the slam of the front door. He looked at his watch: ten-thirty, nearly.

He heard the sound of a heavy briefcase hitting the floor, then the toilet door slamming, then peeing, then a flush, then a cupboard being opened, then the cork going out of a bottle, and the clink and splashing he knew to be wine pouring out into a glass, then some mixed kitchen noises—opening and shutting of refrigerator door, dish rattling, and so on—and then his wife appeared around the hall of the living zone, with a sloppy meatball sandwich on a plate and a large tumbler full of cheap red wine.

Marlene fell into a sling chair across from the couch and kicked her shoes off, sighing.

"Don't ask," she said and took a deep swallow of wine.

Karp took a long, fond look at his wife. Even flustered and worn from a long day working one of the city's more trying jobs, she was good to see, and he always had to suppress, as he had from earliest times of their acquaintance, a spasm of disbelief that she had chosen him, of all people.

Then and now a remarkable-looking woman. Classic features? A phrase used loosely enough, but Marlene actually had them the way they liked them in fifth-century Athens: the heart-shaped face, the straight nose, the rose-petal mouth, the broad cheekbones. Her skin was a dusky bisque, on which she typically wore no makeup, nor did she need any. The sculptor who lived downstairs from them said she looked exactly like the statue of Saint Teresa by Bernini. Marlene had lived a rougher life than the saint. She had a glass eye and was missing two fingers on her left hand.

"*Morgan* again?" asked Karp.

"Needless to say. With his fucking wife, actually."

Morgan and his fucking wife had taken care of a series of foster children in their large Inwood home, model citizens, until a school nurse had become suspicious. What she thought was a bladder infection in the Morgans' seven-year-old turned out to be gonorrhea. All six of the Morgans' fosterlings had it as well; the youngest, age seventeen months, had the oral version.

Marlene chomped away at her sandwich, leaning over her plate,

dripping fragments and talking around mouthfuls. She had been hunting Morgan for weeks now, having the kids examined by psychologists, making sure the evidence they generated was genuine and that the enraged social workers did not encourage them to stretch the truth in any way. Marlene was in charge of a small unit at the DA's specializing in sex offenders, and *Morgan* was the current hot case.

Morgan would admit nothing and he had a good lawyer. His wife was the key to the case.

"I hit her with recordings of the oldest kid's testimony, right. Timeesha, nine years old. The shitbag has been fucking her since she was six. No response. Din see nothin'. He's a good man. Wait'll I nail her as an accessory. Then we'll see."

Finishing her sandwich, she took a long swallow, and sighed. Then she looked up at Karp as if she had just noticed him. "Pretty speedy, huh?" she said, laughing at herself.

"I'd say so. How about a juicy one?"

"Sounds right."

She crossed over and sat on his lap and gave him a wine-and-marinara kiss. "Mmm, good! And the last straw? Ann Silber came into my office as I was just about to leave and totally collapsed. Out of control. I had to stay with her for an hour before she was fit for company."

"The new kid? What happened to her?"

"Oh, she went out with the cops on an abandoned child call. They found this six-month-old boy in a shooting gallery. Skin and bones, with maggots crawling over his eyes." She shuddered. "How's Lucy?"

"Fine. Relatively maggot-free."

"Nice to hear. How was yours?"

"The usual," said Karp. "I got an interesting call about a job."

Karp didn't expand on this, nor did Marlene pump him. Karp got lots of offers.

TWO

Marlene regarded Karp's trip to Philadelphia as merely a good excuse for a day off and had asked him to bring home a cheese-steak and a Liberty Bell piggy bank. Karp was scarcely more enthusiastic as he rode the elevator up to Crane's Market Street office. The car was done in dark, gold-flecked mirrors, with shiny baroque brass rails and trim. A fancy building, and a fancy office, he observed when he got there: dark wood panels set off the shine of the mahogany furniture and the blond receptionists.

Crane had a huge corner office with a good view of Ben Franklin hanging in the cloudy sky. He stood up when Karp entered and so did the other person sitting there, a tall, saturnine man with deep-set intelligent eyes.

"Glad you could make it, Butch," said Crane. "You know Joe Lerner, of course."

"Sure. Long time, Joe." The two men shook hands. Lerner seemed to have aged little in eight years. A little more jowly, the crinkly hair receding and graying on the sides, he still crackled with a nervous, aggressive energy. Karp imagined Lerner was remembering the green kid Karp had been and was doing his own assessment of the current version.

They left immediately for lunch, which was taken in one of those expensive, dark, quiet saloon-restaurants that thrive around every major courthouse in the nation by purveying rich food and large drinks to lawyers and politicians and providing a comfortably dim venue for deals.

Seated in a secluded booth, the three men declined cocktails and ordered carelessly: the "special." No bon vivants, these. There was a period of obligatory sports talk. All were basketball fans, all had played in college, but only Karp had played NBA ball, albeit for six weeks as part of an undercover investigation. Crane wanted to hear all about that.

The food came; they ate. Over coffee, Crane settled back and gave Karp an appraising look, which Karp returned. Crane was a good-sized man in his early fifties, who exhibited the perpetual boyishness that seems to go with being a descendant of the Founding Fathers and rich. He had a sharp nose, no lips to speak of, light blue eyes, and graying ginger hair, which he wore swept straight back from his high, protuberant brow.

"So—to business," he said. "First, some background. What do you know about the JFK assassination?"

"Not much," said Karp. "Just what everybody knows."

"You haven't read the Warren Report?"

"Not really. Just the *Times* stuff and Cronkite on TV. Like everybody."

"All right. Let me say this. If the victim had been a minor dope dealer, and you had Lee Harvey Oswald in custody as a suspect, and the cops brought the evidence presented to the Warren Commission to you, as a homicide case, you would've laughed in their faces and given Oswald a walk. You wouldn't have even taken that trash to a grand jury. And they served this up on the most important homicide in American history."

"That bad, huh?"

Crane nodded. "Worse. All right, it's never been any big secret. As a result, almost from the start the Warren Commission has been under fire. Three main reasons."

He held up a big, freckled hand and counted on his fingers.

"One, it didn't take a genius to figure out that even if the conclusions of the commission happened to be correct, no legitimate case had been presented. The chain of evidence for critical material was a hopeless mess. The autopsy was a joke. There was no follow-up on possibly critical witnesses. Two: The conclusions are inherently implausible. The existing amateur film of the actual assassination locks in the time sequence of the shots striking Kennedy, which means that if you want all the shots to come from Oswald's rifle you have to make some fairly hairy assumptions

about what happened to the three shots Warren assumed that Oswald got off. The magic bullet and all that—you remember the magic bullet? Also, 'assumed' is a word I don't like hearing around homicide investigations, but that's nearly all Warren is made of. Look—you know and I know that crazy things can happen to bullets. I wouldn't want to rule anything out a priori. But you also know that if you're going to make a claim that a missile did a bunch of things that no missile is likely to have done, then your ballistics and your forensics have to be immaculate. Which in this case they are distinctly not. Three—and this is the tough one. It *wasn't* some junkie who got killed—it was the president of the United States, a man with important political enemies, some of whom may have been involved in the investigation itself. Then we have the supposed assassin, who is not your garden-variety nut, but a former radar operator with a security clearance who defected to the Soviet Union, who was involved with Cuban weirdos, who had a Russian wife, and who was killed in police custody by a guy who had close ties with organized crime."

Crane paused, looking at Karp. A cue. "You mean the conspiracy angle," Karp said.

"Yes, indeed, the conspiracy angle. JFK was killed by the CIA, the FBI, the Cuban right, the Cuban commies, the Russian commies, the Mob, or any three working in combination. There's a vast literature on the subject ranging from the plausible to the insane. You'll have to go through it all, along with the original Warren material, of course—"

"Um, Bert, slow down. You're making the assumption that I'm gonna do this thing. I haven't decided I am yet. I still have a lot of questions."

Crane opened his mouth to speak and then checked himself. Karp saw him shoot a quick glance at Lerner across the table. Crane smiled and said, "Sorry, my enthusiasm runs away with me. Of course, you have questions, and I just broke my own rule about assumptions. Please—ask away."

He waited, smiling. Karp said, "Okay, first, why me? If you're really serious about digging up these old cans of worms, you're going to need somebody who knows his way around politics. That's not my strong point, as I'm sure Joe will tell you." Karp glanced toward Lerner, who returned a cool, ironic look.

"Second, I'm not sure why you think you can get to the truth

in this Kennedy thing. You know as well as I do that the chances of solving a homicide go into the toilet after a week, much less a year, much less—what is it?—thirteen years. I'm trying to think of a New York homicide case that got solved after that long and I can only come up with one."

"Hoffmeyer," said Lerner.

"Yeah, Hoffmeyer. Killed his wife, the cops loved him for it, but they couldn't find the corpse. Confessed out of remorse after fifteen years."

"He fed her to his dogs and ground the bones up into the Redi-mix for the patio," said Lerner.

"He did. Oh, yeah, I forgot the serial cases. The Mad Bomber. We catch a guy with an MO used in an old case, we can clear it —sometimes. So—either, you got a guy trying to kill the current president in Dallas with a mail-order Italian rifle, or somebody's confessed, which I haven't heard about either of them. Or, maybe the job is to make a show of activity around this to cool down the Mark Lane types. In which case, I'm also the wrong guy."

Crane was grinning broadly now. "This is just the attitude I want. Look—you've answered the first question yourself. I want you *because* you're a professional homicide prosecutor, and *not* a politician or a bureaucrat. You've been in charge of hundreds of homicide investigations. The whole Kennedy material has *never* been approached from that perspective by a real pro, ever. That's what was wrong with the Warren operation."

"I thought Warren was a DA once," offered Karp.

"Yeah, back when Pluto was a pup. He'd been wearing a black dress for a while by then, and that changes you. Besides, he had another agenda going."

"Oh? Like for instance?"

Crane paused, frowned briefly. "I'll get to that. Also there was Jim Garrison and the Clay Shaw thing, but that was a conspiracy case. Garrison had to show that Shaw, a prominent New Orleans businessman, had been in on the assassination planning. There was all kinds of weird stuff there, too, that Shaw was a homosexual who had a liaison with Oswald and a nut named David Ferrie— all hard to prove, and frankly, screwed up. Anyway, the fact that you're not interested in political wheeling and dealing is a big plus as far as I'm concerned. That's what *I'm* for; I'll run interference while the both of you do the real investigative work. Now, as to

the possibilities for really doing something: I think they're good. The journalistic material has reached a critical mass. That stuff has to be examined by a professional team, and either tossed out for good or confirmed. And the Senate Intelligence Committee, the Church committee, has come up with some amazing stuff. I think that's part of what's triggering the House reinvestigation."

"It's been in the papers," said Karp.

"Not what I'm talking about, and it won't be, either," said Crane.

Karp waited, but Crane said nothing more.

"And you're not going to share it with me?"

"Not until you're in for real," said Crane.

The waiter appeared and asked them if they wanted dessert or coffee. They declined. A brief silence descended. Then Karp said, "Well, in that case, thanks for the nice lunch."

"I don't believe this!" Lerner blurted out after a moment.

The other two men turned to him, startled. Lerner had said almost nothing during the meal.

Now he stared at Karp, tight-jawed. "What is it, Butch? You worried about your pension already? Got a family? Lost the edge? No, you can't believe that. You're not dumb. You know you're living on borrowed time. . . ."

"What're you talking about, Joe?" asked Karp irritably.

"You know what I'm talking about. You think I don't know what goes on up there? You've been lucky. But you're dead-ended. Bloom has you in a box, and he's squeezing. How long can you last? Another year or two? Three? Sooner or later he'll get you out. You'll be lucky if he doesn't scam you into something that'll get you disbarred."

"Joe, I don't need a lecture about Bloom."

"No? Then why the hell don't you jump at this? You're actually telling me you're gonna keep working for fucking Sandy Bloom instead of coming in with Bert Crane and closing the homicide of the century?"

"It's more complicated than that," said Karp lamely. But Lerner had virtually repeated one side of his own internal arguments. The complication was, of course, The Wife. And The Kid. And Moving. Karp had already wrecked one previous marriage because, among other things, he had moved his first wife away from Southern California, where she had been comfortable and happy

and working at something she enjoyed, to New York (because he'd wanted to work for the DA there), where she hadn't much of anything but Karp himself; which proved, in the event, insufficient.

Lerner was looking at him as if he had Karp's number—not a nice look. He asked, "How's Marlene these days, Butch?"

"She's fine," Karp answered shortly. Crane caught the interplay. He said, "I'm sure something could be found for your wife, Butch. I hear she's quite a competent attorney in her own right."

"Yes," said Karp, beginning to steam. "She is. And I'll need to discuss this with her. And think about it some more. Why don't I call you tomorrow or Monday?"

Crane frowned. "All right. But we need to get moving on this."

After thirteen years, why the rush? Karp thought to himself, but said nothing.

On the train back to the city, Karp went through the interview again in his mind, obsessing about what he should have asked, how he should have acted. It was an uncomfortable pattern of thought, and unfamiliar. Nerds did it, playing out witty things never said to snooty girls, going home on the subway to Queens, having failed to score in the Village. *L'esprit d'escalier.* Karp nearly always said exactly what he thought at the moment (except, of course, when he conversed with his wife). Athletics, they say, builds character, and Karp had the sort of character built by bigtime athletics: all-state guard, high school all-American, Pac-Ten star, and that peculiar six weeks in the NBA. You see the opening, you go for it. Roll over anybody who gets in the way. You screw up, you don't think about it, there's always another game. Shoot the ball.

It happens that this sort of character is also well suited to prosecuting homicides, although less so for major life decisions requiring introspection. That's what Marlene was for.

Karp shook himself free of troubled thought and watched New Jersey flow by outside the dirty window. What he should have said, he concluded, when Crane first offered the job was, "Sure. When do I start?" Holding that thought, he dozed.

"What's wrong?" asked Marlene, five minutes after she arrived at the loft. Karp had come back to town, hopped a cab to the day care, picked up Lucy early, for a change, and was now draped

across the red couch watching the news on TV. Karp looked up at her.

"Nothing," he lied.

"How was Philadelphia?"

"Okay. I got a nice lunch."

"What was the guy like?"

"Crane? A good guy. Reminded me a little of Garrahy, if Garrahy had been a WASP. A straight shooter. Joe Lerner was there too. He sends his regards. How was your day?"

Marlene sat in her rocker and threw off her shoes. "Hell on earth," she began, and launched into a familiar litany: witnesses not showing, witnesses fishtailing; the idiocy of social workers and psychologists; the cynical malfeasance of the police. People who prosecute sex crimes rarely have a nice day.

Karp had, of course, heard it all before, and was as a rule no more than passively sympathetic, when he did not offer irritating advice about what Marlene should do or should have done to solve various problems.

Now he was almost therapeutic—considerate, patient, interested. When she started to run down, he asked casually, "It might be nice to take a break, wouldn't it?"

"Oh, like a long weekend? Try me! Like where? Vermont?"

"Um, no, I meant a real break. Doing something else. Do you really want to spend the rest of your life with scumbags? I mean, you come home like this every day, bitching and complaining about the witnesses, the shrinks. Trying to put together child abuse cases, rapes . . . yeah, occasionally, very occasionally, there's a real bad guy, and maybe you can put him away for seven years and he gets out in three and a half, and meanwhile you got all the others. He-said, she-said; who the hell knows what happened in the back of the goddamn Buick?" He looked at her searchingly. "Don't you get tired of it? Wouldn't you like to do something else. I mean you paid your dues. *I've* paid my dues. . . ."

A look of confusion on her face: "I don't understand. What are you saying? I should just quit—or what?"

"I mean we should seriously sit down and think about what we're doing, the kind of life we have—"

At that instant there was a loud, high-pitched shriek from the nursery, of just that timbre that turns parental blood to transmis-

sion fluid. They both sprang up, crashing into each other like the Three Stooges exiting a ballroom, and raced down the hallway, Marlene in the lead.

Lucy was standing in front of her bed, red-faced, in hysterics.

Marlene knelt to embrace her, but the child shook away from her and backed away toward the bed.

"What's wrong, baby! Calm down and tell Mommy what's wrong," cooed Marlene, heart in throat.

Karp, trained observer that he was, said, "It's her foot." The child had all her weight on her left leg, with only the toes of her bare right foot touching the floor. Marlene lifted her thrashing, sobbing daughter and grabbed at her ankle. She inspected the foot and cursed. "Christ, she's got another splinter."

"No needuh! No needuh!" yelled Lucy.

"Baby, *please* calm down! Mommy has to take it out. You don't want an infection, do you?"

"Nooooo! No neee-duh!"

"Hold her," said Marlene, after which ensued Karp's absolutely least favorite paternal chore, that of clamping in a viselike grip the wriggling, choking, screaming, red-faced, snot-bubbling changeling his darling had become, while its mother probed the splinter out with a flame-sterilized number two sharp.

And after that necessary torment, Lucy extracted the maximum of cosseting, as being only her due. After a fretful supper there were multiple tuckings in, expeditions for milk and cookies, story after story read, cramp-backed sittings by the little bed—in short, all the forms of torture imposed upon guilty, loving parents by their innocent young.

The couple collapsed in the living room, having at last seen their kid off to dreamland. Marlene poured herself a stiff one of jug red and drank off half of it.

"God, did I not need that! I've told her a million times to wear her slippers."

"She's only three and a half," said Karp in defense. "She gets splinters because we live in a decaying industrial building. Maybe she should wear gloves too, and a face mask."

"Please, don't start. . . ."

"No, really! It's all part of the same thing. You have a job that drives you crazy and leaves you exhausted, we live in a five-flight

walk-up with splintery floors and leaky plumbing that's freezing in winter and boiling in summer, and you wonder why we're irritated all the time."

"We're not 'irritated all the time,' " snapped Marlene. "Every time something happens you blame it on the loft. Okay, we'll get the floors sanded and refinished."

This was far from a new argument. The loft had originally been Marlene's dwelling. She had constructed it herself, with help from family and friends, tearing out the industrial ruins, cleaning it, painting it, putting in drywall, kitchen and cabinet work. She'd lived in it happily for six years. When Karp moved in it had seemed to him just one of his lover's delightful eccentricities. But as the seat of a marriage, and a place to raise a child, it was, in his often-voiced opinion, a giant pain in the ass.

"Refinishing isn't going to do any good. The damn floor's sagging all over the place. It's probably totally rotted out underneath."

"Okay, we'll *replace* the fucking floor! Why are you *hocking* me about the floor? Why now?" A flush had appeared across her famous cheekbones and she took another swallow of wine. Then she looked at her husband narrowly. He met her gaze for an instant and then glanced away.

"Because," said Karp, "we have to make some decisions. How long are we going to keep pouring money into this place? I mean, is this *it*? We're going to live here forever?"

Marlene wasn't listening. She was still staring at him and the expression on her face was not pleasant.

"What?" said Karp.

"You rat! This isn't about the floor, or Lucy, or how hard I work. They offered you a job in Philly and you want to take it and move and you're afraid to just come out and say it."

Karp felt his face steam in embarrassment. A denial sprang to his lips, but, to his credit, he suppressed it. He *was* a rat.

"Well?" pressed his wife. "Did they?"

He nodded.

"And you want to take it."

He nodded again.

"Christ! What I hate is having to worm stuff like this out of you like you were a little boy. Why don't you just come up to me like a real person and *talk* about it?"

"I don't know," answered Karp, meaning that he did know. "I

guess . . . avoiding. I really started wanting this and I knew there was going to be an incredible explosion when I told you and I was just easing into it. I'm just basically slimy that way."

"I'll say! So spit it out already. What is it, a glossy partnership with the white shoes, down in Philly there?"

"No. It's a government job. In D.C."

"Huh? Schmuck! Darling! You already got a government job. What, you just developed a sudden interest in federal crimes?"

"No, it's with a congressional committee, working for Bert Crane. The House is reopening the Kennedy assassination case and they want me to be in charge of it, Crane does."

Marlene was sipping at her wine when this emerged and her snort of amazement sprayed a purple mist over the nearby area, including Karp.

"I'm sorry!" she sputtered. "That was unexpected. Let me hear that again: they want you to find out who killed Kennedy?"

"Yeah. What's wrong with that?",

"It's looney's what's wrong with it," she laughed. "I mean, I knew you were a caped crusader, but . . ."

"Marlene," said Karp, his tone strict, "it's a serious investigation. A lot of new stuff has come up."

"Oh, yeah? Like what?" She waited. After a silence and some uncharacteristic fumfering by Karp, she added confidently, "They didn't tell you, did they? They sold you a pig in a poke. And you bought it." She struck her forehead to indicate the extent of her amazement.

"I can't believe it! Especially you. Jesus, Butch! It's like some mutt said, 'Hey, let me walk on this one and I'll give you Mr. Big,' and you let him walk and *then* you called him up, hey, Mr. Mutt, how's about coming down and talking about Mr. Big?"

"Bert Crane isn't a mutt, for Chrissake, Marlene!"

"No, he's a *lawyer*," Marlene shot back. "I rest my case."

They glared at each other for an uncomfortable few seconds. Then Marlene rose and went to her closet, where she shed her working outfit and put on a T-shirt and Osh-Kosh overalls and flip-flops. Then she began putting together a meal. Karp drifted into the kitchen. Wordlessly she put on the butcher block in front of him a tin colander loaded with washed salad ingredients. Karp got a salad bowl and tore and cut the vegetables into bits. Marlene threw a mystery casserole into the oven.

They ate a silent meal. Marlene put the little espresso maker on the stove. They listened to it hiss. Then they both said "Look" simultaneously, which made them smile.

Karp said, "Your 'look' first."

"Okay, look . . . I'm sorry. I'm sure what's-his-name thinks it's a great honor to get picked for this job, and maybe you do too. I shouldn't have pissed all over it like I did. But . . . we got to work stuff out like this together, Butchie, like a team. We got to think it through together, the pros and cons, for all three of us, what's best—you know? That's all I'm saying."

"Okay," said Karp. "I should've been straight about it. I'm a cryptic son of a bitch, all right? But . . . if what Crane suggested to me checks out, if we could really crack the assassination . . ." He waved his hands, speechless before the magnitude of those "ifs."

"Big time, huh?"

"Not just 'big time.' If you want to know, it's mainly not working for the clown anymore. It's eating me up. Crane's a real guy. It'd be like Garrahy again."

Marlene took the little silvery pot off the stove and poured herself two ounces of tarry liquid into a squat clear glass cup. She put half a cube of sugar into her mouth and slurped the coffee past it until the sugar was all gone.

"Well. You shouldn't be eaten up. Except by me, of course." She smiled, faintly, not the real Marlene thousand-watt room-lighter, but a smile, and welcome.

"I haven't said I would yet, Marlene," Karp said, smiling back. "It's still not a done deal."

"I see in your eyes it's a done deal, babe. You want it, you oughta go for it."

He reached across the table and grasped her hand. "Okay. That's good. I'll call him tomorrow and tell him we're coming. It'll be okay, Marlene. Moving—it's not the end of the universe or anything."

"No, 'cause I'm not moving."

He cocked his head as if he hadn't heard her. "What?"

"What I said. Go do it! I'll keep a candle burning in our little home against your return. I mean, how long can it take, solve the crime of the century? For you? Couple of weeks, tops."

"Marlene, this is serious. . . ."

"Yeah, you keep telling me. I'll tell you what else is serious. Ripping our life apart is serious. Dumping my career. Taking Lucy away from her grandparents and everybody she knows. Leaving our *home*. Serious stuff, and what's the most serious is that I can tell you haven't thought much about it. You hear crime of the century and Bert Crane, another solution to your perpetual lost-father complex, and you're off and running, and let old Marlene deal with the little details."

"That isn't fair, Marlene."

"No, you're right, it isn't. How about you springing this shit on me? Hey, babe, I got a job in D.C., pack it up! That's fair? Look—you can't stand working for Bloom? Fine! There's four other DAs in the city, plus two federal prosecutors, and half a dozen other county prosecutors within commuting distance. Not to mention, I hear there's one or two private law firms in New York. I don't recall you beating on those doors, you can't stand another minute of Bloom."

Karp stood up abruptly and walked a distance away from her, his hands thrust deep in his pockets. He was angrier with her than he'd been in a good while. It was the sort of rage we experience when we have been selfish under the guise of some pretended generosity, and have been found out. Naturally, what he said then was, "You're really being selfish, Marlene."

She opened her mouth to say something, closed it, took a breath instead, and knocked back the rest of her wine. "I'm going to bed," she said, and walked off.

"We haven't finished this, Marlene," said Karp.

She stopped and turned. There were tears in her eyes but her voice was steady. "No, but in a minute you're going to hit me with 'A man's gotta do what a man's gotta do.' And I agree. A man's gotta. But a woman doesn't, and neither does a little kid. Don't forget to write."

The next day, Karp called Bert Crane and told him he would take the job. Crane made enthusiastic noises of congratulation; they sounded tinny and unreal coming over the phone, and made Karp feel no better. He had a taste like bile in his mouth and his stomach was hollow and jumpy. He was stepping into a void.

Next, he went up and saw the district attorney. Bloom was sitting behind his big, clean desk, in shirtsleeves and yellow sus-

penders, puffing on a large cigar. He was a bland-faced medium-sized man who might have been an anchor on the six o'clock news. He had nearly every qualification for his job—a keen political instinct, the ability to generate ever-increasing budgets, a cool hand with the ferocious New York media, and a*positive talent for bureaucratic management. All he lacked was an understanding of what the criminal justice system was supposed to accomplish and even the faintest ability to successfully try cases.

Karp stood in front of the desk and told Bloom that he was leaving and where he was going. To Karp's great surprise, Bloom seemed stunned and dismayed. He gestured Karp to a chair.

"What's wrong? I thought you were happy here. You got your bureau. You're doing great things. . . ."

Karp had trouble finding his voice. At last he said, "Well, I've been here a long time. I thought it was time to move on. And the challenge . . . Kennedy . . ."

"Crane, huh? What's he paying you?"

Karp told him.

Bloom said, "Tell you what—it'll take some screwing around with personnel, but I think I can beat that."

Karp felt his mouth open involuntarily. "Um . . . it's not really a money thing. It's just time for me to do something else."

Bloom chomped on his cigar and frowned. "You're making a big mistake, my friend. You'll dick around down there for a year or so until they get tired of stirring the pot and they'll get you to write a fat report nobody'll read, and then where are you? Out on your ass."

"Well. I'll have to worry about that when the time comes."

Bloom shrugged and blew smoke. "Think about it," he said.

Karp said he would and walked out. The feeling of weirdness, of being in a waking dream, continued unabated. Bloom being nice to him, Bloom offering him a *raise*, was, more than anything he could think of, a sign that his life had irrevocably changed.

In the headquarters of the Central Intelligence Agency in Langley, Virginia, a small group of men is sorting through stacks of paper. The paper has been removed from filing cabinets throughout the Agency in response to a subpoena duces tecum from the Church committee, a body established by the United States Senate to investigate certain suspected excesses of the CIA. They are obliged by law, and as federal employees,

to comply with this order to yield documents, and they are complying, if reluctantly. The men have been trained in strict secrecy since early adulthood, and more than that, they have been trained to be judges of what must remain secret in order to protect the national security, and more than that, they have come to believe that they themselves are the best judges of what the national security is.

Two of the men are working with ink rollers and thick markers, blotting out the sections of these documents deemed too sensitive for the eyes of United States senators. Some documents have had nearly everything but the addresses and the letterhead blotted out in this way. They have done this many times before and are good at it.

One man walks among the desks, picking up piles of finished documents, indexing their reference numbers, and placing them in a carton for delivery to the Senate. It grows late, but the CIA is, of course, a twenty-four-hour, seven-day-a-week operation. Nevertheless, these are all senior employees and not as young as they once were, when several of them were actual spies. They are anxious to see their suburban beds.

The man picking up the documents yawns, shares a slight joke with one of the men at the desks, and picks up by mistake the wrong pile, a thin stack of paper comprising four brief documents that were by no means ever intended to be seen by senators without being reduced to illegibility. He indites their numbers on his list, tosses them into the carton on the floor, and moves on.

THREE

Karp disliked flying, not because he was afraid of crashing—at this point in his life he might have enjoyed a quick immolation—but because airliners are not constructed with the Karps of the world in mind. From the moment he sat down in his seat to the moment he arose at flight's end, the leg-jamming angle imposed by the cramped coach seats always produced a continuous dull ache in his bad knee. He stared out the window at greasy-looking clouds. It had been raining at La Guardia when he boarded the shuttle and the pilot had just announced that it was raining at National as well. The weather suited his mood. For the past week he and Marlene had maintained a climate of chilly formality: overcast, with no sign of clearing.

The plane lurched and dipped a wing and Karp's window showed woolly whiteness, then glimpses of landscape, a brown, oily river lined with autumn trees; now the famous sights jumped into view, the Monument and the Capitol dome, always a little shocking to see in real life, rather than on the little screen. Another lower swoop across the Potomac and they were down at National Airport.

Karp had been in Washington only twice before, once during a high school class trip and again to give a speech on homicide prosecution to a seminar at an annual meeting of prosecutors. He recalled steamy heat, bland food, large groups of people endlessly walking. The old tag came into his mind, "A city of southern efficiency and northern charm," and then with a little jolt he re-

membered that John Kennedy had said that, and here he was in that city to study the man's death. It made him feel mildly light-headed.

He stepped into a cab at the hack stand and gave the driver the address Crane had given him. Looking out the window as the dripping scene whirled by, he tried to orient himself. It was not easy, even with reference to the little map of the District, encased in plastic and affixed to the back of the driver's seat, which all Washington cabs must carry to show the fare zones. Orientation in Manhattan makes few demands on the intellect; it is like living on a ruler: uptown, downtown, East Side, West Side. The absence of this in other metropolises often produces a form of vertigo in long-time New York residents, that and not being able to find a decent loaf of rye bread.

So it was now with Karp. Over a bridge, across some parkland studded with monuments glowing dimly through the drizzle, through some meaningless streets, and to the door of an unprepossessing office building on Fourth Street off D: the old FBI Annex.

He took the elevator to the sixth floor and entered a scene of noisy disorder. The hallway was redolent with fresh paint, and workmen were moving desks and chairs along on dollies, stacking them in a great jumble at one end of the hallway. Karp eased around the mess, stepping carefully over the spattered drop cloths until he came to a door that bore a neat hand-lettered sign:

HOUSE SELECT COMMITTEE ON ASSASSINATIONS
CHIEF COUNSEL

This gave on a large room full of cartons and desks and chairs scattered at useless angles. Several women dressed in jeans and casual tops were unloading cartons into steel file cabinets. A telephone technician was up on a ladder poking into a hole where a ceiling panel had been removed.

"You must be Karp," said a clear, high voice behind him.

Karp turned and saw a thin middle-aged woman in jeans and a T-shirt, her white-blond hair done up in a neat bun. She wore large round glasses and had a pleasantly bony face.

Extending her hand, she said, "I'm Bea Sondergard. Bert's waiting for you."

Karp shook the hand and followed her down a short hallway.

She said, "What a mess, huh? Bert wanted to get started in

D.C. as soon as possible. The federal government is not used to starting operations in a week. Or a year."

She knocked briefly and threw open a door. Bert Crane, dressed in chinos and a worn blue Brooks Brothers shirt, was sitting on a secretary's chair in the center of a large corner office, using a stack of cartons as a desk.

He looked up expectantly. "Phones?"

Sondergard shook her head. "Definitely by Thanksgiving—no, really, the guy said pretty soon. Look who's here."

Crane rose and greeted Karp. "Welcome to Washington. I wish I could have received you in more splendor. The furniture's on order; God knows when it'll get here. We have no phones, and I'm not sure we're being paid."

"Aside from that . . . ," said Sondergard.

Crane grinned. "Yeah, aside from that. This is what's known as hitting the ground running. Look, here's the plan. I have to make some calls, assuming the phone starts working. Bea will get you started on the paperwork to get you on board. Then we're due over at the Rayburn Building for a meeting with the chairman, show him you can walk and talk and don't drool. Then I've got a lunch with some media people, and you're free until, let's say, two; get back here, and we'll talk. You should be able to catch the four o'clock shuttle."

"Sounds good," said Karp.

Bea Sondergard ushered him out and into her own cramped office next door, where, Karp was not surprised to see, all was in order: a desk, several chairs, a brass lamp with a shade, a typing table on which was a Lexitron word processor, and on one wall, several sheets of white chart paper displaying carefully printed lists of things to do, and flowcharts showing the order in which they were to be accomplished. The woman quickly found a manila file and handed it to him. In it were the forms without which the government would not recognize the existence of its servants. On each of the forms there was a little typed note explaining which forms were most important and offering pithy advice on what to put where.

"Very thorough," said Karp, again not surprised. He realized, of course, that Bea Sondergard was one of the anonymous, self-effacing, and ruthlessly efficient people, almost always women, al-

most always in their middle years, who hold the fabric of modern civilization together by sheer force of will. There must be at least one in every organization, and in order to have any sensible interaction with a bureaucracy, the first step is to find out who she is. Bea Sondergard was the one in Crane's outfit.

"Thank you," said Sondergard. "I trust you won't have any trouble with all that. We're exempt from civil service because we work for Congress—obviously Congress isn't going to burden itself with the nonsense they make the rest of the government go through—but it's twisted enough as it is. Getting purchase orders and stuff through the comptroller—God knows when you'll be able to get furniture."

Karp looked up from "Mother's Maiden Name." "What's wrong with the stuff in the hallway?"

"Oh, that! It's just garbage the previous tenants declared surplus. It's going out to Maryland for storage or disposal tomorrow."

"I'll take it."

"Seriously? It's tacky in the extreme."

"No problem."

"Well, well. You must have flunked bureaucrats school. I thought you looked like class," she said, beaming a smile that showed large teeth and a significant spread of pale pink gum. "I bet you *do* find out who killed Kennedy."

Later, on the short walk up the slope to the Rayburn, Crane, now in a slick gray suit, said, "Let me fill you in on George Flores. Six-term rep from the Twentieth District. That's Dallas, by the way, and probably not by accident. Flores was not a big enthusiast for starting this committee, but once it got the go-ahead from the House leadership, he moved in fast. Why? Who knows? It may just be that he doesn't want anyone stirring up his patch without being able to look over their shoulder.

"As far as the rest of the committee goes, they'll be inclined to let Flores take the lead. Frank Morgan's a solid guy, he's a black caucus leader, but he's mainly interested in the MLK side. On your side, I'd have to say the main guy would be Hank Dobbs."

"Who is . . . ?"

"Representative from the Second District in Connecticut. He's Richard Ewing Dobbs's kid, by the way." Karp gave him a blank

look. Crane shook his head in amazement. "How soon they forget! Richard Ewing Dobbs? Doesn't ring a bell? How about Alger Hiss? Julius and Ethel Rosenberg?"

"Them I know. His father was a spy?"

"Accused spy. One of the great liberal cause célèbres of the bad old fifties. We don't discuss it with Hank, incidentally. He's a little raw on the subject. Anyway, of the committee as a whole, he's probably the strongest supporter of the way we want to do things."

"A friend, in other words," Karp ventured.

Crane sniffed, "I wouldn't go quite that far. You know the saying—if you want a friend in Washington, buy a dog. But an ally, at least—and I think you and he will get along."

They reached the undistinguished sugar-white pile with the acromegalic statues flanking the entrance and went in. Walking down the broad corridors toward Flores's office, Karp was gratified to see actual lobbyists plying their trade, speaking in small confidential groups to one another or surrounding a striding representative in a slowly moving pack, like hyenas tugging at a dying wildebeest.

They arrived at the appointed hour and were told to wait in an anteroom. Karp looked around with interest. He had never been in a congressman's office before. On the walls, posters showed the Dallas skyline and a rodeo. There was a Lone Star flag on display and a Remington knockoff of a buckaroo on a side table, which also held a selection of magazines devoted to Texas, Dallas, government, and Mexican-Americans, several in Spanish. The walls of the waiting area were paneled in dark wood and there was a rug on the floor emblazoned with the congressional seal.

A head-high wall of frosted glass ran across the width of the room, and looking over it Karp observed that it was crowded with cubicles so small that it seemed incredible that any normal human beings could work in them.

He observed as much to Crane, who chuckled. "Those are congressional staff, not human beings. Congressional staff have the worst working conditions and longest hours of anybody in the country. The whole place is one huge sweatshop. The laws of this great nation are written by twenty-five-year-olds in the last stages of exhaustion, breathing the farts of their neighbors. That's why the government works so well."

He glanced at his watch and then at a clock embedded in a bronze longhorn on the receptionist's desk. "George is showing

he's a congressman and we work for him. If we were voters, he'd've been out here ten minutes ago."

Flores made them wait for fifteen minutes. When he emerged it was behind a group of elderly ladies chattering in drawls, patently voters all. The congressman pumped schmaltz without stopping in a thick Texas drawl until the last of the ladies had cleared the outer door, at which time the broad smile, very white against his tan face, faded to mere cordiality.

He shook hands with Crane and turned to be introduced to Karp. The smile lost a few watts as he shook hands. The congressman was only five feet five. Karp had observed this before, the reflexive pugnacity of the short when confronting someone of Karp's size. Flores squeezed a little harder than necessary; Karp pretended to flinch, conscious of being on his best behavior and not wanting to screw things up for Crane.

Flores ushered them into his office. Whatever constraints applied to staff space obviously did not apply to the elected representatives of the people. The private office was large, darkly paneled, and supplied with broad windows looking out across Independence Avenue. Flores sat behind a large mahogany desk, flanked by the flags of his state and nation. Karp and Crane arranged themselves in comfortable chairs facing the desk, which was covered with papers and the sort of knickknacks that public figures accumulate over the years.

There was a side table with various awards and plaques on it, and the usual wall full of framed photographs showing Flores with people even more prominent than he, that or doing something notable, like posing in a hard hat digging a spadeful of earth with a silvery shovel. The three men exchanged pleasantries. Karp thought that he had already discovered one difference between New York and Washington: the social bullshit segment of meetings seemed to go on longer down here. Flores and Crane chatted on about some people Karp did not know and he felt his attention wander.

On the surface of the desk in front of Karp, amid the commemorative medals, flag stands, and objects embedded in Lucite was a rough-looking tool, a dark, mattocklike blade attached to a stumpy handle. Flores caught him looking at it and smiled. "You know what that is?" he asked.

Karp did not.

"It's a short hoe. *La cortita.* The backbreaker. My grandfather used one of those all his life, migrant labor; when he was an old man he was bent over like a question mark. And my father, before he got out of it. And me too, a summer. I keep the goddamn thing there to remind me where I come from."

There did not seem to be anything to say to this revelation, so Karp smiled politely and waited for what would come. In any case, the social preamble seemed to be over.

Flores leaned back in his high-backed leather chair and laced his fingers. He had a large square face the color and texture of worn leather, set off by extravagant gray-shot sideburns and a thick Villista mustache. His hair was dark and swept back, and he had black, shiny eyes that seemed to be all pupil. These now bored in on Karp.

"I've heard a lot about you," Flores began. "Bert here's filled me in and I've asked around. Y'all have quite a record. You seem to be a hard charger." He paused. "And that concerns me. I've already mentioned this to Bert when he brought up your name, and I'm going to have to say it to you. This investigation is not the same kind of thing as a New York street shooting. The whole country'll be looking at what you do. Every move you make'll be raked over by the press and squeezed to see if it's got any political juice in it. Not only that, y'all're working for the Congress now. It's a whole different branch of government. It has . . . different ways of doing things. Political ways. You following me?"

The word "sure" formed on Karp's tongue, but he could not bring it into the air. There were limits, after all. He said instead, "No, as a matter of fact, I don't follow you at all. I'm a homicide investigator and prosecutor. I look at the evidence and shape a case. I don't see what politics has to do with it."

Flores smiled at this statement as he might have at the burbling of a small child. "Son, this is Washington, D.C. Ain't nothing happens here doesn't have some political angle. You might *think* it don't when you do it, but there's sons-of-bitches make it their whole life's work to *find* some politics in it and beat you over the head with it." He paused to let this wisdom settle.

"Now, the reason I'm telling you this is that if you want to work for me we got to get one thing straight from the get-go. Y'all work for Bert Crane here, and Bert Crane works for me. Not only do I expect to be kept informed about what you're doing, but I

expect that you and the professional staff of the Select Committee will be, let's say, *guided*, by me in all of your work. That means one thing's more important than anything else: no surprises. Your chairman does not want to get a call one evening from the *Post* or CBS asking me what I think of the latest thing y'all've done and me not know what the hell they're talking about. You following me now?"

Karp nodded. "Right. No surprises."

The conversation then turned to the details of staffing and logistics. There was some confusion here and Karp could tell that Crane and Flores were fencing. Neither said anything solid about how much staff he could expect and what his budget was going to be. This was something of a shocker; Karp had supposed that it was all greased and ready to go.

The two men got into an argument about parking spaces and then one about how the letterhead of the investigation staff was going to read. Karp felt he had nothing to contribute to this discussion and remained silent, growing ever more bored and irritated, and thinking that working with a short hoe was probably good preparation for this sort of work, although perhaps more stimulating.

After twenty minutes of palaver over trivialities, a call came through and the congressman picked up the phone and snapped at the operator. Then he cradled the phone in his neck and said, smiling, "I got to take this one, boys." He extended a hand to each of them in turn, and Karp noted that this time Flores did not feel obliged to squeeze hard.

"What the hell was that all about?" asked Karp when they were in the hallway again.

Crane placed a hand on Karp's shoulder. "Welcome to Washington."

"No, really. Did he mean that shit about running everything through him?"

Crane laughed, the booming sound echoing in the hallway, drawing stares. "Oh, God, no! Let me translate. What he meant was, if things go well and we don't raise any flak, he gets the credit. If we raise any flak, we're on our own. There's no conceivable way he can oversee our investigation. He's got way too much on his plate, like all these jokers. Matter of fact, any involvement with

government at all takes him away from his real occupation, which is getting elected every two years. That's the full-time job. He didn't really bear down on the staff issues, for which you can be grateful. That's why I kept him on the stationery and the rest of the horse puckey."

"What about the staff?"

"Well, you'll be lucky to hire the main people—your personal secretary, the head of research, the chief field investigator. The others . . . well, congressmen have folks to whom they owe jobs, besides which, everybody on the committee will want at least one personal spy in the organization."

Karp was openmouthed. "You must be joking."

"Not really. They're all worried, especially Flores. This Kennedy thing is a can of worms, with no real political payoff for anyone. The House leadership launched into it *very* reluctantly."

"Yeah, you said that before. So why did they go for it at all?"

"Well, there you have me. My own theory was that it was a payoff to the black caucus in an election year. Launching a King investigation is something they can sell at home, and it's kind of hard for the House Democratic leadership to buck something having to do with King. Once you're looking into King, Kennedy kind of follows. Plus the stuff about federal agencies not being forthcoming with Warren, the stuff that's turning up in the Church committee's work. And the assassination nuts keep yawping at their heels. A lot of people believe it and it has to be answered. O'Neill's the key player, of course, and he hates this kind of thing, and consented *very* reluctantly. Warren is gospel with Tip. The old 'protecting the family' business."

"This is not good for us, right?"

"Right, but meanwhile here we are." Crane checked his watch. "Look, I have to roll. Let me take you by Hank's place. If he's in, I'll introduce you; if not, we'll set up a date to get the two of you together."

This, as it proved, was not necessary. As they entered the elevator, Crane greeted a tall, lean, sandy-haired man already in the car.

"Hank! This is a piece of luck. I have to run off and here you are to take the pass. This is Butch Karp from New York."

One of those Norman Rockwell kids grown up was Karp's first impression as he shook hands with Henry Dobbs, Democrat of

Connecticut. As their eyes met he revised his take. Dobbs had the freckled skin, the even, understated features, the crisp short hair, but the cornflower eyes were not innocent ones. There was a careful intelligence there, a wariness, some complexity of character that was not ever seen on the covers of the old *Saturday Evening Post*.

By the time the car had gone two floors, it was agreed that Karp and Dobbs would lunch together. Crane took his leave. Dobbs led Karp to his own office. It was like Flores's, with different flags, seals, and posters. Dobbs checked his messages, excused himself and made a short call, dealt with several matters pressed on him by staff, and then broke free. He seemed to run a happier and lower-keyed ship than Flores did.

The Capitol has a restaurant reserved for members and their guests during the lunch hours, and Dobbs took Karp there on the little subway that connects the various congressional buildings.

"I hear you met George," he said when they were seated. "What did you think?"

"A great American and a fine public servant," Karp answered.

Dobbs smiled. "You're learning. Keep that up and you'll be a big hit in Washington."

"Well, about that—I'm starting to think this might be a major misunderstanding, me doing this job."

"Oh?"

"Yeah, I tried to explain to Bert about being politically impaired. It's a form of epilepsy. If I think an investigation is being screwed up because of politics, my eyes roll up, I foam at the mouth, and I become uncontrollable."

Dobbs laughed but Karp went on, deadpan. "I'm serious. I don't want to mess things up and destroy lives and careers. I *want* to kiss ass, and go along to get along, and be one of the boys. I just . . . can't . . . do it. It's my personal tragedy, like being one of Jerry's kids. And now you know my shame."

Dobbs wiped his eyes with his napkin. "Thank you for sharing. Actually, I think you're just what we need. Look, in all seriousness, here's the picture on Flores. Like the rest of us, he's got more committee assignments than he knows what to do with. Two things interest him, Hispanic affairs and migrants—to his credit he's sincere about helping out his people—and energy, because he's in the oil patch down there and that's how he stays elected. His interest in the Kennedy thing is twofold: first, if you do come

up with something rich, it'll get him on TV in Dallas, and two . . . that's a bit more complex." Dobbs took a sip of water and continued.

"One assumption some people have is that the mystery behind JFK is a Dallas mystery. Oswald's life there. Ruby and the cops. What really happened in the half hour or so after the first shots. George is connected to the people who run Dallas, and to the extent that the investigation might affect them, especially in a negative way, George has *got* to be on top of it. Does that make sense?"

"Yeah, it does. But the question is, if it turns out that one of his associates needs to be leaned on, will he balk?"

Dobbs grinned. "Oh, yeah. He might balk. He might do worse than that. Which is why you have me."

Karp thought about this for a moment, and then, looking into the blue eyes, asked, "And why *do* we have you, Mr. Dobbs? Are the people of Connecticut burning to find out if old Earl Warren went into the tank on this one? Or what . . . ?"

The waiter came and they ordered. When the man left, Dobbs said, "That's the right question, all right. What's in it for Dobbs. I like you, Mr. Karp, or, if I may, Butch. I'm Hank. You get right to the point, which is sometimes like a dose of oxygen around here, although I should warn you it's a violation of the Federal Anti-Confrontation and Bullshitters' Protection Act of 1973, As Amended." He smiled at the small joke and Karp smiled too.

Dobbs leaned back and looked up at the ceiling. "How to put it? Well, first, my constituents. The people of the great state of Connecticut are mainly interested in keeping the insurance industry happy and making sure that when ships and weapons get built, they get built in the great state of Connecticut, as a result of which I spend most of my time on the Banking and Armed Services Committees. In my spare time, I try to do an occasional favor for the United States. As far as personally goes, in 1963, I was at Yale. I'd worked on the presidential campaign in Hartford, and my family had some connections in the past with Jack Kennedy. I'd actually shaken his hand, once, when he was in the Senate. I remember I told him that I was interested in politics and that I was off to Yale that year, and he laughed and told me that if I worked hard I could overcome even that obstacle. I was in Dwight eating a sandwich when some kid ran into the dining room and

yelled out that Kennedy'd been shot in Dallas. I went into shock
—well, everybody did, really, but I guess I imagined mine was
worse. My dad had just passed on that summer and I suppose I
conflated the two losses in my mind. It was an extremely bad year
for me; I nearly flunked out, as a matter of fact, and had to repeat
the semester. Okay, that's personal aspects. There's a political aspect too. I think practically everyone understands that when Kennedy was assassinated, the country started on a downward slope.
I think it had more of an effect on the country than Lincoln's did,
because Lincoln had mainly finished his work and Kennedy had
barely started his. Not that I'm comparing Kennedy to Lincoln—
that's not the point. The point is that the country was tipped out
of one track and into another, which we're still on and which is
no good."

"Because Kennedy died?" Karp asked.

"Actually, as much as I mourn his loss, no, not exactly. It was
mainly because of what happened afterward. The government
didn't tell the truth about what happened. Some people decided
that a higher national purpose would be served if the facts about
the assassination were bent to prove a point. Have you read the
Report?"

"Not yet."

"Then I won't say anything about it; make up your own mind.
But give me the point for a moment. That lie was the forerunner
of the lies in service of a higher national purpose that got us into
Vietnam, and kept us there until the army and the country were
nearly wrecked. It was the premise for all the stuff that Nixon's
cronies did. The good of the country, as any bozo wants to define
it, is more important than the truth. Hey, the good of the country
demands that Nixon gets reelected? No problem, we'll burgle,
we'll lie, we'll cover up the truth. After a while the people stop
believing *anything* the government says. Hell, we've got a presidential candidate now whose main platform is 'I'll never lie to
you.' Like it was a big thing. It's pathetic! And it all started in
Dallas, and what we made of it in the Warren Report. If we're
ever going to get the country back on the right track, we have to
go back to the point when we ran off the rails. That's why I'm
pushing this investigation, my little favor, as I said, for the United
States of America. Does that answer your question?"

Karp nodded. "Uh-huh," he said. It was a convincing speech.

On the other hand, Dobbs was a politician; his profession was giving convincing speeches. Maybe he had even given this one before, like Flores with his hoe routine. Maybe it was even true. In any case, it was at least possible that Dobbs was prepared to support a serious investigation. Karp found himself liking the man, despite what Crane had said about Washington and dogs. Karp was himself a connoisseur of fine speeches, and lies, and his instinct told him that Dobbs at least believed what he was saying. Also, the contrast between the patronizing, overbearing Flores and the frankness of Dobbs, a man only two or three years Karp's senior, was gratifying. A *congressman*, after all.

The food came and they began eating and resumed talking, the subject having been changed by unspoken agreement to fields less fraught with passion and consequence.

Karp walked back down the Hill to the office on Fourth Street. When he entered, Bea Sondergard was sitting on the floor amid a chaos of file boxes, moving papers among file folders of various colors. She looked up at him over the rims of her spectacles.

"How was lunch? I heard you dined with Congress."

"I had the chicken," said Karp.

"That's the first step. Chicken, then sirloin, then bribes and fancy girls. He's in his office. Oh, and I had some furniture moved into your place. I took the liberty of deciding on a color scheme."

"Gosh, I had my heart set on something in rusting gray metal."

She flashed teeth. "Then you'll be pleased."

Bert Crane was on the phone when Karp walked in. The office had been tidied some and Crane now sat in a high leather chair behind a handsome new mahogany desk. And the phones obviously worked. Karp sat down on a new-smelling black leather couch, and waited.

When Crane got off the phone and turned to him, Karp observed, "You guys work fast."

"Yeah, it's great, if we stay out of jail. Bea sometimes cuts the corners in procurement. I think she paid for all this stuff with an account that's not quite authorized yet. How was your lunch?"

"I had the chicken. How was yours?"

"As I said, I ate with the press. We just went out on the veldt and they found a dead zebra. But, really—how did you make out with Dobbs?"

"Pretty good, I think. He seems like a straight shooter."

"I agree. For a politician, anyway. What did you talk about?"

"He filled me in on Flores, similar to what you said. And we exchanged boyish confidences. He told me a story about why he's serious about doing the Kennedy investigation right."

"The one about JFK and his dad?"

"Just hinted at it. I gathered they were political allies of the Kennedys in some way."

"More than that. Richard Dobbs was with Kennedy in the Pacific during the war. He was some kind of operations or intelligence officer with Kennedy's PT boat squadron. They'd been at Harvard together, although Dobbs was a little older, and I think they were pretty close. He finished the war as a lieutenant commander and then went right into the Navy Department. When the shit hit the fan in the fifties, JFK was the only politician of any stature who stood by him. An unusual profile in courage for Kennedy, I might add. He was not prone to gestures that might have hurt him politically, and defending Richard Ewing Dobbs was sure as hell in that class."

"Well, none of that got mentioned. He also talked about how bad it was for the country, the doubts about Warren and all. He sounded sincere."

"No doubt. Sounding sincere is in his job description."

"Is being cynical in mine?"

Crane laughed enthusiastically. "Yes it is, the *sine qua non,* in fact. But seriously, Dobbs is solid on this investigation, and on most other things too. I didn't mean to denigrate the man. If things get sticky, and they will, I think we can count on him. All you have to remember with Dobbs is, his daddy didn't do it."

FOUR

"I don't see what's so funny," said Karp to the ceiling. He was in his office at the New York DA, his soon-to-be-former office. On a nearby chair, a chunky, milk chocolate–skinned man in a tan, pin-striped, double-breasted suit was bent over with helpless laughter. It was the hiccuping kind of laughter, nearly soundless, the infectious kind, and Karp himself felt it tickling his own face.

"It's a good opportunity—," he added.

The laughter increased in intensity, and the other man, who was a detective lieutenant in the New York Police Department, started to lose control of his limbs and slide off his seat.

Karp started to laugh too, as the thought of trying to convince a hysterically laughing man to take charge of the field investigation of the death of John F. Kennedy suddenly struck him as hilarious.

Several minutes passed in this way, and when the lieutenant, whose name was Clay Fulton, and who was Karp's oldest and best friend in the cops, had advanced to the stage of gasping "Oh, God" and wiping his eyes with his lemon silk handkerchief, Karp took up his case again.

"Seriously, Clay . . ."

"Oh, God, don't start," Fulton groaned. "My heart can't take much of this anymore."

"Seriously," Karp persisted. "I think it's a good deal. You were set to retire from the job anyway."

"You *are* serious about this," said Fulton, sitting up again.

"I keep saying."

"You're going to go find out who aced JFK, and you want me to help you?"

"You got the picture. What's your problem?"

Fulton let out a whoosh of breath and scratched the side of his heavy jaw. He regarded Karp through narrowed eyes. "Well, I got a couple. One, what makes you think we're gonna do any good on a thirteen-year-old investigation, that the guys who were there when the corpse was still warm couldn't've done?"

"Maybe they didn't want to. Maybe they were incompetent. Besides, it was Texas. You ever been in Texas?"

"Yeah, in the army. Why?"

"Well, so you know what it's like. Do they have food? Do they have shows? Do they have clothes? They're hicks, face it. So, get a couple of sharp New York kids like us in there, a little hustle— it'll be a whole different story."

Fulton laughed again. "So what you're saying is because you can't get a knish in Texas, we'll make it happen thirteen years later, where they drew a blank?"

"That's it. I rest my case."

Fulton stared at him for a moment and said, smiling, "You need professional help, not a cop."

"Come on, Clay. You're a homicide investigator. Investigate the homicide of the century! What're you gonna do when you retire? Security for department stores? Teach at John Jay? You'll go batshit."

"This is for *me*, right? You're doing me a *favor*? Just a minute, let me make sure my wallet's still here." He patted at his suit coat pocket. "Okay, wise guy, how long you figure this gig is going to take? Months? Years?"

"This I don't know," admitted Karp. "Say a year . . ."

"Okay, that means I'm gonna have to go to Martha and say, 'Guess what, baby? We're going south. Back to the land o' cotton . . .' "

"Oh, horseshit, Clay! Washington isn't the *South*!"

"Do tell," said Fulton, giving Karp a hard look. "And there's Texas, too. Those old boys're gonna love having a big-city nigger poking around in what they did or didn't do, the heaviest case they ever saw."

Karp was taken aback, and felt himself flush with embarrassment. It had not occurred to Karp that Fulton and his wife would

be at all discommoded by moving from their apartment on the Upper West Side of Manhattan to a city that was still heavily segregated, in fact if not in law, or that poking into a Texas investigation might be a problem for a black man.

Karp said, "Okay, forget it. I wasn't thinking. . . ."

Fulton stood up, leaned over, and placed his hand on Karp's arm. "No, I appreciate being asked . . . I guess."

He perched on the edge of the desk and looked at Karp with the fatherly expression he sometimes assumed with the younger man. He was only twelve years older, but he had spent most of his adult life as a street cop uptown, which worked out to an effective seniority of about a thousand and four years.

"Goddamn," said Fulton, shaking his head and grinning, showing his gold tooth, "our little Butch's really gonna do it. A long time, the two of us."

"Yeah, eleven years. Dr. Fulton's College of Criminal Knowledge for green-ass prosecutors. I would've sunk like a stone, you hadn't grabbed me by the shorts."

"Mooney McPhail."

Karp smiled. "Yeah, Mooney McPhail. An easy grounder to short and I bobbled it."

"You were second seating for Joe Lerner."

"Right, another blast from the past. He's in on this too, by the way, the MLK side. I had a witness said she saw Mooney use the knife, and picked him out of the lineup. That was the case. Holy shit! What a fuckup!"

"Only she didn't. It was her sister saw it and she told—what the hell was her name?—Esther, Ethyl?"

"Methyl," said Karp.

"Methyl, right. She got the whole story from the sister and she decided to be the witness, because the sister had the arth-a-ritis."

"Yeah, it would've been a classic, if it'd come out on cross. Defense would've asked, 'Did you actually observe this with your own eyes,' and old Methyl would've said, 'Oh, no, my sister told me the whole story and she don't lie.' Case dismissed."

Fulton laughed. "Turned out the sister didn't see it either. Took me a month to find the girl who told the sister. . . . Damn!"

"What?"

"It just flashed on me, where I was."

"What, when you found the witness?"

"No, where I was when I found out about Kennedy. I was up on St. Nick, up around 'forty-third, making a collar. Some pimp cut a girl. I was a detective second out of the Two-eight. I had him in cuffs on the street and my partner, Mike Samuels, was just opening the car, and I looked up and there was a crowd of about fifty people around this appliance and stereo store, pressed up against the grilles. They had a bunch of TVs there, on all the time. We locked the mutt in the back and I went over to see what was going on. We'd been in the building maybe forty minutes with this asshole, and in that time Kennedy'd been shot and pronounced dead. The man never meant that much to me personally, but it was a hell of a jolt—the *president* and all that. But the people on the sidewalk, most of them were carrying on like it was Lincoln all over again, a couple of old church ladies hollering, 'Sweet Jesus God . . .'"

Fulton paused for a deprecating chuckle. "It affected a lot a folks up there. I guess it's . . . they've seen a lot of young men die for no reason, just from meanness and stupidity. It must've kind of crystallized the whole thing for them. My mom, now . . . still got a magazine cover of JFK framed, and Bobby too. Right next to Dr. King. And Jesus, of course. Hell of a thing!" He shook his head.

"Anyway, I ran back to the car and told Samuels what was up, and of course, he had to go over and check it out for himself. The mutt asks me what's up and I tell him and he says, 'Well, fuck him! When we gonna move?' Like he was late for a big date."

Fulton stood up and said, "Tell you one thing. I do this, and it works, I'd get my momma off my case. She's been pissed at me for joining the cops from day one. Can you believe, she still introduces me: 'This is my eldest, Clayton, first college graduate in the family and he threw it all away to be with the police.'"

Karp brightened. "So you *will* think about it."

"I'll *think* about it, boss. We're in the thinking stage here. Give me a couple of days. Meanwhile, I'll see you later on at the party."

"You're not supposed to tell me about it," said Karp glumly. "It's supposed to be a surprise."

Four hours later, Karp was in that state of woozy euphoria he obtained through drink, a state that for him lasted about twelve minutes before being replaced by faint nausea and a sick headache. Karp couldn't drink at all, this lapse being a source of keen amuse-

ment to his friends and his wife, all of whom could put it away pretty good.

The farewell party was well under way. The homicide bureau had kicked in for a catered spread—chopped liver, little shrimpy hors d'oeuvres, fried wontons, tiny pizzas—and some decent liquor and beer. There were about fifty people in the bureau's outer office, where the desks had all been pushed to the walls. The secretaries had set up a big boom box, which was now blasting out the Village People's "YMCA" for the fifth time and people were getting funky in the center of the floor, doing the peculiar spastic dancing that made the 1970s such a world of fun.

"No more," said Karp to the man attempting to refill his glass with champagne. "I'll get blotto."

"That's the point," said the man, continuing to pour. "If the guest of honor can walk out steadily, it's an insult to his friends. We'll carry you on a door."

The man's name was Vernon Talcott Newbury. He was a lawyer in the fraud bureau and Karp's closest friend among the people he had started with in the old DA's office. A rare bird, Newbury, in the gritty environs of 100 Centre Street: rich, for one thing, very rich, a sprig of a family of New York bankers who regarded the Rockefellers as pushy newcomers. Yale College and Harvard Law for another, unlike most of the people working at the DA, who were more likely to have come from places like Fordham and St. Johns. A lean, small man with longish, ash blond hair, he had the remarkable good looks, "chiseled" as the expression has it, of one of the gentlemen in white tie that Charles Dana Gibson used to draw in company with his famous girls.

Karp had never figured out what had brought V.T., as he was universally known, into the DA, or what kept him there. V.T. would not give a straight answer. "One slums," he might say, or, "My family are practitioners of fraud; I prefer to study it." It did have something to do with his family, Karp had concluded early on: that great intermarried, extended family of WASPs, with names off the street signs of lower Manhattan and downtown Brooklyn, as exotic as Nepalese to Karp, and as fascinating. Such clans tend to produce at least one maverick in each generation, and V.T. was the one in his. He might as easily, and with about the same level of family disapproval, have chosen to have become a lion tamer at Ringling's or opened a delicatessen in Passaic.

Karp himself had a contracted family, and had he been a re-flective type he might have considered that a vicarious association was one of the things that attracted him to V.T., as well as to his wife, whose clan was also vast.

There she was now, dancing with a young black paralegal. She was wearing a full plum maxiskirt with the bottom three buttons undone, so that as she danced it whirled upward, showing her thin and splendid legs. Her black curls were shoulder length and cut so that they fell over the left side of her face. In that way, if Marlene held her head cocked, as she always did, it would be more difficult for someone to tell that her right eye was glass.

This damage had never interested him; he had loved her before, when she was stunning and perfect, and afterward, when she was merely a gorgeous exotic. As always, when he watched her dance, he was excited and vaguely saddened at the same time. Marlene loved to dance; Karp did not. He hadn't even before his knee had been replaced, thinking himself gawky on the floor and conspicu-ous with it.

As he watched, she caught his eye and winked and went through a set of parodically dirty contortions.

"Marlene's not going down with you, I hear," said V.T.

"Not right away," said Karp, turning back to his friend. "We're being modern."

V.T. nodded and smiled ruefully. He himself had been carrying on for a number of years a hopeless affair with an artist who lived in the Berkshires and who would on no account move to the city. "Yes," he said, "how well I know it! Prisoners of women's liber-ation, a burgeoning gulag. And without even the balm of self-pity, since we richly deserve anything they can dish out, we swine. Sins of the fathers. The best cure is more wine."

He poured himself another glass of champagne. V.T. had sprung for a case of Moet magnums, a typical gesture, and one that had contributed mightily to the current hilarious mood of the party. Nor had he stinted himself in the use of his own gift. A bar of scarlet had appeared across his cheekbones, and his intelligent blue eyes were starting to approximate the cheap plastic glitter of a baby doll's.

"Fuck 'em, anyway," said Karp woozily. "You know, Newbury, you should get out of here, too."

"Why? The party's roaring and we have four bottles of wine left."

"No, I don't mean the party. I mean the DA's." Karp put an affectionate arm across Newbury's shoulder. "Look, V.T., I have a slot for a head of research on our staff. Why don't you take it?"

Newbury cocked his head and looked at Karp out of a narrow eye. "You're joking, right?"

"No, I'm not. You should do it. We'll have a ball."

"But I'm a funny-money man. Fraud is my life."

"The People rest," said Karp.

V.T. laughed, sputtering around a mouthful of champagne. "What? You have the brass to suggest that the Warren Commission and the concept of fraud can possibly exist in the same universe of discourse? It was printed in the *Times*! Walter Cronkite—"

"Will you?"

"Of course," said V.T., without an instant's hesitation.

The party wore on. People drifted away, leaving the hard-core fun lovers, who became more raucous, as if hoping to make up in noise what was lost in numbers. The sun went down; the lights were doused and replaced with candles. Around nine, Karp slipped into his private office and sat down behind his desk. He began rummaging through the drawers, extracting personal items.

There were few of these, or few that he wished to retain, at any rate. A block of clear Lucite in which was embedded a round from an AR-16 that had been removed from his shoulder after an unsuccessful assassination attempt. A softball signed with the names of all the team members, and by Francis Phillip Garrahy, the year the DA's team had won the city league championship. He rose and assembled a carton taken from a stack Connie Trask had provided. He thought he would not need more than one.

Off the wall came his law school diploma and his New York bar certificate, and a framed photograph his friends had signed and given him when he had first been appointed to the homicide bureau back in Garrahy's day.

The door opened and Marlene came in.

"What are you doing lurking in here?" she said, swaying slightly. She was nicely drunk.

"I'm not lurking, I'm cleaning out." He handed her the photograph. "I'm taking this for inspiration," he said.

It was a grainy reproduction of a famous World War II photograph, the charge to destruction of the Pomorske Cavalry Brigade during the Nazi blitzkrieg against Poland. In the foreground were several German tanks, and coming toward them out of the smoky distance was a long line of horsemen in white tunics and *schapskas*, waving pennoned lances. The gift was meant as a comment on fighting homicide in New York.

Marlene looked at the relic, and at her own signature prominent on the bottom. "You still feel like that? Charging the tanks?"

"I don't know. Lately, I've started to see myself as being on the other side—more panzerlike. I guess I don't like it."

"I thought I was supposed to be the intractable romantic in this family," said Marlene petulantly. "You're supposed to be the solid one. You're supposed to be there for *me*."

Karp laughed at that and tapped the photo. "Wait—I thought I was the romantic Polish lancer, dashing into danger."

"Yes, but a *dependable* romantic Polish lancer, who helps with child care and does dishes."

Karp laughed again and went on with his packing. Some personal books and a few papers went into the carton. He walked to the line of bookcases that held the records of his hundred or so murder trials. He pulled out a few at random, and then put them back. "I'll have to get Connie to pack these and send them home."

"God, you're really doing it!" she said, amazement in her voice. "It just now hit me, watching you pack."

"Yeah, packing makes it real. *I* still have trouble believing it."

"Leaving everything . . ."

"Not quite everything. V.T.'s coming along to run the research side. I think Clay Fulton'll go for it too."

"How pleasant for you," she sniffed. "Butch and his gang. What more could a boy want?"

"You could get on the staff too, you know, if you hadn't made up your mind to be a pain in the ass about this. We could all be together. . . ."

"I'd scrub floors before I'd work for you again."

"You don't have to work for me," said Karp heatedly. They'd been through this before. "You could get a slot with Joe Lerner on the MLK side."

"If you ask him to hire me."

"Yeah! What's wrong with that?"

"It *sucks* is what's wrong with it," snapped Marlene, this un-helpful comment being the only way she could bring into words the complex of emotions that whipped her about when both Karp and career occupied the center of her thoughts. She knew she was a decent prosecutor, and had helped to revolutionize the handling of rape and child abuse crime in Manhattan, but she also knew that she was no Karp. Karp had over a hundred successful hom-icide prosecutions, Karp had been featured in a *New York Times Magazine* article as the iron man of the fight against crime, Karp had been appointed a bureau chief by the legendary Garrahy. And Karp was higher than she was in the hierarchy of the DA and always would be, and at some level of her mind anything she achieved in her career lay under the shadow of bimbohood: beau-tiful Marlene—she got where she is through the bedroom.

That this shadow was largely of her own making did not in the least diminish the pain it caused her. She could not tolerate the thought of starting a legal career again in a new city where she did not wish to live, among strangers, where she had not even the modest reputation she possessed in New York, and where she would obtain her job on her husband's recommendation. A bimbo in Washington, like those "secretaries" kept by congressmen you read about in the papers—it was not to be endured.

Karp finished his packing and closed the carton. "Want to go?" he asked. She looked at him and writhed inwardly and then shook her head as if to dispel the oncoming fog of depression. In her saner moments, she was honest enough to realize that it was not Karp's fault that she felt this way, nor his fault that he was a su-perstar, a workaholic, a job-obsessed, macho son of a bitch. . . .

"What's wrong," said Karp, struck by her odd expression.

"Oh, nothing," she said, going toward him. "I just realized I'm going to miss you." The music from the other room had turned slow.

"Let's dance," she said, and they shuffled, locked together, weaving around the furniture.

V.T. Newbury walked into Karp's Washington office, three weeks after his blithe agreement to take the Kennedy job, and

immediately stifled a number of second thoughts. Karp looked up from his desk, which was covered with a stack of gold-stamped blue volumes, some open, some closed, all festooned with scraps of markers made of torn yellow bond. He smiled wanly.

"Good, you made it," said Karp.

"I did."

"Any problems getting away?"

"There was gnashing of teeth from one end of Manhattan to another. Three wine merchants closed their doors and the family went into mourning. Again."

"They don't like you going to Washington?"

"They *love* me going to Washington, but they were thinking of something more along the lines of deputy assistant secretary at Treasury. Where did you get this furniture?"

"It came with the job. Like it?"

"It's very forties. You look like General Wainwright on Corregidor."

"I feel like it too. Have a seat, V.T. It's been sprayed for insect life, I think."

V.T. sat on Karp's couch, an object made from the skin of a large puce nauga. You could still see where it had been shot, the holes now oozing fluffy white stuffing.

"Your office is next door," Karp continued. "Fulton'll be across the hall."

"He decided to come?"

"Yeah, another divorce in the making. He'll start next week."

"Do I get furniture as nice as this, or is yours special because you're the boss?"

"As a matter of fact, I think you have a wooden desk. I saved it for you because I know you're the kind of guy who appreciates the little touches. The drawers don't open, but luckily we happen to have an unlimited supply of these unassembled gray steel shelves"—here Karp gestured at several long brown cartons stacked against his walls—"so that shouldn't be a problem. The good news is we're not being paid."

"We're not?"

"So it seems. They're fucking around with our budget on the Hill. Me and Crane and Bea Sondergard . . . did you meet her? Good lady. We're all on per diem and you and Clay will be too,

until we get it straightened out. That means a hundred and twenty-five dollars each and every day we work, no sick leave, no vacation time, no benefits. Sound good?"

"Irresistible. But what about the staff? If we can't hire . . ."

"Well, actually, we *can't* hire, not yet. The committee'll be staffed with people detailed from the Hill and from various federal agencies. That'll get us started, although we sort of have to take pot luck about who we get. I'm sure we'll get sent the very best people, and not the shitheads every agency in Washington has been trying to dump for years. Besides that, Bea informs me that if the per diem account runs out before we get a budget, we won't get paid at all. Not to mention, if this goes on long enough, we won't have anything in the account to pay our experts."

"That's nice," said V.T. "How am I going to run a research operation without experts?"

"Get with Bea on that. I don't think she actually intends to commit fraud, but she runs pretty close. It's a matter of juggling, according to her. Everybody does it."

"Everybody does it! How often I've heard that in court, just prior to sentencing! Tell me, am I to gather from this that the sun of approval does not exactly shine from Congress on this enterprise?"

Karp grinned. "You could say that. But as Crane keeps telling me, here we are."

"Here we are indeed. So what should I start with meanwhile?"

Karp pointed at his desktop. "You see all these nicely bound blue books? *The Report of the President's Commission on the Assassination of President Kennedy,* in twenty-six volumes. The Warren Commission."

He rummaged through the stacks of books on his desk, jerked one out, and tossed it across to V.T. The rest of them slumped into a new configuration, like geological strata during orogeny. "I'm on volume twenty. Here's volume one, the report proper, eight hundred eighty-eight pages of crisp prose. The rest is hearings and exhibits. You'll have your very own set pretty soon, I hope. Meanwhile, don't lose my notes."

"Read the whole thing, huh?" said V.T., hefting the volume he had just received.

"For starters. Then there're the critics. I've collected the essential ones: Lane, Meagher, Josiah Thompson, a couple others." He

pointed to a steel shelf lined with books. "Read them too. They've done a lot of work and raised some interesting questions. You'll see my notes on them—feel free to make your own. When you're finished we'll get together with Clay and map out a strategy for the investigation."

V.T. said, "Sounds right." He paged through the book on his lap. "So. What's your take so far?"

"Um, let me keep that to myself for now," said Karp after some thought. "I'd like your viewpoint without you knowing what I think. But, obviously, if there weren't serious problems with this beast"—he tapped the pile of blue books—"we wouldn't be here, would we?"

"No, I guess not," said V.T. "It's hard to believe we are in any case. John F. Kennedy! It certainly stirs the old memories. You know, I met him once."

"Oh?"

"Yes, on a sailboat. I was something like twelve, so it must have been fifty-three or fifty-four. My uncle Tally Whitman had asked me on a sailing vacation on his boat, basically to keep my cousin Frank company. He was about my age and the problem was that Frank's sister, Maude, had invited a friend from Brearley along, and Tally didn't want the kid ganged up on by two seventeen-years-old girls.

"Well, we set out from New Haven, where Tally kept the boat—he had a beautiful ketch, an Alden design, a forty-eight— the *Melisande*, it was called. Of course, in the first five minutes I fell desperately in love with Effie, the Brearley friend—who was by the way a raving beauty, in love in the way you can only fall at twelve. We gunkholed along the North Shore for a week and then crossed over to the Vineyard, and put in at Vineyard Haven. And there were the three Kennedy boys and some friends in the next slip. A bachelor outing; they'd come across from Hyannisport that day."

"So you met him," Karp broke in. He liked V.T. a good deal, but he had a limited patience for his stories about life in high society, with endless glosses on who was related to whom, and who did what to whom at Newport in the year whatever.

"Yes," said V.T. "I had no idea who they were, of course, but Uncle Tally had been at school with Bobby, at Choate. I was allowed to serve drinks, life's finest moment up until then. Frank

was nauseated, of course. Well, I was probably a colossal bore to them all, because all I had to talk about was sailing, which I did in the most pompous way imaginable, and I must say they were nothing if not polite. The afternoon, however, wore on, and the gin flowed. I was an efficient little barman. Then I began to notice something very disturbing. I was a sheltered youth, of course, and at twelve my sexual knowledge was at the schoolboy giggle stage, but it was clear to me that Jack Kennedy was making eyes, as we then called it, at the delicious Effie. And hands, too. And she was reciprocating. I was astounded, and devastated. I mean he was an *old man*."

"So did he bonk her?"

"Not that I saw. I'm sure that Uncle Tally would never have allowed it, not on his watch. Of course, he might have bonked her thereafter; apparently he bonked everybody else. In any event, it was decided that we should race across to Hyannis the next morning, and we did. The Kennedys were good sailors, of course, but Tally was an Olympic-class skipper and I worked my young butt off, as did Frank and the girls. And we whipped them, by three boats. Jack was not amused. I mean it was ridiculous; he was *really* angry, red-faced, screaming at Teddy about some goof. A man who didn't like to lose. As he proved in later life, too."

V.T. put his hands in his pockets and looked out the dirty window. "Here's the kicker: ten years later, I was at Yale, a chilly afternoon, I was getting ready to go out in a single scull, when the crew manager came running down the ramp yelling that somebody'd just shot the president. At first I thought he meant the president of *Yale*. There was a radio going in the boathouse and a bunch of us sat around and listened. When they announced that he was really dead, I went back out onto the ramp and pushed my scull into the water and rowed until I was exhausted. And I'll tell you the truth, all I could think about was that day on the Vineyard when he made a drunken pass at a seventeen-year-old Brearley girl. Incredibly shaming and inappropriate, but I couldn't get it out of my head. That and this weird fantasy, about flying back in some way to my twelve-year-old self in the cockpit of the *Melisande* and grabbing him by the shoulders and shouting, 'Forget the girl, asshole! November 1963: don't for God's sake go to Dallas!'"

V.T. let out an embarrassed laugh and made a gesture of helplessness.

Karp smiled and indicated with a wave of his hand the office, and by extension the ramshackle investigation. "I guess this is the next best thing, then."

"Sad to say," said V.T. "Sad, sad to say."

In the headquarters of the Central Intelligence Agency, a man received a disturbing phone call. It was a journalist calling; remarkably, this journalist was not seeking information but supplying it. The CIA has this sort of relationship with quite a number of journalists, both domestic and foreign.

"Are you positive?" asked the CIA man.

"Positive," replied the journalist. "I got it from one of Schaller's staff guys. They were blown away when they read them. Schaller doesn't know whether to shit or go blind."

Schaller was a leading member of the Senate Select Committee to Study Governmental Operations with Respect to Intelligence Activities —the Church committee.

The CIA man cursed briefly, then said, "This will take some controlling. All right, what's your take on Schaller's options?"

The journalist replied, "I think he'll have to use the Castro stuff, but he had some of that already, and it all leads to dead ends. The other thing, the JFK items . . . I don't know. It's not exactly in his line of study, and he doesn't want to look like an asshole a couple of months before election. I think he'll pass it on."

"What, to Flores's operation?"

"Yeah."

"Which is not going anywhere."

"Which is definitely not going anywhere."

The CIA man thought about this for a while and then said, "Still, I'd like some insurance."

"Anything I can do . . . ," offered the journalist.

"I'll be in touch."

After getting off the line, the CIA man made a call to the head of the little team that had prepared the documents for the Senate Select Committee's subpoena, and gave him the reaming of his life. Then he called several other people, including a former CIA deputy director for operations, and told them what had happened. None of them was pleased.

After that, he sat for a while, humming, tapping a pencil, making mental plans and weighing risks. The first rule of secrecy is that every

time you let someone new in on the secret, you increase the chances of exposure by a factor of two. Too many people knew about this thing already, and so if he wished to mobilize people to suppress the inadvertently leaked knowledge, it made sense to use only those who knew the story already. He went to a locked filing cabinet, unlocked it, and drew out a worn notebook. Opening it, he found a telephone number.

He dialed it, and while he waited for the call to go through, he locked the notebook away again.

It took a good while for the call to go through and then the CIA man had to make use of his still-fluent Spanish. Finally, in the town of Quezaltenango, in Guatemala, a phone rang.

FIVE

In the weeks that ensued, Karp each morning left his furnished two-bedroom apartment in Arlington, took the metro to Federal Center, walked to the office, and there spent his days largely in reading. He had finished the Warren material and was now slogging through the recently released Church committee report on intelligence. The office of the Select Committee staff continued stinking of fresh paint and plaster dust, and still sounded with the thumps of heavy equipment being moved about. Increasingly, Karp was running into people he did not know, who claimed to work for him, or almost to work for him. He had nothing as yet for these people to do, which did not seem particularly disturbing to them, since they all seemed to have other jobs of some sort. There was a good deal of motion in the hallways, typewriters and Lexitron printers clattered away, people trailed reels of phone wire, telephones rang and were occasionally answered. Crane was rarely in the office, as he had a series of private legal commitments still outstanding in Philadelphia. Karp had no idea what was going on.

Late in the morning of one of these trancelike days, Karp, befuddled with reading, wandered out of his office in search of coffee. Cup in hand, he went into the small bay that was supposed to hold a reception area and the clerical pool, but which still resembled the site of a terrorist bombing. There Bea Sondergard was standing like a ringmaster, directing a team of phone engineers, a crew building partitions, and three men with huge cartons from Xerox, carrying on at the same time a conversation with a short, bespec-

tacled, red-bearded young man. Sondergard waved Karp over and pointed him at the other man.

"Butch, I want you to meet Charlie Ziller. Charlie's a loaner from Congressman Dobbs. Charlie, Butch Karp, your new boss." She coughed as plaster dust settled in a cloud around them. Karp shook hands with Ziller and said, "I'm sorry, we seem to be a little disorganized. . . ."

At this Sondergard uttered a cackling laugh and raced off after the Xerox people who were, despite her instructions, moving their copier to the wrong room.

"Actually," said Karp, "it's a nonstop Chinese fire drill around here. Do you have a desk yet?"

Ziller grinned engagingly and shrugged. He looked about twenty-five and had small, bright blue eyes. "No, I'm going to have a cubicle when they're built, according to Bea."

"Great. So—you're a volunteer, or did you fuck up something important?"

A polite laugh. "No, I wangled it, in my subtle way. The Kennedy thing—just something I've always wondered about, and maybe this is a chance to be in on the real story."

"Another Camelot fan."

"I guess. My folks were in the administration then and it's something that hit them pretty hard. I was in junior high at the time. Sixth period, they announced over the PA. My math teacher burst into tears. I'll never forget it; it was . . . I don't know, like finding out you're adopted. It shook up the whole world, you know? Especially with us all being in the government. I guess it just feels like a natural thing for me to do."

"So what're you supposed to be doing for us?"

Ziller shrugged again. "The representative didn't specify. I'm just supposed to come over and make myself useful."

"Oh, yeah? Like how? Expand on your talents."

Ziller made a self-deprecating little writhe. "I'm a staffer. I can talk on the telephone. Type on the typewriter. Go to meetings. Have lunch. That's what we do here in the nation's capital."

"Okay," said Karp, "in that case, let's have lunch. You can show me your stuff."

Ziller took Karp to the Green Hat, a small multileveled saloon on Maryland off Third. They walked up the Hill and behind the

Capitol, Ziller pointing out the sights knowledgeably. It turned out he was a third-generation civil servant; his father was a fairly high mandarin at State, his mother a budget officer at the General Services Administration. Ziller had been educated at American U. and was one of the rare natives of the town. He seemed happy to speak freely about himself, Washington ways, and his recent job, which was staffing the House Intelligence Committee. He touched amusingly on the idiosyncrasies of various congressional characters as well, pointing out several who were dining in that very place.

Ziller did this last discreetly, in a low voice. Most of those he indicated were solid-looking men in their fifties or sixties, with graying hair and very pink skin, but there was one woman, an undersecretary of something, lunching with another, an assistant secretary of something else. Karp learned, whether he wanted to or not, that an undersecretary was more important than an assistant secretary, but that a deputy assistant secretary was more important than a deputy undersecretary, except at the Pentagon, where the reverse obtained.

They ordered; food was brought. Karp found himself unexpectedly ravenous, and tore into his meal, a cheeseburger as large as a regulation softball.

"Good burgers here," observed Ziller as he plucked at a shrimp salad.

"Yeah. So—how am I doing? Am I having lunch yet?"

Ziller grinned, showing the small neat pearly teeth you get if you have been covered by the government's generous health plan from birth. "Not quite," he said. "Lunch actually happens when I tell you something I've been sworn not to tell you, and tell you not to tell anyone else, knowing that you will tell exactly the person I want to find out about it, but couldn't tell. *That's* having lunch."

"And . . . ? What's the secret?"

Ziller shrugged and his expression became more guarded. "Avoid the apple pie. It tends to be watery."

"I'm serious," replied Karp, placing the stump of his burger on its plate. He wiped his mouth with his napkin and regarded Ziller unsmilingly. "I appreciate the walking guidebook act, but let's not screw around with each other. Dobbs sent you over here to watch the store for him and also to slide me information he thinks I should have without having to do it officially. Obviously, you don't want to do that on our first date, so to speak; you want to feel me

out a little, learn something about who *I* tell secrets to before you let loose, maybe check out do I know what the hell I'm doing around an investigation. I appreciate that, but here's a tip. The problem with telling me secrets, is I *don't* pass them on. That's because I'm basically a simple country boy. Around here, as I gather, you've got to show what you know to show everybody you're somebody. Like, 'Look at me, I know some Senator is *schtupping* the assistant secretary of what's-its-face, hooray.' But basically, I don't give a flying fuck about being somebody in Washington. I didn't much like it when I was somebody in New York. Plus, I left my family in the city, and as a result I'm horny and generally pissed off. I'm here to do a job and scram, the quicker the better. And I could put all the patience I have with all this shit—'don't mess with that one' and 'respect this one's fucking sensitivities'—in my belly button. I told Crane I had no political skills and it's true, and he said that was okay, and if it turns out it's not, I'm on the next plane out. You can convey the same message to Representative Dobbs." He paused and produced a mild version of his famous stare. Then he grinned, to forestall any tension.

Ziller made a mock swipe at his brow and said, "Well, *that* was a cold douche. Are you always this charming?"

"No," Karp said, still smiling, "sometimes I'm extremely obnoxious. For example, when I think somebody is not telling me stuff I need to know."

"Which is certainly not the case here. Look, we're on the same side. I'm from the federal government and I'm here to help you."

"Help me how?"

Ziller laughed, "No, it's a joke—the third biggest lie."

"Meaning?"

"That's right, you probably haven't heard it eight million times: What are the three biggest lies in the world? Answer: I'll respect you in the morning; the check is in the mail; and I'm from the federal government and I'm here to help you. Ho, ho. Well, I really *am* here to help you."

Karp waited, his expression neutral. Ziller took a breath and resumed.

"Okay, I got this from a buddy of mine who shall remain nameless. He's a staffer with the Church committee."

"The Senate Intelligence investigation."

"Yes, the Intelligence investigation. Church is the chair, but Dick Schaller is the leading light. They subpoenaed a shitload of stuff from the CIA and most of it was either trash or blanked out—par for the course with the spooks—but there was one incredibly juicy little package that came through untouched. Some of it bears heavily on the JFK investigation."

"In what way?"

"This I don't know, but my guy says it's dynamite."

"And Schaller is going to give us this stuff?"

"Yeah. What he wants is to get rid of it. The investigation is finished, the report is out. The last thing he needs is to be sitting on something this big that he didn't use."

Karp frowned. "Wait a minute. What you're saying is that a U.S. senator had information germane to the assassination of the president and he's playing footsy with it? He's not going public with it immediately?"

"That's not the point. It was ancillary to the intelligence investigation proper, and if he used it, he'd have had to branch off down a line of investigation he chose not to pursue."

"Why not?"

Ziller paused and said meaningfully, "Because in certain quarters of this town, getting excited about who did JFK is considered on the same level as having food stains on your tie or walking around with your fly open."

"That's good to know," said Karp, and then asked, "So what do I do? Beg him?"

"No, we'll set up an appointment, you'll go over to the Dirksen Building, you'll chat, talk about the weather, and when you leave the stuff'll be in your briefcase."

"Great," said Karp. "Is that it?"

"No, Mark Lane has some dynamite stuff he got on an FOIA request from the FBI, another miracle. There must be a rat in the public information office there," said Ziller. He looked at his watch and beckoned to the waitress for the check. "I have to run; there's a staff meeting over at Rayburn in ten minutes."

"Wait a second—what's this about Mark Lane and a rat in the FBI?"

"Yeah, it's a long story. It's another document, and I'm sure

Lane'll be around to see us. It's apparently signed by J. Edgar Hoover's own soft, pink hand." He stood up. "I should be able to start full-time next week, if that's okay."

"Yeah, sure, fine," said Karp, feeling vaguely one-upped and unsure about whether it was fine or not.

Back in the office, Karp found a message from V.T. on his desk. V.T. himself was in his own dingy room poking into one of several heavy cartons made of a dark, waxy-looking cardboard.

"What's up, V.T.?"

"How was your lunch?"

"I had the cheeseburger special. What's in the boxes?"

"National Archives," said V.T. "Your research director has been researching, and I had these sent over. It's the photographic stuff, copies they let us have. The actual stuff, they send a guy over and he watches it. I imagine we'll need to do that when we go to hearings."

"What actual stuff?"

"Oh, the Rifle. The Bloody Shirt. The Magic Bullet. I went over there this morning. They let me Handle the Items. You get a chill."

"I bet. So you got all the evidence and autopsy shots?"

"Those they had. Plus the films. That's what I wanted to show you. I set up a projector already."

V.T. led the way to a freshly painted bare room down the hall, in the center of which he had a projector set up on a metal typing table. There were two straight chairs on either side of it. The blinds were closed, and when V.T. shut the door and clicked off the lights, the room became quite dark.

"What are we watching?" asked Karp, sitting in one of the chairs.

"You're a trained investigator—see if you recognize it."

V.T. flicked the projector switch and sat down. The white wall opposite lit up. The usual leader numbers counted down and there was a message informing the viewer that this film was copyrighted by *Life* magazine and a brief look at the seal of the National Archives. Then bright sunlight, a road, a crowd, a motorcade coming down a street, led by motorcycle cops, preceding an open limousine in which two men and two women are waving and smiling.

Karp realized that he had never actually seen the film shot by

Abraham Zapruder on assassination day, although he had seen the grainy color stills made from it. It was different, more chilling, in motion. He asked, "This is the original?"

"No, that's in a vault at Time-Life. This is the archival copy. Let me slow it down for you."

V.T. turned a lever and the scene slowed to a nightmare crawl. The Kennedy limo passed behind a large sign and emerged, the president grimaced and snapped both his hands up to his throat, elbows high, then John Connally puffed his cheeks out in pain and slumped to the side, then Kennedy's head exploded in a pink cloud. Jackie scrambled out onto the rear deck of the car, a big Secret Service man leaped up on the rear deck and thrust her back into her seat, the car accelerated and moved away until it vanished under a freeway overpass. The screen went white again and the most famous snuff film ever made was over.

"Like to see it again?" asked V.T.

"Yeah. Can you stop it on a particular frame?"

"No, not with this projector. I want to get us a Moviola for that and for some other film material I have. There are eight-by-ten prints of each frame, of course, but they're not as . . . compelling as seeing the real thing. I'm also going to go back to the city and take a look at the original. What I hear is that it's got detail you can't see on the archival copies."

"That's interesting. I mean why take any trouble to make a good copy? It's just the most important piece of film in history. If Zapruder hadn't shot that film, we'd both be back in the city, eating bagels and putting asses in jail. There wouldn't be an investigation. There wouldn't be any single-bullet theory because you wouldn't need one, because without the film to time the bullet impacts and show their order in detail, all you got is a dead guy, a wounded guy, and a rifle in a high building. Let's see it again."

V.T. rewound it and they watched the Zapruder film again at normal speed. It took twenty-two seconds. They were silent for the few seconds it took to rewind.

"Again?" asked V.T.

"Not right now," said Karp. He rose, stretched, and turned on the lights. "We have a photo tech yet?"

"Uh-huh. I convinced Jim Phelps to join the cause. You don't recognize the name? He's the guy who liberated the Zapruder film and he's done some interesting enhancements. He impressed me.

A certain passionate sincerity that ought to balance my own blithe amateurism.''

"I'll need to meet him."

"I'll set it up. Also, I have that list for the autopsy panel you wanted."

"Murray's heading it, right?" Newbury bobbed his head in assent, but with a sour expression on his face.

"What's the matter, you have something against Murray Selig?" Karp asked.

"No, not as such. The credentials are fine. You can't beat chief medical examiner in New York City. On the other hand, you and he have been pretty tight over the years. His objectivity may be called into question. It might have been better to give it to someone with whom we have no prior connection."

"Come on, Murray's the best in the business. You think he's going to shave the findings to make me happy?"

V.T. shrugged. "You're the boss. Okay, next: I'm going to set up an index for the materials we're gathering. I'll base it on the index Sylvia Meagher made in sixty-four, of course. We'd really be even further up shit's creek without that. And I'll make a separate list of the stuff we should have that's missing, not that I have very high hopes of finding it." He rose and sighed and ran his hand through his fine pale hair.

It struck Karp that V.T. had been putting in hours as long as his own and even after a few weeks his face was beginning to show the strain.

"Fulton's coming on Monday?" V.T. asked.

"Yeah. He called yesterday. He's got his little mafia of retired cops ready to start as contract investigators. Speaking of which, first thing Monday we should have a meeting. I'll get Selig to come down, and you should get your photo guy in. I'll try to figure out which of the people wandering around here knows what the hell they're doing."

V.T. nodded unenthusiastically and went to the door. Karp said, "I'd like to see that list of missing stuff as soon as possible. I'm going over to see the Senate Intelligence Committee. Maybe they'll know about some of it."

"Tomorrow morning all right?"

"Sure. Like what kind of stuff, by the way?"

V.T. shot him a glum look. "Like Kennedy's brain, for starters. And it's probably not in the Dirksen Building."

Karp read for the rest of the day until his eyes burned. He reached the end of a chapter and threw the heavy book on a pile. He'd gone through three yellow pads making notes on the Warren Report, cross-checking his reading with the critical works also spread out across his desk: Meagher's *Accessories after the Fact*, Thompson's *Six Seconds in Dallas*, Lane's *Rush to Judgment*, Epstein's *Inquest*. He reviewed his notes and distributed more little yellow slips among the critical books. As always, he finished these sessions with an incipient headache and a queasy sensation in his belly.

Having entered this work without any prejudgment of the Warren Report, he had never concerned himself particularly with its critics. He had read the *Times* and watched Uncle Walter on CBS like millions of Americans, and the idea that a lone nut had shot the president was perfectly reasonable to him. He also had a deep-seated reluctance to accept the idea of conspiracy on the part of government agencies, even though he had in his career exposed several such conspiracies.

That was the point, in fact. If *he* had exposed conspiracies, and *he* was a law-enforcement official, it was difficult to believe that other law-enforcement officials could not have done likewise. Since none had, in the last decade, it had seemed to him probable that no conspiracy existed. He also had a professional's reluctance to accept the conclusions of amateurs. In his long experience at the DA's office in New York, and in contradiction to the great mass of popular culture pertaining to the subject, no amateur, no Miss Marple, no Poirot, no Sam Spade, no Lew Archer, had ever contributed in the slightest to the solution of a homicide. Private investigators were a joke among the pros he worked with.

After three weeks of study, however, these beliefs had been seriously eroded, and he had conceived a ferocious resentment against the people associated with the Warren Commission. His reading had shown him what any experienced homicide prosecutor would have gathered. The commission report was not an investigation that might have substituted for a trial of the dead Oswald, but merely a prosecutor's brief, and not a very good one at that.

As Crane had suggested at their first meeting, Karp would have laughed out of his office a junior ADA who had waltzed in with something of this quality as prep work for the trial of a street mutt accused of popping a whore.

He had seen a similar botch any number of times in training ADAs: love at first sight. The cops provide a likely suspect; the kid gathers evidence that aids in convicting that suspect, and shows up at Karp's pretrial meeting with a fat file and a big grin, which grin Karp demolishes by pointing out all the things the defense is going to bring up that the kid didn't think about, or didn't think were important. The autopsy. Did you see the films? Are the wounds consistent with the weapon we say he used? What about that weapon? Chain of evidence? Do you have it, an unbroken written record of everyone who touched it from the time it was found in possession of the defendant to the present instant? You "think" so? Not good enough. What about the witnesses? You got "most of them"? Why not *all* of them? They didn't see anything or they didn't see what you thought they should have seen? Better apply for a continuance, kid. You're not ready for court.

And that was what happened on Karp's watch in a cheap street killing of a nobody. This—he glanced in distaste at the nicely bound blue volumes—was an investigation of the murder of a president in front of umpteen thousand people, supervised by the chief justice of the United States. Karp recalled what Bert Crane had said about Warren and his report—that Warren was rusty, that the problem with the report was the peculiar life histories of both the main suspect and the guy who'd shot him. The critics made much of that too, but Karp thought both they and Crane were off the mark. The problem with this thing was that it was a lousy investigation. A third-year law student could've come in off the street and walked Lee Harvey Oswald through its gaping holes.

Karp rose, put his suit jacket on, grabbed some more reading material, and threw it into an accordion folder. He walked through the deserted office and out into the darkening streets. The Federal Center metro station was a block away, and he took the Red Line train to the Court House stop in Arlington.

The Federal Gardens Apartments consisted of four two-story red brick buildings with tacky and pretentious white colonial porticoes, despite which they remained easily distinguishable from Mount Vernon. Most of Karp's neighbors appeared to be noncom-

missioned military on temporary assignments or the kind of working stiffs that dressed in uniforms with embroidered name tags. There was a rusty playground set in the worn grassy quadrangle, which was littered with trash and forgotten plastic toys. There were lots of children in the complex, although Karp, who left for work at seven and returned after dark, saw them mainly on weekends. He heard them often enough, though. The interior walls were thin.

He entered his apartment and turned on the light. A small living room contained a nubby plaid couch, an easy chair with a reddish flowered slipcover worn at the arms, a scratched blond wood coffee table, a standard lamp with a rusty nylon shade. In the rear of the ground floor there lurked a tiny dim kitchen and a dining alcove with a table of the same blond wood and four chairs. There was a dark stain on the table in the shape of a map of China, where someone had once spilled ink, probably during the second Roosevelt administration. Up a narrow flight of stairs were two bedrooms and a bath. The place was dark and low-ceilinged, but it was cheap and ten minutes by train to Karp's office.

Cheap was the main thing. Housing prices in the District had exploded in the seventies and Karp had vastly underestimated the cost of keeping two households. As it was likely that he would be unemployed after the committee concluded its work, he had resolved not to touch his small savings until then. He now understood why congressmen took bribes.

Karp changed into comfortable clothes, went down to the kitchen and heated up and consumed, without tasting it, a TV dinner. Then he went into the living room, lay down on the couch, and read for ten minutes before falling into a profound sleep.

He awoke with a start to the sound of a violent argument in the apartment next door. Screaming, breaking things, and an unfamiliar sound, the whining and barking of a dog. The quarrel reached a crescendo and then abruptly terminated with a slamming door and a final crash of something breaking. The whining and barking, however, continued. Karp cursed and checked his watch. He was late for his nightly phone call.

Marlene was cool when she answered, as if she were speaking to a distant relative.

"How're things?" he asked.

"Not bad." And, away from the mouthpiece, muffled: "It's Daddy."

"Got a new husband yet?"

"Yeah, I just picked this dude off the street, name of Frank or Ralph, something like that—anyway, he's far better than you in every possible way."

"Good. As long as you're happy."

"I'm euphoric," she said, and then after a brief pause, "I was on TV yesterday."

"Yeah? What, you hosted 'Saturday Night Live'?"

"Almost as good. I talked to the National Association of Attorneys General about rape. One of the locals picked up about twelve seconds of *moi* for the local news. I did my line about how after the legislature changed the law on corroborative evidence, our conviction rate went up thirty percent."

"That's great, Marlene! God, Bloom usually hogs that whole thing for his buddies and his own self."

"Yeah, well apparently, I'm one of Bloom's buddies now," she said.

"Oh?"

"Yeah, a bunch of feminists had a rally in front of the courts building and the TV gave them a big play. Apparently, car theft gets something like eighty times the investigative resources that rape gets, and forget about narco. Also there was a series about rape in the *Voice* and a piece in *New York* with a couple of juicy horror stories. Mr. Bloom was very glad to have his very own pet feminist talk to the press."

"So you're famous."

"Please! Quasi-famous at the most."

"Like it?"

A pause. "Yeah. Yeah, I do. It's nice to get some recognition, and I think it'll be good for the program."

"You get any new staff yet?"

"No, but . . . what's that supposed to mean?"

"It means don't hold your breath. Bloom is a master of the meaningless gesture. He could be setting you up."

"I can take care of myself," Marlene snapped, with more edge than she had intended. "Just because you've had a running war with him for all these years doesn't mean I have to. We're separate people, something which has been getting a lot clearer to me since you left."

"Marlene, what are you talking about?" Karp demanded, his voice rising. "Bloom is a corrupt fuck, and you know it."

A pause. "Let's change the subject, Butch," said Marlene coolly. "What's going on down there? Solved the crime of the century yet?"

"Yeah, well, it would help if I had a staff, or money to pay one, or an office that worked, but besides that it's going great. Why don't you come down here for the weekend? I miss you."

"I have stuff to do and no money. Why don't you come up here?"

"Same answer."

"Great. Well, in that case, I'll see you when I see you. Here, talk to your daughter."

Clunking of phone, sound of tiny running feet. His heart clenched.

"Daddy, I have an elephant balloon."

"That's great, baby," said Karp, and chatted with his daughter for a few minutes, in the sort of unrewarding and stumbling conversation possible with a three-year-old who is really only interested in when you're coming home.

"Lucy, good night now," said Karp. "Let me talk to Mommy again."

But the child placed the phone carefully back on the hook, and Marlene did not call back. After some moments of agonized waiting, Karp punched up their number, but hung up before it could ring.

On the Monday following another miserable work-clogged and lonely weekend, Karp for the first time marshaled his investigative staff. They met in a small windowless office that had been designated the conference room. It was bare and dusty except for two long folding caterer's tables placed end to end and a motley collection of chairs, which the attendees had dragged from their own offices. There were little piles of dead cockroaches on the floor and the room stank of a recent extermination.

It was not, Karp thought, a particularly impressive group for the task at hand. Most of them were young, in their mid to late twenties, congressional staff types, all of them, male and female, wearing neat career suits in muted colors. There were also several

older men in cheaper suits who exuded the vague bonhomie that marked them as political hacks. Karp was sure that none of them had ever investigated a homicide or worked a major criminal case. Bright or slow, ambitious or defeated, they were paper pushers all.

V.T. Newbury was, of course, solid, but Karp had his doubts about whether Newbury or anyone else could form this mob into an effective research organization. Karp glanced across the table at Clay Fulton, who gave him a hooded, eye-rolling look. Fulton was solid too, but even under his supervision none of these people was going to be able to hit the streets of a strange town and ferret out secrets from the lowlifes. Ziller was there—Karp still didn't know quite what to make of him—as was Jim Phelps, V.T.'s photo expert; short, bearded, wearing a cheap tan safari suit. At the end of the table sat a small dapper man with a brush mustache and heavy black horn-rimmed glasses—Dr. Murray Selig, former chief medical examiner of New York and the chairman of the forensic panel.

Karp began, "This is our first general meeting and I hope it's our last. I hate meetings." Muffled, polite laughter. "This staff is still small enough so that we can talk to each other just about every day. I also want to minimize written reports and bureaucratic garbage as much as possible. I assume you've all met V.T. here. He'll lay out the research assignments for each of you. The well-dressed gentleman sitting across from me is Clay Fulton, on leave from the New York PD. He'll handle all the fieldwork with such of you as he thinks can help out. We've divided the work into a number of lines of research in two big groupings. First, we want to know to the extent possible what really happened in Dallas that day. We're therefore going to reexamine, one, the ballistics and other forensic material, two, the photographic evidence, including the various amateur films, and, three, there'll be a special reexamination of the autopsy evidence by Dr. Selig and his team of forensic pathologists.

"The second grouping is concerned with why Kennedy was shot and whether the actual facts of the crime were covered up by either governmental or nongovernmental sources, or a combination of the two. The recent Church committee report gives us some reason to believe that neither the CIA nor the FBI was perfectly forthcoming with Warren. We're going to look into, one, the

Cuba connection, right- and left-wing versions, and the CIA involvement; two, we're going to review the investigation of Oswald's background; three, we're going to check out the organized crime connection; and four, we're going to see what we can find out about Jack Ruby."

Karp then read off a list of assignments and looked up. Everyone except Fulton, Selig, and Newbury was scribbling away on pads. Karp continued, "V.T. has set up a filing system and an initial set of leads for each group. We'll expect you all to use your heads in following them up. I'm available any time for a conference on any particular problem, but I'm not going to have time to nursemaid you through this. One other thing: I intend to run this as a professional investigation. You'll hear a lot about political sensitivities and pressures. I want you to ignore them. The reason we're here, the reason the Warren Commission screwed up, was just that kind of knuckling under to politics, and I'm not going to be party to a repetition of that. All we're going to be concerned with here is evidence and the best interpretation of that evidence, on the basis of our professional judgment and not a damn thing else."

He paused and looked around the table. Some of the faces bore faint smirks or incipient expressions of disbelief. Then he added, "Some of you may have problems with that, in which case you're welcome to leave. And I can guarantee you this: if you sign on here and I do find out you're crimping the investigation to suit somebody's political agenda, you're out and I don't care who your patron is. I know Bert Crane will support me on this. Okay, any questions?"

A silence, then a series of anticlimaxes. Somebody asked about furniture. Another asked about travel funds, and a third raised the critical issue of whether congressional staff parking privileges would be retained. It was a replay of the conversation between Flores and Crane. Karp referred these matters to Sondergard. Nobody seemed to have any substantive questions about who shot JFK. The meeting broke up in the usual burble of cross-conversation, centering around V.T. Karp slipped out feeling tense and irritated.

Later, Karp sat in his office with Fulton and Murray Selig. "Welcome to the funhouse," he said.

"You got yourself a problem, boychik," said the pathologist. "Comparatively, I got it easy."

"You're satisfied with the panel?" Karp asked.

"Oh, yeah, all good people. That's not the issue, though."

"What is?"

"The material. If the material isn't there, how are we going to come up with anything different than Warren did?"

"Oh, come on, Murray!" Karp snapped. He reached for the summary volume of the Warren Report and flipped it open to the famous ugly profile drawing of JFK with the trajectory of the magic bullet going through its neck. "Are you going to endorse this crap?"

Selig smiled and placed his hands over his ears. "I don't want to hear it. We'll look at the evidence available and we'll judge from that. You know how I work."

Karp tossed the volume down with a bang that raised a little flurry of plaster dust. "Yeah, right. Sorry, I know you'll do what's right."

Then the three men, who had worked together on hundreds of violent deaths over many years, chatted briefly about the simpler cases of the past, until Selig had to leave to catch a plane back to the city.

When he had gone, Fulton observed, "He's right, you know. Autopsy could draw a blank on this one."

Karp shook his head. "I don't believe it. This"—he motioned at the blue book—"is a lie. Murray won't be party to a lie. I don't expect him to get the full story, but I'd be willing to bet he'll explode this one."

Fulton shrugged. "Maybe. I hope so. Meanwhile, what are we going to do about this investigation? That crew in there couldn't find a cat in a grocery bag. You in deep shit here, Stretch."

"We in deep shit, you mean. Any ideas?"

Fulton rubbed his hand slowly over his close-cropped head for a moment before he replied. "Well, there's you and me and V.T. Maybe a couple of the crew'll turn out to be some good. They can't all be as useless as they look."

"You mentioned ex-cops on the phone."

"Uh-huh, cops on pensions, here and there. They'd be willing to pitch in."

"Like who?"

"Al Sangredo, used to work the Two-five?"

"Yeah, way back. He still alive?"

Fulton chuckled. "Al better not hear you say that. Yeah, he's down in Miami. Got a private license, still dabbles a little. He's up for it. He's a Spaniard, but he can get into the Cuban business down there. He was Fidel's bodyguard for the cops when he made that New York visit back in the fifties, so he knows the other side too. Apparently they hit it off, him and Fidel."

"Oh, great! That's a desirable reference in Little Havana."

Fulton laughed. "Then there's Pete Melchior in New Orleans. . . ."

"What about here?" Karp asked impatiently. Fulton gave him a disbelieving look and shot back, "Man wasn't *killed* here, son. We don't need no more people here in D.C. We're damn lucky that New York cops hit the warm climates a lot when they throw in their tin. Spend the bribe money in peace. This is gonna be cleared up in Texas, probably New Orleans, maybe Miami, if the Cubans are connected up to it, like the Senate Intelligence report says. I think I got a guy in Dallas too. What I mean is, we need folks *know* those towns, which I don't and neither do you."

Karp shook his head as if trying to throw off sleep and sighed. "Yeah, sorry. That's what this fucking place does to you. I been here a lousy month and I'm starting to think the world ends at the Beltway, like everybody else." He looked at his watch. "I have to get over to Schaller's office."

"The CIA stuff?"

"Yeah."

"You want me to come with you?"

Karp gave Fulton a puzzled look and opened his mouth to say something like, "No, why should you," when the other man's implication struck him, generating an unwelcome shiver.

Karp laughed unconvincingly. "You think Langley is going to gun me down on Independence Avenue and steal back their files?"

"It's been known, if you believe half what these assassination nuts say."

"Fuck it!" said Karp. "I'm not that paranoid yet." He picked up his briefcase, shrugged into a suit jacket and his raincoat, and headed for the door.

Fulton issued a rough laugh. " 'Yet' is the right word, baby. We're just starting out."

Karp reached the Dirksen Senate Office Building six streets away without being gunned down by Cuban paramilitaries or Texas fascists, nor succumbing to the more likely ambuscade from one of the dozens of Kennedy-assassination nuts that had started to haunt the Select Committee's staff.

The interview with Senator Schaller did not go quite as Ziller had predicted. Schaller proved to be a bluff, square-faced, stocky man with thinning reddish hair, who presented himself in the antique Trumanesque style that had been abandoned by many of his colleagues for the blow dryer and the spin doctor. He had the papers right on his desk and made no bones about what they were. He regretted not having used them himself, cursed the CIA in earthy barnyard terms, and wished Karp good luck. The whole thing took eight minutes, and involved a crushing handshake that seemed to last nearly a third of the entire interview.

Karp walked back to the Annex at a good clip, making one detour at Third Street to avoid the guy with the funny orange hair who had counted thirty-eight shots in Dealey Plaza. His first stop was the Xerox room, where he made a copy of the Schaller papers. His next stop was Fulton's office.

Karp handed the thin stack of originals to the detective and sat down in a creaky wooden swivel chair to read the copy. For the next twenty minutes there was silence but for the rustle of pages and the creak of Karp's old chair as both men read. Karp finished his reading before Fulton did and, taking out a pen, began to re-read, making notes.

Fulton indicated he was done reading by scooping up the pile of pages on his desk and neatly squaring the edges of the stack. He placed the documents in the center of his steel desk and looked at them with an odd expression. Karp studied his friend's face curiously. Was it fear he observed? Unlikely. Clay Fulton possessed more physical courage than any man Karp had ever met. Disgust? Maybe. Karp was fairly disgusted himself.

He asked, "What do you think, Clay?"

Fulton met his eyes, his expression one of the most profound bafflement. "What do I think? I think we should've stayed in town.

We're way over our heads here, boy. Way, way, *way* over our heads."

In a small whitewashed room in Quezaltenango in Guatemala, a thin, bearded man packed his suitcase. The phone call from Washington had been unexpected but not disturbing. The man was used to phone calls interrupting his life and asking him to travel to another part of the world to do odd things.

This is what he does for a living, goes places and does things in response to phone calls. He is not exactly a professional assassin. There may, in fact, be no such thing, despite the fantasies of fiction writers, and were there to be such a profession, it would not be staffed by elegant men who wear dinner clothes and drink champagne in tony resorts. This is simple economics: it is so easy to kill people, and there are so many who will gladly do it cheaply, that it would be hard to command a high living from that trade. The thin man has, however, killed any number of people for money, but only as an ancillary, if critical, activity, just as a chauffeur may wash a car, or a waiter may wipe down a table.

He is not exactly a spy either, or a mercenary soldier, although he has spied and fought for gold. He has also run a bar in Honduras and managed a small air-shipping service. Essentially, he does what certain people tell him to do. It is the only fixed point in his life, and it gives him the closest feeling he ever has to a feeling of security.

He completed his packing, put on a khaki baseball hat, turned to leave the room, but stopped at a cracked mirror tacked up by the door and looked at his face. He was nearly forty. He had brown eyes and crisp, short brown hair. He did not think that anyone will recognize his face at his destination. He had aged and grown a beard and it had been a long time.

The thin man walked down a narrow flight of stairs and entered a room with several desks and chairs in it. A brown-skinned soldier in green fatigues sat in one of them, tilted back against the wall, reading a magazine, his rifle leaning against the wall next to him.

The thin man asked, "Has Chavez gone out to the airstrip yet?" His Spanish was quite good, almost unaccented.

The soldier said, "No, the truck's still outside." He took in the suitcase. "Going somewhere?"

"Yes. I have to meet a plane."

"What should I tell them?"

"Tell them I'll be back, but I'm not sure when," the thin man said, and walked into the steamy evening.

SIX

Five in the morning and Marlene Ciampi lay sleepless on her back, studying the stamped tin pattern of the loft's ceiling. She was dying for a cigarette, but she had decided to ration herself to five per day, and the first one was going to be with coffee in a few hours, when she officially rose to start the day.

Much of her energy recently had been going into this sort of self-torment. She had become obsessive not only about smoking, but about food and booze and schedules and shopping. She thought about this, lying in bed. I'm counting everything, she thought. People are starting to look at me funny. I bought a Day-Timer in a little leather case. That's a joke. I never seemed to need one before; now I write down everything, schedule everything to the quarter hour. I'm not like this, she thought: happy-go-lucky, anything-on-a-dare Marlene. It's like I'm back in high school with the nuns.

During such musings, Marlene did not dwell on the source of these disturbing changes. She did not want to believe that Karp's leaving for Washington was involved at all. She loved Karp, although she was angry with him for leaving, but that didn't mean she was dependent on him. Dependency was the death of love, so Marlene believed, and she also knew that she *should* be able to do it all on her own. She had been on her own for a long time before she got together with Karp, so what was the problem now? The kid was no problem; Lucy was an angel—healthy, cooperative, a delight.

And, of course, other women did it, including black single working mothers with many fewer resources than she had; also, there were those women you read about in the magazines, "Sharon Perfect, single mom, thirty-five, cooks French cuisine for her three kids, vice-president of a major ad agency, plays cello in the local orchestra, training for the Hawaii Triathlon. . . . (picture) Sharon's a size five, blond, the three kids are gorgeous, snapped at the family table as they discuss nuclear physics in Chinese."

With these thoughts stoking her already red-hot guilt and urging her to improve each shining hour with ever more zeal and efficiency, Marlene flung herself from bed, made a hasty ablution, and started her exercise regimen. This was an hour each day of the sort of conditioning that prizefighters use to prepare them for their literally punishing sport. Marlene's father had been a likely welterweight just after the second war and had worked his way up to a match with Kid Gavilan, and lasted one and thirty of the first round, which was why he had decided to become a plumber. He had, however, taught all of his six kids (including the three girls) how to box.

Marlene was the only one who had kept it up. She had a body bag and a speed bag set up in a corner of the loft she and Karp called the gym, and now she slipped into shorts and a T-shirt and sneakers and speed gloves, and pounded away at both bags for forty-five minutes. Then she skipped rope with all the hand-crossing, pace-changing frills you see in boxing movies, tossing her head to snap the sweat out of her eyes.

She stripped and plunged into the huge black tub. She felt better, as she always did after her violent exertions. There was nothing in fact wrong with her or her life, she decided, only with her thinking. She'd stick it out for as long as that idiot wanted to waste his time in Washington. She would flourish, in fact.

Actually, she reflected as she lolled in the steaming water, things were getting better. Bloom was paying attention to her, he had invited her to a meeting of a national advisory committee on sex crimes. And deservedly: she had racked up some nice convictions, her staff was terrific and getting better, she had earned some nice ink recently. A disloyal thought . . . maybe Karp's intransigence had been screwing up *her* career?

She left the bath and dried herself and washed her empty eye socket with saline and inserted the glassie, then walked naked to

the closet area under the sleeping loft. There was a full-length mirror there and she stopped to look at herself appraisingly. Nice boobs, smallish but high yet, and well proportioned, nipples the color of Bing cherry jam. She lifted her breasts with both hands and let them drop, checking the jiggle factor. Acceptable. She turned sideways and struck a bodybuilder pose. Some good def on the biceps and triceps, belly still flat, although the washboard ridges she had boasted at seventeen were nearly gone, butt still high and solid. She turned face-to again and slumped, letting her arms hang down like an ape's. A little thickening in the waist maybe, incipient love handles. Tough shit, thirty wasn't twenty, but she was still a five and many couldn't say that. She struck a sex goddess pose and hip-twitched toward the mirror, making the sort of masturbatory breast- and crotch-rubbing motions beloved of soft-core pornographers. Hmm, better stop that; she was horny enough as it was, another reason to be irritated with the absent Karp. She must be sending out pheromones, too. Guys had started to hit on her with a regularity and intensity unusual since her mating. It was irritating and nice at the same time. The image of an affair formed itself in her animal brain and swiftly faded.

She pushed her face up against the mirror, examining it for blemishes and wrinkles. No, that was still okay; one thing, the Ciampi women had good skin. They ran to fat, but they had good skin. Her mother at fifty-seven looked under forty. Marlene herself still got carded in dark bars.

She made faces, seeking the traces of wrinkles to come. She curled her lip back and pulled her ears out, chimp fashion. Soon she was cavorting in front of the mirror, grunting and dangling her knuckles against the floor, waggling buttocks, and singing "Alley Oop."

"What're you *doing*, Mommy?" said her daughter, appearing from behind, her voice tinged with alarm.

Karp said, "You're going to have to get this started, guys. I have to get back to the city this weekend. In fact, I'm thinking of splitting early today."

The three of them, Karp, Fulton, and V.T., were sitting in Karp's office going over the documents from Schaller and trying to figure out what to do about them. Clay Fulton gave Karp a concerned look and asked, "Something wrong back home?"

Karp shrugged. "No. Maybe. Marlene's been sounding strange on the phone this last week."

"Marlene *is* strange," said V.T. "You just want to get laid while we do all the work."

"That too," said Karp. "Okay, where are we on this abortion? V.T.?"

Newbury adjusted his gold-rimmed half-glasses, the ones that he said made him look like a foreclosing banker, and consulted a sheaf of notes. "We have five documents, which we have labeled A through E. I know you've read them all, but I want to summarize them so we can all agree on what they say and what's significant in them. Document A appears to be an internal CIA report from the winter of 1962 describing the composition and capabilities of a Cuban emigré group called Brigada Sixty-one and its involvement in Operation Mongoose—where do they get these names?—which was designed to launch guerrilla raids on Cuban targets and which included a plot to kill Fidel Castro. The burden of the report is that even though President Kennedy had ordered the end of such attempts as part of the Cuban missile crisis deal with the Soviets, Brigada Sixty-one, with the help of the CIA, or some parts of it, had continued to try to infiltrate Cuba and do the regime some damage. The key section for our purposes is a list of CIA contract agents working with Brigada Sixty-one, among whom we find the name 'Lee Henry Oswald.' Also mentioned in this report is the name of the project's CIA handler, somebody named Maurice Bishop, and the name of a Cuban banker named Antonio Veroa. Veroa apparently was the leader of Brigada Sixty-one.

"Document B appears to be an after-action report, to this same Bishop, in which an actual attempt on Castro's life by Veroa and a gentleman named Guido Mosca, with some others, is described. This was in 1961. Apparently Mr. Veroa was able to rent, in his mother-in-law's name, an apartment in Havana overlooking a plaza where Castro was scheduled to give a speech, and was able to install Mosca and the others there with a hunting rifle, a machine gun, and a rocket launcher. The attempt failed, obviously, for reasons that are not covered in the text. It just says that Veroa decided that it had to be called off. Both Veroa and Mosca returned to the U.S. via Mexico. I called Ray Guma about Mosca. Goom says he's known as Jerry Legs, and was at that time an

enforcer for a loan-sharking and gambling operation run by Carlos Marcello in New Orleans."

Karp nodded. Ray Guma was the homicide bureau's resident expert on the world of organized crime, or at least its Italian provinces. "Where is Mosca now? The city? Miami?"

"Guma said he'll check and get back to us."

V.T. continued, "Documents C and D are two-page memoranda on CIA letterhead. C is dated November 30, 1963, from Richard Helms to a group of CIA senior staff, directing them, in so many words, to stonewall the Warren Commission about any connection between Oswald and the Cubans working for the CIA and about any connection between anyone that turns up in the assassination investigation and Mongoose or any later CIA operations against Cuba. D is dated June 12, 1968, from Clyde Peterson, who was a special assistant in the office of the director of Central Intelligence at the time, to a group of senior CIA personnel, directing them to harass certain witnesses being called by Jim Garrison for the Clay Shaw trial.

"The last one, E, is my favorite. This is a transcription of an interview conducted by one of Schaller's investigators. The subject is Milton Thornby, one of Earl Warren's law clerks. There are two interesting sections. According to Thornby, during an early meeting of the full commission, Allen Dulles informed Warren that he had evidence that Oswald was a Soviet agent, and that if this got out, the American people would demand a retaliation that would certainly lead to a thermonuclear exchange. The other item is a report of a colloquy between old Earl and some of the senior commission staff. The staffer was objecting to taking at face value the CIA's assurance that Oswald had no intelligence connections. Were they justified in ruling out a conspiracy so early in the investigation? Warren replied with heat that there was to be no investigation in that area and that, quote, 'Our purpose is to assure the American people that the president was killed by a single man acting alone.' "

Newbury removed his glasses and rubbed his face. "So. What do we have? Evidence of a conspiracy? No, not quite. Evidence of an interest on the part of the CIA to suppress a thorough investigation? I guess. The question is, why?"

He looked at the others so they would know that this was not

merely rhetorical. After a moment, Fulton said, "I *hate* this, but okay: because the CIA set up the hit on Kennedy."

"Okay, that's one," said Newbury.

Fulton said, "Or they didn't have anything to do with it, but Oswald worked for them or associated with some people who worked for them and they didn't want the trail to lead back to their door."

"Good. Two. Butch?"

Karp snapped back to the business at hand. He had been thinking about Marlene and the last phone conversation they had shared, about false laughter and long silences with the dead line whispering bad things to his imagination. He said, "Three, they had nothing to do with Kennedy's murder, and they didn't even know Oswald was connected with them, but the trail from Oswald led back to the Cuban involvement, and Mongoose, and using mafiosi, and the stuff they did after Mongoose, *after* JFK told them to stop. They couldn't let anyone follow on that trail."

"Why not?" asked Fulton. "That stuff got out anyway. And who the hell cares about some spooks playing war games. Especially as they totally screwed up the hit on Fidel."

"That might be just the point," said Karp. "I have a feeling these guys felt they had a reputation to protect. Also, the Warren Report critics who say the whole thing in Dallas was totally organized and carried out by the CIA never explain how come these guys tried to kill Castro about a dozen times and tripped all over themselves and then got Kennedy the first time out. On the other hand—"

V.T. broke in. "Stop! Now *we're* doing it. This is how people go crazy over this business. Look, there are ten thousand facts, or quasi facts, that have been dug up about this assassination. They've been arranged in about four hundred books and God knows how many articles, of which every one contradicts every other one, because each one selects out a group of facts and ignores others that are inconvenient to its initial thesis: the CIA did it, the Mob did it, Castro did it, and so on, of which the Warren Report itself is the most famous example. If we start doing the same thing we're going to wind up with something that's not much better than Warren in some different direction."

He took off his spectacles again, wiping them absentmindedly on his tie. The two other men exchanged a look, and Karp asked, "So what do we do, V.T.? Hang it up and go home?"

V.T. grinned. "Don't ask me twice. No, I can think of two things. One is this stuff." He tapped the sheaf of documents. "It's new and it's a break. It's the very first documentary evidence that someone called Lee Oswald was actually connected with the CIA, actually on somebody's payroll. So we have to explore the CIA connection for all it's worth. We have to find these three guys, Veroa, Mosca, and their CIA contact, Maurice Bishop. Or whoever Bishop really is."

"What do you mean?" asked Fulton. "It's an alias?"

"Yeah, I checked already. Nobody named Maurice Bishop ever worked for the CIA. Okay, that's the first thing. The second approach is through Oswald himself."

"How do you mean?" Karp asked. "I thought he was dead. Or am I still being a dupe of the Warren Report?"

They all laughed, a relief of tension. V.T. said, "That, or a conscious tool of malign forces. No, what I mean is this. Oswald is the sole connector that links all the usual suspects, even if he was just a patsy, as he himself said when they grabbed him that day. Who are the usual suspects? CIA, commies, anticommies, Mob. Okay, Mob first. Oswald was raised by a minor Mob figure in New Orleans, his uncle, Dutz Murret. Murret's best buddy was Carlos Marcello's bodyguard and chauffeur. There's all kinds of hearsay evidence that Oswald knew Jack Ruby before, so maybe he kept his connections up with the wise guys.

"Next, commies: Oswald claimed to be a Marxist nearly all his life. Whether true or not, he certainly made the marines believe it and he did move to Russia and then married the niece of a Soviet Interior Ministry official."

"And he went to Mexico and tried to get to Cuba," added Karp.

V.T. paused and gave him an odd look. "Yes, so it seems. Although . . . no, let's not get into it now. Where were we? Yes, the anticommies. In Dallas, Oswald was welcomed with open arms by a group of violently anticommunist White Russians, like George de Morenschildt, Viktor Bezikoff, Armand Gaiilov, and others—not something you'd expect them to do for an actual Red. Also, on his return to New Orleans in 1963, Oswald hooked up with

Gary Becker, a notorious right-winger, and Becker apparently re-cruited him to infiltrate pro-Castro student organizations. That seems to be the origin of the famous Fair Play for Cuba incident. Oswald hands out pro-Castro leaflets and gets into a scuffle with anti-Castro Cubans and gets arrested. He even goes on the radio to debate some anti-Castro Cuban about communism. Unfortu-nately, when he printed up the leaflets he used the address of Beck-er's organization, the Anti-Communist League of the Caribbean, 544 Bank Street, on the pro-Castro leaflets. Very odd. Finally, there's the Sylvia Odio incident. Three men identifying themselves as members of an anti-Castro organization show up at the Odios' Dallas apartment one evening in September 1963. Odio's dad is a big anti-Castroite and a political prisoner in Cuba. Two of these guys are Cubans, one's an American who calls himself Leon. They talk a lot about killing Kennedy because of how he betrayed them at the Bay of Pigs and after the missile crisis. When Kennedy is shot the next month, Odio IDs 'Leon' as Oswald. Everybody who's ever talked to Odio swears she's right on, but of course Warren discounted her evidence."

"This is old stuff, V.T.," said Karp. "What's the point?"

"Wait. Now we come to the CIA connection. Oswald works at one of the most secret bases in the military, Atsugi, Japan, where they launch U-2 spy planes against Russia. He has a secret security clearance. Atsugi also happens to be the regional CIA center. At this time, although Oswald is boasting he's a commie and a Rus-sian spy, nobody does anything about it. In fifty-nine he gets out of the marines, and despite the fact he has almost no money, he somehow gets the fare to fly to London. Then he gets to Helsinki in some way on a day when there's no commercial London-to-Helsinki flight, crosses over by train, goes to Moscow, and talks with an embassy official with strong CIA links. He defects, works in Minsk for a while, marries a Russian girl, redefects to the U.S., all without an instant's difficulty with passports or transit. This is in an era when famous people are getting their passports pulled for even the faintest pink associations. The capper to all this is that Marina Oswald paints a picture of her late husband as a feckless schmuck who could barely keep a job, just the kind of nutty loner who typically assassinates presidents of the United States. The guy apparently has no talent at all, except a talent for making big, powerful bureaucracies do anything he wanted. Oh, yeah: one

other useful little skill. He can be in two places at once. In the month before the assassination, nearly a dozen witnesses have placed Oswald in interesting places—a firing range shooting his rifle, a rifle repair shop, a garage, a gas station—at times when we know he was somewhere else. And in all those places whoever it was made sure that people would remember him as Lee Oswald."

"You're buying the double-Oswald story?" asked Fulton.

"I don't know. It's one explanation of the facts, with the only other one being that a bunch of unconnected people, solid citizens, lied in concert for no reason. But that's not crucial at the moment. What *is* crucial is that whoever Oswald really was, he's still the key to the mystery. All the threads cross on him, and that's why the most exciting thing we've uncovered so far is this document actually naming him as a contract CIA agent."

Fulton stood up and stretched. He said, "Well, you know, V.T., this is all very fancy, but I'm just a simple street cop. Maybe before we elaborate any theories we should locate this guy, what's-his-face, Veroa, and have a chat with him. And the wise guy, Mosca. That's what I'm gonna get started on, as soon as I come off the drunk I'm gonna go on now for getting into this pile of shit in the first place."

"While you're at it," said V.T., "you could find out what old Lee was doing from August 21st to September 17th, 1963. The whole FBI was trying to find out his daily activities from his date of birth to the time he died, but nobody's ever been able to determine where he was or what he was doing for those twenty-seven days. Marina, naturally, says he was napping on the couch, but nobody else saw him during the period in question. All we know is that he was in the country on Labor Day; he visited his aunt."

"His aunt, huh?" Fulton chuckled, a rumbling noise that could be by turns delightful or threatening. Now it was somewhere in between. "That the same aunt that was seen coming out of the manhole on Dealey Plaza with the silenced forty-five? I'll check it out—it sounds like a real break." He left.

V.T. stared at the closing door. "He's pissed off. Not at me, I hope."

"No, but like he said—he's basically a street cop. He gets ner-

vous when he doesn't know the players or the neighborhood."
Karp rose, walked over to the greasy window, and stared out at
an unpleasant vista of railroad tracks and freeways.

"Speaking of neighborhoods, this is the worst view available
from any federal building in the area. Whoever decided to put us
in this dump knew how to make a point." He stopped as a familiar
scratching noise sounded behind one of the walls. "It also probably
has more rats per square yard than any building they had available."

"The FBI used to be here."

"That explains it," answered Karp with a brief laugh. V.T. did
not join in. Karp looked more closely at his friend. Newbury met
his gaze briefly and then turned his eyes away, as if ashamed at
what they might reveal. In the moment Karp had seen something
he didn't like, something he had never seen in the man before.
Exhaustion? No, like Karp, he had gone through the same mur-
derous training in the old criminal courts bureau, and he had always turned up in court crackling fresh with a jest on his lips—he
was famous for it. It was something deeper—a psychic depletion,
the investigator's equivalent of the thousand-yard stare that afflicts
infantrymen too long on the line.

"You look beat," Karp offered. "You should take the rest of
the week off." A joke; it was Friday afternoon.

V.T. said, "I *am* beat. This defeats me. I believe I've contracted
Oswald's Syndrome. Symptoms: a chronic and progressive inability to discern fact from fiction and role-playing from personality.
Distinguishable from common psychosis by the odd fact that the
underlying structure of reality gradually comes to mimic the imag-
inary world created by the sufferer. An occupational disease of
spies, counterspies, and the people who study them. Speaking of
spies, did you ever hear the odd story of Evno Azev? Doesn't ring
a bell? Well, around the turn of the century Azev was the most
successful terrorist leader in Russia and the head of an anarchist
band called the Terror Brigade. These guys carried out dozens of
successful assassinations of public figures, including the minister
of the interior, von Plehv, and the czar's own uncle, the grand duke
Sergei. In 1908, however, it was revealed that Azev was also a
senior agent of the Ohkrana, the czarist secret police. He was planning all those assassinations, see, to get in better with the terrorists,

so he could betray the terrorists. So it turned out that the chief antiterrorist agent was, in fact, the best terrorist of them all. When he was exposed, in fact, the terrorist movement totally *collapsed*. What am I getting at? Well, compared to Lee Harvey Oswald, and his many confreres, old Evno was . . . I don't know—who's authentic any more? Martin Buber? You? Maybe Oswald was his own double."

V.T. got up and placed the CIA papers back into a folder. "I think I will take the rest of the week off. And perhaps more. Call me when we get a budget."

"Yeah, right. But aside from this new stuff, what else can we do meanwhile?"

"Find out who Bishop is," said V.T. "Although how to begin doing that I have no idea. Aside from that, we're dredging through the Senate material, making lists of follow-ups from the Warren stuff, Phelps is trying to get his hands on the autopsy photos and X rays . . . but it's all indoor sports. We need fresh stuff that hasn't been dragged over a million times, stuff from the field, stuff from new material, like this." He rattled the papers in his hand. "And without a settled budget . . ."

"Yeah, I know. We can't do serious investigation."

"Any word on when we'll get one?"

"No, but I have a meeting with Crane later today. That's on the list. And I'll tell him about this CIA stuff, too. Maybe he has some ideas."

V.T. started to leave.

"Take care of yourself," said Karp. "And be careful with that material. There's only three copies and I don't want any more made."

"Leaks?"

"That, and theft."

V.T. mimed an elaborate terror, clutched the file to his breast, and scurried out crabwise, looking rapidly from side to side over his shoulder.

When Karp arrived for his meeting, Crane was engrossed in a newspaper, cursing under his breath. "Did you see this shit yet?" he demanded, tossing the paper across his desk. Karp took it and read the obvious story, a short piece above the fold on the front

page, headlined "Congressmen Balk on 'Police State' Tactics of Assassination Committee Chief."

"It's started," Crane said bitterly. "Yesterday I had a closed-session meeting with the full committee. I finally got them to focus on getting this damned show on the road and outlined my approach. Those two old bastards must have been on the horn to the press the minute I walked out of the room."

Which particular two old bastards Crane referred to, out of the many in Congress, was made clear by the article. Congressmen Peller and McClain expressed "grave alarm" at the plans disclosed by the committee's chief counsel to use a variety of investigative devices, including phone taps, concealed taping, lie detectors, and voice stress analyzers, in the course of the investigation.

"Big on civil liberties, are they?" Karp asked when he was done reading.

"Don't make me laugh! Peller was some kind of hanging judge down in Alabama and McClain is an ex–Un-American Activities Committee lawyer. They wouldn't know a civil liberty if it bit off their left nut. No, there's something else going on. I mean it's unique; I've been blasted plenty in the press for things I've done, but I've never been blasted for things I *might* do. What it is, somebody's running scared and they're putting on the pressure. I wish I knew who it was."

"I think I might have an idea who," said Karp after a moment's thought, and he told Crane briefly about what was in the new CIA documents. Crane grew increasingly excited as the story unfolded. "That's terrific stuff, Butch. It's our obvious line of inquiry. And you're right—somebody must have leaked to the committee that we've got something solid linking Oswald to the CIA."

"So our next move is . . . ?"

"Subpoena the bastards. Helms and the rest of them down to the cipher clerks. Grill 'em. Wave their own damn documents in their faces."

"Why won't they stonewall it, like they did in sixty-three?"

"Let 'em. We'll hit them with contempt citations. Somebody'll crack, when they're looking at jail time. Not the big boys maybe, but the little fish. This is great! We can start weaving a real net."

"Um, I hate to bring this up, but with what for money? Weaving is fine, but I got no weavers. I need investigators in the field, with

travel and phone and equipment budgets to support them. . . ."

"That's coming," said Crane irritably. "Bea is working up the formal budget, and I'll submit it to Flores by close of business today. He'll read it over the weekend, present it to the committee next week, and I'd expect closure on it no later than a week from now. I've asked for six and a half million. That'll support nearly two hundred people for both assassination investigations."

Karp was stunned. "That's a lot of money," he said, thinking that the typical homicide in New York was solved by two good cops with some minimal canvassing and lab work. The JFK business would need more, being spread around the country, but . . . Tentatively, he suggested, "Will they give us that much? I mean, if we had just a little to start, we could make some progress and then go back for more."

"That's not the way I work," Crane said with some force. "They asked me what I needed and I told them. If they don't want to shell out, it's on their heads."

To which Karp generally agreed; still, his political warning lights, dim and unreliable bulbs though they were, had started to flash. Crane was supposed to be the political mastermind of the project, but even Karp understood that a time when you were in trouble in the press was not exactly the best time to ask for a huge shitload of money from a guy who didn't like you in the first place.

The thin man did not have to wait long at the landing strip. Just after the appointed hour, he heard a droning sound and the DC-4 broke out of the clouds over the mountain and landed in a cloud of red dust. He waited while some crates were unloaded and then entered the plane and strapped himself into an uncomfortable jump seat jutting from the bulkhead.

The flight to Guatemala City took forty minutes. He walked from the military section of the field to the commercial terminal. There was a ticket waiting for him under the name he gave the girl at the Avianca counter, and he took the regular evening plane to Miami.

There was a man there waiting for him outside of customs, a short Latin man in sunglasses (though it was night) and a flowered shirt worn outside his pale lemon trousers. They went to a blue van parked outside and drove from the airport down LeJeune Road to Eighth Street, Calle Ocho, the heart of Little Havana, where they turned left. In a few minutes, they arrived at the driveway of a house painted apricot with

white trim. *The thin man from Guatemala got out of the van and went into the house.*

In the living room, a good-looking older man of about sixty rose from a sofa and extended his hand in greeting.

"Hello, Bill," he said, smiling. "Welcome to Miami. Long time."

"Hello, Bishop," said the thin man. "Yes, a long time. Years."

SEVEN

"I can't *believe* I did that!" cried Marlene in anguish. "I yelled at a secretary. In *public!*"

She was in private now, in her tatty little office, with Luisa Beckett, her deputy. "What happened?" asked Beckett.

"Oh, nothing, just stupidity. I was in a rush to get to court to answer motions on the Schaffter thing, *People* v. *Melville,* and I just reached into the drawer and grabbed the red-tabbed file that's supposed to have all the motions and responses in it and of course I didn't check it and when I got there I looked and found it was full of Q and A's. No motions."

"Marva mixed up the tabs again."

"Right. And so I got chewed out by the judge, who was fucking Hannegan, who hates me anyway, and I had to run back here and get the motions and run back and get there all sweaty like a kid on his first day in criminal courts. And of course got snickered at by all attending, and then I got back here, and Marva and Beverly were lounging around comparing nails, and I guess I just lost it. Good Christ! I called her a . . . a. . . ."

"Not a dumb nigger, I hope," said Beckett.

"No, a *stupid bitch!*" wailed Marlene, and pressed her face against her desk, with her arms wrapped around her head.

"She'll get over it," said Beckett soothingly. "Don't take it so hard. Everybody gets mad sometimes. You've been under a strain."

Marlene looked up. "Yeah, I have. So have you, so has every-

body on the staff, so has fucking *Marva*, probably, but we don't all carry on like that. Face it, I'm losing my mind."

"No you're not," said Beckett automatically. Marlene stared at her more closely, searching her face for signs of the sort of patronizing looks people use to calm the loony down before punching 911. But Beckett seemed merely embarrassed. As well she might be, Marlene thought miserably. One of the very rare black female ADAs, and Marlene's protégée for the past four years, Beckett was a rail-thin, pale tan woman who might have been extruded from Kevlar, and who had never been observed to exhibit any emotion except fury at rapists. Marlene figured there was a personal story behind that, but she had never asked and Luisa had never volunteered. They were close comrades on the job, but not really friends.

Marlene swallowed hard and said with a sigh, "Oh, I'm being a baby. I didn't mean to lay a trip on you. Just, lately—it's like someone's running fingernails over my blackboard all the time. I can't relax. I'm obsessive. Like this filing system that Marva screwed up. Did I really need it? I don't know—I sort of got on all right before I set it up. I mean, I was never famous for losing stuff. But lately, I feel everything's slipping away, that if I don't keep track of things, minutely, everything will sort of dissolve—*I'll* dissolve, or crack, or fall into little pieces. . . ."

Her voice died away. Great! Now Luisa would be *positive* her boss was crazy. Marlene's face colored with embarrassment. Out of the corner of her eye she could see Beckett, looking at her impassively, as if waiting for this display of weakness to be over so that they could get down to business again. A good prosecutor, Beckett, but not much of a confidante.

Marlene cleared her throat and said, as briskly as she could manage, "So. You came in here for a reason, right?"

The relief was clear on Beckett's face as she placed a file on the desk between them. "Yeah, rape and assault. I think the vic might need protection."

Marlene took the file and skimmed it, which included glancing at several color Polaroids of a forlorn-looking woman, young, blond, pretty, with a fat shiner on one eye, a lumpy jaw, and a cut lip. The woman's name was Maddy Merrill, twenty-three, a dancer and model. According to her statement, the accused, Albert Buonafacci, twenty-four, a tourist from Miami, had picked her up in a

bar in the East Forties, bought her a nice dinner, and taken her to some clubs in a white limo. He had seemed like a nice guy. He had driven her back to her place in Chelsea, and she had invited him in for a drink. The nice guy had rounded out a magical Manhattan evening by beating her up and raping her.

"And the perp is where?" Marlene asked.

"The cops picked him up at his hotel. His story is she was a pros who tried to rip him off so he slapped her a couple. I got a hundred K bail, but he paid it without a twitch and walked out."

"What's the problem? Did he threaten her?"

"No, but she says he's connected, or so he told her. She's nervous about testifying against a Mob guy."

"But he didn't actually threaten her."

"Not that she said, but . . ." Luisa checked and gave Marlene a penetrating look. "What, you have a problem with this? The guy's a bastard, a violent son of a bitch. And he's, um . . ." She hesitated.

"He's Italian, right? Hence a mafioso?"

"That's not what I meant," said Beckett.

Marlene made a dismissive gesture with her hand. "Yeah, you did. It's okay, we get it all the time, like black men are muggers and black women are welfare sluts. Welcome to the melting pot. Let me say this: I grew up around guys who are now actually with the Mob—not a lot, but some. But for every guy who's really with, there are a dozen sleazebags that talk about how connected they are. So our boy could be one of these. Or he could be for real. Okay, say he's for real, there's no guarantee that he'll carry out on a threat. A threat is business, and the dons are not hot on mixing business with pleasure, and he'd be a lot more scared of them than he is of us. Meanwhile, there's not even a solid threat, so . . ."

"No protection?"

"Not now," said Marlene; and observing that Beckett's fine-boned face was solidifying like a pour of epoxy, she added, "Come on, man! We have women being actively stalked and we got no place to put them."

Luisa stood up and gathered up the case file. "Thanks for the lecture on the Mob," she said bitterly. "I'll pass it on to Ms. Merrill. I'm sure it'll make her feel a lot better."

"Oh, Luisa, for crying out loud . . . ," said Marlene to the back of the departing woman. The door slammed shut.

A good day, thought Marlene: I've alienated my secretary and my deputy. What next?

But next, as it turned out, was a nice lift. The DA called her directly, an event about as rare as a thank-you from a New York cabbie:

"Marlene? Sandy Bloom. Are you busy?"

"Umm . . ."

"If you can spare a moment, I'd like you to drop by. I'm having an interesting meeting and I'd like your views."

It happened that Marlene could just spare a moment for the district attorney. She stopped by the ladies' to make sure that her face and outfit bore inspection, and of course, to check that her glassie was straight in its socket. Glass eyes tend to rotate and you have to check them often, unless you want to depend on the horrified looks of your interlocutors to cue you in that something's wrong. Marlene claimed she was used to the thing and it didn't bother her. This was a lie: besides the hair that fell artfully over her bad right eye, she was careful in public to obscure that side of her face with various practiced gestures and postures.

There were two other people sitting in the comfortable brown leather chairs in Bloom's office when Marlene arrived, both of whom were vaguely familiar: a thin, spectacled man and a blocky, fair-haired woman in a denim suit. The DA was behind his desk, leaning backward in his thronelike judge's chair. He stopped talking, warmly beckoned Marlene over to them, and made the introductions. The man was a prominent criminal justice scholar working on a project for the Vera Institute of Justice. The woman was the president of the New York State chapter of a national women's organization. Marlene had seen both of them recently on a talk segment of the "Today" show.

"I was just telling Paul and Beth about you, Marlene," said the DA, gesturing expansively toward her. "This woman has revolutionized the prosecution of sex crimes in Manhattan."

Marlene bobbed her head at the fatuous remark, and the two celebrities beamed at her.

Paul said, "We were just talking about the possibility of identifying potentially violent sex offenders. We have some data that show violent sex offenders often have a history of misdemeanor arrests—public nuisance, exposure, sexual battery—before they

become violent, and we were exploring the possibility of a program to track these people from their first appearance in the criminal courts."

They all looked at Marlene, the revolutionary, for a brilliant response. Though feeling short on brilliance today, Marlene understood her new role as the DA's pet smart girl. She paused for a moment to order her thoughts, and then said, "Well, that's an interesting idea, but just because some violent sex offenders started small and went on to bigger things doesn't mean all of them, or even the worst of them, did. Ted Bundy was clean as a whistle. So was John Wayne Gacy. The main problem we've had is that not potential but *actual* rapists walk on misdemeanor charges because we can't nail them for a rape, or because we haven't felt like going to trial. They plead to misdemeanor sexual abuse, or 130.20, sexual misconduct, which is a class A misdemeanor. They might get off with time served or serve at the most sixty days."

The woman said, "Yes, but if we had some way of tracking them, we could either get them into some kind of enforced treatment program, or, I don't know, warn people about them."

Marlene nodded impatiently. "Yes, we could, if the law were changed, but the problem is we have no basis for assuming that these guys are any sicker than the average mugger, or that therapy would do any good. As far as tracking them, yeah . . ." She paused. An interesting notion had just popped into her head. "If the same people, the same staff of prosecutors, dealt with misdemeanor sex crimes in the criminal courts bureaus as well as the felonies, maybe then we'd get some perspective, maybe then we wouldn't let these guys walk when they've already raped or abused some people. I mean, it wouldn't be just another case on the calendar: like"— Marlene here imitated the monotone of a court officer calling out cases—"burglary, plead to trespass, bang, next case; dope dealing, plead to possession, bang, next case; rape, plead to sexual abuse two, bang, next case. It'd be more like, well, homicide. Something that stood out."

The two visitors were interested in this prospect, of course, and they discussed at some length how it might work. During this interchange, Marlene cast an eye on the district attorney, and got a knowing and appreciative look. What the visitors didn't quite understand was that the proposed unit that they were discussing, that would deal with sex cases in the criminal courts bureau as well as

more serious offenses, would naturally be Marlene's unit, which would require perhaps a tripling of her staff. But the DA understood it very well.

The meeting wound down, with the usual promises to keep in touch. As the two rape fans were leaving, Bloom motioned Marlene to stay behind. He said, "That was very good, Marlene. With you around, I got my ass covered on sex." He grinned charmingly, showing the neat white perfect teeth of the wealthy, and patted her arm. "And real tricky too," he continued. "You know, you set me up a little there."

She felt her face heat. "I didn't mean—," she began, but Bloom interrupted with a gesture.

"No, I understand. And I tend to agree with you. But what we're talking about here is a fairly massive reorganization of staff. The criminal courts bureau chief is going to be involved, and maybe the bench too. I'm going to have to stroke a lot of guys' balls on this one."

"You mean you're interested in doing it? Actually?"

"Well, we need to talk some more," said Bloom expansively. "But it could be done. It would put you in the big leagues around here, that's for sure." He tossed a sincere look into her eyes. "But you're a big-league player, aren't you?"

"Uh-huh," she said, putting some wattage behind her return smile.

"Yes. Well, here's the thing. I'm tied up for the rest of the afternoon, and then I have a five-thirty with some of the governor's people, but . . . how about coming by my place around, say seven-ish, with a preliminary plan. I'll have a light supper prepared and we can talk about this idea of yours. Nail down the bodies and the numbers. Then you can draft something up over the weekend, a proposal, with all the figures estimated, and so on, and we can start passing it around on Monday."

Yes, things had definitely turned up, Marlene thought with pleasure as she rode down on the elevator. She wouldn't, of course, tell anyone about this coup until it was a done deal. After that . . . she basked prospectively in the praise to come. She could get Marva a promotion, as a real bureau secretary, and there'd be something in the pot for Luisa too. People looked up as she strode humming happily down the hall to her office.

She had just settled herself when the phone rang.

"Hi, it's me."

"Butch?"

"Yes, your husband. You sound surprised."

"Um, yeah, you usually call later, at home. Is anything wrong?"

"Not a thing. I'm just about to leave for National. I'll get the four-thirty shuttle and I should be home by six, six-thirty. I figured we'd have dinner out."

"Um, dinner out?"

He caught her tone. "Yeah, like real people. You know, nothing fancy—in the neighborhood, the three of us. We can go to Bobo's, or Villa Cella, they don't mind kids."

"I'm sorry, I can't," Marlene blurted out. "I have, um, a meeting."

A pause on the line. "You have a *meeting*? At seven p.m.? What kind of meeting?"

"A meeting, Butch. It's work. I'm a DA. Not everybody in the business keeps office hours. Remember?"

"Uh-huh, and I remember that one of the nice things about being a bureau chief was that you didn't have to hustle around after hours. Who's the meeting with?"

"With the person I'm going to meet," snapped Marlene. "What, I'm under suspicion, Counselor? I'm getting *grilled*, as we used to say?"

"Hey, I'm sorry I asked," said Karp quickly. "So, calm down."

"I'm calm."

"Calm down, and I'll see you tonight, okay? I'll hang out with the kid and I'll . . . ah . . . see you when I see you, all right?"

"Yeah, and I'm sorry I bit at you," said Marlene. "I'll try to get away early. No kidding, I really do miss you."

"Me too," said Karp, huskily, not quite succeeding in keeping the worry out of his voice.

Marlene hung up the phone feeling vaguely remorseful, but not remorseful enough to call Karp back and tell him the truth. She would present him with the fait accompli: a huge new sex crimes bureau, a tamed and amenable Bloom. Marlene was not, of course, consciously devising a way to get one up on Karp. She would have denied it, if charged, and copped to a lesser: that she was entitled to her own life, her own career, that she was just doing what everyone did to get ahead, that Karp had nothing to do with it. She

even believed this at times, and despised the creeping edge of guilt she now felt as she worked at the preliminary plans for her expansion.

A knock at her door, and without a pause a thin man walked into the office. He was wearing a shabby brown jacket over gray slacks and his face was putty-colored and heavily lined, with eyes like damp, dark stones. He was a hard fifty-five years old.

"Hello, Harry," said Marlene. "I was just going to call you."

Harry Bello was a cop who worked for Marlene. He had been a star at Brooklyn homicide for nearly twenty years before his descent into drunkenness. Marlene thought he was, when sober, as now, the best detective she had ever met. He was also Lucy Karp's godfather.

"Tonight's okay," said Bello.

That was another thing about Harry Bello, and it took some getting used to. Harry not only didn't waste words, sometimes he eliminated both sides of whole conversations. Marlene would have said something about having a late meeting and asking whether it would not be too much trouble for Harry to pick up Lucy at day care and to watch her while she was out. How Harry knew that Marlene was about to call him to ask just that favor, and not something else, was a mystery. Another one was how a man with eyes that dead could light up and be such a sweet godfather to her daughter.

"Thanks," she said. At least one problem was taken care of. She looked up at him expectantly; Harry did not drop by for small talk; barely for large talk. "What's happening?" she asked.

"Mrs. Morgan caved."

"*She did?*" Marlene shouted, springing to her feet and clapping her hands together like a little girl. "Oh, Harry, when? What happened?"

"I told her Morgan wanted to pin it on her son, kid's eighteen. Messing with the little girls. So . . . she gave him up."

"What? When did Morgan try to pin it on the son?"

A slight tilting of the lips; Bello's working smile. "After I suggested it to him," he said.

Marlene shook her head in admiration. "Harry, you're a piece of work."

Harry said, "That protection argument. The guy's definitely connected."

Marlene switched gears. "Argument? Oh, yeah, Luisa's wise guy. He is?"

"He's Tony Bones's oldest kid."

"No kidding? Did he threaten her?"

A shrug.

"So do you agree with Luisa, or what? Protection?"

Another shrug. "I'll look into it. When'll you be home."

"Ten or so, probably, but Butch should be home way before that. Thanks, Harry."

He nodded and was gone.

Marlene had a final visitor, around five-thirty. She was deep in the most difficult task of public administration, figuring out how many people are required to do something that nobody has ever done before. Thick bound printouts of court records spread out across her desk, personnel manuals gaped open on chairs, and Marlene was punching a desk calculator with enthusiasm, one pencil clenched in her teeth and another, forgotten, stuck in her hair, when Raymond Guma walked in after a perfunctory tap on the glassed door.

She looked up, not pleased, and removed the pencil from her mouth, saying, "Not now, Goom."

"This'll just take a second," said Guma. He was a stocky man in his late forties with a monkey face, large spreading ears, and a greasy mop of black ringlets that had just started to recede back from a low forehead. The shadow of his beard was more than Nixonian, giving him a seedy appearance that was reinforced by the big tie knot pulled down to the third button and the bagginess of the trousers. He looked at the cluttered desk. "What're you doing, your taxes?"

"Just some admin shit," said Marlene snappishly.

He stood staring, in no hurry to leave.

"What *is* it?" she asked.

"Oooh, who's got the rag on today? I heard about your little display this afternoon. Maybe you're suffering from lack of nooky too."

"Fuck you, Guma! Is that what you came in here for, to bust my hump?"

Guma rested a pudgy thigh on the edge of her desk. "No, it's

business. Guy charged with rape and assault, name of Buona-facci?"

"Tony Bones's kid."

Guma's eyebrows lifted. "You know already?"

"Yeah, Guma, even though we're a bunch of dumb cunts around here, we occasionally get the message. What about him?"

"Tony called me. He wants to know can anything be done."

"Done? What is this, Guma? Since when are you running errands for the *cugines*?"

Guma pulled his chin in sharply, spread his hands, and frowned. "Hey! What're you talking 'errands.' One, the guy's a friend, the father, it's a courtesy, find out what's happening to his kid. What's the difference he's a don? Two, Tony could do us a lot of favors on open cases. It'd be nice having him owing us a big one. Three, he's willing to make it right with the girl."

Now, of course, this sort of thing happens all the time in DA's offices. Criminals know more about crime than anyone else, and in most of the major crimes that do get solved, critical information comes from the bad guys, for which reason the law likes to cultivate favors among them. On any normal day, Marlene might have been receptive to Guma's proposal, but this was not a normal day, nor was Marlene her normal self. Her deputy already suspected her of favoritism toward her supposed tribe, she had dissembled with her husband, she was about to go to dinner with a man she disliked in order to advance her career: she felt, in short, sufficiently corrupt without doing a big one for Tony Bones.

So she said, "Forget it, Guma. The woman's marked up, she made a complaint, we have a good rape case. He wants to plead to the top count, rape one, I might drop the assault and I'll see about putting in a word with the judge, but that's it."

Guma slapped the side of his head with the heel of his hand. "Jesus! Marlene? Earth calling Ciampi? The girl is a 'model'; she's a 'dancer.' What does that tell you?"

"I don't care if she's got a sheet for soliciting, Guma. This sweetheart beat her and raped the shit out of her and he's going for it."

Guma's color was rising and his voice became louder.

"Marlene, what the fuck you mean 'he's going for it'? The kid's gonna waltz in there with Di Bennedetti or Schoenstein, or some

other distinguished criminal member of the criminal bar, tell his sad story of misguided youth and a thieving whore, and walk out of there with a suspended sentence and probation for sexual mis and assault three. The girl'll get nothing and you all are gonna have wasted your fuckin' time preparing a bullshit case."

"No deal, Guma," said Marlene.

"You're serious?"

"Yeah."

"Then fuck you very much, and I'll try to do the same for you someday!" he shouted, and slammed out of the office. Marlene sighed and went back to her columns of figures, hoping that Luisa Beckett would be happy about this. Marlene certainly wasn't.

District Attorney Bloom lived on Park Avenue just north of Sixty-fourth Street, in a duplex on the top floor. His family had made a pile as meat-packers during the Civil War and an even greater pile later when the meatpacking district had become Sutton Place and their stockyards had turned into the most gilded real estate on Manhattan Island. Bloom also owned a large spread in Westchester, where he kept his family, preferring to spend the bulk of his time in his pied-à-terre. He was the kind of person who actually called it that.

Marlene arrived shortly after seven, having splurged for a cab. She was wearing her working clothes, a plain gray wool suit, and a cream silk blouse, with a tan raincoat on top. She carried a large leather bag and a briefcase, in which rested her work of the last four hours.

A green-coated doorman smelling lightly of drink ushered her in and told her she was expected. The elevator was brass, rosewood, and mirrored. Marlene checked her face and adjusted her eye.

The door to Bloom's place was opened by a short middle-aged Latina woman in a tan uniform and apron, who took Marlene's coat and bag and directed her silently down a hallway lined with lit paintings. Marlene spotted a small Hockney and what looked like an Utrillo.

Bloom was waiting in a large room fitted out as a library: two walls book-lined floor to ceiling, an oriental rug on the floor, and on the third wall two large windows decked out with pale drapes and showing the lights of Park Avenue and the East Side beyond

it. In the center of the room was a long mahogany library table with suitable chairs and an arrangement of side tables, standard lamps, dark leather couches, and club chairs, in one of which sat the master of the establishment.

Bloom looked up from the book he had been reading. He was wearing a baby blue knit golfing cardigan with the seal of a country club on it, an open-necked tattersall check shirt, tan whipcords, and Gucci white loafers, no socks. He rose and greeted Marlene warmly, which included a lingering squeeze on the arm and some remarks about how good she looked, as if he hadn't seen her for months, instead of just a few hours ago. He offered her a drink and she accepted a white wine. Bloom opened a bottle of Pouilly at a small bar hidden behind a panel made from phony books, placed it in a silver ice bucket, and brought it over to a coffee table. He made a little ceremony of pouring it out into crystal goblets, accompanied by some wine-snob chatter. His eyes were bright and it was obvious that this was not his first drink of the evening.

They sat at the coffee table, Marlene on the couch, Bloom on the club chair opposite, and drank. Bloom refilled their glasses. He described his meeting with the "governor's people": they wanted his support on a big anticrime bill now before the legislature. According to Bloom, Bloom was the pulsing center of criminal justice clout in the state of New York. The actual content of his talk was not, however, about legal or judicial ideas and plans, but about politics, specifically the politics of personal relationships, about which Marlene was ready to agree he was a reigning expert. One guy was out to get him, these two were in collusion because one owed the other a sleazy favor. That one was fucking his colleague's wife. Bloom went on, and did not spare the bottle.

Finally, at one of the infrequent pauses, Marlene said briskly, "Well, should we get going? I've worked up a lot of stuff and I don't want to be out too late."

Bloom stared blearily at her, as if he had forgotten the ostensible purpose of their meeting. He said pettishly, "Yes, well, but supper. We haven't had our supper yet. I'm starving, aren't you?"

No: what Marlene was was irritated and starting to get woozy from the wine. But "Sure," was what she said, imagining a pizza or a plate of sandwiches. Wrong again; the DA ushered her down the hallway and into a dining room, where a table had been set

for two. Candles were lit. They sat, and the Latina servant began to serve a full meal: lobster bisque to start, an arugula salad, little fillets with roast potatoes and asparagus. And more wine, of course. The DA went to a wine closet built into the paneled wall of the dining room and brought out a Chateau Petrus. Marlene learned what it had cost, and what a hard bargain Bloom had driven with the wine merchant, and how hard it was to get first-growth seventies, and so on and on until Marlene wanted to throw something heavy at him. Instead, she drank three glasses of the stuff, which was, she was still able to admit, truly marvelous.

A familiar feeling struck Marlene about then, almost a déjà vu. This was exactly like a bad blind date with one of the stuffed shirts she had spent evenings with in law school. Marlene had been living with three other poor students in a New Haven fleabag, subsisting on peanut butter and spaghetti, and from time to time, when she was feeling unusually resentful of her poverty and the squalor in which she lived, she would allow herself to be picked up by some rich jerk and fed lavishly at a fancy restaurant, after which the main problem was how to keep him out of her pants. Marlene had never actually let herself be fucked for a nice meal, but she knew any number of distinguished and brilliant women, in both college and law school, who had, and thought little of it.

The dishes were cleared at last. Marlene said, "Can we get through this now? I really have to go soon." Karp would be waiting at the loft now; Lucy would be fast asleep. She was struck by a powerful desire to be away from this bore and sitting in comfy clothes in her own kitchen talking to her husband. Or in bed.

She had interrupted one of Bloom's insider anecdotes. He frowned petulantly and said, "Yes, yes, all right. My God, you're relentless, aren't you? You should relax more, my dear. Go with the flow, as the kids say. I tell you what—I have a Zabar's cheese-cake. I'll have it served in the library, with coffee and brandy. How would that be? Cozy? And you can at long last unburden yourself. Sound good?"

"Fine," said Marlene, rising. Okay, she thought, be polite, be correct, people do this all the time, you have to learn to get on with people you don't particularly like, be a grown-up. She lifted her chin and constructed a smile on her face, and forced a little self-deprecating laugh.

Bloom returned the smile and chuckled. See! she thought. It's easy. They removed to the library.

The servant brought a tray with a whole, perfect blond disk of cheesecake and a silver coffee service. Bloom went to the bar. Marlene arranged her papers on the mahogany coffee table and waited. After a while, Bloom returned with two snifter glasses, each containing a hefty shot of amber liquid. Bloom poured out the coffee and sliced the cheesecake, and sat down on the couch next to her. Marlene ignored the cake, and the pressure of his thigh next to hers, took a quick sip of coffee, slipped on her specs, and went into her spiel. She felt curiously detached now, as if she were floating back among the towering bookcases watching a windup version of Marlene making the pitch. She glanced at Bloom from time to time to see how he was receiving it. He seemed all right, with the same bland semismile he usually wore stuck like a cheap decal on his pink face.

She finished and looked up. "That's it. Any questions?"

Bloom shook his head. "No. I'm overwhelmed. A terrific job, Marlene. I think that's a really good base to go on with. Very feasible."

"You think so?"

"I do. You've got a great, great future with the office. Onward and upward," he said, patting her thigh several times. "Let's drink to it!" He raised a snifter, Marlene raised hers, they clinked, they drank. Marlene liked cognac, and this was the best she had ever tasted, a bubble of smooth fire in her throat.

They had another. They talked, and now she started to talk, about herself, about Karp. Bloom seemed interested. He drew her out. The conversation became more intimate. There was something avid about his interest in Karp, in "what he was really like," something disturbing. Marlene found herself talking automatically, without thinking. She experienced once again that feeling of detachment, of not being herself, in her body, in charge.

It was hot in the room, and Marlene slipped out of her suit jacket, for some reason not feeling it was an odd thing to do. Bloom removed his golf sweater.

A hiatus here, blankness. Marlene drifted off into a dream. She was naked in a cage, in some sort of zoo. Karp was in the next cage. There were people watching them expectantly. She was full

of sexual desire and so was Karp, but she was nervous and embarrassed. Then, in the strange way of dreams, it became all right, natural. She pressed against the bars, spreading her thighs. He stroked her thighs and belly. She squirmed.

She awoke, gasping. She was lying on her back, on the couch, with her skirt hiked up and her legs asunder. Her shirt was open to the waist and her bra had been unhooked. The district attorney was kneeling over her, breathing hard, with one of his hands under the elastic of her panty hose, groping at her crotch.

In a convulsive movement, she sat up and thrust him away. She stood up, tottered, her head spinning, and fell back against the arm of the couch. Bloom stroked her leg and said soothingly, "Relax. Relax, there's nothing wrong. . . ."

She struggled again and found her feet, in deep panic now, disoriented and feeling ill. There was a peculiar medicinal taste at the back of her throat. Drugged. Something in the brandy. She saw her jacket and snatched it up and shoved it under her left arm and did the same with her bag. With her right hand, she held her blouse closed. She started to walk away, but Bloom reached out and grabbed her left arm. His face was flushed. He said in his best avuncular tone, "Hey, look, let's sit down and talk about this. Before you run off and do anything rash, let's just sit . . ."

Marlene set herself, hauled back, and threw a solid right cross into Bloom's mouth. It was not an artful blow and her father would have disapproved of the right hand lead, but it was a sincere one, with all her meat and considerable skill behind it. Bloom staggered away from the punch, caught the backs of his calves against the coffee table, and crashed down on it. Two of its legs collapsed, dumping him on the carpet, so that the cheesecake and everything else on the coffee table slipped down the slope thus created, covering him with a mess of glutinous dessert, cold coffee, cream, sugar, and shattered crockery.

Marlene ran out of the apartment, without stopping to pick up her coat or her briefcase and her carefully prepared plan. She adjusted her clothing in the elevator, and raced past the lobby without disturbing the nodding doorman in his chair. On the sidewalk she was overcome with nausea. She knelt and puked her expensive meal into the gutter. Then she wobbled herself upright, whistled through her fingers, and snagged one of Park Avenue's plentiful yellow cabs.

Once in the warm and deodorant-scented taxi, the shock caught up with her. She came apart. One part of her, that is, stood apart and analyzed the situation with a cold and well-trained logic. She had, of course, been a fool to think that Bloom was interested in her ideas. Bloom might have actually used the rewards available to him to help her career, if that was necessary to get her into bed, but the main thing was the sexual titillation of fucking the head of the rape unit, and not just that, no, not just, or even principally, for love of Marlene's sweet body, but to put it to Karp. To fuck Karp.

And there was, of course, no way of getting back at him, even though she was almost certain that she had been drugged. What would she tell the police, for example? That she had gone to a man's apartment while her husband was away, and he had what . . . grabbed a cheap feel? And who was the guy? Oh, the *district attorney*? Did you talk to the rape unit? Oh, you *are* the rape unit? Delightful. And of course, her career was now in the toilet, permanently.

Another part of Marlene was balled up, screaming in shame and rage. Marlene was, needless to say, no stranger to sexual violence. She had, in fact, once been kidnapped and subjected to various intrusive rituals by a gang of satanists. This was different, and, in a way, worse. She herself had written this script. What had Karp called him? A corrupt fuck. Yes, and of course she had known that, and of course she had conspired to hide that from herself, to pull off a coup, to show that she could succeed where Karp had failed, in controlling Bloom, in getting—what was it?— *past* Butch in a way? Because that would mean that she didn't *need* him in some pathetic fashion, that their relationship was purely voluntary, that she was in control, and free.

As she had been since she (sort of) stopped believing in God at the age of twelve. This thought crossed her mind quickly, but not quickly enough, for now the taps were opened and the vast reservoirs of shame and guilt supplied as part of her Catholic girlhood and held back these many years by her worldly success, by her confidence, burst forth and flooded her spirit. She blubbered noisily down Broadway, prompting a nervous look in the rearview by the cabbie.

The final part of her was barely conscious. This was the part that knew that, if only fleetingly, she had considered letting Bloom

screw her, for the advantage it would bring. That she had instantly rejected it did not in the least balance the horror of having made the calculation, having considered it at all. It was indelible, like a bloodstain on white silk.

Marlene was now moving toward a state that, as she well knew, the Church calls *acidie*: the condition of believing that one is beyond salvation, which is itself a mortal sin, and unique among the sins in that the indulgence in it is its own punishment.

Arriving at Crosby Street, she thrust a ten-dollar bill at the cabbie, double the fare, and staggered through her door and up the stairs.

In the dark loft, she checked the child, stifling her sobs so as not to wake her. Karp was asleep too; she could hear his heavy breathing. It was past two. She rinsed her mouth out at the sink and brushed her teeth for a long time. Then she curled up on the red couch in the living room and drew a quilt around her against a chill that was as much from within her as from the air in the loft. That was how Karp found her in the morning, wide awake and staring at nothing.

The thin man settled easily into the house in Little Havana. He watched a good deal of television and slept late. It was fairly cool for Miami, nights in the sixties, but the thin man kept the air-conditioning set high, and slept under blankets. He had a serious air-conditioning deficit, almost thirteen years' worth. The Cuban brought him his meals, takeout from American places, Kentucky Fried Chicken, McDonald's, Dairy Queen. Another deficit to be made up. The man who called himself Bishop had told him not to go out, which he thought somewhat peculiar, because he would have to go out sometime, or there was no point in his being there at all.

One day, a little over a week after his arrival from Guatemala, the Cuban went out and returned with Bishop. They sat at the Formica table in the kitchen and drank American beer. For a few minutes they made small talk about how they both were doing, how the country had changed, about sports and television.

Bishop slid a paper across the table. It was a list of names. All of them were familiar to the thin man.

"You want all of these done?" the thin man asked.

"No. I wish we could leave all of them alone, but that may not be

possible. The point is, we want the minimum possible hangout here. It'll depend on how much the investigation learns before it collapses."

"It's going to collapse, though?"

Bishop smiled. "Assuredly. That operation's already under way. We just need to stay one step ahead for a relatively short period." He tapped the list of names. "We may not need to do anything. I'd prefer that, frankly."

The thin man thought about that for a moment and drew the obvious conclusion.

"So you have people inside. The investigation."

"Oh, yes, our sources are quite good," said Bishop. "That's what we do, after all. We're spies." He laughed, and the thin man laughed too.

EIGHT

"It must be nice to have your wife and kid here in Washington," said Bert Crane conversationally. "How are they settling in?"

"Oh, just fine," said Karp. "It's an adjustment."

"I'm looking forward to meeting her. You'll be at the Dobbses' tomorrow night, right?"

Karp had forgotten the dinner party. He always forgot parties. In the city, Marlene had kept track of their social obligations. He hoped she had kept track of this one, and secured a baby-sitter. Somehow he doubted it; Marlene wasn't into tracking anything anymore. He said, "Oh, yeah, we'll be there."

"Good. Dobbs is doing us a favor on this one, you know. Parties are where things happen in this town, or so I'm given to believe. We haven't quite burrowed in on the social side the way I'd hoped we would. These damn loose ends up in Philadelphia—I haven't stroked egos and bought lunches to the extent I should have." He rubbed his face and stared briefly out of his window at the train yards. Karp thought he looked more drawn and tired than he had in his plush Philadelphia office that first day. These were changes similar to those Karp saw every day in his own mirror. The expression "pecked to death by ducks" popped into his mind.

"Things are looking up, though," Crane resumed. "I've just been invited to address the Democratic caucus. This could be a turning point for us, but we need something splashy, some breakthrough, to throw to the dogs." He looked at Karp speculatively. "That CIA stuff we got from Schaller, for example . . ."

"You're not serious."

Crane flushed and opened his mouth to say something else, but instead sighed and grumbled, "No, damn it, now they've got me doing it. I never thought I'd be in a position where leaking material in an investigation would look good. No, obviously, once that stuff gets loose, everybody remotely associated with any leads it provides will head for the tall timber. Or worse. Of course, they know we've got it."

"Of course," said Karp, "but they don't know how we plan to use it. They might even be hoping it's still buried in that pile of crap they gave the Senate committee. Once it's out . . ."

"Yeah, the shit hits the fan. So what *do* we have to throw to the dogs?"

"In the way of progress? Nothing, frankly. The investigation hasn't really started, because I can't do any investigating, because I don't have any money."

"Yes, yes, I know that," said Crane testily. "I'm working on it. But I have to give them a taste, a scent of something that's worth the budget I'm asking for." He thought for moment, leaning back and considering the little dots in the stained acoustic tiles of the ceiling. "How about this? We've uncovered conclusive evidence that shows the CIA was involved with Oswald before the assassination. Just that. And that we believe a thorough independent investigation of the Central Intelligence Agency will be a key first step in our work. I could use that in my speech to the caucus. What do you think?"

Karp made a helpless gesture with his hands. "Hey, what do I know? I told you I was out of my depth here. Sure, try it. It probably won't make things any worse."

They turned then to administrative details, and the meeting lasted only a few more minutes. Crane had a TV interview to go to and Karp had a meeting with Charlie Ziller.

Back in his office, Karp called Marlene at the Arlington apartment, but she was out. He was glad of that, having urged her for many days now to get out of the house and do something. It was starting to irritate him. She was a few blocks from the metro and a few stops on that from the wonders of tourist D.C., most of which were free or near enough to it. And, God knew, she had all the free time in the world, while he was working eighty-hour weeks.

Restless, he got up and moved through the warren of offices. Everyone he looked in on seemed to be doing something, although Karp could not have said with assurance what those things were. In the corridor, he spied V.T., dressed for the outdoors in a double-breasted camel hair coat.

"Going out?" asked Karp.

V.T. looked down at his coat and then, quizzically, at Karp. "I can see you're still a sharp investigator. You know, there was a dead rat in my office this morning."

"No kidding? A big one?"

V.T. regarded him bleakly. "Let's say it was larger than any rat I have found in my office heretofore, and *far* larger than any rat I expected to find in my office when I graduated from Harvard Law School. No, make that any rat who was not a paying client."

"What can I say, V.T.? It's hell on earth and it's my fault. Where are you off to anyway?"

"Away from rat-land, mainly. No, I'm going over to Georgetown to follow up on something. Maybe a lead on Lee's lost weeks."

"Oh?"

"Yeah, August 21 to September 17. We've been checking out the people that Oswald knew at that period and seeing if we can develop any secondary sources—on people like Gary Becker, David Ferrie, the New Orleans Cubans on both sides. Nearly all the principals are dead now. So, in checking out David Ferrie, we came up with the name of a small-time reporter named Jerry James Depuy . . ."

"Who got this?"

"Pete Melchior, our guy in New Orleans. He's really good. Anyway, Depuy was apparently doing a story on Ferrie, except Ferrie died in 1967. Depuy was well known in New Orleans saloons for bragging about how when his book on Ferrie came out, he'd be rich and famous, and so forth, the usual failed reporter stuff. Nevertheless, worth checking out—he did know Ferrie, maybe Ferrie knew something about where Lee was, that he hadn't told anyone else but Depuy. But Depuy died too, in seventy-four. Pete went out to his house, and the widow told him that she'd cleaned out all Jerry James's stuff, and that should've been that, another dead end, except I recalled that the Associated Press had a program of checking the estates of reporters who had kicked off

and seeing whether they hadn't saved stuff of historical significance—original notes and so on. The AP also has a JFK archive at Georgetown, full of that same sort of original material and I thought just possibly . . ."

"That's quite a long shot," said Karp.

"Long shots are the only shots we have, my child," replied V.T. "See you."

Ziller was waiting for Karp in his office, standing by the desk. The young man offered his usual bright smile. Karp said, "Hello, Charlie," and sat behind the desk, while Ziller went over to the foul green couch. Karp caught himself looking at the papers and folders on his desk, checking whether anything had been disturbed. Nothing seemed to be, and Karp felt foolish and paranoid.

"What's up?"

Ziller said, "A small victory. I saw Mark Lane today and he handed me this little gem. I think I mentioned it. He got it from a FOIA dump from the Bureau."

Karp took the paper. One of the original Warren critics, Lane was to the Freedom of Information Act what Menuhin was to the violin. He could get stuff out of it that seemed impossible for most others.

"God, it *is* signed by Hoover!" Karp exclaimed.

The paper, dated November 23, 1963, the day after the assassination, was a memo from J. Edgar Hoover to FBI supervisory staff, in which Hoover said that the FBI had determined that the voice of the man identifying himself as "Lee Henry Oswald" on a tape recording of a conversation recorded in October 1963, between that man while talking on the phone inside the Soviet embassy to an official of the Cuban embassy in Mexico City, was not the voice of the accused assassin, Lee Harvey Oswald.

"Interesting, huh?" said, Ziller, grinning broadly.

"You could say that," Karp agreed. He tapped the memo with a finger. "Do we have this tape?"

"Unfortunately, no." Ziller leafed quickly through a thick stack of notes. "According to Lane, and I checked this with the Warren testimony, the CIA claimed that they routinely destroy the embassy bugging tapes every week. Of course, at the time of Warren, nobody knew that the FBI thought it wasn't Oswald."

"The FBI doesn't have it?"

"No—according to them. You think the tape itself is critical?"

"I don't know about critical, but assuming we had an investigation going here, and assuming we happened to find a guy who was in Mexico City on that day and had some ties with Oswald, or the CIA, and assuming we could get a voiceprint off of him and it happened to match the Soviet embassy tape, we might be in a position to ask the son of a bitch a couple of questions. But since we don't have an investigation . . ." He shook his head and flipped the memo onto his desk. "Another one for the files."

Ziller asked, "No word on the budget, yet, I take it?"

"Yeah, the word is soon. Crane's all excited about going to speak to the Democratic caucus, he thinks that'll help."

Ziller looked startled. "He's going to *what?*"

"Speak to the Dems. Why, what's wrong? Apparently they invited him."

"I bet they did. You realize Flores is gonna go ballistic over this."

"Why? Isn't he a Democrat?"

"Sure," said Ziller, "and he's just going to love having somebody he regards as his personal employee speak to his own leadership and, probably, ask them for a shitload of money, for something ninety percent of them wish would crawl back under a rock. It's a neat scam, though. I wonder who thought it up."

"Scam? You think it's a setup of some kind?"

"Most assuredly," replied Ziller with confidence.

"But why would Bert . . . ," Karp began and then stopped with a curse. He'd had exactly the same thought. "No, I'm not going to get started on this shit. Crane's the political guru; let him do it his way. Meanwhile, let's go back for a minute to J. Edgar here. Okay, it's a day after Kennedy's shot. The FBI and the CIA are going crazy, they're running around like chickens with their heads cut off. Who is this schlemiel who just shot the president? The FBI says, 'Oh, my God, he's on our list! One of our guys visited him in Dallas. How do we cover our ass? Oh, yeah, he must be a lone nut, no politics, no spying—that's the story, stick to it!' Now over to the CIA. They're going, 'Oh, my God, we got a contract with this little fucker. Bury it! Uh-oh, he showed up in Mexico, we got him on tape. No, it wasn't really him!' There's chaos. Helms and the big boys are trying to find out what really happened at the same time they're trying to cover up the Oswald connection, and

cut the trail that leads back to the Cubans and the Mob business with Castro. They're going crazy and they start to fuck up. A picture of some short, stocky guy who's obviously not Oswald gets sent to Washington. Then a tape gets sent to the FBI that's not Oswald either. But Oswald *has* to be in Mexico—that's right away part of the legend, he has to be this marginal commie trying to get back to Cuba. Besides, if he wasn't down there, where the fuck was he? Who *was* in Mexico City pretending to be Oswald, and why? So all this stuff gets buried. The bus ticket is conveniently found in his stuff by the amazing Marina. It goes into the Warren Report as gospel: Yeah, boss, Ozzie was south of the border."

"You think he wasn't?" asked Ziller.

"The fuck I know!" snapped Karp. "But V.T. said that Oswald is the key, and it's true whether it's the real one or the fake one, if any. This whole cover-up is designed to do just two things: one, make it impossible to determine exactly how and why and by whom JFK was shot, and two, to obscure who and what Oswald was. The things're connected, and they're connected through the Central Intelligence Agency. Crane just told me he plans to blitz the Agency for starters, so let's do it."

Ziller nodded after a moment's hesitation, and asked, "Starting where?"

"With whoever it was at the CIA who supplied the phony picture and the tape to the FBI. That guy, what's his name? Two first names. You know—he testified to the Warrens back then."

"Paul Ashton David," said Ziller.

"Yeah, him. Let's get him in here and talk to him. Crane wanted something to show to the committee; let's show them Mr. David."

The fourth week in purgatory, thought Marlene as she pushed the stroller down the rutted sidewalk alongside Wilson Boulevard; only a thousand years to go.

After that evening with Bloom, she had dragged herself to work for a few days, increasingly depressed and ineffective. Of course, she was no longer invited to nice meetings in the DA's office, and she could not tell anyone why. Not Karp. Not any of the women in the office. Not her relatives. Friends? Well, did she really have any friends? Who would want to be friends with such a degraded

slimeball as Marlene? She had called in sick for a day, then a week, and then she cleaned out her desk. Let Luisa run the unit. Let him try and get into *her* pants.

On this morning, Marlene was in her full crazy-lady regalia, wearing her brother's old army field jacket over a red T-shirt she had slept in, and a misbuttoned tan acrylic cardigan. Below this were gray sweatpants and ragged black high-top Converse sneakers. On her head was a venerable New York Yankees hat. Her hair was unwashed and pulled back with a rubber band, and she wore, as she had for some weeks now, the black patch over her missing eye.

The child in the stroller, in contrast, was immaculately turned out, in a darling lined and belted cherry-colored raincoat, a soft felt hat with a fabric rose in its band, a rust turtleneck jersey with little birdies embroidered on it, nut brown corduroys, red Mary Janes, and fuzzy woolen leg warmers. Lucy's hair shone and her face was scrubbed pink. The message was clear to anyone with the faintest grasp of sidewalk semiotics: *I may be a wreck, but I am not a Bad Mother.*

The two of them were going to a playground Marlene had discovered during an earlier expedition. The playground at Federal Gardens was in her opinion unsuitable even for a kid raised in New York, its equipment rusty and covered with lethal surfaces and its sandbox full of cat turds. Besides that, it was frequented by chain-smoking women in their twenties who came out in hair curlers and tatty bathrobes, and talked with one another about daytime TV and about how dumb their husbands were, and screamed in harpy voices at their grubby kids. Marlene had rediscovered the difference between being Bohemian and being white-trash poor.

As mother and daughter rumbled along they sang, or rather Marlene sang and Lucy pitched in when she knew the lyrics. They sang Lucy's favorite rock classics: "Heart of Gold," "One-Trick Pony," and "Hotel California," all of which Marlene considered to be superior to "Itsy-Bitsy Spider."

They arrived at the playground, which was built off a side street to the main boulevard, and which served a newish middle-class district of large wooden or brick homes, the kind that have black metal carriage lamps in front of them, to indicate that the owners could afford a coach-and-four if they so desired. The playground

equipment was new and artistically woody. Big aircraft tires were also used, for climbing and swinging, and to contribute the proper environmentally responsible effect.

There were several women and children in the playground when Marlene and Lucy arrived. Unlike the women in Federal Gardens, these were either well dressed in conservative sweater and slacks combos or obvious nannies: one black woman and two Latinas. The nannies sat separately and stared dully at their charges. The four mothers chatted on a bench. Marlene sat on a bench with the black woman, who was young, thin, and wore a pale green uniform with a pink cardigan draped over her shoulders. A baby slept wrapped in woolens in a large gleaming maroon baby carriage, which the nanny jiggled from time to time with a white-shod foot.

Marlene stretched out her legs gratefully and pulled a cigarette pack out of her bag. It was turning into a fairly nice day. The sun was a bright coin shining down through the leafless maples and there was no wind. Lucy had gone immediately to the sandbox and was playing happily there with her Barbie and her lavender My Little Pony. Two husky boys of five or so were constructing piles and ditches with Tonka trucks and shovels. They ignored her, and she them.

Marlene lit her Marlboro, blew out a cloud of smoke, and gradually became conscious that the nanny on the other end of the bench was looking at her.

Marlene nodded. "Nice day," she observed.

"Sure is. I can't stand it when it rains all day and you get cooped up in the house. Say, I left mine back at the house . . . would you . . . ?" She gestured toward her mouth.

Marlene moved closer to her and handed her the pack and matches.

"I ain't seen you around here," the nanny said after lighting up. "Where you work?"

"I'm sorry, work . . . ?"

"Yeah." The nanny cocked a hand toward the sandbox. "Where's the kid live?"

Marlene pointed vaguely. "Oh, east of here. Off Wilson."

The woman looked Marlene over and chuckled. "How you get away with that? They cut me loose I showed up dressed like y'all."

Marlene shrugged. "Different strokes. I guess it makes them feel liberal, I dress like I want."

"You lucky, girl. People I work for—they like, Lincoln didn't free no niggers. But they pay pretty good. How about y'all? You makin' it?"

"Barely," said Marlene. "My husband got a job down here and we just moved."

"Yeah, I'd move too, but I ain't got the coins yet. Good thing, though: I got my mama here. She watches my two, and I watch the white folkses'. But not for long. Jerome, that's my husband? He got a job in a factory down in Raleigh. I save up enough, we gonna all move down there, get me a good job, maybe a house."

"You sound like you've got your act together," said Marlene.

The woman grinned, showing a flash of gold. "We just startin' in, sister. They got a community college in Raleigh. I figure I could study X-ray technician. That or dietician. Get me a qualification, a AA degree, you know? And then, while I'm working, my husband'll go to school." She went on in this vein for some time, and Marlene was content to let the chatter wash over her, sitting in the weak sun and smoking and watching the children play. Time drifted by.

The nanny stopped abruptly, and smiled sheepishly at Marlene, as if embarrassed to have blown too loudly on her own horn. "You could do that too, you know," she said. "Go to school. You speak real good English. Them over there"—she motioned to the Latina nannies—"they some kinda Guatemalas. Hell, I don't even think they speak Spanish. So, how long you been here?"

"In Washington?"

"No, the country. The U.S."

"Um, oh, years and years."

"Where from?"

"Ah, Palermo?"

"What's that, one of them islands?"

"It's on an island."

"Well, if you don't want to be watching other folkses' kids all your life, go to a school. Get you some qualification—"

This useful advice was interrupted by a loud shriek from the sandbox. One of the little boys had snatched Lucy's My Little Pony and, sporting the bully's nasty grin, was dangling it by its long acrylic mane. Lucy stood in front of him with her fists clenched. "That's mine! Give it back!" she yelled. The boy ignored her and started to twirl the toy horse around by its hair.

Lucy made a grab for it and the boy pushed her hard in the chest. She staggered back a few paces, and looked over at Marlene, who had tensed but hadn't moved.

Lucy dropped her raincoat, crouched, adopted the boxer's stance she had been taught from infancy, took two steps forward and hit the kid twice in the mouth with straight left jabs. Startled, the boy dropped the pony and threw a roundhouse preschool right. Lucy checked this easily with her left, stepped in close, and crossed a solid right to the nose. And again. Blood spurted and the kid collapsed howling in the sand. Lucy picked up her My Little Pony and began unconcernedly currying the sand from its tresses.

The mother of the wounded child now came racing from her klatch, crying "Jason! Jason!" and swept up her kid, who was now blue with howling and still pouring with what the sportswriters used to call claret. The woman pulled a wad of tissues from her pocket and held it to the child's nose. After a few minutes, she put the still-sniveling boy on the ground and leaned over Lucy menacingly. "Did you see what you did!" she shouted, grabbing Lucy by the shoulder and waving a finger. "You made Jason bleed. You're a very naughty, naughty girl." Lucy looked at her wide-eyed, and then over at Marlene, who was up and over to Lucy's side in a flash.

"Hands off my kid, lady," she said flatly.

"Did you see what your kid did?" said the woman. She was a slim aerobic blond dressed in a style Marlene always thought of as neatsy-keen: a navy blue car coat, red crewneck, a little pin, blue slacks, new Adidas. Under Marlene's baleful one-eyed stare, she released Lucy.

"Yes," said Marlene matter-of-factly, "I did. Little Jason here ripped off my daughter's toy, my daughter asked for it back, and when she tried to take it, he pushed her. Then she decked him. You've got blood on your nice coat."

"Is that what you're teaching her? To hurt people?"

"In self-defense, yes," said Marlene calmly. "Little Jason's learned a valuable lesson today, madam, one that might keep him out of prison some day, provided it's reinforced: if you take by force things that don't belong to you, you get your lumps. Good day to you."

Marlene took Lucy's hand, picked up the raincoat, and strode out of the sandbox with as much dignity as such striding allows.

Jason's mother stared openmouthed after her; except that she was not dripping ropes of saliva, she looked much like a fighting bull stupefied by a skillfully brandished muleta.

Marlene steered Lucy back to the bench and put her into her raincoat. "That, that lady was yelling at me," Lucy said, her voice uncertain. "Was I bad?"

"No, baby, you did good. You remembered never hit once when you can get two shots in. Only next time remember to keep your thumbs tucked." She demonstrated with a fist. "You keep slugging with your thumbs up, one day you're going to break them off."

"Then I would have broked-off fingers like you?"

"Yeah, right," Marlene said, and kissed her.

The nanny, observing this, put in, "You did right, sugar. Don't let them boys push you around."

Marlene smiled at her and said, "Well, I think we'll be going while the going's good. Always leave 'em bleeding is our motto."

Jason's mother had joined her group over at the other bench. They were talking animatedly and looking daggers at Marlene and Lucy.

"Okay, you take care now," said the nanny. "Nice talking to you, and hey—mind what I told you, get yourself some school!"

Marlene waved at her and she and Lucy headed down the path, Lucy pushing the stroller, singing her version of "One-Trick Pony," which, when she got to the part about a herky-jerky motion, required her to throw her body into a Dionysiac spasm, giggling madly. Marlene was required to join in this, which she did gladly, feeling better than she had in weeks.

The healing power of justice was what it was, she thought, even playground justice. Maybe especially playground justice, which seemed like the only kind she was likely to see again in this life.

She felt oddly free and she knew why. She was feeling bad, as she had when, as a schoolgirl, she had come home to Queens on a Friday night, shucked out of her blue serge Sacred Heart livery, raced competently through her homework, slipped into skintight black toreador pants, a sleeveless blouse with the collar up in back, over a wired bra that transformed her young breasts into hard little conical gun turrets, between which hung the little gold cross; applied scarlet lipstick and blue eye shadow; put on gold hoop earrings; and booked out the back door to meet, waiting at the end

of the block, the sideburned and leather-jacketed Rocco in his chopped and channeled 1950 Ford Fairlane.

They would cruise Queens Boulevard, hitting a sequence of drive-ins, pizzerias, and vacant lot hangouts in an order as nearly formalized as the stations of the cross. They would race their engines and lay patches of rubber. They would trade friendly insults and use phony draft cards to buy beer, and after enough beer the insults would turn less friendly and there might be scuffling, clumsy fights. A car might be stolen for a joy ride. This was what was meant by being bad, in Queens, in the early sixties.

That, and parking out by the runways at La Guardia for a bout of similarly formalized sexual groping. Of this activity Marlene was entirely in charge. She had no intention of letting the passionate bad boy go, as the saying then was, all the way, and had discovered, at fourteen, that any importunate demands in this direction could be easily forestalled by direct attention to the actual fount of desire. Marlene's fascination with Rocco's organ, and those of the various Roccos that succeeded him, was (if such a word is not entirely inappropriate) innocent. She regarded penises (how different each one!) much as the air force regarded its X-15 at the time—as experimental instruments, from which much might be learned. A skilled and enthusiastic *fellatiste* by fifteen, Marlene never heard any complaints about being denied the ultimate liberty from any of the Roccos.

The Church to one side, Marlene simply could not accept that the Creator of the Universe was overly concerned about the odd blow job. That she had finessed the virgin-whore business by becoming both and neither seemed to her a practical application of the Thomistic synthesis she had learned about in Religion 2, in which she had received an A.

Throughout this period, therefore, Marlene remained a regular communicant, both at Sacred Heart and at St. Joseph's in the neighborhood, and a frank and voluble confessor, adding much interest to the lives of several elderly priests. Her reputation did not suffer at all, owing to both the sanctity of the confessional and the convenient fact that she went to school miles from where she hung out on weekends. At Sacred Heart she was a model student, demure, and submitting cheerfully to discipline. The Mesdames could hardly have realized that much of her good humor derived from imagining what they would do if they only knew.

Lucy had now switched songs to "Heart of Gold," which she rendered with something approaching a genuine Neil Young whine. Marlene joined in, her thoughts turning from the past to her present situation and to Karp. Karp was not bad, ever. He had, in addition, a true heart of gold, honest and loving. Occasionally priggish, perhaps, but never would he have sucked after Bloom the way she had, never *betrayed* himself as she had . . . *Stop!* she told herself, that was quite enough of that. She was paying for her mistake, had ditched her job, was living in a rat hole, was dead broke, but on the other hand, she was at long last starting to recover a taste of free. Free to hang out with Lucy, who was more enjoyable company than anyone she was likely to meet in the criminal courts, or official Washington, and free to fully explore bad Marlene, something that she now discovered filled her with a certain anticipation.

Back in Federal Gardens, Marlene left Lucy snoring gently in her stroller in the living room and opened a beer for herself. She could hear loud voices and heavy movements from the apartment next door. Marlene and Karp called the couple who lived there Thug 'n' Dwarf. Thug was a hulking long-haul truck driver, and Dwarf was his tiny bride. Their relationship seemed to consist of silence, violent arguments, and noisy fucking. Lately the arguments had grown more violent, as Dwarf had brought home a dog without Thug's permission. The barking and whining of this dog now added its note to the audio channel. A final burst of screaming and the door slammed next door: Thug going off to get his load. He'd be back at midnight, ready for action.

The phone rang and Marlene went into the kitchen to get it.

"God, Marlene," said Karp, "I've been calling all day. Where have you been?"

"It was a nice day. We took a long walk. Why, is anything wrong?"

"No, but I just wanted to remind you that we have a dinner party to go to tonight. At the Dobbses'."

A pause. "That's 'remind' meaning 'to inform for the first time'?" asked Marlene sweetly.

"Yeah, well, I lost track of it; Bert reminded me yesterday. Is that going to be a problem?"

"No, not really. I have nothing to wear, no baby-sitter, and we

have no means of transportation. I tell you what, why don't I just huddle in the cinders and sniffle while you go to the ball?''

"You're sounding more feisty, anyway," said Karp. "Last couple of weeks I thought it was *Invasion of the Body Snatchers.*"

"Yeah, well, it's probably just the manic phase. Couple of days I'll try to break into the White House with a secret plan for world peace."

"Please, don't joke!" said Karp. "Meanwhile, smarty-pants, dumb old husband happened to take care of the baby-sitter and the car both. Clay's going to watch Lucy, and we can borrow his car."

"Great!" said Marlene. "Does he have a dress I could wear?"

The truth was that Marlene had packed hardly any of her own clothes during her precipitate flight from New York. She had dragooned her younger brother into leaving his comfortable Village apartment and moving into the loft, at a ruinously low rent, carefully packed all of Lucy's clothes and toys, and, as an afterthought, emptied some of her own drawers and shelves almost at random into an army duffel bag, lest she have to walk the streets of Washington literally nude. Tony dinner parties in McLean were not uppermost in her mind during those dreadful days.

Thus, she was well supplied with undies, but the only shoes in the house, besides sneakers, were a pair of knee-high, floppy boots suitable for appearing in performances of *Der Rosenkavalier.* As for dresses and suits, Marlene had grabbed a handful of summer items, having picked up that Washington was swelteringly hot in summer, but having somehow forgotten that it was now closing in on winter. As these were obviously unsuitable, she chose a quilted grayish purple long skirt of some vague central Asian ethnicity, and a good silvery-colored French silk blouse from Saks that unfortunately had a large and indelible wine stain under the right breast. Easily solved: she had a paisley Edwardian waistcoat, moth-holed, yes, but the moth holes did not match where the wine stain was.

Having selected her outfit, Marlene bathed and washed her hair, and put in her glassie. She paused to inspect herself in the small and blackened bathroom mirror. Her hair was an impossible mess. The lock that was usually sculpted by her hairdresser to distract from her bad eye was long grown out. She dragged a brush

through the worst of the tangles, and then gave up, laughing hysterically. The errant lock she grabbed and pulled back, and looked around for something to hold it with. Ah, Lucy's Little Orphan Annie plastic barrette—perfect! She snapped it in.

She was dressed and watching the blurry black-and-white TV with Lucy when Karp and Fulton arrived.

"Daddy, I coldcocked a asshole!" shrieked Lucy, running into Karp's arms.

He hugged her and shot an inquiring look at Marlene, who shrugged casually.

She kissed Fulton, and said, "Thanks a million for this, Clay. Make yourself at home, such as it is. There's beer in the fridge. Try to keep Lucy under a quart. She's a mean drunk."

Fulton chuckled, and said, "No problem. Speaking of which, don't wreck my car."

"You still driving that T-bird?"

"Uh-huh. I would've traded for a Caddie El Dorado last year, but my mama gave me all kinds of grief about it. Ford hired her brother in 1938 and since then everybody in the family's got to drive their shit."

"What is this about 'coldcocked,' " asked Karp.

"What she said," answered Marlene indifferently. "Some brat tried to boost her toy and she flattened him." She twirled. "How do you like my outfit?"

"Great, Marl. You look great," said Karp automatically, in the fashion of husbands.

"I look like a clown," said Marlene cheerfully. "Let's go to the circus!" she cried, literally skipping to the door, the clunky boots thumping, the tacky skirt flapping.

Karp followed with a measured tread. He had seen tiny glimpses of his beloved in this state from time to time; now it looked like becoming nonstop entertainment. To his credit, Karp preferred this version to the recent zombie. Manic. A good word, he thought, as he went through the door. Marlene was in the car and honking its horn in a boogie rhythm. Maniac, another good word.

In Miami, the thin man grew bored. He shaved his beard, leaving the mustache. Beards weren't real big in this neighborhood. In violation of instructions, he went out and walked around Little Havana, and had

a late meal at La Lechoneria: steak with a foot-high stack of curly fried potatoes. It was bright as day in the place, as in all Cuban restaurants, but he wore his ball hat and dark glasses. With those and the mustache, he doubted anyone would recognize him. It had, after all, been thirteen years. And, of course, everyone thought he was dead. The thin man enjoyed his meal, left a nice tip, and walked back to the house.

NINE

They had valet parking at the Dobbs house. The Karps alighted from the T-bird nonchalantly, as if they always went to parties with valet parking, and let the teenage kid drive it away. The house was a three-story, red brick, Federal–style structure, with two generous wings, its face embellished with white trim and a white-columned portico, set on two acres of landscaped grounds. There were several outbuildings, each with a white spire and a weathercock.

Past the door, in the circular entrance hall under the glittering brass-and-glass chandelier, Butch and Marlene had their coats taken by a maid in uniform—no throwing on the bed for the Dobbses—and were greeted by a small woman who introduced herself as Maggie Dobbs. As Marlene shook the proffered hand she noticed the woman's eyes widen and her smile stiffen as she absorbed what Marlene was wearing. Marlene absorbed Mrs. Dobbs too: a fine-boned woman not much older than herself, with delicate china-doll features, a shining blond Dutch boy, and blue eyes to match. She was wearing a jacket and trousers outfit of vaguely oriental cut, in embroidered yellow brocade. Marlene judged the outfit stylish, and absurdly expensive, but somehow Maggie Dobbs failed to bring it off in the manner that Halston, or whoever, had intended. The vivid yellow washed out her pale coloring, and besides that there was something in her eyes, a faint-heartedness surprising in a good-looking woman, the chatelaine of this rich place, a look more comprehensible in an unattractive teenager on the wallflower line at the junior prom.

"I love your outfit," said Marlene.

The woman colored and murmured, "Thank you, I . . . ah . . ." She reached for a return compliment, baffled.

Marlene said gaily, "Oh, it's just something I threw together," and tripped off to the brightly lit living room, where the dozen or so guests had gathered for drinks before dinner.

A small bar had been set up in one corner of the room—a cloth-covered table with a young black man in attendance—and Marlene headed straight for it. She needed a drink; her bravado had quite collapsed upon entering the room and checking out the people gathered there. The men were all in early middle age, dressed in good dark suits, and all had the easy confidence that comes from wielding political power. The women were all suited in various ways as well; they had obviously all just come from important jobs—all, that is, except the hostess in her unfortunate golden pj's. Aside from the expensive clothes, the women were a mixed bunch. Some were gorgeous, others were plain, and there were two enormously fat ones. It was clear that they had not been invited because of their looks or charm, but because of who they were. This should have delighted Marlene the feminist, but it did not—another source of shame. It had been easy, she realized, to be blithe about status when one had it. It shocked her how different she felt now, being nobody.

Marlene threw back half her iced vodka in a gulp, and felt Karp come up and take her arm from behind. She was being introduced to a good-looking man with sandy hair, their host. Andy Hardy, with an edge, Marlene thought. Another introduction, this time to Bert Crane, hearty and smooth. Crane told her how great Karp was. Then she was passed off to the nearest group, two women and a bald, short man with thick glasses. All of them were senior staff on committees Dobbs had an interest in. In a few moments, Karp was led away by Congressman Dobbs and Crane.

Marlene had been introduced simply as Karp's wife, which was new and which she did not much appreciate, but there it was. There was some more commentary about how good everyone thought Karp was and how they had heard so much about him.

"What do *you* do?" asked one of the women.

"I'm a lawyer," said Marlene.

The woman smiled. They all did. "How unusual!" she said humorously. "Who with?"

"Nobody," said Marlene. "My daughter's four and I'm at home with her."

"Do you live around here?" asked the other woman. "There's some wonderful day care in McLean."

"No, we have a furnished apartment off Wilson in Arlington. And I'm planning to stay home with her."

The smiles jelled. Then they began to talk again, not exactly ignoring Marlene as if she weren't there, but each time she made a comment there was a brief pause and then the conversation would start up again as if she hadn't said anything. This had never happened to her before. That she was smart, that she had graduated from Yale Law School, that she had something to say, apparently did not count anymore, not with these people. She was "wife-of," and nothing else, occupying the capital's lowest status rung. She looked over to where Maggie Dobbs was being gracious to a group of men. The men laughed at something she had said. There was the exception; if she had a house like this one, she could give big, expensive parties, and then she would be a person again.

Marlene had to think about this, the realization that for the indefinite future the only people who would talk to her would be her daughter and nannies. Such thoughts required a drink. Another vodka, please. And another.

A bell rang, an actual dinner gong. Everyone trooped into the dining room. Marlene caught a blurry glimpse of her husband talking to Dobbs and Crane. Karp waved to her, and she nodded briefly back to him. He had a worried, distracted look.

There were little place cards. Marlene found hers down at the end of the table, far from the head, where Dobbs and Crane and Karp sat, interspersed with some of the power women. The people at her end seemed distinctly junior, congressional staffers of both sexes, and, of course, Maggie Dobbs at the foot. Marlene had never been to a dinner party like this in a private home; she had scarcely imagined that they still went on, but here she was.

A caterer had, of course, been engaged: no guests hanging around the kitchen and helping with the guacamole. Black men in maroon monkey jackets served turtle soup, then a radicchio salad, then little birds en brochette, with stuffed potatoes and some sort of bland orange vegetable sculpted into flower shapes. The servers also circulated with chardonnay; Marlene politely drank when they filled her glass, which was often.

Animated talk flowed around her. After a few perfunctory attempts to engage her in their conversation, the two men on her flanks chatted for a while to each other around her as if she were a pillar at a hockey game.

The dessert was served, a banana mousse. The conversation between the two men having flagged, the one on Marlene's good side turned his attention to her, and seemed to notice for the first time that, although unimportant, and absurdly dressed, she was stunning. He was a fair, small, even-featured man of about thirty with a supercilious eye. Marlene recalled having been introduced to him; Jim Something.

"So," he began, "what do you do in the government? No, let me guess—something arty, National Gallery? Kennedy Center?"

"I'm a housewife," said Marlene in a dull, low voice.

"Please! Nobody's a housewife anymore. You're highly decorative. Fix yourself up a little and you could walk into any front office in town and get hired. Where did you go to school?"

"Smith."

"Oooh, very Seven Sis! And you majored in marriage?"

"I guess."

"Well, it's never too late, my dear," said the man in a hearty and patronizing tone. "We need to get your juices flowing again. You don't want to be a Potomac widow, getting wan and shriveled while hubby conquers the world. I'm sure some deep fire still burns within that domestic exterior." He reached over and kneaded her arm.

She froze, then looked up from her dessert into his watery blue eyes. "Oh? How can you tell?"

"Men know," he said. "They can sense the heat."

"Can they? Sense the heat. Can *you* sense the heat?" The booze seemed to hit her all at once and she laughed, louder than was usual at such tables. "*Now* I know who you remind me of," she cried to her dinner companion. "God! I can't remember his name. I remember the name of the Kool-Pop artist, though. Mary Ellen Batesy."

The man looked at Marlene, polite confusion on his face. "Pardon, who is . . ."

"Mary Ellen Batesy. A big blond whore, walked the stroll on West Street and when she got a little old for it went into specialty work. You saying 'heat' was what reminded me. See, some men

like hot women, as you were so suavely informing me, but others don't. Others like to fuck dead women, and in the Kool-Pop trade, also they call it a slab job. See, the whore usually gets a couple three bags of ice and takes a bath in them to get the skin temperature down and get her looking blue, and then she stuffs the Kool-Pops up her snatch, and asshole and in her mouth—not the *same* Kool-Pop, three *different* Kool-Pops, until they melt, according to Mary Ellen. Anyway, Mary Ellen had this gurney in her crib, just like in the morgue, and when she was chilled down and ready, she'd lie on it and cover herself with a white sheet and the john would sneak in, and jump on her and do his thing. Mary Ellen said that aside from the risk of getting pneumonia it was a better gig than regular whoring, where they wanted you to pretend you liked it. And more money too."

Marlene was now talking in quite a loud voice, the sort of voice they developed in New York City to cut through the screaming of badly ground subway car wheels, and her end of the table had grown silent. People had stopped eating their mousse; they were all staring at Marlene.

"But that's not what I wanted to *tell* you about, not Mary Ellen, but the guy. Christ! What was his name—Osgood, Oscar, Oswald . . ." Then she raised her voice to a still higher pitch and shouted down to the other end of the long table, "Butch! What was that guy who liked to fuck dead women? With the rent-a-cooler. Oscar somebody?"

Now the whole table fell silent, and into this silence, Karp's voice said evenly, "Oscar Sobell."

"*Oscar Sobell!*" shrieked Marlene. "Yeah, Oscar. Whatta guy!" She looked right at Jim Something and said, "Yeah, Oscar. He was a little washed-out blondie like you, maybe a little more chin than you have. Oscar was one of Mary Ellen's clients, only after a while it started to get old because as good as Mary Ellen was, she wasn't really dead. I mean, he *knew* that. Also, Oscar was blowing a good chunk of his paycheck on Mary Ellen because she got a hundred a pop for a slab job, plus ice. So, what he did, he rented a cold locker, like people do for their furs and all, and then he went out and found a *regular* girl and he *customized* her for his special needs. Well, great, except he had to sort of wear a parka while he got his rocks off, which was inconvenient, but the real problem was—how to put this delicately . . . ?"

"Say, Marlene . . . ," Karp rumbled from down the table. She ignored him. A murmur from the guests had begun.

". . . delicately, as I was saying," she declaimed in her powerful, clear, courtroom voice, "the problem was that after a few months, his girlfriend was becoming, ah, *gummy*, from all the jelled *semen*, which apparently cut into the quality of the experience he was after. So he racked her, hung her up by the mouth on one of the hooks they supplied there, and went out to the stroll and customized another one. And another one, and another one. Well, what happened then is that the warehouse made an error and gave Oscar's key by mistake to a nice old lady who wanted to store her minks, and of course she complained to the management, because naturally she didn't want to share her cold space with a pervert and four dead whores, you could see why, and they called the cops. Oscar had, needless to say, given a phony name and address, and it was all over the papers, so Oscar didn't come back to the warehouse. The police were baffled, as they say. They circulated a description to the other cold-storage places, but no luck. Oscar didn't show. Which was when the kid herself here thought of Mary Ellen Batesy and the other ladies who specialized in slab jobs. There are more of them than you'd think. Anyway, Mary Ellen remembered Oscar. And there he was at his place on Staten Island; he'd just ordered a big cold locker for his basement. My brilliant and famous husband, only he wasn't my husband then, just screwing me on the side, put him away for consecutive life terms. And a good thing too, because, who knows, with his tastes, he might have started on *Jewish* American princesses. . . ."

"Marlene . . . ," said Karp, more sharply. The table remained silent except for embarrassed whispers.

Marlene paused, not because of Karp's interruption, but because of the insistent nausea rising from her stomach, the result of pouring unaccustomed rich food and a lot of alcohol, quickly drunk, into the seething acids of despair.

"Silly me," she said in a lower voice, "I've monopolized the conversation again." She rose shakily and pushed back her chair with a rattle that now seemed as loud as gunfire. "Be right back," she muttered, and stumbled out of the room.

Dinner resumed in her wake as if nothing had happened, and the truth is that such scenes are not at all unusual in the more refined precincts of the capital. Washington, as Alice Roosevelt

once remarked, is full of brilliant men and the women they married when they were very young. Being a wife-of is a harder career than one might imagine, and many of these women, suited by nature, if not society, for different work, get drunk a good deal as a result, sometimes publicly. Remarkably, this nearly always generates substantial sympathy, not for them, but for their husbands.

Everyone at the party was, in fact, especially nice to Karp after dinner. The guests returned to the living room, where coffee and after-dinner drinks were served. Karp had decided not to think about Marlene for a while. No one seemed particularly concerned about her behavior, and Karp was, in truth, happy that it hadn't been worse. That Marlene could be a gigantic pain in the ass, he well knew, and he accepted it as a fact of nature. That her behavior could have a specific cause never entered his mind.

Besides, he was enjoying himself. There is a form of flattery worked on people in important positions in Washington that only a saint well advanced in humility will be able to resist; sadly, few of these are summoned to government service. Karp was perhaps less susceptible than most, but still far from Zion.

Now he sat comfortably on a love seat with an intelligent, pixie-faced woman in her early forties. The woman, whose name was Felicity McDowell, had her silver-blond hair cut short and was dressed in a splendid blue silk pants outfit that had not obviously been thrown together at the last moment, nor was she drunk and disorderly. They had a nice conversation. She knew who Karp was, of course, not just his current job, but his former one. She had lived in New York and was familiar with some of his more spectacular cases. Admiration flowed. She was a journalist and a documentary filmmaker. The possibility of doing a film about the DA's work arose. Difficulties in doing this were explored. Interesting possibilities were dangled.

The conversation turned, as if reluctantly, from Karp's glory to her own modest achievements. McDowell had just completed a feature on, of all people, the Lee Oswalds.

"Oh?" said Karp when she announced this. "It must have been hard to do."

"You mean Marina? Oh, no, she's quite good with her English now. She's a smart woman, actually. Lee didn't want her to learn any English, you know. He was afraid it would loosen her attachment to him."

"No, actually, I meant Oswald. His character. A very strange and complex man."

"You're joking," she replied with a charming laugh. "He was a . . . a . . . *putz*—is that the right word? A nonentity. Nobody at home."

"Maybe. A guy I work with says if he was such a schmuck, he didn't kill the president, and if he did kill the president, he wasn't such a schmuck."

She laughed again and put her hand casually on his knee. "Oh, God! Please don't tell me you're one of those!"

"One of what?"

"An assassination nut, silly."

Karp said, with some stiffness, "Well . . . yeah, I guess. I guess I'm *supposed* to be a kind of *official* assassination nut."

"So, you honestly don't think Oswald did it? Forget about the obvious defects of Warren. Let's say it was a sloppy investigation because everyone was running around terrified. The fact remains that they came up with the right guy."

Karp shrugged. "Well, they haven't proven it by me. How come *you're* so sure?"

"Because I'm a journalist and this is the story of the millennium. If there was anything there that was *real*, that couldn't be interpreted in sixteen different ways, then serious journalists would have dug it out within weeks of the assassination."

"Wait a minute!" Karp objected. "There are dozens, hundreds, of books digging at the thing."

"No, I meant by serious journalists. All these buffs—they're all lawyers, or politicians, or sociologists, or historians. Or 'experts.' None of them ever made a dime out of any writing except writing about the assassination. There's not a real hard-rock working journalist in there. Why? Because journalists are suspicious—the good ones, anyway. They check their facts. And they can read people."

She looked hard at Karp. "Just like I can see you don't believe me—you're becoming a conspiracy buff yourself." She smiled at Karp in a way he didn't much like, the smile of a mom patronizing a preschooler.

"Look," she said, "I spent hours and hours and hours with Marina Oswald. This woman is just what she says she is. Lee Oswald is just what she says he was and what every reliable record of him says he was—a bum with delusions. He's *exactly* the kind

of person who has been the killer in *every* presidential assassination: Booth, the failed actor and disgruntled southerner; Guiteau, a petty office seeker with a grievance against authority; Czolgosz, an anarchist, whatever that means. Zangara, the guy who tried to kill FDR, when they asked him why he did it, he said he had pains in his stomach. Oswald was cut from exactly the same cloth. Believe me, I spent some time with the man, so I know."

"You knew Oswald?"

" 'Knew' is a little strong. I was a stringer for the *Post* in New Orleans in September 1963, when he was arrested and went on the radio to debate the anti-Castro Cuban. The peak of his life until then—people actually paying attention to him, the little shit. I interviewed him after the program, but he was so boring and inane that I didn't bother to write it up. What *was* interesting was what he told me about his wife. I thought it might be interesting to talk to a Russian defector—a defector*ess*, actually. I was thinking of a piece for the woman's page as we then called it, so I went to Dallas and looked her up. I did the piece, but the paper didn't use it, and weren't they sorry the following month, when Lee pulled the trigger! In any case, after the hassle died down and the FBI quit holding her hand, I renewed our connection, and did some articles and now this film." She laughed. "Who am I to criticize? I've done pretty well myself off the JFK hit."

They were silent for a moment, and then Karp asked, "And you have no problem with all the discrepancies, the lost evidence, the—I'll say apparent—cover-ups?"

"Problems? Of course I have problems!" she replied sharply. "Who wouldn't? Do I know that Lee never talked to anyone who worked for someone who worked for the CIA or the FBI? That his name isn't stuck on some obscure file? Of course not! Christ! The Hosty thing alone would cause conniptions. FBI agent Hosty visits the assassin a couple weeks before the killing, and he knows he's a nut, who threatens violence, *and* a political wacko, who just *happens* to work in a place that's on the president's motorcade route, and nobody thinks to check this guy out while the big man is in town? So were there cover-ups? Probably. But not of conspiracy; the cover-ups were about incompetence. Like I said, Warren messed up, my boy, messed up big-time, but they got the story right."

"Well, there I can't agree with you. Obviously, right? I mean

that's what the House investigation is for, isn't it? To figure out what went wrong with Warren, and fix it."

She looked surprised. "Surely you don't believe that? In fact, the point of your committee is to dispose of the criticisms of Warren and come up with approximately the same results."

Karp bridled and snapped, "That's not what Bert Crane thinks."

"Yes, I know," McDowell said darkly. "That's the *problem*. Look—you seem like a very nice man, honest and forthright and all that, so I'm going to give you some free advice. Don't hitch your wagon to a falling star. Hello, Blake."

The man standing over them and smiling was large and built on an angular plan. His shoulders were squared off and broad, his jaw was sharply drawn, there was a sharp line dividing a short crop of crinkly black hair, graying on the side, from a flat, smooth forehead. Below that were thick eyebrows straight across and black squarish glasses like Clark Kent's. The lines in his face and his wide mouth seemed also to run rectilinearly, as if drawn on graph paper. He wore a sharply cut, expensive dark suit, pin-striped, of course. Karp knew who he was: next to Jack Anderson and perhaps James Reston, Blake Harrison was at the time the most influential political newspaper columnist in the country.

Harrison said, smiling, "Hello, yourself, Felicity," and then said his name to Karp and stuck out his hand. Karp rose and took it, and said his own name.

Harrison said, still smiling, "Felicity, would you mind terribly if I poached a bit? I have to get somewhere and I do need to have a few words with Mr. Karp here."

"Not at all," said McDowell, her smile a trifle forced. "Nice talking to you, Butch."

Karp nodded and voiced similar sentiments, and was led away, noticing that no one had asked him. Apparently, when Blake Harrison wanted to talk to you, it was not a negotiable issue.

Karp followed Harrison out of the crowded living room and down a hallway. Harrison was hailed by several people on the way, and returned their greetings, but refused to stay for conversation. He also seemed to know his way around the Dobbs house. They reached a doorway and Harrison ushered Karp into a small room that appeared to be some kind of den: wooden bookshelves along one wall, a desk, an elaborate stereo system, sporting prints and

political cartoons on another wall, two large red leather library chairs flanking a coffee table piled with magazines. Harrison sat in one of the chairs and propped his feet up on the coffee table, seeming quite at home. He motioned Karp into the other.

Harrison said, "So . . . Butch. They still call you Butch, don't they?"

"Or worse."

Harrison smiled briefly. "Yes, I'll bet. I'm Blake, and they call me worse things than they probably call you. Well, I could butter you up with tales of what I've heard about your reputation, but knowing that reputation as I do, I know that you have no use for flattery. So I'll get to the point. Your boss is going down. It may be this week or the next one, I don't know, but for sure he's finished. The question—"

"Why?" Karp interrupted. "What's he done?"

Harrison smiled, the same smile that McDowell had given him, the patient smile of an adult addressing the question of a child. "Why does anyone fail in Washington? He has not made happy the people he ought to have made happy, and he has made unhappy the people he ought not to have made unhappy."

"I thought he was supposed to run an honest investigation, not put on *A Chorus Line.* Who exactly are these people he's pissed off?"

"His committee, for one. Elements of the press."

"You mean Flores? He's a jerk."

Harrison chuckled. "Doubtless, but that does not disqualify one from a position of power in Washington. No, Bert made a very serious mistake in accepting this invitation to speak before the caucus without clearing it with Flores. Flores is hurt and he's going to lash out. Bert could have opposed him if he himself was in a position of unassailable power or if his own record were absolutely clean, but such is not, apparently, the case."

"Crane is *dirty?* That's bullshit!"

"Let's just say that there's a cloud. On Monday, two major papers, one in Philadelphia and one in Washington, will break stories about Bert Crane. The Philadelphia story will explore unsavory connections between Crane and various organized-crime figures that took place while he was a DA in Philly. He let a mobster named Johnny Serrano off on a corruption charge and some-

time later there were contributions made to his campaign from a union known to be influenced by the Serrano crime family. The Washington story will focus on the operations of the committee staff. Apparently a good deal of money has been spent without legal authorization, and the comptroller general is starting an investigation."

Stunned, Karp paused a moment before responding, aware that the other man was examining his reaction. "That's ridiculous!" he said at last. "Crane never did any deal with mob guys. And the only money that's been spent is on essential items for the office. What, they think he's ripping off paper clips?"

"That's not the point. It is a fact of political life that you can survive accusations if you have a strong political base, or, if you have a weak base you can survive by ensuring that no accusations are made against you—as I said, by making the necessary people happy. But Crane has made people angry without a political base, and that's fatal."

"I can't believe this," replied Karp stubbornly.

"For the sake of argument, then, assume he'll be forced out. The question I wanted to raise with you, Butch, has to do with *your* position."

"My position?"

"Yes. Assuming Bert has to go."

"Well, obviously, I hadn't thought about it. I don't agree that Bert's going."

Harrison waved a dismissive hand. "Yes, yes, very loyal, of course, but let's cut the crap. Crane *is* finished and the only problem that remains is who replaces him. I think you'd be ideal. No —let me finish. One, you're as apolitical as a lamppost. That's essential. The report the committee writes is going to have to be salable to the public at large and that means no detectable political influence. Two, I've checked you out pretty thoroughly, and I've been unable to find a cloud. In fact, on several occasions you've dug up nasty stuff that could've been used to good advantage in building a career for yourself and you haven't used any of it. Very commendable, and useful in the present case. Incorruptibility is a salable commodity in this town, but it's as perishable as oysters. It requires, let us say, a certain protective shield. Let's say that I can arrange such a shield."

"I don't understand," said Karp, and he meant it.

"What I mean is that Crane's job is yours, if you want it. If we can come to some understanding."

"Which would be what?"

Harrison checked and grinned and fanned his hand in front of his face. "My God, such frankness! It takes my breath away. Okay, I'll be blunt, as much as it violates my sensibilities. You take Crane's job. I'll use my influence and the influence of people who owe me favors to make sure you get it. I will ensure cover for you in the press while you do your work. In return, you will provide me with a first look at everything you turn up. Also, if you're as smart as you seem to be, you'd also accept such political guidance as I may offer from time to time. How is that? Blunt enough?"

"Yeah. Tell me, you're a reporter—how come you can offer political guidance?"

Harrison laughed at that. "How? My friend, you might as well ask how a telephone can transmit stock market tips. I am a conduit for powerful people. They tell me things. I tell them things. Everyone knows that, which is why my column gets read, and why it's influential. It's the way this town works, as I'm sure you'll find out, if you survive. So—what do you say?"

"I say I'll think about it."

Harrison nodded his cube of a head several times. "Good. But don't take too long. The train is pulling out of the station and those who aren't on it will be left behind."

Karp was tired of this sort of advice. He said, "Well, Blake, the fact is that I really don't give two shits about whether I'm on the train or not. I came here to find out what the truth was about the Kennedy assassination, which is a legal and forensic investigation, a job that, with all due respect, I don't need any advice from you about. If I can do that, fine. If I can't, for whatever reason, I'm out of here."

Harrison rolled his eyes and brought his fist angrily down on his knee. "The truth! Yes, of course you want the truth. Don't you think that's what I want too? I was in Dallas when Jack was shot. I was at Parkland when they brought him in with his brains spilling out of his head. Nobody ever forgets something like that. My point, if you'd care to listen, is that without some experienced political guidance and some cover, you will not *get* to the truth.

You will not be *allowed* to. So the choice I put to you is whether you want to remain a 'legal and forensic' choirboy with an unsullied heart, and get kicked out on your ass, or whether you want to play this game and win. Let me know when you make up your mind which.''

He rose from his chair and stalked out of the room, leaving Karp sitting there thinking about what Clay Fulton had said those many weeks ago: indeed, he *was* way over his head. And in muddy water too.

After vomiting copiously in a primrose yellow toilet, Marlene washed her face, dried herself on one of the charming flowered guest towels, and went looking for a place to lie low until the wretched party had reached its end and she could sneak out.

She walked away from the sound of well-informed conversation, down a darkened hallway and through a door. She found herself in an echoing room with tall windows and a flagstoned floor, smelling oddly of both earth and chlorine. The windows on the left side were lit, those to the right, dark. To the right, then, obviously a pool; to the left a greenhouse, or, she supposed one should say, a conservatory. There was a door and she went through it.

The room was large, about fifty by thirty feet, and had one wall all of glass, which by night threw back the reflection of the overhead fluorescents and the variously shaded greens of the plants, mingled with the brighter hues of their blossoms. There were large specimens of the usual indoor plants—impatiens and prayer plants and tradescantia—but also more exotic growth. Huge staghorn ferns hung from the sprinkler pipe supports. Ficus and hibiscuses, oleanders and eucalypts grew from pots, and there were tables covered with weird aloes, and euphorbias and other fleshy, striped and waxy-flowered items that Marlene could not identify. A faint scent of jasmine floated over the bass note of the moist earth.

She saw a flash of a remarkable lavender color through the dense branches of a large croton and went around a potting table to see what it was. The plant was in a pot on the floor. It had dark green shiny leaves like a rhodie, but its flowers looked like giant purple pansies. She poked under its branches to see whether there was a label.

Behind her a voice said, "It's *Brunfelsia floribunda,* from Brazil."

Marlene jumped back six inches and whirled, startled. Maggie Dobbs was sitting on a low green wooden bench in an alcove made by a pair of potting tables.

"It's lovely," said Marlene, recovering her composure. "Do you, um, do all this?" she asked, gesturing to the conservatory.

"Yup. Me and Manuel the gardener. I have a green thump. Thumb." She held up her hand with the thumb sticking out. The fingers, Marlene saw, were wrapped around a squat brown bottle. Maggie looked at the bottle as if she had just noticed its attachment to her hand. "Want a drink? It's B and B."

"Um, I think I had enough already tonight, thanks. As I'm sure you observed. I have to apologize. . . ."

"Nah! Life of the party. It was worth it to see the expression on that jerk Jim Royce's face when you started talking about fucking corpses. Oops! Excuse my French!" She placed her hand over her mouth and giggled. Marlene wondered how long she had been hiding from her own party behind the potted plants. Apparently, and contradicting her previous thinking, the ability to give nice parties was not a perfect recipe for the good life.

"Mind if I join you?" Marlene asked.

"Sit," said Maggie, and she took a swig from her bottle. There were two bars of hectic red across her cheeks and her blue eyes were bleary, but aside from this, she still looked neat and doll-like in her golden hostess costume. Marlene did not want to think about her own appearance; she thought she had removed all of the vomit from her hair. Some people are neat from the core out, she decided, of which happy company Marlene was not a member.

Marlene leaned back against the wall behind the bench, drew out her Marlboros, and lit one.

"Oooh! Ciggies! Thank God!"

"You want one?"

"God, yes! I'm quitting."

On impulse, Marlene finger-palmed the cigarette and used a standard sleight-of-hand production, seeming to pluck it out of thin air with a snap of her fingers.

"Yikes!" cried Maggie. "Do that again!"

Grinning, Marlene hummed an upbeat version of "Tea for Two" and did a little routine of vanishes, acquitments, and productions using her own lit cigarette.

"That's terrific!" Maggie screamed. "How did you learn to do that?"

"I had a lot of time to practice. A physical therapist I had after I got blown up thought it was a good way to strengthen my hands." She held up her hand and wiggled the mutilated fingers.

"Blown up?" Maggie said, her eyes widening.

"Yeah, by a letter bomb."

"Oh, God, she was blown up, she knows corpse fuckers, she does magic. . . ." She hung her head and her golden Dutch boy covered her face. "I'm so *dull* I could scream."

"Well, I'm dull too, now, invisible, in fact, at least according to what's-his-face—that Royce asshole. Wife-of-hood."

"Yeah, he treats me like I was Twiggy, only not as socially valuable."

"Well, at least you're dull and rich," said Marlene. "It beats being dull and poor." It was a cruel thing to say, and Marlene immediately regretted saying it.

Maggie let out a wail. "I *know*! I'm so *ashamed*! I have *everything* and most people have *nothing* and I'm still *miserable*. And, of course, even saying that makes me feel even more ashamed. I have a marvelous husband and two marvelous children. There's no end to it." A fat tear plopped onto her cheek.

"Well, I'm miserable too," said Marlene, thinking once again of the first conversation she had had that day with a cigarette-bumming woman on a bench, and what she had concluded from it, "but I'm damned if I'm going to be maudlin. Come on, fuck 'em all! We'll join the . . . Wife-Of Self-Defense Association."

Maggie gave her a long unfocused look. "Is there one?"

"I think we just formed it. You can be the first president."

"No," said Maggie instantly. "*You* be the first president. I have to be the secretary."

That started them giggling. Marlene exclaimed, "I love it! It's even got a good acronym. WOSDA."

"Yeah," said Maggie, "as in 'Darling, WOSDA matter with you *now*?'"

By the time Karp tracked Marlene down, an hour or so later, they were still laughing like banshees, clinging to each other on the green bench, the empty bottle stashed behind a potted oleander.

Bishop visited the house in Little Havana over the weekend. The thin man was watching golf on television when he strode in.

"Interested in a little work?" Bishop asked.

"No, I like sitting on my ass watching golf," said the thin man sourly.

"Jerry James Depuy," said Bishop, "may have become a tiny problem."

"I thought he was dead."

"Yeah, he's dead. His works have apparently outlived him. Apparently some ex-cop was asking questions of the widow. It turns out this guy works for the House committee on contract. She told him that she'd given all his stuff to the AP and they'd given it to Georgetown U. for their Kennedy archive."

"So? Aside from that bullshit with Ferrie, he didn't know dick."

"Yes, well, we always knew Ferrie was one of the weak links. Secrecy was not his strong suit. He liked to brag. The point is, it turns out that among the material passed on to the archive were several spools of eight-millimeter film."

The thin man looked away from the TV for the first time. He stared straight into Bishop's eyes. "I got that film, if that's what you're thinking. When Ferrie went down."

"Yes, you did, the original reels. But film can be copied. It's entirely possible that the little asshole showed the film to Depuy and Depuy copied it. I went to the archive myself the other day and found that the committee staff had already grabbed Depuy's material."

"But you don't know that the film they have is Ferrie's film."

"No, I don't," Bishop agreed. "But the possibility is extremely disturbing. We're going to be busy people if a copy survived. And if the people looking at it understand what it means."

TEN

"What else did you find besides this film?" asked Karp, as V.T. threaded the Moviola editor in the dim room.

"Some notebooks, mainly concerned with Depuy's coverage of Garrison's prosecution of Clay Shaw, lots of clippings of same, the original manuscripts of his filed stories, an address book. Notes for a book on Ferrie and the New Orleans right-wing scene that never got past the interview stage. Like that."

"Anything there?"

"I haven't really scoured it, to be honest. This film hit me in the eye right away and I've been looking at it ever since."

After threading the film, V.T. cranked the handle for about fifteen seconds, taking up film until a piece of yellow paper popped out of the spool and fluttered to the floor. Then he switched on the screen light.

"It's show time," he said, and began to crank the Moviola. Karp leaned forward in his chair and concentrated. The small square screen showed a shadowy landscape, some bushes and trees, then a road. The film was black-and-white and grainy, or perhaps the graininess was just an artifact of the ground-glass screen of the editing machine. In any case, the film seemed to have been shot in bad light, at dusk perhaps, or in moonlight.

The camera panned across dark woods that seemed vaguely tropical—palmettos, Spanish moss, and hanging vines—past an open field, and onto the road again. A line of two-and-a-half-ton military trucks appeared, moving slowly, their headlights cut to

thin slits. The trucks stopped and soldiers leaped out and lined up on the road. They were dressed in fatigues and soft caps. Most carried rifles, but there were some with machine guns and mortar components, and Karp spotted one with a folded bazooka.

The film now cut jerkily to maneuvers: the soldiers rushed across the field and flung themselves down, while others provided covering fire. The film was silent, but you could see the pinpoints of fire from the rifles and the shimmering gouts of muzzle blast from the machine guns. It cut to a mortar team firing, dropping the shells in odd silence down the tubes and shielding their ears from the blasts. Karp was no expert, but they seemed well drilled.

"Where is this happening, V.T.? And what's the point?"

"Patience. Aren't you interested in how we trained all the brave anticommunist Cubans?"

"Is that what this is? The Bay of Pigs?"

V.T. stopped cranking. "No, they trained those in Guatemala; this is Louisiana, and if we assume that the film was processed shortly after it was taken, from the markings on the leader it's the early summer of 1963. It's an illegal operation."

"How do you know where it is?" Karp asked.

"Watch."

V.T. started the film moving again. Now the camera was obviously in a vehicle of some kind, an open vehicle because the camera could pan around 360 degrees. A jeep: the well-known square hood flashed by and then the backs of the heads of two men with military caps on. A white road sign loomed up and started to whip by. V.T. stopped the movement again. The road sign had the shape of Louisiana and a number.

"We know just where this is, right by Lake Pontchartrain, near New Orleans. Okay, this part is important." He cranked slowly. The jeep ride ended and the camera cut to a group of five men standing around a jeep, talking, as troops filed by in the background. V.T. froze a frame and pointed with a pencil.

"Okay, these two guys look like Cubans, we haven't identified them yet. This stocky guy with the round face is Antonio Veroa, of Brigada Sixty-one fame—the star of document A. The tall, ugly guy here is Gary Becker, the head of the Anti-Communist League of the Caribbean."

"Who's the other guy in civilian clothes?" asked Karp, indicating a tall man with dark hair, a prominent nose, and deeply im-

pressed wrinkles under his eyes. He was turning away from the lens as the shot opened, as if more interested in some background object than in the conversation the men were having; that, or he had a predisposition to avoid being the subject of photography.

V.T. said, "Also a blank. It's a little hard to ID him because he's turning away like that. Now watch this."

He edged the film forward. In the treacly movements of slow motion, the camera's view moved to another group of men standing by a truck. One of the men in the group turned around and smiled at the camera. It was actually more of a smirk than a smile, the famous smirk.

"Holy shit!" said Karp. "It's him."

"So it seems," said V.T. "Perhaps a sort of private ROTC weekend away from the lovely Marina, or maybe this was during the time he was actually living in New Orleans."

Karp was looking at the other men in the group around Lee Harvey Oswald. "Who are they?"

"It'd be nice to find out. I'll have portrait blowups made of every identifiable face in this film and get my people on it. But there's more."

He turned more quickly now, the figures moving with the comic velocity of Keystone Kops. The screen brightened. It was full day. Some men were shooting pistols at a crude outdoor firing range, firing at man-shaped targets nailed to trees. Karp recognized Veroa, in civvies this time, holding an army .45 and smiling. The view moved unsteadily back to the shooting; the camera jumped slightly at each soundless explosion. Two men, grinning, held up a well-punctured target. A man in a black T-shirt and ball cap sat at a table loading bullets into pistol magazines. He looked up for an instant, frowned, spoke briefly, and lowered his head again so that the bill of the cap obscured his face. V.T. backed the film to the few frames that showed his face.

"Oswald again," said Karp.

"Looks like it," said V.T. "It's got to be some time later than in the first scenes, because his sideburns've grown longer."

V.T. cranked the film forward for another few seconds. More shooting, men posing with weapons, then a close-up of a round-faced man with a fright wig and patently phony, impossibly thick eyebrows.

"David Ferrie," said V.T. Unnecessarily: nobody else looked like Ferrie.

The film moved on and then Oswald in his ball cap and black T-shirt returned. The shot was taken from the rear and showed him standing, aiming at a target twenty-five yards downrange and firing off seven shots rapidly. V.T. slowed the film. The thin puffs of smoke from the pistol, his arm moving up in response to the recoil, took on a ghastly slowness. The camera moved in for a close-up of the head of the target silhouette. It was shredded and flapping away from its fiberboard backing.

"Terrific," said Karp tightly. "It's like a coming attractions trailer for the Zapruder film." They looked at the frozen target in silence for a while. V.T. moved the film again through another twenty seconds of paramilitary dullness. He stopped cranking, pulled the film from the viewer, and began to wind back.

"What's on the front end of the spool?" he asked.

"Nothing," said V.T. "Home movies. A barbecue somewhere. A Kiwanis award of some kind."

"Ferrie was in Kiwanis?"

"No, but I doubt the cameraman was Ferrie. Ferrie didn't own a movie camera that we know of and of course he's there in the picture."

"So who took the film and how did Ferrie get hold of it?"

"This we don't know," said V.T. with a sigh. "In fact, we don't know its provenance at all: who took it, why they took it, or how it got from whoever took it, to Ferrie, to Depuy, or why." He grinned without humor. "In short, it's just like all the other fucking evidence in this case."

Karp rose stiffly and wiggled his bad knee. "But it's great stuff. It puts Oswald with the Cubans."

"Assuming it's Oswald. Assuming it's real."

"We could show it to Veroa," said Karp.

"We have Veroa?"

"Yeah, I didn't tell you. It was no big thing—he was in the book. Al Sangredo, Fulton's guy in Miami, just talked to him in Little Havana. I'm going to get Clay to go down there and pick him up."

"He'll cooperate?" asked V.T., surprise in his voice.

Karp shrugged. "He's on parole on a federal drug charge. You have to assume he's interested in helping the government."

V.T. let out a bitter laugh. "Yes, he would be—in real life. In this investigation, on the other hand, it might be just as well to assume the opposite."

"That's a point," said Karp. "We'll have to see. Meanwhile, and in the same vein, make a copy of that film and bury it. And V.T.? Don't show it to anyone else but Clay. Oh, yeah, and I guess Ziller too. He's a spy for Dobbs, but, hell, if Dobbs is bent we might as well pack it in anyway. He's the only friend we got on the committee."

"Are you serious about restricting access? I mean I'm paranoid too, but that's a little extreme."

"Yeah, I'm serious. Have blowups made at a private lab, and you can show those to your photo-analysis people, but keep the actual film to yourself."

"Can we afford a private lab?"

"*You* can," said Karp.

"Still no budget, huh?"

"Afraid not."

V.T. switched on the lights and collected the film. "You going to see Crane? Yeah? Ask him if we can have a bake sale and a dance at the gym. I mean, this sucks!"

When Karp arrived for his regular Monday meeting, Crane was talking to Bea Sondergard. They both froze for an instant and stared at him, as if they had been deep in conspiracy against the Republic. Sondergard's face seemed drawn, and her eyes lacked their usual tolerant good humor.

Karp hesitated in the doorway and said, "Sorry—I'll come back later. . . ."

But Crane waved him in. "No, we were just finishing up. Come in and sit down." To Sondergard he said, in a lower tone, "Stop worrying—we'll be fine."

The woman sighed and said, " 'We' is not the problem, Bert. As far as I'm concerned they can all kiss my sweet patootie. It's you I'm scared for."

"What was that about?" Karp asked when Sondergard had gone out.

"Oh, administrative horseshit, the usual crying and moaning," Crane said, waving his hand in a limp circle to indicate the triviality of it all.

"I heard it was more serious than that."

Crane gave a snort of derision. "You and Bea both. Am I going to have to hold *your* hand too? Look—what it is, there was a piece in the *Post* today. Flores sent me a letter citing irregularities in staff expenditures and of course the son of a bitch leaked it simultaneously to the press. He told me I am to incur absolutely no further expenses until this issue has been resolved by the committee. According to him, I'm encouraging some kind of sybaritic lifestyle off the public fisc without doing a damn thing to earn it." He smiled and tapped his desk. "This desk was specifically mentioned along with its cost. I guess I thought when they hired me that I'd have a desk, but I guess I was wrong. So Bea's pretty upset. She feels responsible for her usual efficiency. And then there's this."

Crane reached into his wastebasket and pulled out a folded newspaper and waved it. "Have you seen this piece of shit yet?"

Karp had not, but of course he knew what it was.

"Philadelphia," he said.

"You read it?"

"I heard about it. You're in with the Mob."

"Trash, a total lie. I'm going to bring a libel suit that'll kick their teeth in. My only worry is that this and the budget thing are going to occupy the caucus and the press so much that they'll totally forget why they got me here in the first place."

"You're not still going to the caucus?" Karp had blurted it out without thought and he was dismayed when Crane gave him a searching look.

"Yeah, I'm still going," he snapped. "Why the devil shouldn't I? I haven't done anything wrong. If I lie low, it'll just give them something else to yap about."

Karp nodded and held his tongue. He knew Crane was wrong and that Harrison had been right. The man was doomed. The worst thing he could possibly do now was to continue his defiance of Flores. He should have canceled his appearance before the Democratic caucus, should have apologized to Flores, should have sucked ass for all he was worth, so that they would let him alone. He should have then proceeded with the investigation, in secrecy, covering the real work with a cloak of supine amiability until he had some politically potent findings, preferably some that implicated Flores or his cronies, or that were so explosive that they

couldn't be suppressed. But Crane, it seemed, was just like Karp. That was the problem. And nothing could be done.

After a brief, empty silence, Karp rattled his notes, cleared his throat, and launched into his briefing. Most of it was concerned with the film V.T. had found, the Cuban connection, and the proposal to have the CIA man Paul A. David testify.

"When is he scheduled?" asked Crane.

"Wednesday, day after tomorrow."

"Any problems?"

"No, except for the usual CIA stuff about not violating secrecy."

"Mmm. On that score—he'll be our first major witness. Do you think it's a good idea to start out with the CIA?"

This startled Karp. "Bert, we had this discussion. You said we should bear down on Langley, and that's what I'm doing. I didn't think good idea or bad idea. Our only new material—the documents from Schaller, the letter from Hoover, and now this film— all suggest CIA connections, and participation in suppressing evidence. It makes sense to start off with a senior CIA guy who might have been directly involved with concocting a phony story."

"I take your point," said Crane, "but I've been thinking about it some more. It's starting to strike me as, well, backward. It might make more sense to start with the assassination proper: the shots, the trajectories, the witnesses, the evidence inculpating Oswald, the autopsy . . ."

"You mean present it like Warren," Karp said, and when Crane nodded, he continued, "No, the problem with that is that there's no point at all in most of the forensic stuff. It's all corrupt. Every piece of it. We don't have reliable chains of evidence for anything. The bullets, the photographs, the X rays—God knows where they came from or who handled them. The autopsy was totally fucked. We have no access to the body. The tissue slides are missing. The witnesses? All interrogated originally by people we know had some sort of ax to grind—the FBI or the Dallas cops or the Warren people—oh, yeah, and the assassination buffs, of course. The surviving witnesses have told their story so many times that any connection between what they're saying and what actually happened is probably coincidental. So, absent actual, legally probative evidence, we have to rely exclusively on experts, which means, as you

know as well as I do, that for any three experts saying one thing, I can get three other experts to say the opposite. Even so, ninety percent of Warren and ninety percent of the anti-Warren writing has focused on the minutiae surrounding a single question: Did the shots that killed Kennedy come from a single known rifle on the sixth floor of the Texas Book Depository? That question is a waste of time. Oh, yeah, we'll go through the motions, but it's going to be essentially a dead end, and irrelevant. Any real advances we make will be made through completely fresh material, stuff that hasn't been totally mangled, like the evidence I just mentioned. It tells us two things: one, the CIA was actively involved in stonewalling on this case; and two, Oswald was definitely involved with anti-Castro Cubans and with the CIA. Whether Oswald killed Kennedy alone, or with help, or was just a patsy is something that can't ever be established from the existing Dallas evidence. But there's at least a slight chance that if we follow up this new stuff we'll find something that'll give us the real story."

Crane was silent for a long while after this. He swiveled his chair around to stare out the window, at the rail yards, or perhaps at nothing. Finally, he said, "You're right, of course. But . . ." Crane looked directly at him. "I don't want this degenerating into a Jim Garrison circus. I won't have that."

"No, of course not," said Karp vehemently. "Garrison's problem was the fact that he *didn't* have anything documentary like we have now. He had to rely on testimony from sleazebags against the word of Clay Shaw, who, whatever his sexual predelictions, presented himself as a solid citizen. Garrison's star witness was a petty hustler and known perjurer. Another one was a known crackpot. And he was trying to prove Clay Shaw's involvement in a conspiracy, which is always a hard case to prove. Okay, so what if Shaw knew Oswald and Ferrie and denied it? It doesn't generate guilty knowledge of, or participation in, the assassination, which is one reason Garrison's case collapsed. One thing, though: Garrison was right on about the importance of the New Orleans connection. Something *was* going on in New Orleans in the late summer of 1963, even if Garrison got sidetracked about what it really was. If there was a plot at all, it was hatched there, because Oswald was there and active, and guilty or innocent, Oswald is *involved.* He's still the key to everything."

Crane nodded distractedly. His mind seemed to have passed over to some other subject. "Okay, do what you have to and let me know as soon as anything breaks. But, Butch? Don't spend any money."

After his meeting with Crane, Karp walked over to Independence Avenue and spent money. He bought two hot dogs, an egg roll, and a root beer from one of the trucks that parked in the driveway in front of the Civil War Memorial. It was long past the tourist season, but the sun was out, and it had turned into the sort of fairly pleasant late-autumn day Washington sometimes gets. The trucks still came at noon, their immigrant drivers hoping that hungry people with slender means and no fear of stomach cancer would show up in sufficient numbers to pay for the daily rental.

As Karp was entering his building, a small man in a red stocking cap and a shopping bag darted out from the cover of one of the marble lamp supports and accosted him. Karp shied away and kept moving. The man followed him into the building, waving a ragged pack of xeroxed sheets and raving his assassination theory. The security guard at the desk inside rose to intercept him.

"You're making a big mistake," the man shouted. "I have the evidence right here. . . ."

Karp moved toward the elevator. Red Hat was a well-known figure around the building. He believed that Kennedy had not been assassinated at all, that only a double had been killed in Dallas, and that the former president was now living in Georgia. It was, oddly enough, not the least-plausible story Karp had heard while at this job; it did not, for example, involve beings from other planets.

He was at his desk, eating his egg roll, with his head down over a paper napkin placed on the desk to catch the falling debris, when Clay Fulton came in and sat down on a side chair.

"Is that good?" Fulton asked, curling his lip in distaste.

"It sucks."

"How come you don't get none of these fancy lobbyist lunches I keep hearing about?"

"I don't know," said Karp through egg roll, "but it's a real disappointment. I mean, I'm a Washington lawyer, right? Maybe

those guys you hear about with the big lunches are just bragging. Maybe they're really grabbing franks off the hot trucks."

"Could be," said Fulton, chuckling. "I saw that movie V.T. got. That's some interesting movie."

"Yeah. He pointed out Veroa? Good. Now you know what he looks like, you can go down there and get him."

"*I* should get him? Why don't we just have Al Sangredo bring him up?"

"Because you're the official investigator and Al isn't, one, and two, I got something else I want Al to follow up on. I think it'd be a good idea if Al used his contacts to see exactly how this drug beef that Veroa's got hanging actually went down—how dirty is he, is it a legit beef—like that."

Fulton chewed his mustache, ruminating. "You think it might've been a setup?"

"I don't know, but I make it a point that when I talk to a guy I want information out of, I know where and how hard he can be squeezed."

The detective rose and went toward the door. "Okay. I'll get Bea to cut some travel."

"No, you can't do that. No further expenditure. Apparently we're under investigation."

Fulton stared at him in disbelief. "*We're* being investigated? I thought we're the investigators."

"Yeah, but they're on our ass for spending money that Congress hasn't appropriated—I forget what it's called, but it's a big deal. Put it on your card. Don't worry—you'll get it back."

"I got to fly to Miami and pick up your Cuban on *my own card*?"

"You got it, chief. Consider it a little vacation. Take a few days. Play the ponies. Eat some stone crabs."

"Yeah, right," said Fulton sourly. "And I'll work on my tan."

Marlene and her daughter looked through dusty blinds out at the courtyard of Federal Gardens, watching a small woman being dragged across the dead grass by a big black dog. The woman was their neighbor, the one Marlene called the Dwarf. Mrs. Thug. She was not, of course, an actual dwarf, merely a small, thin woman,

too small and light to control an athletic and untrained dog that was delirious with joy at this brief respite from its nearly perpetual confinement.

"That lady is yelling bad words at her dog, Mommy," observed Lucy.

"Yeah, I hear," said Marlene. The woman had tripped over a grass hummock and gone down and the dog was racing around her, capering and barking. The woman and the dog ran around in circles for a while until she managed to snag the dog's lead, after which she dragged it back into her apartment. The cute puppy had become an unmanageable adolescent. A common tale, and Marlene thought it was just as well that they hadn't tried the same script with a human child. A door slammed, and Dwarf strode across Marlene's field of view, with a purple car coat thrown over her aqua-colored supermarket checker's uniform. The dog had already started its endless whining. The dramatic high point of my day, thought Marlene, that and, *I have to get out of the house.*

The phone rang, and Lucy cried, "I'll get it!"

Marlene followed her into the kitchen and poured herself another cup of coffee. It was probably Karp. In the wake of the Dobbs party, they had just concluded one of their bad weeks— silence, interspersed with coldly formal interactions. Karp was distracted, worried about something, probably to do with work. Marlene's share of the marital responsibility had always been to worm these worries out of him, but she no longer had the energy. Something vast and soggy hung between them, compounded of Marlene's isolation and feelings of uselessness, and the Big Secret, the Bloom thing. And sex. They had only done it once since Marlene had arrived in Washington, and remarkably—for the Karps had until then enjoyed a delicious and imaginative life of the flesh—it had fizzled. Karp had withdrawn into the despondency he exhibited when he didn't know what was going on in their relationship, favoring her on many occasions with the sort of long-suffering, whipped-Airedale looks that drove her batty. A dozen times she had opened her mouth to confront, to tell all, to break through into real life again, but each time she had lost courage.

This can't go on, she thought, and lit a cigarette from the butt of the one she was smoking—a bad sign—but what could stop it? She wasn't going to sink down into ultimate depression; the crazy

scene at the Dobbses' showed that well enough. But was she going to keep on being naughtier and naughtier until something broke? She thought of Maggie Dobbs and the mad laughing in the green-house . . .

"It's a lady," said Lucy. Marlene took the receiver, knowing that it was Maggie calling, ready to give her "this is amazing, I was just thinking about you," and was oddly shocked to hear in-stead the voice of Luisa Beckett.

After some stilted preliminaries, Beckett said, "The reason I called, I thought you'd want to know. Morgan got sentenced on a 130.65, three counts. Max of fifteen."

"Oh, honey, that's terrific!" cried Marlene. The 130.65 was first-degree sexual abuse, a Class D felony; the baby raper would be away for at least seven years, if he survived at all at the very bottom of the Attica pecking order.

"Yeah, well, I thought you'd like to know. It was your case." Luisa's tone was dull and tired, and vaguely guilt-making.

"So. How're things?"

"Okay. You know, the usual."

Marlene brought up some cases, as conversation, but Luisa did not seem to want to converse. Why the hell had the woman called anyway? What did she want, an apology for leaving them in the lurch? For fucking up? Marlene persisted mulishly, picking at the scab.

"What about that mobster, Buona-something? What happened with him?"

"Buonafacci. We're not handling that anymore. Your old buddy Guma's got it."

"Guma? Why's he got it? It's a rape case."

"Yeah, well he must've pulled some strings with narco or one of the *real* bureaus. They figure they can hold the rape over him, Buonafacci, and he'll help them out somehow. Don't ask me, I just work here."

There didn't seem to be much to say after that. Marlene fin-ished the call feeling, if possible, worse than she had before it. The dog was howling again. Marlene got Lucy dressed and threw on her own rags in a concentrated fury, scattering sparks and cigarette ashes over everything, leaving the breakfast dishes in the sink, which she herself considered the very lowest level of sluthood, and was just wheeling the stroller out when the phone rang again.

"This is amazing," Marlene said to Maggie Dobbs. "I was just thinking about you."

Karp noticed the change when he walked in that evening. There was music playing, one of Marlene's tapes, and instead of the sour old-paint and steam-heat smell that was the base pong of the Federal Gardens, the apartment was redolent with the perfume of a Marlene dinner in preparation—garlic, onions, oregano, wine— that and patchouli incense, also a Ciampi trademark. Lucy came dashing out of the kitchen and leaped into his arms. "Daddy, we went to the zoo!"

"Really? Who did you go with?"

"Um, Laura, she's my friend. And a lady. We saw monkeys. They were throwing their *poop*!"

Karp carried her into the kitchen, where Marlene was setting the table with the cheap ware provided by the building management. There was, however, a bunch of yellow mums in a mayonnaise jar in the center of the table, and there was a checked red-and-white paper tablecloth. Two green Coke bottles held tall candles. Karp put his daughter down and leaned over and kissed his wife.

"I'm impressed," he said.

"You like it? You don't think it's too *Lady and the Tramp*? Pathetic?"

"Not at all. Are we celebrating something?"

"No, why? Oh, you mean why the switch from Blanche DuBois to Betty Crocker?" Leaning down to check the oven. "I just had a nice day, and I thought, after reading the *Post*, that you probably didn't have a nice day, so I thought maybe I would take vacation from self-pity and make a real dinner and have some wine and pretend that we're still alive down here." Interruption by Lucy on the subject of the great apes. Microlesson in natural history supplied.

"Who's this Laura?" Karp asked.

"Maggie Dobbs's six-year-old. Maggie called me up and invited me for a day at the zoo since we got this nice break in the weather. So we went."

"She came here?"

"Of course not. I have some pride left. No, I arranged to meet her at the Rosslyn metro and she came by in her big blue Mercury

wagon and off we went. Lucy and Laura fell in love. We saw the zoo, we went shopping in a nonpeckerwood supermarket up on Connecticut, where I bought real food. What can I say? It was magic."

"You like her? Maggie Dobbs I mean."

"Yeah, she's okay. Not my usual type of pal, but nice. Sweet-natured, generous. Funny too. I think she's a little dominated by the congressman. He's real ambitious, wants to be a senator or in the cabinet, for starters. Anyhow, it's a lot of pressure on her, parties, waving to the crowds, doing good works. She showed me how to wave to a crowd for two hours without your arm falling off. It's a real technique." Marlene demonstrated, also miming a fixed and glassy smile, through which she said, "I think dinner's ready."

So it was. They ate: meat-stuffed shells with sauce and cheese on top, salad with roasted peppers, and a bottle of reasonable do-mestic red. Lucy nodded off at the table. They stashed her in bed and moved to the living room, and sat on the tatty couch and finished their bottle.

"Well, this is indeed very similar to real life," observed Mar-lene, sighing contentedly. They sat in their old companionability, speaking of the day's events. Marlene mentioned her call from Luisa, Karp talked about the film and his meeting with Crane. Suddenly he broke off and looked directly at her, his gaze intense.

"All right. Now that you got me drunk I'm going to make a confession," he said. "It was a serious mistake coming here, taking this job. You were right and I was wrong. It's totally fucked. Crane is going to be out on his ass in a fairly short time and then I don't know what I'm going to do. I screwed up and I screwed you up and I'm sorry."

Marlene, who would have given anything to hear this a couple of months ago, found herself curiously unaffected, and certainly nowhere near a disposition to gloat. She snuggled closer to her husband and said, "Well, it could be worse. Maybe we both needed a break from the DA, and this is better than a stretch in a mental hospital." Laughing. "Marginally better, anyway. You think the investigation is *totally* fucked?"

"I don't know. I think there'll be a narrow window for doing decent work between now and when whoever comes after Crane clamps down. Something could break."

"You don't think *you'll* get the slot if Crane goes?"

Karp considered this for a moment in silence, thinking about Harrison's offer. "I might get it offered but I don't know if I'd take it. I think it'd come with too many strings. It's a political job, and I probably wouldn't be much good working the politics of it, not even as good as Bert, which as we now know isn't good enough. I mean, what I am is a prosecutor. That's all I really know how to do."

"Well they definitely have the right film," said Bishop over the phone. *"And one of their investigators is headed for Miami to see Veroa."*

The thin man turned the sound down on the movie he was watching on television and repositioned the handset against his ear. "Do we need to do something about Veroa?"

"No, Veroa's solid. I doubt he'll identify me with what we have hanging over him, and he doesn't know the rest of it at all."

"Others do."

"Yes. Although I'd say there are no more than two who could be damaging enough in the short run to require extreme intervention," agreed Bishop.

"So you want me to . . ."

"No. Not yet. Let's see what emerges."

"You're cutting it close. If they find out about P—"

"Shut up! For God's sake, man, this is an unsecured line. And yes, close is how I like to cut it. As you should know."

ELEVEN

Karp stood in front of the counsel's table and looked down at the witness. Behind and above Karp sat Flores and four other members of the subcommittee, barricaded by their high dais. From his chair at the first witness table Paul A. David projected an air of irritable boredom. The bony face with the heavily ringed eyes told all who watched that a hardworking public servant was being subjected to unwarranted abuse.

Karp almost believed it himself. The guy was good, you had to give him that. Karp had ducked a million lies from culprits of various types in his career, but he could not recall a more bland and skillful liar than Mr. David. David was sticking to the same story he had given the Warren people. A man identifying himself as Lee Harvey Oswald had arrived in Mexico City on September 27, 1963. Thereafter, he had gone to the Cuban embassy and asked about a transit visa to Cuba, when told he had to go to the Soviet embassy for clearance, he went there too. The CIA had photo surveillance of both places and telephone taps and wall bugs as well. Oswald's voice, asking about applying for a visa to visit the Soviet Union through Cuba, had supposedly been recorded on tape, and the tape shipped to CIA headquarters.

"And what happened to this tape, Mr. David?" Karp asked.

"As I've said many times before, since we had no idea Oswald would become important later, the tapes were routinely destroyed by recycling, approximately a week after they were made."

"That would be early October? Assuming, of course, that the call was made on or about October 1, 1963. Yes? Good. Now let's turn to the photographic evidence. It's clear that the photo forwarded as being Oswald bears no resemblance to Oswald. Why was that?"

"It was a mix-up," said David in a tired voice. "Our cameras had malfunctioned."

"All the cameras at both Communist embassies broke down just as Oswald walks in? In all the time he was in Mexico City flitting back and forth among the embassies, you don't have a single clear picture of him?"

"Yes. As I said, we couldn't know he was going to be important."

"So, no pictures, but you did have a tape of his voice. That's how we know he was in Mexico, right?"

"Yes, that and identification by people working in the Cuban embassy."

"Yes," said Karp, "all those identifications. Well, obviously someone went to Mexico City and asked about those visas, and got his voice recorded. Mr. David, are you aware that shortly after the assassination, and a full month after you have testified that this tape was destroyed, the FBI listened to that tape and concluded that it was not the voice of Lee Harvey Oswald?"

You had to give him credit. He didn't blink. "I'm not aware of that," he said.

"So the tapes were in fact not destroyed."

"They were destroyed."

"Not according to J. Edgar Hoover," said Karp, brandishing a photocopy of the FBI memo. It was entered into evidence and David was given a chance to study it.

"So," Karp continued, "if the tapes were routinely destroyed as you claim, Mr. David, how do you explain the FBI listening to them a month afterward?"

"I can't explain it," said David.

"Does the CIA have a copy of this tape still in its possession?"

"Not to my knowledge."

"Then who, if you know, ordered this evidence destroyed, *after* Lee Harvey Oswald became a suspect in the murder of President Kennedy?"

"I can't answer that," said David.

"What does that mean?" asked Karp sharply. "You haven't the knowledge or you refuse to share it with the committee?"

Then occurred the oddest thing that had ever happened to Karp in the course of questioning witnesses. David said, "I don't care to answer any more questions." Then he rose, turned, and walked out of the room.

Karp gaped, his brain frozen. He thought inanely of calling out to David to stop, and checked himself, thus avoiding seeming even more of a fool than he now felt himself to be. Flushing pink, he looked frantically up at the dais. There was no help there. Flores was conferring with Representative Morgan. The other members seemed bemused, including Dobbs, who was staring vacantly at the door closing behind David.

"Mr. Chairman," said Karp at last, "I think we have cause for a contempt citation here."

A frown and a significant pause. "The subcommittee will take this under advisement. Call the next witness."

Who was an official of the FBI; as it turned out, he didn't know where the tape was either.

When the hearings at last adjourned, Karp returned to the Fourth Street building in a foul mood, bit the heads off two junior staff who approached him with minor problems, and retired to his office, seething. Crane was not in. Sondergard was closeted with a trio of suits from the comptroller general. V.T. was with the photo analysts.

Karp tried to get interested in a report about nuclear magnetic resonance as a technique for comparing bullet fragments and found himself reading the same paragraph for the third time.

He was not, it appeared, interested in nuclear magnetic resonance. What he was interested in was Paul Ashton David. The man's face swam into his mind's eye, its calm assurance irritating even in memory. And something else about it, something he couldn't pin down. A face from the past?

He shook these maunderings away and refocused on how to nail David's slick CIA ass to the wall. On this too he was drawing a blank. The problem was secrecy. If the CIA was allowed to be the sole judge of what could be revealed and what could remain hidden for reasons of national security, then the committee might as well hang it up. Karp was willing to bring it to the test of a

subpoena, and he thought that Crane would back him on it. The CIA people might claim that their oath of secrecy took precedence over the obligations under a testamentary oath. Fine—they would jail David on contempt charges, and then get the next guy in line and jail him, and so on. Obviously it would be subject to judicial clarification, maybe even a Supreme Court case. Karp started to feel better. He got out a pad and began making notes for a succulent piece of legal research.

The phone interrupted him.

"Butch? Clay here. I'm at National, just got in. Where do you want me to bring Veroa?"

"He's with you? How is he?"

"He's fine. Doesn't say much. Didn't give me any trouble about coming up either. Kind of a mild chubby little guy, an accountant. Doesn't strike me as much of a terrorist leader. You sure we got the right guy?"

"What did you expect, a slouch hat, flaming eyes, a beard, and one of those round bombs with a smoking fuse? Believe me, he's no sweetheart. I tell you what—stick him in the TraveLodge down the street—no, why don't you bring him over to the office. I want him to watch our movie."

They arrived forty minutes later. Veroa did indeed look like an accountant: tall for a Cuban, about five-nine, mustached, with thick black-rimmed glasses and a soft-looking pear-shaped body. Karp went into the file room, and from a locked file in a drawer labeled Administration Forms withdrew the spool of film. He called Charlie Ziller in to run the machine. Fulton, Karp, and Veroa grouped themselves in front of the screen while Ziller cranked the film up to the point marked by the little paper slip. The screen lit up on the road through the swamp.

"This is you, right, Mr. Veroa?" asked Karp when the right frames came by. "Freeze it right here, Charlie."

Veroa peered at the dim scene of the men around the jeep. "Yes, that is me. Younger, of course."

"Could you identify the other men for us?"

"Some, I think." He placed his finger on a squat, pop-eyed man standing near the jeep. "This is Angelo Guel. And here is Gary Becker." He rattled off some more Cuban names. He had forgotten who the driver was. Fulton wrote down the names in a notebook, also marking down the frames they appeared in.

"Who's the tall guy with his face moving away from the camera?" Karp asked. "Near the front wheel."

"That is Maurice Bishop."

"It is, huh? Are you sure?"

"Oh, yes. He was in charge of the whole operation. I knew him quite well."

"Good, okay roll it slow until I tell you to stop. A little more, more, stop! Do you recognize this man?" Karp pointed.

"It looks like Lee Oswald, but it is dark. I can't be sure."

"You never met him at these exercises?"

Veroa shrugged. "No, but there were many hundred men, and many exercises. He was not active, if he was there at all. I did actually meet him once, though."

"You did? When?"

"In September of sixty-three. I went to meet with Bishop at a hotel in Dallas, and Oswald was with him."

There was silence in the little room while they all digested that. "Let's, uh, move on, Charlie. Okay, Mr. Veroa, here's a scene in broad daylight. Let's see what you make of this."

The man in the black shirt and ball cap appeared.

"Oswald again, right?" Karp asked.

Veroa shook his head. "No, I know who that is. That is Bill Caballo."

"A Cuban?"

"No, not Cuban. But he spoke Spanish, I think with a Central American accent. An American. Bishop gave him to us, for weapons training. He was an expert with small arms, and an armorer." They were all staring at him. Veroa glanced back at the screen. "He resembles Oswald, certainly, especially in the shape of the face and the coloring. But Caballo was thinner. He had many . . . what? *Pecas*—freckles on his arms and his hands. Also, he was shorter than me, and Oswald was perhaps a little taller than me."

"But it might have been possible to confuse one with the other, huh? If you had never seen both of them together?"

A slight nod. "Yes, in that case, perhaps. I knew Caballo more than I knew Oswald. I met Oswald only that one time, with Bishop. Really, I didn't even remember that he was on this exercise, on this film. So *I* would not have confused them."

They watched the film a few times more, with Veroa filling in as many details as he remembered on the recognizable people

shown in it. Then they grilled him for some additional hours about his long association with the man he knew as Maurice Bishop: the initial contact while Veroa was still in Cuba, the conversion of an unassuming but patriotic Cuban accountant into an underground agent, the failed assassination attempt against Castro, the escape from Cuba, the foundation of Brigada 61, the raids, the additional attempt on Castro's life in Chile, in 1971. Bishop had been closely involved as a planner and financier throughout his clandestine career, purportedly as the representative of "anticommunist businessmen." The CIA had never been mentioned.

"And are you still in contact with Bishop?" Karp asked. Veroa confirmed that this, at least, was too much to hope for.

"No, in 1971, after the Chilean thing failed, we . . . no longer trusted each other too much," said Veroa. It seemed to sadden him.

"How did that happen?"

"I had set up an organization in Caracas to run the operation. We had, the Cuban resistance, I mean, many assets in Venezuela, in the police and so forth. And we had a good deal of money too. The plan was that after Castro was killed in Valparaiso, the Chilean army would arrest the two assassins and allow them to escape. But the assassins didn't trust that plan; they thought they would be killed instead." He paused. "Actually, it was because of Caballo."

"Caballo? The man in the film?"

"Yes, he was in charge of the escape, in Chile. The assassins, they didn't trust him, so they arranged their own getaway plan. Which they kept secret from me. But somehow this other plan was betrayed to the DGI—"

"That's the Cuban counterintelligence agency," said Ziller.

"Yes, and then the assassins refused to go through with it."

"Who betrayed the new plan, do you have any idea?"

Veroa shrugged. "It was—how can I say—a cloudy situation. The Cubans on both sides, the Venezuelans, the Chileans, all penetrating one another, and the CIA penetrating them all. I have heard, although I cannot vouch for the report, that it was Caballo himself who sold them to the DGI, and then let it be known to them that they were sold."

"Why would he do that? Why should he care how they escaped? Didn't he want Castro killed?"

Veroa shrugged again. "Fidel is still alive, yes? And many other people are dead."

Karp glanced at Fulton and Ziller, who both looked blank. "Mr. Veroa . . . ah . . . help me out here. I'm not sure I understand what you're saying. Are you trying to tell us that all these plots against Castro that you were involved in were in some way phony? That the CIA guys you were working with, Bishop and Caballo and the others, were running some other kind of game?"

Veroa spread his hands in a gesture of helplessness and shook his head slowly from side to side. "It would be hard for me to believe that. Bishop I worked with closely for over ten years. He made it possible for us, for the Brigada, to do much damage to the Fidelistas. On the other hand . . . there were times when he did things that I did not comprehend."

"Like what?"

"Oh, once we were asked to deliver a briefcase to a couple of men sitting in a bar in Caracas. As our man left the meeting he heard them talking in a language he did not know. Later we learned that these were both Russian agents. Another time we were on a raid at night on the Cuban coast. We were involved in a firefight with the militia. Many of our people were wounded and several were killed, but we drove them off. We destroyed a power plant and left. Later, back in Miami, I heard rumors that another Cuban anticommunist group had been in a raid that same night on the same part of the coast, and had been badly hurt. I thought it was possible that these were the people we had fought. When I asked Bishop about it, he laughed and told me not to worry. He said that all this was coordinated at a level above him and they would not make such a stupid mistake."

"Did he ever identify this level above him?" Karp asked.

"No. We never talked about it."

"And you never worked with any other CIA contact?"

Veroa looked at Karp quizzically. "No, and I am not entirely sure that Bishop was a CIA contact. He certainly never said so. He always presented himself as an agent of private business interests."

"What about Caballo? The same?"

Veroa shrugged dismissively. "Caballo I always thought was Bishop's dog. He was a man with no conversation, a blank, a technician. Bishop was very different, a man of a certain quality, a

thinker. But he was certainly getting orders from someplace, you understand. We knew this because often, when we had planned an action, he would say he needed a go-ahead. Then there would be a delay, and we would either do it or not."

"Do you still have contact with him, with Bishop?"

A shake of the head, and Veroa answered in a slow, reflective voice, like that of a wife abandoned for no reason. "No. He began to distance himself from us, from me personally, after the failure in Chile. He contacted me in the summer of 1973. We met in Hialeah, at the racetrack parking lot. He told me that the people he worked for no longer wished him to continue his relationship with me. He was sorry but this is the way it had to be. Then he handed me a briefcase and drove off."

"What was in the briefcase?"

"About a quarter of a million dollars," said Veroa.

Twenty minutes later, Karp and Ziller were still talking in the file room, by the light of the small blank screen, when V.T. Newbury strode in, his cheeks bright pink from the brisk outdoors. He held up a thick manila envelope.

"Our stills. Want to take a look?"

V.T. spread two dozen or so eight-by-ten glossies across a table. Consulting the notes Ziller had made during the recent viewing of the film, they were able to put names to most of the portraits. V.T. examined the picture of Bill Caballo with interest and they filled him in on what Veroa had said.

"So it's not Oswald after all," said V.T. "Fascinating! So now we have a guy who looks like Oswald, who's an operative with the anti-Castro movement, connected to the infamous Bishop, and is apparently an expert shot. My stomach is tingling."

"Yeah, this is a break," agreed Ziller. "I'll tell you one thing I'd like to do with these pictures. Take them out to Miami and let Sylvia Odio look at them. It'd be interesting as hell if she was able to identify the guys who showed up at her place as one of them." He looked at Karp as he said this, expecting some response, but Karp was staring fixedly at one of the photographs.

He said to V.T., "A couple of weeks ago, when we were talking about getting testimony from Paul David, you showed me a picture of him that they took when he appeared before Warren. Could you get that for me?"

V.T. went to the filing cabinet and brought back a folder. Karp pulled out a yellowed clipping and placed it beside the photograph Veroa had identified as Bishop.

"What do you think? David is Bishop, right?"

V.T. and Ziller studied the two portraits. "It's hard to say," said Ziller. "The one from the paper is a full face and the one from the film is a side view, and it's dark and blurry too."

"But I saw the guy in the flesh today," replied Karp. "It's the same guy. It has to be." He took the folder V.T. had given him, shuffled through it, and drew out a sheet of paper. "Look at his record," he continued, excitement starting to show in his voice. "David was a major player in the Bay of Pigs. He was a covert agent in Havana at the same time that Bishop contacted Veroa. He spent his whole career, practically, doing covert work in Latin America, *and*, of course, he was in charge in Mexico City when the fuckup about the tapes of Oswald's supposed visit happened."

"Yeah, the only thing missing is a link between David and this guy Caballo. If it turned out Paul Ashton David just happened to have a faithful Indian companion who just happened to look like Lee Harvey Oswald . . ."

He didn't need to finish the thought. They all rolled their eyes and made other gestures indicative of astonishment.

"I think this is what the poet meant by looking at each other with a wild surmise," said V.T. "This could be the road out of the swamp. It seems to me that the next steps are, one, getting Veroa close to David in the flesh to see if he'll make a positive ID of him as Bishop, and, two, putting the hounds out on Caballo."

"And three," added Karp, "getting that fucker back in front of the committee with a contempt citation ready if he tries the trick he pulled today. Charlie, why don't you get that started with Flores and his people, and get Clay to set up the ID run with Veroa."

When Ziller was gone, V.T. said, "Something else interesting in this Depuy material from Georgetown. Let's go into my office."

"This is the last notebook that concerns David Ferrie," said V.T., bringing out a tattered steno pad from the recesses of his desk. "Depuy interviewed him on February 12, 1967, about two weeks before he was found dead, apparently of a drug overdose. Ferrie was drunk or doped up—he usually was, toward the end—but Depuy wrote down everything he said, whether it made sense or not. Ferrie was complaining about being broke and abandoned

by all his friends. He says, 'I was supposed to get ten grand on that PXK thing. It wasn't my fault. I could've . . . what the hell, I could still get whatever I want out of those bastards.' Interesting sentence; what does it mean? In the margin Depuy wrote 'PXK? Check out.' He must have asked Ferrie right there, but Ferrie says, 'No, the time isn't right. I gotta think what to do.' Then he starts rambling again. A little later, Depuy must've brought up the subject again, because Ferrie says, 'I need to talk to Term on that first. Goddamn Term won't talk to me anymore, none of those PXK cocksuckers.' Then more drivel. Depuy's got a marginal note, 'Term who dat?' "

Karp thought for a moment, mentally shuffling through the hundreds of names associated with the case, concentrating on the New Orleans subdivision.

"Wasn't there a guy named Termine, a Marcello hood from New Orleans?"

"Yeah, actually Marcello's driver, Sam Termine," said V.T. "I thought of that too, but I doubt it's him. Depuy was a New Orleans police reporter and he would have checked that out, or asked Ferrie right there if he meant Sam. No, this is a new name: I'll start a folder on it."

"Okay, but why is this interesting, V.T.? The guy was obviously nuts. It could've been a business deal that went sour in 1958. PXK sounds like a company, like TRW or LTV."

"Yes, that's true," V.T. agreed. "On the other hand, Depuy obviously thought it was something to follow up on. One last thing. In Depuy's pocket diary there's a notation in mid-1967, way after Ferrie kicked off. It says, 'Term in N.O. 9-63' and there's a phone number. I had it checked out. In 1963 it was the number of Gary Becker's Anti-Communist League of the Caribbean. So there's a string of connections: Oswald with Bishop and Caballo and Veroa; Oswald and Becker; Oswald and Ferrie; and now Ferrie and Becker and whoever or whatever Term and PXK is."

Karp paced for a few moments, thinking. Then he shook his head irritably and said, "Yeah, but so what? It doesn't get us any further unless we get more on this PXK and Term. Have you got any ideas on how to do that? No? Plus, this Ferrie thing is a miasma—it sucks us down into Garrison territory: innuendo, he-said-I-heard, and all the rest of the conspiracy bullshit. It's just another pair of loose threads."

V.T. gave Karp an appraising look and replied in a sharper tone than he ordinarily used, "Yes, but at least they're new loose threads. You've been telling me all along that the minutiae of the assassination weren't going to advance the cause. So we're concentrating on Oswald and his merry friends, which now you're calling conspiracy bullshit. Fine! But if you don't mind, I'll keep pulling on whatever threads I turn up, in the hope that sooner or later something will unravel. I mean, what else can we do?"

Karp had no good answer, and almost as a punishment, spent the rest of the day buried in that minutiae. By four, the transient excitement occasioned by Veroa's story had quite faded.

Clay Fulton tapped on the doorframe and came in. "You look beat," he said. "You should be up behind this. I thought we just got a good break."

"Veroa? Yeah, the entrance to another set of blind alleys. Did you set up the ID on David yet?"

"Yeah. David's speaking at some national intelligence officers' association thing in a hotel out in the burbs day after tomorrow. I figure I'll drive Veroa out there and let him loose. Antonio should be right at home in an old spies' convention. Anything else happen today?"

"The usual. Crane is still talking to that damn caucus, so God knows what's going to happen. Bea's still getting grilled by the bureaucrats. Everybody else is tracing witnesses or farting around with experts. Speaking of which, one of the kids went out to Aberdeen and found a film archive of people getting shot. No, seriously! Apparently the army collected films from the Nazis or wherever, showing people getting executed, mostly with head shots. Wound research. We're having a showing tomorrow."

"Great!" said Fulton after a heavy sigh. "All right if I bring the kids?"

"No problem. There's a pool on how many times we'll see an actual human being getting shot in the head and flinging himself toward the gun like Kennedy did on Zapruder. All the shots came from the rear, says Warren, but after the guy's head explodes he goes flinging backward."

"The old grassy knoll."

"Right. Old grassy knoll's got me. How was Miami?"

"Warm, with a chance of Cubans." Fulton snapped his fingers. "Oh, yeah! Speaking of Miami: I found our mobster."

"Which mobster?"

"Mosca, Guido. Jerry Legs. The Castro thing . . . ?"

"Oh, right! God, this is really important now. The Mob . . ."

"They were in on it you mean?"

"No, but did you ever see the film from the first press conference? Henry Wade, the Dallas DA, held it the day after the assassination. No? Interesting. He made two factual errors, one about Oswald's middle name and the other about the name of his phony Cuba committee. In both cases he was accurately corrected by a man standing in the rear of the room. It was Jack Ruby, the guy who never met Oswald, but somehow knew the exact name of an obscure organization Oswald was running. Yeah, I'd like to talk to Mosca about that. So . . . he's down in Miami? I thought he was a New Orleans boy."

"Was. He was with the Marcello organization back in the sixties, like we heard, then I think he must've got traded to Miami, for an aging left-hander and two utility outfielders. Worked for Trafficante and then ended up with the Buonafacci organization in South Florida. He still keeps his hand in a little but he's mostly retired now—he must be pushing seventy."

"You saw him?"

"Yeah, he's got a nice little place in Surfside, on the bay. Friendly guy, as a matter of fact. He made me some ice tea."

"What'd he tell you?"

"Not one fucking thing. He was very apologetic. So, unfortunately, unless he's been raping babies and we catch him at it, and put on the squeeze, the guy's a clam. Another dead end."

"Maybe not," said Karp.

"How so?"

"Mmm . . . it's a long shot, but when you said rape I thought of something I just heard about. Ray Guma may be in a position to do Tony Buonafacci a big favor. I think Mosca will talk to us if Tony Bones tells him to, don't you?"

"I feel like I'm back in college," said Maggie Dobbs happily. She was perched on a chair in front of her dressing table, a pile of blouses on her lap, watching pale bubbles rise in a flute of straw-colored wine. "Why is that?"

From her comfortable position on Maggie's bed, Marlene put down her own wineglass, now empty, stretched luxuriously, and answered, "Oh, I don't know. No kids whining. We're talking about men in a bedroom with clothes scattered all around. We're drunk. Feels collegiate to me."

She had known girls like Maggie at Smith, pale, arty creatures, inevitably engaged to embryo stock-and-bond men from Amherst, cashmere-sweatered, plaid-skirted, circle-pinned, who dashed blondly through the campus walks like flights of pallid doves. In the usual cliquishness of college life, she had not had a great deal to say to these creatures. Marlene wore black under army surplus, smoked a lot, scowled, talked dirty, and hung out with U Mass boys, or even (shudder) townies from Northampton.

That was, however, long ago, and the two women had both experienced an odd attraction to each other, as if catching up on some missed experience. Since meeting her at the big-shot party, Marlene had shamelessly parasited herself into Maggie's elegant and well-ordered life. Lucy was installed in a tony play group, hobnobbing with the Ashleys and Jennifers of McLean, under the eyes of perfect mommies or French nannies.

"No hitting," Marlene had said before dropping Lucy off. "You queer this deal and you'll go three rounds with me."

"But, Mommy," Lucy had complained, "what if they're mean?"

"They won't be mean. These are high-class kids; they already know how to kill with a look. In any case, if you have to slug somebody, body-punch. I absolutely don't want blood on the walls. *Capisc'*?"

Now the two women were lounging in Maggie's boudoir (and it *was* a boudoir, done in jonquil frillies) with a cold bottle of a nice Moselle nearly down the hatch, and a long afternoon of nothing much ahead.

"Are husbands the same as men?" Maggie asked musingly.

"Well, unlike in school," Marlene said, "the mystery is gone. It's like Christmas. You're in a delicious agony wondering what you're going to get, and then you tear the paper off and there it is—just what you always wanted. Or, not, as the case may be. Whatever, the thing is, the fascination after that is learning how to play with it. Or him. A different kind of agony, if you're into it.

Which, as it turns out, I am. How about you? Where did you hook up with old Hank?"

"Oh, we met at a freshman mixer. I was at Connecticut and he was at Yale. We got engaged my junior year. Ho-hum. How about you?"

"Oh, Karp? We worked together in the old homicide bureau. No sparks or anything. Then we were at this party and he got plastered and I had to drag him home. I crashed on his bed. The next morning I was taking a shower, and he came stumbling in, hung over, and there and then, to the surprise of both of us, we fell on each other like animals and fucked our brains out. The rest is history."

"Oh, see, that's what I mean!" cried Maggie. "Nothing like that ever happens to me."

"Like what?"

"Oh, the unexpected. The dramatic. The exciting."

"Well, as to that, it's not all it's cracked up to be, the so-called exciting life. A lot of it is pissing in your panties. And besides, my life, ninety percent of it, is just like yours. Shopping, cleaning, taking care of the kid, working." She paused and looked at Maggie. "If you're bored you could get a job."

"Oh, right, that's what *he* always says. It's not being bored. Besides, I had a job, until Jeremy came. It's more like—I don't know—my life is in a, like a railroad siding, just waiting for an engine to pull me along the track again. And Hank is like some kind of express train roaring along the other track getting farther and farther away." She reached for the bottle and refilled her glass.

"What did you do, when you worked?" asked Marlene.

"Oh, some job in O'Neill's office. Hank got it for me, of course. Just, basically, your D.C. job: sitting around answering phones with other wife-ofs and the little hard chargers starting their Hill careers. Then when I quit, it was supposedly to start working on the files, getting the book ready, but I haven't honestly had the energy. And Hank hasn't said anything, but when I try to talk to him about the way I feel, he gives me this look, like I'm letting down the team."

"But you're still basically okay. You and him."

"Oh, like do we love each other. Oh, yeah." She twirled a lock of her shining hair, looked toward the heavens, and laughed. "Still madly in love!"

"What with? What do you like about him besides that he thinks you're letting down the team?"

"Oh, see, I didn't really mean that," explained Maggie in a nervous rush. "Actually, he's wonderful. The minute he looked at me, I went all squooshy."

"What was it? Body?"

"No, although that was all right—he was on the crew at Yale. No, it was something about his head, or his face. A look. You know, it was sort of intelligent, but not smart-alecky, and noble, and with depth. Like he was injured somewhere inside and hiding the wound. You know what he reminded me of? That central figure in Picasso's *Saltimbanques*, the one in profile?"

"Yeah, I know what you mean. It's one of my favorite paintings," said Marlene, thinking that guys who had that look probably got unbelievable amounts of pussy off little blond art lovers. Or Italian tough girls. Karp, of course, had it too.

"Oh, mine too!" said Maggie, delighted. "It's in the National. We have to go see it."

"Yes, two aging housewives standing rapt in front of a seventy-year-old painting, our knees trembling, our undies slowing getting damp . . ."

"Oh, stop it!" Maggie shrieked, and threw a blouse at Marlene.

Marlene caught it and glanced at the label. "Mmm . . . nice silk. From Bloomie's." She sat up and held the sleeves wide, framing Maggie's face over it. "It's not your color, really. What do you wear it with?"

"Nothing!" Maggie wailed. "I never wear it. I have cubic yards of clothes and I never have anything to wear."

"Drag 'em out," said Marlene, focusing her attention. "Let's see what we got."

An hour or so later, the two women stood looking at a gaudy pile of fabric three feet high, stacked on the bedroom floor.

"God, this is so embarrassing!" said Maggie with feeling. "I feel like such a jerk."

"I still don't understand it, really," said Marlene. "You know you can't wear all these saturated colors and wild prints with your coloring. And besides"—she lifted up a scarlet brocade jacket and a chrome yellow skirt—"none of this stuff makes outfits. Why on earth did you buy it all?"

"I don't know. I go into a store to shop and something hap-

pens—I become a zombie. I feel this pressure crushing down on me, and I guess I just buy the flashiest thing in sight and dash out. Or else, maybe I desperately want to be someone who can wear an acid green pantsuit."

"Well, at least you'll make Goodwill happy. I bet a lot of their customers *can* wear this stuff." Marlene held a red-white-and-blue bulky-knit sweater up to her chest, struck a Foreign Legion salute, and started to hum the "Marseillaise."

"Oh, stop!" laughed Maggie. "Actually, that'd look great on you. Why don't you pick out what you want and take it?"

Marlene dropped the sweater and gave Maggie a sharp glance.

Maggie blushed rosily and put her hand to her mouth. "Oh, God, I didn't mean . . ."

"No, I appreciate it, but the funny thing is I really have lots of clothes. I just didn't bring them with me into exile." She quickly related the story of her hasty departure from New York, leaving out the shameful proximate cause.

This, of course, was exactly what Maggie wanted to know. It struck her as astounding that someone with Marlene's extraordinary life, and moreover, one with impeccable *Waffen*-feminist credentials ("You ran a *rape bureau?*"), would dump it to go be a wife-of in Washington. She probed uncomfortably close to the real reason, and rather than snapping out that it was none of her business and perhaps adding that they were *not* actually schoolgirls pouring out their little hearts, Marlene changed the subject.

"What was that all about, what you said a minute ago—about files and a book?"

"Oh, that!" Maggie seemed to slump. A tiny, worried indentation appeared beneath the glossy bangs. "You don't want to hear it."

"Yeah, I do. It's something to do with your husband?"

"Oh, all right," Maggie sighed resignedly. "My husband, prince that he is, whom I love dearly, has this little obsession. I assume you're familiar with the Dobbs case?"

"No, what case?"

"See? Everybody in the known universe has forgotten about it but Hank Dobbs. Oh, yeah, and, of course the Widow Dobbs. Hank thinks it's on everybody's mind as soon as they meet him. Of course, he's been elected to Congress three times and nobody's so much as mentioned it, but there it is."

"What'd Hank do, anyway?"

"Hank? Nothing. This is about his father, Richard. Ewing. Dobbs." She said the name portentously, like a butler announcing a belted earl. She was fairly wasted by now, sitting tailor-fashion at the foot of the bed, with the second bottle of wine tucked in the cavity of her crossed legs. They had dispensed with glasses by this time. Maggie continued in the same exaggerated "Masterpiece Theatre" diction.

"Mr. Dobbs, as I never stop getting told by my husband, and the Widow, and all my in-laws, was . . . a prince. A perfect prince. Brilliant? *Of course.* Yale blah-blah, Harvard blah-blah. Brave? *Of course!* Decorated for bravery in the Pacific, Navy Cross blah-blah. Every little boy's dream of a daddy? *Of course!* Riding fishing boating skating baseball blah-blah-blah. I am not privy to the secrets of the marriage bed, but I have no reason to believe he would not have won the Distinguished Service Medal there too.

"Okay," she adopted a more normal tone, "after the war, Richard and Selma Hewlett Dobbs, that's the Widow, and little Hankie, go to Washington, to make a career. Richard gets a job with naval intelligence. Very important, hush-hush work. He rises, he has a brilliant career ahead of him—secretary of the navy, probably, and who knows? The sky's the limit. The family's wealthy and well connected in Connecticut politics, not the Kennedys quite, but in the same general zone. Richard, of course, knew Kennedy, knew him quite well, and didn't think all that much of him. According to report."

"Did you ever meet him? Richard, I mean," Marlene interrupted.

"Yes, a couple of times. He died in sixty-three. Right before Kennedy. Of course, by then he was totally destroyed by what happened. I remember a shy man with tinted glasses, who didn't say much. A sad, sad man, around whom everyone walked on eggs. Excruciatingly careful not to disturb him through word or deed."

"You know, now that you remind me, the name does ring a faint bell. Wasn't he involved in the Joe McCarthy business—some kind of communist accusation?"

"Oh, it was far, far more than an accusation, my dear. Richard Ewing Dobbs was tried for and nearly convicted of treason black as night."

"My God! This was what, during Korea?"

"Yes, indeed, and they'd just fried the Rosenbergs. It was a capital case. But what happened was that Harley Blaine stepped in and saved the day." Seeing Marlene's uncomprehending look, she added, "The lawyer. From Texas?"

The name stirred vaguely in Marlene's memory. One of the great defense lawyers of an earlier decade. She asked, "He was the defense."

"Yes, but there's more to it than that. Harley and Richard were biddies. Buddies. God, I have to lay off this wine. The kids will be back any minute. Well, they were friends from college. Went to Yale and then Harvard together and they were in the navy together. Started in Washington about the same time too. Anyway, what you have to understand is, when the thing happened to Richard, he became a pariah. That was how it was in the fifties. People he'd known for years cut him dead on the street. People wouldn't let their kids play with Hank anymore. Like that. Except for Harley. And apparently John Kennedy. Harley quit his government job in the Pentagon and took up Richard's defense. Kennedy didn't do that, but at least he didn't go out of his way to shun him. That was important."

"What had he done? I mean, why did they accuse him?"

"Well, that was the strange thing about it. Basically, the FBI had caught an employee of the Soviet embassy, a guy named Viktor Reltzin. Reltzin was an actual spy, no question about it. They caught him with top-secret technical data on the nuclear submarine–building program, which was getting started then. Reltzin claimed that he was just a courier. The way they worked it was, on a specific day each week, Reltzin would go out to Arlington Cemetery and check out a particular grave marker. There'd be a special arrangement of flags and flowers on the grave and that'd tell Reltzin where to pick up the secret stuff, a wastebasket or a hollow tree, whatever. And Reltzin would use the same method to communicate with his contact. 'Dead-drops' is the term, I think. You sure you don't remember this? It was a big scandal—using the graves of American heroes to commit treason and all. No? Well, believe me it was a big thing at the time. We have the clippings. Anyway, they put the screws on Reltzin and he gave them the name of his contact, who was a low-level Navy Department clerk named Jerome Weinberg. So the FBI set a trap. . . . My God! Look at the time! The play group will be over by now."

"Uh-oh—don't tell me we have to drive over there and pick them up?"

"No," said Maggie, with a silly grin. "The Winstons have a driver. A *drive-ah*. Claude. Claude will deliver our little dears in the Caddy. Let's go downstairs so we can greet their smiling faces at the door. Or their shrieking faces, as the case may be."

The two women walked unsteadily down the stairway and into the kitchen, a big cheery, light-filled room with built-in everything of the latest design, and divided by a long butcher-block counter. Maggie got coffee and hot chocolate efficiently started. Marlene was mildly surprised that Maggie could still function. Functionality while stoned was apparently a quality required in the wife-of business.

"So what happened then?" Marlene asked. "With Reltzin and what's his name? Weinstein."

"Weinberg. Oh, they nailed him delivering a package at Arlington. He cracked right away and said that he got the secrets from Richard Dobbs. That was it. They came and arrested him the day before Thanksgiving, 1952. No bail, of course. He was in jail for nineteen months while the trial went on. But Harley got him off in the end."

"How did he do that?"

"Well, all the government had was Weinberg's say-so, that and Richard's fingerprints on the documents. But they were his documents to begin with, so that didn't mean much. Then there was some secret stuff that I'm not really clear on. Harley Blaine found out that the CIA had this Russian defector, and that the defector claimed that Richard was innocent, that Weinberg had made the whole thing up to cover himself, to play that he was just the delivery boy. 'Agent Z' they called him, the defector. Very cloak-and-dagger. So the CIA said they couldn't let the agent testify because of national security, and Harley said he was going to subpoena him anyway, and they went eyeball to eyeball on it and the CIA said no go and that was it. The judge threw out the case. But that didn't help Richard much. He was 'accused traitor Richard Ewing Dobbs' for the rest of his life."

"That's some story," said Marlene. "So what does Hank want you to do with it after all this time? You said a book. . . ."

"Yes, the book. He's collected boxes of stuff over the years. The trial transcripts, clippings, papers written about the case. It

was quite a thing for a while among the liberals. Richard was what I think they called prematurely coexistent. He was opposed to the nuclear sub program. He thought it was a provocation, especially if the subs were going to have nukes in them. He thought it probably wasn't a good idea to have a navy captain who might be cut off from communications with the outside be responsible for pushing a button that might blow up the world. Richard didn't think much of most navy captains. There was a lot of talk about a dark conspiracy. Dreyfus Two."

"You're saying somebody set him up?"

Maggie shrugged. "What do I know? It's the family myth, anyway. Rickover and the hard-line cold warriors did him in. That's what the book's supposed to be about, but"—she shrugged again, helplessly—"I've made a start, an index of the material we have, and I've made a trip or two to archives, but Christ, Marlene, I did some research in college, but this needs a pro, a lawyer preferably, or a real investigative reporter."

"Why doesn't he hire one?"

"Control. He wants to keep total control. And *I* am apparently the only person he considers under total control, lucky me." She let out a bitter laugh. "Maybe when the kids are grown, if I still have a brain in my head . . ."

"Or . . . ," said Marlene tentatively.

"Or what?"

"Well, my dear, not to blow my own horn, but beneath these colorful rags is a fairly hotshot criminal investigator. I could maybe take a look at your stuff—at least get you started."

Maggie's eyes went wide. "Oh, God, would you *really*? Oh, but Hank might, I don't know . . ." She stopped in confusion.

"Object?" offered Marlene, raising an eyebrow. "To a woman who made a total ass of herself at his party delving into the intimate family secrets? Well, you don't have to tell him unless you want to."

Maggie was pacing back and forth behind the counter, conflicting emotions playing over her small features. Finally, she whirled, jutted her sharp chin, brought her fist down on the counter, and said, "Yeah! Let's go for it!"

The women shook hands and laughed. Then a doubtful look appeared on Maggie's face. "But, Marlene, I mean you can't just do this, like, for nothing . . . your time . . ."

At that moment a heavy car door slammed and they heard shrill voices and the sound of footsteps on gravel. The back door flew open with a crash and the children dashed in, Laura dragging a sniveling Jeremy behind her. "Mommy!" she yelled. "Stupid Jeremy wet his pants!"

Marlene said, "Maggie, I tell you what. Just handle the three kids for half days. I'll take care of the investigation, and *I'll owe you.*"

The thin man stood at the Eastern Airlines counter at Miami International and passed a stack of cash over the counter. The clerk printed out his ticket, and said, "Did you want to make your return flight arrangements now, Mr. Early?"

"No, I don't know how long I'll be staying there."

The machine whirred and spat out the ticket, which was snapped into a folder and handed over with a smile. "Boarding in fifteen minutes, Mr. Early, and thank you for flying Eastern."

The thin man walked toward the gate. He was tired. Bishop had mobilized him early in the morning, after a night spent at jai alai and drinking in Cuban after-hours places, noisy, garishly decorated rooms lit like supermarkets. He had recognized several people, from the old days, but nobody had recognized him.

James Early was just one of the four aliases he was able to adopt with the various ID papers he had stashed in his soft nylon carry-on bag. He hadn't used Bill Caballo in a dozen or more years, although people who knew him from those days usually called him Bill. It had been longer than that since he had used the name his parents had given him at birth. Had anyone shouted that name out now, as he moved slowly toward the gate, he wouldn't have looked up, or indicated by the slightest movement that he recognized it. It was not training that enabled him to do this, but a peculiarity of mind, a vagueness of the sense of identity. The thin man was like a boat. It didn't matter what name you painted on the stern; the important thing was that it floated and went where you wanted to go.

The thin man passed his ticket to the stewardess at the mouth of the jetway, and boarded flight 54 to National Airport in Washington, D.C.

TWELVE

Flickering screen, grainy image, the whir of the projector on a rickety wooden desk, four men sitting around the desk on uncomfortable straight chairs, watching people die. Three Chinese men in gray pajamas kneel before a pit, three soldiers shoot them in the back of the head. They fall forward in unison. A machine gun mounted on the back of a truck shoots down a row of naked civilians of all ages and both sexes. Nazis in Poland. Old NKVD footage: a prisoner brought into a small room, is seated on a chair, as at a concert. Behind the prisoner's head, a little door like a dumbwaiter opens: a slight puff of pale smoke and the man falls forward. Various African executions next, obscure and degrading. One famous one: the Vietnamese colonel executing the prisoner with a pistol after the Tet attacks.

"Watch this one, it's the only nonexecution," said V.T.

Wartime, a trench filled with men dressed in motley uniforms, many sporting crossbelts, bandoliers, and odd black, tasseled hats. The men scramble out of the trench and one of them, on rising above the protection of the earth, is struck in the head by a bullet. His head jerks away from the shot, a cloud of dark material seems to rise from his skull like a departing soul, the tassel on his hat bounces up, obscenely playful, and he is flung backward into the trench.

For nearly twenty minutes they watched gunshot deaths representing nearly every one of the monstrous governments and antigovernments the century has produced in such profusion. Karp,

watching, wondered how the victims kept their apparent equanimity. None of them looked like they were going to the beach, but neither did they seem particularly concerned. One woman, standing in her underwear before the guns, smoothed the hair of her daughter, as if they were posing for a photograph. All the victims had but one thing in common: when the bullets struck them, they fell or jerked *away* from the shots, which was the point of the present show.

The film whipped out of the slot and chattered, the screen went white. V.T. clicked off the projector and switched on the lights. Karp and the two other men blinked and stretched. To break the silence, Karp said, "What, no cartoons?"

The laughter was brief and uncomfortable, and Karp was annoyed at himself for the flippancy. He looked around the room at the men. V.T. displayed his usual bland, contained exterior, although there were still those dark circles under his eyes that Karp did not recall from their years together in New York. Jim Phelps, the photo expert, appeared grim and suspicious, as he did when viewing any film that he had not personally examined with a hand lens. He tapped nervously on a pile of manila envelopes he had brought with him, as if anxious for his part of the session to begin. The fourth man, Dr. Casper Wendt, seemed most affected by the film. The coroner of a large midwestern city, Wendt was a vociferous member of the forensic pathology panel Karp had set up. Although he had seen any number of dead bodies in his practice, he was obviously less familiar with the actual process that rendered them so, although he was also one of the great students of all the Kennedy assassination amateur films. Wendt was thin and tall with glabrous blue eyes and a prim, reserved expression. Pale and distracted now, he absently polished his glasses on his tie.

Karp now addressed him. "So, Doc, what do you make of all this?"

Wendt carefully donned his glasses and said, "Very . . . I'm not sure 'interesting' is the correct word. No, informative, in a hideous way. These are armed forces archival films?"

"Yeah, from Aberdeen," said Karp. "There's a group out there that studies battle wounds. They have a lot more than the ones we just saw, but I thought these might give us the idea. I guess you noticed the main point in all these shootings."

"Quite," said Wendt. "It is obvious that we do not observe in

any of these events a movement in the direction from which the shot originated. Such a movement on the part of Kennedy has, of course, been noted by some observers in the Zapruder film. Nevertheless, I would hesitate to call these examples probative in the present case, as confirming that the backward movement of the president was the result of a shot from in front."

"What do you mean?" asked Karp, surprised.

"I mean only that because the actual autopsy was so badly botched, we cannot re-create the possible neuromuscular sequelae of any of the shots that struck the president. Thus we cannot absolutely exclude the possibility that the observed motion was, in fact, the result of a shot from the rear. The various theories that have been put forward, that, for example, the pressure built up by the shock of the bullet, when expelled from the front of the skull, acted as a jet, propelling the body backward, or that some odd neurological event occurred that caused the muscles of the back to contract, with the same result, can therefore not be entirely contradicted. I personally think such sequelae are unlikely, highly unlikely, but they cannot be scientifically ruled out without extensive further experimentation."

Wendt always talked like this, as if he were reading from a double-columned, small-print forensic pathology text. Karp tried to conceal his frustration, asking calmly, "What sort of experimentation? I thought the Warren Commission already did that."

"They shot a goat, with inconclusive results," said Wendt, not disguising his contempt. "Essentially, they were hoping to demonstrate that a bullet such as Warren exhibit 399, the famous magic bullet, could penetrate layers of bone and tissue and emerge as relatively unaffected as 399 was, which, if one believes the single-bullet theory, went through the president's back, emerged through his neck, went through Governor Connally's body, shattering a rib, exited his body, went through his wrist, producing a comminuted fracture of the radius, and penetrated his thigh. In this they were entirely unsuccessful, as, in my opinion, anyone is bound to be. You cannot make such wounds and end up with a bullet that looks like that."

"Yeah, right, but we're not talking about the magic bullet now. We know the magic bullet is garbage, not so much because it couldn't do the things you said, or because the shot trajectories are doubtful, but because we have no damn idea what the bullet

really is. All we know about it for sure is that it was fired from Oswald's rifle. It was found on a stretcher at Parkland? What stretcher? Who found it? Who handled it? If it was pulled from Connally's body and popped into an evidence bag in the operating room, then fine, we'd have to deal with it seriously, but since it wasn't—well, I wasn't brought up to consider crap like that real evidence."

Wendt seemed taken aback at this, since he had devoted years to criticizing the magic bullet's anomalously pristine appearance. Karp continued, "No, what we're about today is the shot or shots that *killed* Kennedy, the head shots. Specifically, what're the possibilities of a head shot from the front?"

Wendt pursed his lips, as if loath to let a speculative remark pass through them. "As to that, I would allow the possibility of an explosive or fragmenting bullet arriving from that direction, simultaneously, or nearly simultaneously, with the shot from the rear. But since we do not have the brain correctly preserved in formalin, nor any sections that might have been made from the brain, we can never arrive at a definitive conclusion on this point."

"But you do have *something* to work with," Karp pressed. "I mean we *do* have an autopsy panel under way."

Karp had been hearing odd things from the autopsy panel. Murray Selig had been uncharacteristically oblique on the few occasions that Karp had reached him by phone, and so he had invited Wendt, the maverick, and famous for his critique of the Warren procedures, for an informal consultation to try and get some straight answers. Which, in the event, he was finding hard to extract.

A smile suggested itself on Wendt's thin lips. "Yes, assuredly, but an autopsy panel without a corpse to work on is more of a debating society than a panel of scientists. Essentially, we are limited to perusing secondhand evidence and with photographic material only, the Parkland and the autopsy photos and X rays. I have suggested, without much success, a program of—"

"The photos are faked," said Phelps, loudly and confidently. "So are the skull X rays."

He had their attention.

Without another word he pulled a packet of eight-by-ten glossies out of one of the envelopes and spread them across the desk.

"This is supposed to be the back of Kennedy's head," Phelps said, "with the entry wound of the head shot near the cowlick." He indicated a photograph of the back of the dead man's head, the hair damp and matted, a rubber-gloved hand holding it in position by a lock of hair. "This is an obvious composite forgery. You can see the matte lines where it was pieced together. That was done, of course, to hide the huge exit wound in the back of the skull."

Karp stared at the photograph while Phelps traced the supposed join with a pencil. Karp shrugged and said "Okay, let's say I take your word for it—"

"You don't have to take my word for it. I spoke to Floyd Riebe, the photographer who took the photograph at Bethesda. He said there was a huge hole in the back of Kennedy's head. The Parkland doctors said the same thing originally too. Also, look at this blowup of frame 335 of Zapruder." He dealt a color eight-by-ten from the stack. "The top of his head is obviously missing." They all stared at the blurry horror. Karp turned to Wendt. "Doc, what do you think?"

Wendt paused judiciously, then responded, "This is obviously inconsistent with the X rays we have been given."

Phelps had an answer to that too. He pulled out a positive print of an X ray and placed it next to a different glossy, the most gruesome picture yet. It showed a three-quarter right-side view of the corpse's face, with the brains bubbling up out of the skull like a party hat. "This is supposed to be a right-side lateral X ray. It shows massive damage to the right front side of the face. But no damage to that side of the face was ever described by any witness, either at Parkland or at Bethesda. And obviously, from this photograph, there's no such damage."

"Did the Warren people see this stuff?" asked V.T.

"Justice Earl Warren saw them," replied Phelps in a sneering tone. "The story is, he was so shocked by them that he refused to allow them to be made public, and they were never shown to the commission."

While they thought about this, Phelps brought out some more pictures and added them to his gallery on the wooden desk. "This is a picture of the top of the head. See this line? It's surgery. And nobody ever mentioned a surgical procedure on the top of the

head. The Bethesda autopsy team said that the skull was so shattered that they were able to lift the brain out without any further
cutting of the skull."

"What are you saying?" asked Karp uneasily.

"I'm saying that between Parkland and Bethesda, somebody
worked on the body. They cut out the brain and modified the skull
to make the single-shot-from-the-rear theory plausible." This was
said with profound assurance, as if anyone with eyes could plainly
see it.

Karp snapped a lidded-eye look toward V.T., who kept his face
blank. It was Wendt who responded first, and with some vigor:

"There is absolutely no evidence for any such interference.
None. Nor would any such alterations be feasible in the time allowed, even if we assume that the president's body was so poorly
guarded that it could have been removed from its coffin on the
presidential airplane and spirited away to a secret dissecting room
before being delivered to Bethesda."

"What about this photograph?" snapped Phelps. "There is
clearly evidence of surgery and—"

"So you say," replied Wendt, "but I see a badly shattered cal-
varium from which nearly anything could be construed. I am not
a photographic expert, of course, but I believe that interpreting
autopsy photographs as to forensic content is well within my professional purview. You say the X rays and some of the prints are
faked. It may well be so, but until I and the other members of the
forensic pathology panel are so informed officially, we will continue to base our findings on them."

"What, on faked evidence?" Phelps retorted. "What's the goddamn point of that!" He addressed Karp, his eyes sparking. "This
is big, damn it. This is evidence of conscious treason by a huge
conspiracy involving people close to the top of the government.
How else could they have—"

"Stop!" said Karp, holding up his big hand like a traffic cop.
Dueling experts, the prosecutor's nightmare, and he was sick of it.
"First of all," he said sharply, "treason is not a word I want to
hear around this office. We're not investigating treason, we're investigating, if that's still the right word, a homicide."

"But, it's the *president* . . . ," Phelps began.

"Assassinating the president is not treason," said Karp force-
fully. "Even a coup is not treason. Treason shall consist in levying

war against the United States and giving aid and comfort to its enemies. It's in the Constitution, the only crime defined in the Constitution. So forget treason. Conspiracy to commit murder, interfering with an investigation, tampering with and withholding evidence—that's different, and we may have found evidence of all of that. It's enough." He shot the famous stare around the table. Nobody spoke, and he resumed. "Now, as to these photos: Jim, write your report. We'll get some independent source to confirm or reject your findings and then we'll see. Dr. Wendt—I'll try to get funds for the sort of experimental testing you're interested in, if you'll give me an outline of the sort of stuff you want to do."

This speech was delivered in a tone of finality. Phelps, still bristling and muttering, shoved his photographs back into their envelopes. V.T. took him aside and spoke earnestly to him for some minutes in a low voice. Karp turned to the coroner. "Sorry about this, Doc. Things are apt to get heated around here."

Wendt tried on a smile. "It was sweetness and light, I assure you, compared with some of our panel's meetings."

"Oh? What's the problem? Murray throwing his weight around?"

"Not at all. But there seems to be a certain . . . reluctance to stray too far from the Warren findings. Whether Mr. Phelps's theories about the documentary material will have any weight with them I can't say."

Karp couldn't say either. Wendt took his leave and Phelps left too.

"Well, that was certainly fun," said V.T. when they were alone. He fussed with the projector and began to rewind the film. "Don't mind Phelps. He really is a top-notch photo analyst."

"Yeah, with a good imagination. Did *you* see the back of Kennedy's head missing in that film?"

V.T. shrugged. "Like you said, we'll get somebody else to check it out."

"Right. Meanwhile, the inmates are in charge of the asylum. The secret dissection, my God! You know we're doomed, don't you?"

"Semidoomed, maybe. One still has hopes. One of the little threads might pull something loose."

"Maybe, but I doubt it," said Karp. "And you know why?" He clenched his fists and adopted a Job-like pose, his arms and face

raised to the uncaring heavens, and shouted, *"Because this isn't a real investigation!"*

"My, my, Butch," said V.T. in a soothing tone. "You seem to be having a nervous breakdown. Would you like to watch the executions film again? It might settle your nerves."

Karp snorted and rumbled, "Speak for yourself, buddy. You look like shit—you must've dropped ten pounds since you got here."

"Yes, well, as you know, you can't get a decent knish in this town."

There was some more of this weak humor, and they were laughing companionably when a secretary stuck her head in and said Fulton was on the line and did Karp want it sent in here.

"What's happening, Clay?" said Karp when they were connected.

"I'm at the Sheraton in Reston," said Fulton. "This old spooks' meeting's just breaking up."

"And?"

"Zilch. I waltzed our boy up to Mr. David and he introduced himself as Antonio Veroa. David didn't bat an eye. He just said, 'I'm happy to meet you. I know the name, of course.' Then Veroa moved on. When I asked him if David was Bishop, he looked sort of funny, and he said, 'They are very similar in appearance but that is not Bishop.' "

"Oh, shit!"

"My feelings exactly. So—what should we do with Mr. Veroa now?"

"Crap, I don't know! We might as well ship him back to Miami. Did Al Sangredo pull up anything on the drug charge against Veroa?"

"Yeah, it's apparently some heavy weight of coke, found in his boat. He could go away for a long time."

"Want to bet he doesn't as long as he sticks to this line of bullshit? Want to bet they'd throw away the key if he testified that David was Bishop?"

"You think the fix is in, huh? Want Al to try and check it out?"

"No, fuck it," said Karp wearily. "Why screw up *his* life too. I know when I'm whipped. Just thank the little bastard, kiss him for me, and stick him on a jet back to Miami."

"What was that all about?" asked V.T. when Karp had finished the call. Karp told him.

"Well, then," said V.T. brightly. "A perfect day."

Marlene now found herself transported to a somewhat higher circle of purgatory. Early, yet not *too* early, she packed young Lucy up and made her way, via several buses, to the Dobbs home in McLean. Lucy played with the Dobbs children while Maggie and Marlene had coffee and cake and discussed the day's research plans, and chatted amiably. Thereafter, Maggie disappeared, as did the children. Maggie either took them somewhere nice, or else she went on her own wife-of rounds, and left them to the efficient and grateful Gloria of El Salvador. Afternoons were spent at play group, except when it was Maggie's turn to be hostess, at which time Marlene abandoned her duties on the book and helped out with the kids.

During most of most working days, however, Marlene was left delightfully alone, in a well-appointed and cozy little room that Maggie called "the study." (This was different from "the den," a larger room, where the congressman had his home office.) There were two windows looking out at an alley of bare and graceful dogwoods; inside, the room boasted built-in walnut bookshelves, several wooden filing cabinets, a long, shiny refectory table, a blue IBM Selectric on its own stand, lighting from desk and standard lamps, a worn chaise lounge of the Dr. Freud-in-Vienna type, and a working fireplace. This last was supplied daily with logs and kindling by Manuel, the Dobbses' gardener and houseman. Marlene was thus often to be found working away in front of a cheerful blaze. In one corner of the room there was set up, incongruously, a movie projector on a rolling metal stand, and there was a folding screen that went with it.

The romance of the situation was not lost on Marlene. A poor but honest lady, down on her luck, finds genteel employment in the home of a powerful aristocrat with a dark secret—it was pure Brontë, and she luxuriated in it: the comfortable and elegant surroundings, the freedom from drudgery, the refuge from the ignominy of Federal Gardens. In that she regarded her Washington exile as a catastrophic hiatus in her *real* life, she had no trouble in slipping into the persona of a sort of upper servant. Sitting in front

of her fire, laboring at her papers, she thought that, to complete the image, she lacked only a floor-length brown dress with buttons up the front, and a ring of keys at her waist. That and her hair in a neat bun with a center parting.

The work itself she attacked with an energy born of months of enforced intellectual idleness. Maggie had made a perfunctory start at organizing and indexing the Richard Ewing Dobbs archives, and Marlene spent several weeks updating this and becoming familiar with the material. This comprised several drawers full of clippings related to Dobbs and his arrest and trial, and the political arguments and commentary that resulted from that event; boxes of photographs, letters from prison, and other personal memorabilia; the transcript of the trial itself, with all the documents produced by discovery, and notes made by Harley Blaine, the defense lawyer; a thin sheaf of material yielded by the FBI under the Freedom of Information Act; and finally, a large archive of 8mm home movie film.

The senior Dobbs, it turned out, had been an avid home cameraman, from almost the first period in which such equipment had become available to the general public. There were four library shelves stacked with neat green file boxes in which were stored hundreds of spools in Kodak yellow cardboard sleeves, all neatly labeled with dates from the late thirties to the late fifties. Marlene had watched dozens of these films selected at random from each year of the record. At first, she ran film when she was bored with reading; later she became fascinated with the vérité aspects of the record. She watched a young, soft-looking, but handsome Yalie in sleeveless sweaters, saddle shoes, and slicked-down dark blond hair become a studious grad student and then a pipe-puffing New Deal bureaucrat in baggy three-piece suits. She watched his play: horses, croquet, tennis, engaged in with other men of the same type and clouds of bright young things, that cloud gradually resolving itself into one, a slim, elegant girl with good bones, a corona of blond hair, and a dignified expression. After 1938, she appeared on nearly every reel: Selma Hewlett Dobbs, the wife, now the Widow. Marlene saw the courtship, the wedding (two reels), the honeymoon (Havana, Rio, eight reels), the new house on L Street, a more subdued Selma, her belly swelling from one reel to the next, and finally, in 1939, the infant congressman, little Hank (six reels).

Dobbs had taken his camera to war too. A whole box was devoted to shots of jungles, airstrips, warships, planes landing and taking off, and any number of what appeared to Marlene to be exactly similar views taken from the rail of some sort of vessel, of the sea at night, with flashes in the distance. Only the labels indicated that they were distant prospects of the great night battles that raged around the Solomons in 1942.

The most interesting parts of these films to Marlene were those depicting the men of the Pacific war, all deeply tanned, many pitifully thin, crop-haired, incredibly young. Like most Americans, Marlene derived her understanding of World War II from war movies, where the soldiers had been played by thirtyish 4-Fs like John Wayne and Ronald Reagan. From Dobbs's films she realized for the first time, and with some shock, that the Japanese Empire had been crushed largely by pimply teenagers and their slightly older brothers.

Dobbs had caught these young sailors and marines at their daily work, or relaxing, or lying wounded in tent hospitals, grinning often, smoking perpetually. There were shots of Dobbs too: at a desk, with a small fan cooling his sweat, in khakis boarding a PT boat, inspecting a submarine, photographing something through the nose bubble of a bomber. The most remarkable sequence was a scene in which Dobbs was shaking hands with a group of young naval officers, with PT boats in the background. One of the officers was a startlingly young Jack Kennedy.

Marlene had mentioned this to Maggie, who had rolled her eyes and said, "Oh, yes, the meeting of the giants! I'm surprised the image isn't worn off the film. That's one of the ones they show you when they're checking you out to see if you're fine enough to be a Dobbs. The poor old bastard used to watch it over and over again, that and the other Meetings with the Great."

She had directed Marlene to an indexed list of film spools bearing shots of Dobbs and famous people: FDR, Hopkins, Nimitz, Spruance, the Dulles brothers, Bob Hope.

And then, of course, there was Harley Blaine. Blaine was in nearly as many of the films as Dobbs's immediate family, from the Yale years onward; during the war, he was in more of them. Blaine had apparently served with Dobbs during some part of his service. There was a long series of them in navy whites working and ca-

rousing around wartime Pearl Harbor, and another series of the two of them poking around in ruins and interrogating Asians; the film labels identified Saipan and Okinawa as the venues.

Blaine apparently shared Dobbs's interest in moviemaking. They traded cameraman duties when they were together, and after a while Marlene was able to recognize their individual cinematic styles: Dobbs flitted from one subject to another in quick cuts. Blaine provided a rock-steady camera platform, focusing on one subject for long seconds and then slowly panning to another. She even learned to recognize the shadow of their heads and upper bodies when they were using the camera: Blaine had huge shoulders sloping upward to a bullet head; Dobbs had a small round head on a graceful long neck.

Maggie confirmed this observation. "Yeah, the two of them were real pests, according to Hank and my mother-in-law. They'd sneak up on anything, one or the other of them, and get it down on film. Selma said the only place you were safe was in the toilet, and maybe not even then. When there was nobody else around they took shots of each other cutting up. Just boys at heart!"

Blaine was, of course, a key to Marlene's investigation, not only as Dobbs's lawyer at the trial, but as a lifelong friend. On a day, perhaps three weeks into her task, having read all the material in the archive and having watched dozens of hours of film, she asked Maggie whether it would be all right to call him in Texas.

They were in the kitchen; Maggie had just brought the kids home; Jeremy was napping and the girls were playing quietly in Laura's room. Maggie's reaction was not what Marlene had expected.

"Oh, my!" she exclaimed, holding her hand to her mouth. "Call him? Is that absolutely necessary?"

"Well, yeah, Maggie. I'm looking into a case that's twenty-five years old, I guess I need to talk to the lawyer."

A worry line dug itself deeper below Maggie's golden bangs. "Yeah, yeah, you're right, of course. But . . . oh, I don't know what to do now. . . ."

"You're worried about Hank finding out I'm doing this."

"Yes! I know it's *stupid*, but . . ."

"But what? Tell him! I mean, it's not like it was illegal. Besides, I'm going to have to talk to Selma too, and I doubt that she's going to swear secrecy. The worst that could happen is that he'll

yell at you and tell me to stop. I mean, he doesn't strike me as such a tyrant."

"Oh, no, he's not, not at all. It's just he's so sensitive about this whole thing with his dad."

She hemmed and hawed for a time, but under Marlene's cold eye, and not wanting to look like a jerk in front of a woman she regarded as the epitome of courage (and of course Marlene would *never* try to hide stuff from her husband for fear of an argument), she gave over Blaine's private number and said that she would break the news to Hank.

The call to Texas was answered by a man with a soft accent. Marlene explained who she was and what she wanted. The man asked her to hold. There was a hiatus of perhaps three minutes. Then another voice came on the line, with a similar accent but a different and more impressive timbre, a voice that reminded Marlene of Lyndon B. Johnson's: cast iron with a coating of honey.

"So you're gonna write all about Dick Dobbs," said Blaine after the brief pleasantries were concluded.

"Well, I don't know about 'write,'" said Marlene. "Maggie's asked me to do the research. Find out the facts, and so on."

"Find out the facts, hey? That'll take some doing. I hope you're not an *old* lady."

"No, sir, but I'm working on it. Tell me, do you get to Washington much? This kind of thing might be easier to do face-to-face."

"Oh, no, I stick close to home nowadays. I been under the weather."

"I'm sorry—I hope I'm not disturbing you."

"No, that's fine. I don't get many calls lately either. I'm always glad to chat with a lady. So, tell me, what've you made so far of the great case of *U.S.* v. *Dobbs*?"

"I've gotten as far as confusion, as a matter of fact," said Marlene, not particularly amused by the "lady" business.

A gravelly laugh. "I'm not surprised. I guess you been reading all the commentary?"

"Yes. And it's either a right-wing plot to destroy a patriotic American who was a premature peaceful coexistence advocate or a foiled left-wing conspiracy to disarm the United States and deliver it into the hands of the Soviets. It's impossible to figure out which because, as you know, the case was never resolved. The

right-wingers claim it was dropped as a part of the conspiracy, with the treacherous Harley Blaine threatening to blow the whistle and reveal national security secrets. The other side claims it was a victory for civil liberties in the dark days of McCarthyism, won by that great civil libertarian Harley Blaine. So my first question is, which Harley Blaine am I talking to?"

Another laugh, and then a long coughing spasm. "Sorry 'bout that," Blaine said. "Guess I'm not used to having my aged ears jangled by impertinent remarks—no, don't apologize—it's good for me—gets the old juices flowing again. Which Harley Blaine, huh? Well, miss, here's the main thing you have to understand. Dick Dobbs was my best friend. He was the one interested in politics, not me. When he got into trouble I figured my job was to get him out of it, whatever it took, and I did that. Whatever a bunch of eggheads and pissant hack writers said about it afterward—hell, I never paid any mind to it at all and neither did Dick. The Harley Blaine you're talking to is the only one there ever was, a good friend and a damn good lawyer."

"Okay, fine, but how did you get him off. There was something about a defector you uncovered—"

"Hell, the government's case didn't amount to a hill of beans," Blaine interrupted. "What they had was the uncorroborated testimony of an admitted spy, that Weinberg fella, and a bunch of papers. There was no question that the papers came from Dick. The question was, did Dick give 'em to Weinberg or did Weinberg steal them? They didn't have a scut of real evidence that Dick had turned them over. Weinberg had no messages, no communications from Dick at all, and he had free access, as a clerk, to everything in Dick's office. Of course, in those days an accusation was about the same as a conviction. They got Alger Hiss and fried the Rosenbergs on cases just about as bad. I wasn't about to let that happen to Dick."

"So you short-circuited the process with this mysterious defector."

"I did. You'll want to know how I pulled it off?" Teasingly.

"Yes. According to the articles and books I've read, you've never been straight on the issue. That's what's fed the conspiracy accusations over the years."

"Well, Miss Ciampi, I don't reckon a smart girl like you would've swallowed much of that old horseshit—pardon my French."

"Does that mean you're going to tell me the real story, Mr. Blaine?"

There was a long pause on the line, long enough to make Marlene think she might have been cut off. But Blaine remained connected. He cleared his throat heavily and said, "Matter of fact, I told Selma the whole thing, back then, Selma and Dick both. I told them what I'd found out, and how I'd found it out, and I said I wasn't going to use it unless they thought it was right. I said, and I remember this like it was yesterday, the two of them holding hands, sitting on straight chairs in the interview room in that damn prison they had him in, and I told them that the government was bound and determined to see Dick convicted of treason and that they would find some way to do it, and that they'd probably ask for the death penalty. And Dick asked me, would it hurt the country, what I was planning to do, and I said, no, I didn't think so, and he told me to go ahead with it. Damned if I knew if it'd hurt the country. About then I wouldn't've cared if it meant the Russian navy could steam into New York. I just wanted him out of that place and safe."

He paused again, and Marlene heard the sound of drinking and a clunking noise, as if a glass had been set down. "So there's no reason not to let you in on the conspiracy after all this time. Everyone's dead, just about, except me and Selma, and a bunch of the small fry. The judge and prosecutor gone; Dick, of course. The chief witness, Weinberg, died in prison. Lord knows where Reltzin and Gaiilov are, dead too, probably. And as far as national security"—he drew the word out long and mockingly—"I expect the Republic will survive the revelation."

"Gaiilov?" asked Marlene.

"Hah! See, you've wormed it out of me already. Yeah, that was the boy. Armand Dimitrievitch Gaiilov. Talk about your conspiracy! My Lord, you couldn't start a conspiracy in this country if your life depended on it; folks here just like to talk too much. They ain't comfortable with secrets. How it happened, I was sitting in the Navy Club in Washington worrying about how I was going to get Dick out of this mess, when I heard two fellas talking. They were huddled together at the bar and I was sitting in a club chair about six feet away with my back to them. They were sort of arguing in a polite way about something or other and then I heard a name that made my ears perk up. I had good hearing back then;

getting deaf as a post now. I got this thing makes the phone louder. Anyway, one of 'em said something like, 'But he says that Weinberg was the only contact,' and the other one said, 'Well yes, that's the point. He's trying to protect Dobbs. It means he's a mole.' And the other one said, 'Damn it, Gaiilov's no mole. He's given us loads of stuff that checks out,' and then he went on to name all kinds of stuff with names like Hatrack and Boneyard, secret files of various kinds, I imagined, but by then I wasn't really paying too much attention. When they left, I asked the barman who they were and he gave me a couple of names and I checked them out and sure enough they were CIA."

"How did you do that—check them out?"

"Oh, it wasn't much of a problem. Washington was still a small town back then. I'd had some connection with naval intelligence, being a former naval person and all, and I asked some friends and they asked their friends and that's how it was done. What it was, anyway, was that an employee of the Soviet mission to the UN in New York had just walked out one day and stopped in at FBI headquarters and said he wanted to defect. He claimed to be KGB. Of course, the CIA got into it right away, and of course they leaned on this guy something fierce to make sure that he wasn't a phony defector. It stirred up quite a ruckus in the Agency, so I learned, because one faction, Bissell and them in operations, thought he was genuine, and another faction, Angleton and his friends, thought he was a phony, a double agent. Anyway, the real kicker was that this joker, Gaiilov, said he knew all about Reltzin and Weinberg, and yeah they were spies, but he'd never heard anybody in the KGB mention Dick Dobbs."

"The point being," Marlene put in, "that if you thought Mr. Gaiilov was a double, then you'd expect him to try to cover for Dobbs, the master spy, but if you thought he was on the level, then Dobbs had to be innocent."

The man chuckled, a dry rustling sound. "Yep, you got it. I reckon you can figure out the rest. I called a meeting in Judge Palmer's chambers with the U.S. attorney, Paul Gerrigan, and I told him that I intended to call Armand Gaiilov as a witness. Well, when that got back to the CIA it let the skunk loose in amongst the choir. There was a great gnashing of teeth, I expect, and it must've brought the internal battle to a head. The last thing they wanted was a fella who they didn't know whether he was a spy or

not getting hauled up in open court under oath to testify about Dick Dobbs. So they said they wouldn't do it, couldn't do it, for national security reasons, and I said in that case, I'd settle for a *subpoena duces tecum*—the transcripts of all their debriefs of Gaiilov. Well, of course, they said I couldn't have that either. Judge Palmer hemmed and hawed, and I got shouted at a good deal, and accused of being a Red communist myself, but after Palmer had stared down the barrel of the Sixth Amendment for a while, he told them they had to let Gaiilov testify. He said, 'Gentlemen, the Constitution in the instant case allows me no leeway. The witness may indeed refuse to answer on grounds of national security or prior oath, at which point I will make a determination as to whether such refusal is justified, but there can be no prior bar to Mr. Dobbs's right to call whomsoever he will to his defense.''

"And the government dropped the case.''

"They did.''

"Very fancy,'' said Marlene, with sincerity.

"Why, thank you kindly, miss. I thought so myself at the time.''

"Weren't you worried that he might get up on the stand and lie for the Agency and say that Dobbs was the one?''

"Oh, that was a possibility, of course. On the other hand, a good half of the CIA had staked their reputations on the idea that Gaiilov was genuine. If he lied about Dick, I would've treated him as a hostile witness, and then I'd've had reasons to call the CIA big shots up there to confirm, or try to deny, Gaiilov's original exculpation of Dick. No way they were going to open up that bag of cats. They'd've looked like a bunch of fools. And, my dear, if there's one thing the CIA can't stand, it's public embarrassment. They don't mind one bit walking out there to the wall with a blind-fold and a last cigarette, but make 'em look like a horse's ass? Hell, they'd do anything on God's earth to stop that.''

"Well, this has been real interesting, Mr. Blaine, and I don't want to take up any more of your time. I'd just like to ask: do you have any material you think would be useful on this project—from the case, or from your association with Mr. Dobbs? And could you give me the names of anyone who might've been familiar with the case that I could talk to?''

The was a pause while the man thought. "No-o, as for the papers, I think I already sent the case papers and all some years back, when Hank started this thing. I told him then I didn't think

it was a good idea to dredge all this up again, but he was determined, so I just sent him a whole stack of stuff."

"Films too?"

"I guess there might've been some films. Hell, Dick and I could hardly ever tell which of our stuff was whose. He's probably got nearly everything I do. On the people side: hell, it's been a quarter of a century, near about. Like I said, judge, prosecutor, and defendant all in their graves, and the defense's got one foot in. The little fry? Well, any of them who had something to say, they've said it already in books and such. Look, miss, I got to go. This damn nurse's pestering me again, I reckon she found some poor inch of my hide without a needle hole in it and it offends her."

"Oh, sure, sorry—one last thing. Would you know how I could find out what happened to either Reltzin or Gaiilov? Even if they're dead, they might have had friends or family. There might be papers left behind. . . ."

"Oh, Lord! I couldn't even guess at how to help you there. Reltzin probably got shipped back to the Soviets. They got most of their nationals back in exchanges. Gaiilov? I heard he passed on, the lucky man."

After she'd hung up, Marlene paged through her notes, puzzled. She found it odd that a man who recalled the exact words of a judge's decision a quarter century past should be so hazy about so much else, for example, about what had become of the Russians. Of course, he was obviously ill, and memory got funny when that happened; for all Marlene knew he had a brain tumor. But that business about overhearing the two CIA guys in a bar—that sounded funny too. She drew a circle around that section of her notes, and around the Russian names, and then made a note to herself to call on Mrs. Selma Hewlitt Dobbs. The Widow.

Karp got through to Ray Guma in New York late in the day.

"Goom? Butch."

"Butch?" said Guma in exaggerated puzzlement. "Do I know a Butch?"

Karp said, "I'm sorry, perhaps I have the wrong number; I was trying to reach the Association of Chubby Italian Attorneys with Mob Connections."

"Oh, *that* Butch. You never call, you never write. . . . So, how the hell are ya, buddy? You solve the big one yet?"

"We expect an arrest momentarily. Actually, that's why I called. I'm gonna offer you a rare opportunity to serve your country."

"Wait a minute, let me put my hand on my wallet. Okay, I got it. Shoot—what can I do for you?"

"The Buonafacci kid you got on that rape charge. I could use a little favor from Tony and I thought it might be better if the ask came from you."

A loud noise, like the sucking of a gas pump at the dregs of a tank, came through the receiver.

"What's the joke, Goom?" snapped Karp.

"The joke, sonny boy, is that you got to take a number on that one. Stand behind the velvet rope. Narco's drooling, racket's got their nose so far up my ass I don't have room for my hemorrhoids. I'm the queen of the prom on this one. I got to pick and choose."

"Goom, for Chrissake, it's not the Gambinos' next smack shipment; it's a lousy phone call to a retired wise guy, a soldier, is all. We just want to talk to him, and not about anything that's going to involve Tony or anybody current in any of the families."

"Who's this soldier?"

"Guido Mosca. Jerry Legs."

"Oh, yeah! V.T. called me about him a while back. So you found him, huh? I personally never had the pleasure. What, he's in Miami?"

"Yeah. We figure it'll jog his memory if Tony asks him."

"Yeah, I guess," said Guma reflectively. "What do you want to ask him about? Like, did he pop a cap on JFK?"

"No, just some other stuff. About some things that went down in New Orleans in sixty-three. Mosca's name showed up on some documents. He was pally with some guys that Oswald was pally with—it's just background, painting in some of the numbers."

"You're not off on this horseshit that it was a Mob contract on Kennedy, are you?" Guma asked.

"Well . . . I'd say it's still on the table. Why?"

"Because it's total garbage," said Guma angrily. "The Mob whacks their own guys or guys who take their dough and then try to fuck them. If they whacked people who just pissed them off or put them in jail, Tom Dewey and Estes Kefauver wouldn't have lasted long, not to mention you and me. You know why that is? Back in the nineteen-tens, I forget where, Cincinnati, or Columbus, some old-time wise guys knocked off a crusading police chief,

a straight-up guy, just like they used to do in the old country, and what happened was a mob came stomping into the Italian section of town and burned it down and lynched any guinea they could get their hands on. So, since then, it's been a no go: don't fuck with the government guys, except with bribes. The other reason is, the Mob couldn't pull it off, not like whoever actually did it did it."

"I don't see why not," said Karp.

"Come on, Butch! It ain't their style. They don't go in for long-gun shots. Bugsy Siegel excepted, I don't know a case in this country where a Mob hit used a rifle. Short range is what they like, or a big bomb."

"What about Jack Ruby? That was short range."

Guma chuckled. "Ah, well, Jack Ruby. I'll give you Jack Ruby."

"So why did he kill Oswald, if the Mob wasn't involved in the JFK thing?"

"I didn't say they weren't *involved*. Fuck I know if they were or weren't involved. They're involved in everything else, they might've been involved in this too. They do stuff for money, you know? What I said was, the JFK hit wasn't a Mob contract."

"Okay, whatever," Karp said. "I still need to talk to Jerry Legs. And don't tell me I got to stand on line, because if you do, I'll get on a plane and fly down to Miami and talk to Tony Bones myself, and if your name should come up in the conversation, I don't know, some of the smart shit you've pulled on him over the years might slip out. . . ."

"Ah, Butch, come on, don't even joke about that business," said Guma, genuine alarm in his voice. Guma had for years walked the delicate line between relations with the Mob for which armed response was highly unlikely and those for which it was far too likely for comfort. Karp remained silent, and after a long moment, Guma breathed out a sigh and said, "Okay, you rat, I'll see what I can do."

"How was your trip?" asked Bishop. His voice over the phone seemed to come from far away, although he could have been in the next room in the Alexandria motel.

"It's fucking cold here, Bishop," said Caballo. "I hate the cold. I'm a sunshine soldier."

"It's only about forty."

Caballo ignored this. "What's the deal?"

"You need to pick up a package."

"Black bag?"

"No, our contact will collect the necessary material and give it to you."

"I can't believe this! You brought me up here to be a fucking courier?"

"No, of course not! They made a copy of the film. The other items, the documents, are neither here nor there and can be explained away. Not the film. So . . ."

"That's the black bag."

"Yes," said Bishop. "A man named Karp. It should be easy."

THIRTEEN

"What do you *mean* he won't allow a contempt citation?" Karp shouted.

Bert Crane, in whose office Karp had shouted this, recoiled, and then flushed with anger. "Could you keep yourself under control, please!" he snapped.

Karp resumed his seat, from which he had sprung when Crane informed him that George Flores had point-blank refused to cite Paul Ashton David for contempt of Congress.

"Did he give you any reason?" Karp asked in a tight voice, but at a lower volume.

"Not as such," said Crane. "The congressman and I do not have a cordial relationship. 'Witch-hunt' was the word he used to describe your citation. It's irrational. I simply don't understand what's going on."

Which was just the problem, thought Karp uncharitably. He asked, "What about Dobbs? He's on our side, isn't he? Can't he get it moving?"

"I spoke with him this morning," said Crane. "He's rallied a minority of the Select Committee over to the way we see things, but he can't oppose Flores openly yet. And you need a clear majority to vote a contempt citation, and you'll never get that as long as Flores is recalcitrant."

"So what do we do, give up?"

"We wait for a break. Maybe something will turn up that'll give Hank the leverage he needs to roll a majority in spite of Flores.

Meanwhile . . ." He left it hanging, like, it seemed, the investigation itself.

That subject being dead, Karp asked, "Any word on the budget?"

"Yeah, the word is no. Not until this cockamamy comptroller general investigation is finished. It shouldn't be too long."

There was a blitheness in the tone of this last remark that annoyed Karp. Crane was independently wealthy and had besides just come from a lucrative private practice, which he still spent a good deal of his time tending.

"It's been too goddamn long already!" snarled Karp. "I have no money. I'm cashing in CDs. We've been paying for consultant services out of our own pockets. If there's no closure within the next week or so, I'm going to have to start looking for another job, one with a paycheck."

Crane seemed taken aback by this outburst. "I'm sorry," he said, "I hadn't realized that you were so pinched. Would a loan help?"

Karp shook his head, suddenly embarrassed for both Crane and himself. "No, no, I'll survive. The main problem is the consultants and the travel. *We* may be assholes, but the labs and the docs and the airlines aren't."

"Well, I'm sure it's just a matter of days," said Crane soothingly. "This crisis can't continue indefinitely. Flores can't want the public to see him as an obstructionist, and Hank will keep up the pressure on him to get the project rolling. Honestly, I think time is on our side."

Karp had his doubts. Later in the morning, these were confirmed when he received an unexpected call from Hank Dobbs—unexpected because Dobbs usually dealt officially with the staff through Crane, and unofficially through his minion, Charlie Ziller. The congressman came quickly to the point.

"I understand you've had a breakthrough," said Dobbs. "This mobster, Guido Mosca."

"I don't know about 'breakthrough,' " said Karp cautiously. "It's an interesting lead."

"But you're pursuing it?"

"Yeah, right now we're looking into the best way of getting Mr. Mosca to talk to us. Speaking of which, Bert tells me that you're pushing Flores for a contempt citation on David."

"He does, huh? I wish Bert would learn that he's supposed to run the staff, and not speculate on, or involve himself in, the politics of the Select Committee. My God! The man is a bull in a china shop. And he hasn't cleared up this Philadelphia Mob connection business yet either."

"But that's nonsense!" protested Karp.

"Of course it's nonsense. Bert Crane is as honest as a brick. But it hasn't been laid to rest, and obviously, if there's even a hint of an organized-crime angle to the assassination, as it now appears to be with this Mosca character, we're in deep trouble unless it *is* resolved, permanently. Also, he's still spending a couple of days a week in Philadelphia on private issues, and that doesn't look good either. Sometimes I wonder whether he really wants the job."

"This is pretty awkward, Hank, you telling me stuff like this. Why don't you tell it to Bert?"

"You think I haven't? I *have*, again and again. I'm on his side, and believe me, if I wasn't, he would have been out of here weeks ago. Look, I have a quorum call and I have to run. But I want to get together with you soon, for a long talk. Maybe a dinner at my place; God knows, the girls are thick as thieves lately, you're the only one who's missing. And one more thing: I appreciate the work you've been doing over there under very stressful conditions. And I'm going to see that you get proper recognition for it."

"I could use some actual money," said Karp, but Dobbs seemed to ignore this remark and got off the line before Karp was able to ask him what he imagined proper recognition to be. Also left unresolved was the relationship of Dobbs and Crane; the congressman was obviously not the staunch ally Crane thought he was. Karp wondered what Dobbs wanted to discuss at the intimate dinner he was planning.

He turned his mind with an effort to more concrete maneuverings. Guma was out, or feigning absence, when Karp called him in New York, so Karp left a message: "Tell him it's about my trip to Miami; he'll understand."

A few hours (spent on desultory paperwork) later, Karp's phone rang.

"It's all set up, wiseass," Guma said without preamble.

"He'll talk to us?"

"He'll sing 'La Donna è Mobile' in the key of C—whatever. Don't say I don't come through for you."

"I'd never say that, Goom. My only problem is how to pay for getting him up here. We're having a little problem with our budget. You don't think Tony would spring for a couple of round trips?"

"Ask him yourself, you're such a buddy of his," snapped Guma, and he broke the connection.

Karp was therefore actually musing on travel budgets, and budgets more personal, when the phone rang again a few minutes later and it was the columnist, Blake Harrison, and thus when Harrison asked him how he was he said, flippantly, "I'm flat broke."

Harrison chuckled briefly. "Still haven't been paid? That's what happens when your boss is an unskillful, rather than a skillful, peculator in the public fisc."

"Is that going to be the subject of your next column: the great Select Committee paper clip and stationery rip-off?"

"Hardly. Have you thought any more about what I said?"

"Some," said Karp. "But I think it's sort of moot at this point. I've just about made up my mind to quit."

"Quit?" said Harrison in a tone of astonishment. "You can't quit now. Why are you talking about quitting?"

"Um, for some reason I have a hard time getting people to understand this, but I have no money. I haven't been paid. The prospect of my being paid remains dim. And when I say I have no money, I don't mean that I can't afford to lunch at the Palm this week. I mean I can't buy the necessities of life for my family. I have a few pathetic CDs which I am going to have to cash in early to keep us alive in New York while I look for a job."

"You're serious? *That's* the hang-up? You're that broke?"

"Oh, yes," said Karp, wondering where this was leading.

"No problem, then. Good, very good. I'll be speaking with you later."

He hung up, leaving Karp with the uncomfortable sensation that a deal had been closed, in which he himself was a fungible commodity.

"I need a car," said Marlene, shaking off her raincoat in the Dobbs kitchen. To journey from Federal Gardens to McLean, not a burden when the weather was fair and warm, was a serious trial now that the fall nastiness had set in with damp vigor.

This complaint had been voiced with increasing frequency. Maggie looked sympathetic and said, "Why don't you buy one, then?"

Marlene shot her an uncharitable glance. "With what for money? And no, I don't want to borrow from you either. The problem is that transit authorities understand that the only people likely to be traveling from Lower Arlington to McLean in the morning are domestic servants, so who gives a shit if they're waiting for hours and slogging through the freezing rain. Keeps them from getting uppity."

"Stop it!" laughed Maggie, and then more thoughtfully, "You could probably get the Mollens' car pretty cheap."

"Who're the Mollens?"

"They live down the street. It's a VW and he's a Member from Milwaukee." Seeing Marlene's incomprehension, she added, "They make auto parts in Milwaukee. Can't have a foreign car anymore. They're hot to get rid of it and it's a darling car. Yellow, one of the kind with a square back."

"A D Variant," said Marlene. "What do they want for it?"

"I could call Sheila and find out," said Maggie helpfully, going for the phone.

The call did not encourage. "Twelve hundred!" Marlene said. "That's about eleven hundred more than we have in our checking account. Oh, well, fuck it anyway! We were going to go into town today, right?"

So they were and so they did. The children were left with Gloria, and Marlene and Maggie climbed into the deliciously warm and mighty Mercury wagon and headed for the GW Parkway.

They went first to the East Wing of the National Gallery, where Marlene had never been before, and cooed or snarled appropriately at the various treasures, and had lunch in the restaurant there, next to the little waterfall, and then went out onto the sodden and dripping Mall and hailed a cab to take them downtown for some shopping.

Actually, Maggie shopped; Marlene only advised and by dint of sincere argument, delivered with a passion she had not required since last she stood in a courtroom, kept her friend from making the sort of egregious mistakes that had left her with a bale of pricey but useless garments. Marlene found she enjoyed this vicarious shopping. There was no guilt involved, for one thing, and there

was the Pygmalion-thrill of reshaping someone who had unlimited money and zero fashion sense.

They spent nearly four hours at it, ending up at Woodies on F Street, and at last, having had most of the packages shipped, and having spent enough to buy two used Volkswagens, the two women emerged, exhausted, onto the crowded streets.

The weather had improved in those hours. The front that had brought chilling rain for the past week had apparently moved away east. The air was clear and fresh, if chilly, and blue sky was trying to pop out between masses of swiftly moving, ragged clouds. They decided to walk east on G Street to Ninth and catch a southbound cab back to the National Gallery, where they had left the Mercury.

"Feeling depressed?" asked Marlene, noting Maggie's glum expression.

"Yes, it's like postpartum psychosis. A huge mass of money has moved out of my account and all there is in exchange is a bunch of new clothes, which I will have to *wear*, after which they will have been *worn*. It seems so futile."

"Gosh, I thought we were having fun."

"Oh, yeah, I didn't mean . . . I don't know *what* I mean! I guess I just need a kind of fun that doesn't involve spending money. If there *is* any of that kind left." She halted and turned to face Marlene. "I'm just another discontented rich Washington matron, aren't I? The truth—am I *pathetic*?"

"Oh, don't start!" said Marlene, grabbing her arm and hustling her along the street. "You just need something to jazz you up a little. There's no risk in your life, is the problem." They were at the corner of Ninth. The sides of the streets were occupied by street vendors selling a variety of cheap articles—hats and scarves, African trinkets, knockoffs of expensive handbags, umbrellas. Marlene looked up the street and spotted the decorative lanterns that marked the precincts of Washington's small Chinatown. She clutched Maggie's arm. "Dim sum! I could kill for a dozen dim sum."

"Do we have time?" asked Maggie nervously.

"No, if we're not back on the dot, Gloria'll ditch the kids and go back to El Salvador, but who cares? It's just what you need; we'll probably be poisoned and then you can stop sweating the small shit like you do and worry about something important, like your liver rotting out. Let's go!"

They headed north on Ninth. At about the center of the block, a crowd of about a dozen people had gathered. They were representative of that quite large proportion of the citizens of Washington, D.C., who are neither tourists nor officials; nearly all of them were black, Latino, or Asian. Marlene felt a rush of nostalgia for grubby New York and pushed forward to see what they were looking at.

"It's three-card monte," she told Maggie in a low voice. The monte man was a heavily built, swarthy Latino with a spade beard and a black leather coat and cap. At the table, betting, were a huge black construction worker with a yellow hard hat worn backward and multiple dusty sweatshirts, a smaller construction worker, similarly attired, and a thin, ocher-colored man in a greasy black raincoat with a jerky manner and an avid look in his eye. This last was doing most of the betting, crumpled fives and ones thrust decisively down beneath a flat and heavy piece of metal on the army blanket that covered the tabletop. He won more often than he lost, cackling each time he found the ace of spades among the two red aces. The construction workers were betting too, but not winning nearly as often.

"The point is to pick the black ace after he does his shuffle. The little guy in the raincoat is the shill," Marlene informed Maggie in the same low voice. "He's winning most of his bets. The other guys are getting skinned.".

Marlene turned her attention to the monte man. As she suspected, he was using the standard monte hand switch. After each round he did a show, holding the diamond ace and the spade ace faceup in one hand, widely separated, and the heart ace faceup in the other. Then he'd throw them down with an exaggerated motion, so that everyone could see he was throwing diamond, spade, heart, and then he'd move the cards around a few times, to "confuse" the suckers, take bets, and do the reveal.

Of course, the "confusing" maneuvers on the table that attracted the closest attention from the bettors were entirely irrelevant, because on the initial throw-down, the monte man had switched the diamond and the spade in his hand with a lightning motion of his fingers. If you knew where to look, and Marlene did, you could spot it every time, despite the distracting motion of the other hand, the one with the ace of hearts.

Now the big construction worker uttered a cry of dismay and a

curse. He'd been worked up via a few two-dollar wins to risk a twenty-dollar bet, and he'd just lost it. The hustler scooped up the bills and wrapped them ostentatiously around a thick roll of cash he pulled from his pocket. "Who wants it, who wants it?" he cried. "Double you money if you pick the black ace, double you money, les go, les go!"

"Marlene?" said Maggie, "I, um, thought you wanted to get some Chinese food."

"Yeah, but I just had an idea," Marlene replied, steering Maggie out of the crowd. "I can beat this guy."

"What do you mean? I thought it was fixed."

"It *is* fixed. That's the point. I know how he fixes it. The problem is, how to pull it off without getting our throats cut. . . ."

"My God, you're serious!"

"You betcha. I'm tired of riding the bus. Oh, hey mister!"

This was addressed to the larger of the two construction men, who were pushing their way out of the crowd. Marlene got up close to him and flashed a smile. "Look, um, I got a way you can get your money back. Interested?"

The big man looked doubtful. "Yeah, how'm I gonna do that?"

"Me and my partner here are gonna take that sucker off. When we do, they're gonna try to come after us. I need a couple of blocking backs to slow them down for a couple of minutes. What'd you blow, around fifty? Yeah? Okay, it's worth that, plus fifty on top."

"A hundred each?" A suspicious look. Two suburban white ladies were going to take off a fairly heavy street dude? "We don't got to *give* you any money before we get our hunnerd do we?"

"No, man, it's a straight-up deal. Cash in hand up front. All you got to do is stand there and be big when they make their move."

Maggie was standing there listening to this with her mouth half-open. It opened all the way when Marlene said to her, casually, "I need twelve hundred dollars. Do you have a bank nearby where you can get it?"

"Um . . . sure, I mean, I can get it on my Visa. Across the street. But, Marlene . . ."

"No buts," snapped Marlene. Make it twenty ones, twenty tens and the rest in fifties and hundreds. Hurry!"

Maggie scooted off without another word, and Marlene re-

turned to the table to watch the action. Ten minutes passed; Marlene was starting to get nervous; the cops would have to come by soon to break up the scam. Then she spied Maggie, looking flushed and wild-eyed, trotting across the street.

Marlene took a fat bank envelope from her and whispered, "Just stand right here and don't say a word. When I signal, run out on Ninth and get a cab and have it waiting on the corner at G Street. Can you do that?" Maggie nodded, her eyes wide and frightened.

Now Marlene slipped the promised money to her two blockers, told them to stay close on either side of her, and then moved right next to the shill at the table. She asked the monte man shyly, "Can I play?"

Big smile, gold glinting. "Why, sure you can, sugar, just takes two little dollars, get four if you win."

Marlene laid her money down and picked a red card. She gave a little shriek of dismay and quickly placed another deuce on the blanket. When she had lost about twenty dollars in this way, growing more and more agitated, she cried, "Oh, God, my husband will kill me. Can I, um, bet higher, like ten? Do I still get double if I win?"

The monte man's smile was dazzling. "Sure, honey, It's the same, ten dolla, fifty dolla, hundred dolla, what you want." Marlene bet ten, and as she expected, the man left out the switch and she won. She gave a cry of delight, and the monte man said, "See what I mean, everybody got a chance to win." The shill came in on the next round, and "lost" ten, as did Marlene and a heavyset black woman with thick glasses. Marlene lost four more tens; the black woman dropped out after three rounds. Marlene reached into her bag and pulled out a fifty. "Oh, Lord, I just *knew* it was the right card! Please, mister, give me a chance to get even?"

She felt the crowd getting thicker around her, as if the people on the street could smell the presence of serious money. The monte man graciously allowed her to risk a fifty. She placed a bill under the bar, the monte man covered it with his own bills and went into his deal. Marlene lost, and a sigh went through the crowd. Marlene cried out and danced around in a circle in what seemed to be frustration, during which she signaled Maggie to get the cab.

"A hundred, a hundred!" yelled Marlene, waving currency. The monte man's eyes were getting wide now, and he snapped a

look nervously over his shoulder. It'd be just his luck for the jakes to come along now before he could take this bitch's whole paycheck. He slapped four fifties under the bar and did his deal. He was automatically reaching for his winnings, when the crowd cheered and he looked down at the ace of spades showing in Marlene's hand.

"I won, I won!" shouted Marlene, jumping up and down like a six-year-old.

The monte man didn't change expression. It happened sometimes. The suckers made a mistake and picked the right card instead of the "right" card. He'd just have to shift them a little slower on the table.

Marlene went back to losing tens to kill some time, until she saw a D.C. cab pull up at the corner and wait. Then she went back to fifties, lost twice and won once. She pulled her stack of bills from the bank envelope and ostentatiously thumbed through them, arranging the denominations. She needed his greed pumped up to the max or this scam wouldn't work.

The monte man wasn't smiling much anymore. He let the shill play a round and win, and then it happened just as Marlene had hoped. In moving to collect his money the shill stumbled and tipped the table over. The cards fluttered to the ground and the monte man and the shill both knelt to pick them up. The shill got up first with the black ace in his hand, and Marlene saw him crimp one of its corners before he placed it on the blanket, just as she was meant to.

The shill then had a run of success, building his bets up to hundreds, always picking the crimped card, which the poor monte man somehow failed to notice. Marlene won a hundred dollars too, picking the crimped card. The monte man made jokes about how he must be losing it today. Marlene tried to put a look of greedy cunning on her own face and asked, "Ah, how much can I bet?"

"Anything you want, sugar," was the casual answer.

"Okay," said Marlene, "I bet eight hundred." A gasp and murmur from the crowd. She placed her wad under the bar and the monte man counted out sixteen hundred and added it to the stack.

He picked up the three cards, showed them, did a little shuffle as if nervous, showed them again, the black ace partly covering the heart in one hand, the diamond alone in the other. Marlene knew

that in that little shuffle the monte man had smoothed the crimp in the black ace and made an identical crimp in the corner of the diamond, concealing it with the ball of his index finger. As he snapped the cards down he also rotated the spade so that the formerly crimped edge faced his way and not toward Marlene. What appeared on the table was two uncrimped cards and one crimped one, just as in the last half dozen rounds, except that now the crimped ace was the diamond.

Marlene poised her hand over the false winner and then in a single darting motion, flipped over the black ace, scooped up the stack of bills, and darted between the two construction men. The monte man shouted in rage, knocked the flimsy table aside, and made to chase Marlene down. An arm like a log held him back. "Where you goin', man?" asked the big construction worker. "We want to play some more."

The monte man yelled, "Fuckin' bitch got my money!"

"Ain't your money no more, man, she beat you," replied the big man reasonably, and the crowd murmured assent.

"Hijo de puta!" screamed the monte man, and reached into his back pocket, bringing out, with the same practiced snap he used with the cards, an eight-inch butterfly knife. The big man backed quickly away a few steps. The crowd opened up like a flower, amid shouts and screams. The smaller construction man picked up the steel weight from the monte table and, coming in on the blind side, swiped its owner across the temple. Blood gushed, the monte man staggered but stayed on his feet. With wild swings of his blade he cleared a path and took off at a clumsy run down Ninth, toward the spot where his quarry was just entering a cab.

Marlene threw herself breathlessly into the seat next to Maggie and looked out the back window. She saw the monte man break out of the crowd and come running toward them, screaming imprecations in Spanish, waving his blade and spraying blood. Marlene pressed down the door locks on both sides and shouted, "Move this cab!"

The monte man had reached them. Maggie looked out the side window and saw a bloodstained, shrieking face pressed up against the glass. She saw the waving knife, and then the man's fist crashed against the window.

Marlene dangled a twenty-dollar bill in front of the driver's face. "Come on, beat the light. Do it!"

The driver, lately of Cairo and its fabled Darwinian traffic system, had no trouble with this request, and might even have done it gratis. He hit the gas, darted into the intersection, through which the G Street traffic had already started to move, grazed a panel truck, provoked a chorus of horns, caused a Mercedes to swerve and slam into a gray government car, and got through to clear pavement.

Maggie was white and shaking. There was a smeary bloodstain on her window. She stared at Marlene, who was calmly counting the take. Marlene looked up and grinned.

"Having fun yet?" she asked.

At five-thirty, Bea Sondergard walked into Karp's office wearing a toothy grin. Such grins had been in short supply lately, and Karp returned it.

"Ta-daaaaah!" sang Sondergard, and flipped a thin brown window envelope onto Karp's desk.

"It can't be!" said Karp, picking it up.

"It is! It's a miracle. I've alerted the Pope."

Karp opened the envelope and read the amount on the green Treasury check within. "What happened?" he asked.

Sondergard shrugged. "Search me, Jack. About three-thirty the guy from the CG took a call and they packed up and left. A half hour ago a messenger arrived with these checks. I made some calls, but nobody could tell me what was going on. Basically, they just cleared our budget, pay, admin, travel, the whole nine yards. The word is, it came direct from Flores. In any case, we're in business!"

When Bea left, Karp called Hank Dobbs's office and was told he had gone home. He called the Dobbs home.

When the congressman came on the line, Karp said, "I like the way you work. Our budget came through just now. We have checks."

The was a peculiar pause on the line, as if Dobbs had forgotten the issue. "Oh. Oh, yeah, that's great," said Dobbs vaguely.

"No, really, I appreciate it a lot."

"Good, fine, glad to help—so, how are you going to spend your new riches?"

"For starters, I think a trip down to Miami to see Mosca, and if he's got anything good, bring him back."

"He's agreed to talk to you?" said Dobbs. He sounded surprised.

"So it appears. I'd like to get down there before he has second thoughts. In any case, with money, it's a whole new ball game. So tell me, how did you roll Flores on the budget? From this end it looked like somebody just flicked a switch."

"Oh, you know—tricks of the trade, tricks of the trade. I guess water wears away a stone if it drips long enough." Abruptly, Dobbs changed the subject. "By the way," he said, "your wife is here. I believe congratulations are in order."

"Excuse me? Congratulations?"

"Yes, she just bought my neighbors' car. I don't know how they do it, but the ladies know when we're flush even before we do. Do you want speak to her? She's right here."

"Yes," said Karp, baffled. "I think I do."

"How did it go?" asked Bishop.

"No problem, the guy showed up, dropped the package in the waste can, and left. It looks like it's all there. The film looks right too, but I guess you want to check out the whole thing."

"He didn't see you? You weren't followed?"

"No, like I said, it went okay, a good dead-drop, like the old days. I guess the next job is to start scoping this Karp character out, right?"

"Yes, but not now. You need to fly to Miami first. I think it's time to close out some of our former assets there."

FOURTEEN

The alarm clock brought Karp up out of confused dreams. He tried to cling to the dream state before it faded—something about Oswald, a lineup of Oswald clones in some dark police station, Karp peering into each identical face in turn, all smirking, a feeling of imminence, of some disaster that would strike if he couldn't pick out the real one. Men standing around, impatient, important, and there was something about Marlene in there too. . . .

"What's wrong?" This was from Marlene herself, warm in the bed beside him.

"What? Nothing, I'm just getting up."

"You were groaning."

"Oh! Was I? I was having this weird dream." He told her about it, as much as he could remember, and then shrugged and laughed. "I have Oswald on the brain."

"Your subconscious is trying to tell you something," she offered sagely. "This guy you found . . . what's his name . . . ?"

"Caballo."

"Yeah. You think he's the double. Maybe the real hit man."

"Oh, crap, maybe, who knows?" said Karp, stretching, but reluctant to leave the warm bed for the barely heated bathroom. "V.T. said maybe Oswald was his own double," he added sleepily. "Whatever that means. I'll believe anything at this point."

Marlene rolled over so that her face was above his. "Actually," she said, "I'm Oswald."

"You are?"

"Yes, I had a sex change operation right after the shooting, and also plastic surgery and secret drugs to make me younger. Then, I manipulated you into marrying me, and the master conspiracy organized your entire life so that you would be picked for this job, where I could thwart the investigation by draining your vital bodily fluids." She demonstrated some draining action on his mouth.

"If you're really Oswald," he asked, "how come you give such good head?"

"Oh, puh-leeze!" she crowed. "Look at the pictures of him, or me, that is! Is that every ten-dollar male hustler you ever saw on the Deuce?"

"I guess you've got me there . . . Lee. Well, this is certainly going to add some piquancy to our sex life from now on."

"Speaking of which," she said, wriggling her upper body onto his chest, "what time does your flight leave?"

"Eight-twenty."

"Oh, good, we have time for a quickie." She threw a hot thigh over his midsection. The oversize T-shirt she wore to bed had ridden up and Karp could feel the amazing heat of her sex pressing against his hip.

"I guess this means you don't hate me anymore," he said among the kisses. She straddled him and set herself up, bouncing lightly on the tip before the first delightful drop.

"No, I still hate you a little," she said, "especially since you're running off to bask in the sun."

"I'm not basking," Karp objected, not very seriously. "It's business."

"Don't be silly, you'll bask your ass off, while I'm stuck in the freezing rain, but as you can see my hatred has fallen below my fuck threshold," she said, and then she said, "Aah!"

"Well, this sure as hell beats chasing muggers through the sleet on St. Nicholas Avenue," said Clay Fulton brightly. They were driving across a sparkling Biscayne Bay on Broad Causeway in warm sunlight, Fulton at the wheel of the rented Pontiac, Karp beside him, studying a road map.

"Make the first right you can, onto Bay Drive," said Karp.

"Hey, I been here before, remember? Nice neighborhood," Fulton observed as they drove down a street lined with palms and

clipped bushes flowering pinkly with oleander and hibiscus. "We're in the wrong business."

"Yeah, we should've been mobsters," Karp agreed. "On the other hand, he probably suffers from skin dryness due to overexposure to the sun's rays. It's a trade-off."

Fulton made a turn and pulled to the curb. "Okay, this is it, we're here."

Karp grabbed a battered cardboard folder and stepped out of the car into the bright warmth of the street and the odors of flowers, hot stone, salt water.

It was a small stucco house, two-story, colored sun-faded pink with white trim. There was a low wall around the property, topped by a tangled bougainvillea vine. They walked through a wrought-iron gate and entered a small courtyard that contained a kidney-shaped pool, some chairs and loungers, a round table with a Cinzano umbrella stuck through it, and a redheaded woman in a yellow bikini, sunning herself on one of the loungers.

She lifted her sunglasses and peered at them, squinting. She was leather brown from the sun and her skin had the smooth and slightly oily look of an old saddle. Karp judged her to be in her late thirties. She had the sort of lithe body you get if you danced professionally in youth and you work out a lot after youth has fled.

"We're here to see Guido Mosca," Karp announced.

The woman cupped her hand around her mouth and shouted, at surprising volume, "Hey, Jerry, you got visitors!" Her vowels were from south Jersey. She gestured to a pair of white-painted steel chairs with flowered cushions, and said, "Have a seat." They sat and she went back to reading *The Racing Form* and working on the tan.

In a few minutes, they saw a glass door at the back of the house slide open, and Guido Mosca walked out onto the flagged patio. He was a medium-sized man in his early seventies, with a deeply lined face, small, bright eyes set close together, and a wide lippy mouth. He was bald save for a fringe of silvery hair, and his skin was the same tanned-leather color as the woman's. They might have been sprayed out of the same can.

Mosca approached them and shook hands without smiling. His eyes flicked toward the woman, who ignored them, and he said, "Come on, I'll show you around."

They walked around the side of the house down a narrow path lined with crotons, and out onto a lawn facing a broad channel, a large island park with a golf course in it, and the bay. The property was small but well maintained: the lawn green and crisp under foot, the bordering shrubbery clipped square. There was a little dock with a white powerboat tied to it under a striped awning. It was the kind of modest setup that might have belonged to a small and successful businessman in his retirement. Which Mosca was, in a way.

A white wrought-iron umbrella table and four chairs sat on the lawn. When they were seated, Karp said, gesturing to the place, "So, Jerry, you look like you landed on your feet—nice house, a boat. What's the secret of your success?"

"I kept my nose clean, my mouth shut, and I put a little money away. Look, what's the deal here? Tony says I got to talk to you guys and go testify."

"Yeah, provided you have something we need," said Karp. "Why don't you start by telling us what you were doing in New Orleans in 1963?"

Mosca leaned back in his chair and played with his lower lip. "Sixty-three, sixty-three . . . okay, sixty-three I was working in a crew with Jackie Colloso and Chick Fannetti. We had some money on the street, also some girls, punch cards, like that."

"This is in Marcello's outfit?"

"Yeah, Marcello. He was the capo there."

Fulton asked, "Jerry, so how did a Philly boy get to be working for Carlos Marcello?"

"Out of Cuba. I used to go down there a lot when it was open, the fifties. I took care of some things for Trafficante, as a favor, you know? And he offered me a job, watch his interests in some of the casinos. And while I was there I met Sam Termine."

"This is the one who worked for Marcello?" asked Karp.

"Worked for Marcello. Yeah, he was his driver and, like, his bodyguard."

"You ever meet Termine's friend, Dutz Murret?"

"The bookie, right? Yeah, later he was a, like a client."

"Meaning you collected for him."

"Yeah, later, when I was with Marcello, him and the other bookies."

"Did you know his nephew?"

Mosca nodded, slowly, as if realizing that this was the point of the whole thing, the nephew of an insignificant part-time bookie for the New Orleans Mob. "Lee Oswald. No, that was before my time, when he was a kid, hanging around in New Orleans. Sam Termine knew him, though. Sam used to go with his mother."

"So, you met Termine in Cuba," said Karp, switching back. "What happened then?"

"Well, Castro took Cuba, we had to get out. Trafficante asked me to stay. He couldn't leave because Castro wouldn't let him. They were gonna put him on trial or something. So some of his people got some big shitload of money up, then Jack brought it in, and I gave it to some Castro guys, and we flew out that night. After that—"

"Wait a second," Karp interrupted. "This was Jack who? The bagman . . ."

"Jack Ruby," said Mosca blandly. "Worked for Carlos as a bagman at the time, and then he ran a nightclub in Dallas."

"I know who Jack Ruby is, Jerry," said Karp. "I was just surprised that he was the guy who bailed out Trafficante. Okay, go ahead."

"After that, I worked for Trafficante for a while, and then one day, must've been the summer of sixty-one, Termine calls me up and says there's something going down, they want to get some of the old Havana fellas together, could I come. So I ask the boss about it, and Trafficante says he heard about it too, and yeah, I should go. They're gonna whack Castro, they need muscle for the job. So I get to New Orleans, and I see Sam and he introduces me to a guy, Johnny Roselli, out of the Chicago outfit. He's setting the whole thing up. He's talking about how the CIA is behind the deal, which doesn't make me feel too fucking relieved, because look how they fucked up the invasion, you know? He asks me can I do a machine gun, can I do a bazooka. Right then I know this is gonna be fucked up, but what can I say? It's a contract. Okay, so Roselli says the CIA guys want to see us, we're supposed to go to such-and-such a bar at such-and-such a time and they'll pick me up. So Sam and me go out and we end up at this bar we were supposed to be at, I think it was Armand's on St. Charles. And we see Dutz Murret and we sit down at a table with him, just shooting the shit, waiting for this CIA guy."

He stopped and looked at Karp, a faint smile on his face. "You

know, it's funny you asking me about Dutz just now, and Oswald, because what happened was, this guy walks in the front door and looks around, and Sam spots him and says something like, 'Holy shit, Dutz! There's your nephew.' And Dutz looks over and he kind of jumps and starts to get up and then when the guy gets a little closer he says like, 'Nah, it ain't him. Besides, he's in Russia, the little prick.' Then this character spots me and walks over and says his name's Caballo and I should come with him, and he notices Dutz is staring at him and he asks him if something's wrong, and Dutz says, 'No, but you're a ringer for my sister-in-law's kid,' and Dutz tells this guy how Lee had gone over to the commies in Russia. Okay, then we got up and—"

"Wait a second, Jerry," said Karp, and brought out an eight-by-ten print made from the Depuy film. "Is this him?"

Mosca studied the photo, holding it at a distance from his face in the manner of elderly men who need glasses.

"Yeah, that's the guy."

"What was your take on him—then?" Fulton asked.

"Caballo? Just a guy. Hard kid, though. If I didn't know he was G, I'd've said he was one of ours, you know? Anyway, we left Armand's and he drives me to this motel out on Hayne by the old airport. There're some guys there in a room, Roselli, a couple guys I knew from the old days, Cuban muscle."

"Names?" said Karp.

"Oh, one of them was Angelo Guel, used to work out of the Hotel Nacional, ran girls, the other one—I can't recall his name—Chico something. And then there was the government guy, Bishop."

A quick look passed between Fulton and Karp. Karp pulled another photograph from his folder. "Is this Bishop?"

"Yeah, that's him," said Mosca after a quick look, and Karp felt a jolt of elation. Mosca had identified a photograph of Paul A. David. Karp spread out several other stills from the film. Mosca picked out Angelo Guel as one of the men who was riding in the jeep, confirming Veroa's ID.

"So anyhow," Mosca continued, "Bishop starts in with these charts and plans and shit, how we're gonna whack Fidel. He's got this tame Cuban to rent a place that's got a clear shot of this platform where Castro's gonna give a speech. The Cubans are supposed to go over in a boat at night and land the gear, and some

other Cubans're supposed to take the stuff to Havana and set it up in the apartment. So while he's talking, I'm thinking, How come these guys need us, they got the whole thing figured. So I ask them.''

He paused dramatically, until Karp said, "And . . . ?"

"Deniability," said Mosca, pronouncing the word carefully in a tone touched with sarcastic contempt. "Deniability is they're using Cubanos we used as muscle around the casinos, they got Roselli to front it, which means Giancana and Chicago is in on it, and Santos is in on it, with me there, so whatever happens the government's in the clear. It's a revenge hit from the outfits, Castro fucked them so bad, you know? Horseshit, but that's the plan. So I say to Bishop, 'Yeah, but you're involved, you got people there in Cuba, the guy who rented the apartment for the hit, that's your guy. You're the CIA.' They all looked at me like I laid a fart or something. Bishop says, 'Who said I was CIA? I'm not CIA.' Then he gives me this line that he's representing some businessmen who want to see Castro whacked. Anticommunist types from Texas.''

"You didn't believe him?" asked Karp.

"Hey, the fuck I know! Roselli sure as shit thought he was working for the G. He was fucking proud of it. So we bullshit some more. They tell war stories. Roselli's got all these schemes he tried to get Castro. A poisoned cigar, stuff to make his beard fall out. Totally fucked up, it sounds like to me. The Cubans are saying all about being in on the Bay of Pigs deal, why it went wrong and fucking Kennedy, how he fucked it up, they would've taken over if he'd've let the bombers work over the commies. Bishop was on the Bay of Pigs too, he says, and they're all crying in their beer what a shame it was. I'm getting bored here, listening to all this crap, so I ask Roselli when we're gonna do him, Castro, and what'm I supposed to do. Sometime in October, he says. So, I say, that's two, three months from now, let me know when you're ready, and I get up to go. They say, wait, we gotta do a picture for your passport. So they take some Polaroids of me and Guel. Then Bishop says they'll be in touch and I shouldn't talk to anybody about it." He smiled. "Like I got a big mouth, you know?

"Anyway, I get back to my hotel, I right away call and leave a message for Santos at this phone booth we use and about an hour later, he gets back to me. I tell him, Santos, these people are fucked up. I say, hey, you want to whack Fidel, I'll get some people to-

gether, we'll go there and whack him, but these people, especially Roselli, they're a fuckin' joke. Santos, he laughs, he says, yeah, he knows that, nothing's gonna happen to Fidel, but we got to stay involved with these fuckheads because whatever goes down, we got a piece of the government's ass forever, they'll owe us to the next pope. So that makes sense, so I go back to Florida and wait. Next thing, the end of September, I get a call from Caballo, the thing's on, get my stuff and go down to the airport, the commercial terminal. They got this plane there, a little private jet, I never been on one of those things before. Guel's there, and Caballo. Caballo's not coming but he gives me this envelope. It's got money in it, American and Cuban, and tickets for a regular Cubana flight out of Mexico City and phony passports for me and Guel and for this other guy we're supposed to pick up in Mexico City. The passports were perfect, but, why not? These guys are the government, right? And we take off. You guys want a beer? No? Well. I'm gonna have one.''

Mosca got up and went to the house. Karp said to Fulton in a low voice, "This is real, right? I'm not having a wet dream?"

"If you are, I'm in it too, son. This guy is from heaven. He IDs Bishop as David, he puts Paul David together with a guy who's a ringer for Oswald, and puts Guel with Bishop way before the film, before the assassination even, and they're all sitting around jiving about what a bad guy JFK is. I love it! All we need now . . ." He fell silent as Mosca returned, clutching a can of beer.

"So. No problems in Mexico City," Mosca resumed after a long swallow. "We fly to Havana and—"

Karp interrupted. "Who was the guy you picked up in Mexico City?"

"I don't know. I never seen him before. He didn't give his name."

"Okay, go ahead."

"Havana. We make contact with Bishop's Cuban, the guy who's setting up the apartment we're gonna shoot from. Name's Tony something, Verana . . ."

"Veroa," said Karp. He showed another photograph.

"Yeah, that's the guy, Veroa. Anyway, I check the setup and it's complete amateur hour. There's one escape route. One! We're gonna have to run down eight floors after we do the job. He got us two cars, but no switch cars, which means we're gonna have to

race to this dinky port where there's a boat waiting for us, he says, with every cop and soldier in Cuba looking for us, in the same goddamn cars we left the apartment in. Plus, the jerkoff rented the fucking place in his mother-in-law's name, so of course he has to get her out of the country before the hit, only he finds out the Cuban cops are looking funny at the boat he's supposed to use and he gets nervous and, of course, Guel and the other Cuban get even more nervous, and they call the thing off the day before it's set to go. And that was it, the story of the great hit on Fidel. Assholes!"

He finished his beer and was silent for a moment, looking out at the water. "Veroa takes off in the boat with his mother-in-law, Guel and the other guys disappear, and I fly back to Mexico and then Miami. Santos had a big laugh over it. I say to him again, like, Santos, you want Castro hit, I'll put some guys together, we'll do it. A bomb is what I would've used, none of this bazooka crap. But he says, I got to check with Giancana, it's his thing, the thing with Roselli and the G. Which is fucked, because Miami's open, it don't come under the Chicago outfit, why should Santos give a shit what Giancana thinks? But I figure, what the fuck, they got some kind of deal working on it, I don't need to know about it. It ain't my affair. Meanwhile, after that, Santos is telling everybody he's gonna get Castro, he's in on the hit, it was all horseshit as far as I could see, but you know Santos, he likes to blow smoke like that."

Karp thought of something Veroa had said and asked, "Jerry, tell me one thing. Did you ever get the feeling that the Castro thing was a scam, that Bishop and the other CIA people didn't really want to hit Castro?"

Mosca shrugged broadly. "Hey, the fuck I know! Like I said, I didn't think it was a serious operation, from what I saw. And Fidel's still around."

"Did you ever see any of these people again?" Fulton asked. "Bishop, Caballo, the Cubans, or the other guy, the one in Mexico City on the plane?"

Mosca thought for a while, and then nodded, looking directly into Fulton's eyes, with a cynical smile on his wide mouth. "JFK. That's what this is all about, right? Well, the fact is, I don't know squat about any of that. You guys are out of luck."

With some effort, Fulton kept the confusion he felt from ap-

pearing on his face, and said casually, "Yeah, we understand that, just tell us what you *do* know."

"Okay, along about sixty-two, late, I got into a situation in Miami, we thought it would be good if I spent some time out of town. So Sam Termine arranged I could work with one of Marcello's crews for a while. I'm there a year or so. So, one night, this is like fall of sixty-three, me and Sam and a couple other of the fellas are standing around outside Gella's on Canal and a bunch of guys get out of the car and start walking down the other side of the street. Sam looks over at them and waves, and one of them walks across the street and comes over to us. First thing I think, it's this guy Caballo, but no, it turns out this is the real Oswald. He shakes with Sam and then Sam introduces him to me. So they bullshit for a while, how's your mom, like that and then Oswald goes back across the street. But while he's talking, I'm looking over at the guys he's with; they look, like, familiar, you know? And I see it's the bunch from the Castro thing, Guel, and another Cuban shooter we had in Havana, name of Carrera, and the other guy, the third guy from the plane. It stuck in my mind because here's three guys connected with a guy who's a ringer for Oswald, and here they are with the real Oswald. Funny, huh?"

"Yes, it's real funny," said Karp through a drying throat. "Um, this third guy. Can you describe him?"

"I don't know," said Mosca with a shrug. "Just a guy. Pretty well put together—looked like he could handle himself in a fight. Didn't say much. I remember he had thick, wavy hair like those old-time movie stars."

"And you don't remember his name?"

"No, like I said, he didn't give it."

"But you were with him on the plane ride and for most of the week planning the Castro assassination," Karp persisted. "You must've called him something."

"Oh, yeah. When I gave him the phony passport, I said, 'That ain't your name, is it?' And he looks at the passport and says, 'It is now.' So we called him Frank."

"Frank what?"

"Frank Turm."

"Term? Like a prison term?"

"No, it sounds like that, but on the passport they spelled it T-U-R-M."

Karp wrote this down on his pad, his hand shaking with excitement. "Um . . . one other thing, Jerry. What was PXK?"

A puzzled frown passed over Mosca's face. "What? What is that, like a company?"

"Maybe. We don't exactly know. It's come up in connection with what went down in New Orleans back then. Maybe this Turm guy was involved in it."

Mosca shook his head. "I never heard of it. Like I said, I just saw the guy twice."

While Karp was writing, Fulton asked, "In Havana, Jerry, what was this Turm guy supposed to do. He was one of the triggers?"

"Nah, he was like the organizer. Like I said, this Veroa character didn't know his ass from a hole in the ground about how to set up a hit. Turm was supposed to be the detail guy: who went in what window, timing, getaway, the cars, the hideouts. We talked about it a little. I got the feeling he did it a couple times before, down in those South America countries."

"But the hit never came off," Fulton objected. "If he was such a pro, how come he didn't fix it up?"

"Yeah, well, that was another fucked-up thing about it. We get to the airport in Havana and Turm says he's got to make a phone call and he'll catch us later, and that was the last I saw him, until that night in New Orleans."

Marlene had seen so many movie images of the red stone house on L Street that it looked entirely familiar when at last she saw it in real life. She was sure that with no help at all she could have found her way around inside it, almost as if it were a house she had lived in as a child. The mistress of the house, Selma Hewlett Dobbs, had aged more perceptibly than the blood-colored sandstone, being made of a softer material, but not that much softer, as Marlene found out a few minutes into her interview.

They were sitting in the old study at the rear of the house, a room Marlene recognized from the films, of course: *his* study. It looked unchanged, like a room in a museum. The books in their cases were neatly ranked and dusted, the bay windows that gave on the small back garden were clean, the desk and an oak filing cabinet and the other furniture were polished, gleaming dully in the thin light, and smelling faintly of lemons. Mrs. Dobbs sat at

her husband's desk, facing Marlene, who sat in a leather chair before her. She was being dressed down.

"Miss Ciampi, is it? I want you to understand that I have not given an interview since my husband's death and I would not being giving one now had not my daughter-in-law asked me to see you. I think it was unwise of her to involve a stranger and I told her as much. Maggie is prone to enthusiasms about people that may overcome her judgment."

The voice was firm and vibrant with the accent and timbre made famous by Katharine Hepburn. There was a Hepburnesque look about the woman herself, Marlene thought: cheekbones like rails and a sharp little chin. Her eyes were blue and bright, although the once red-gold hair had faded to a grayish dun. It was combed straight back with a bun. She was sixty-five and looked ten years younger.

"I'll try to justify her confidence, Mrs. Dobbs," said Marlene.

Mrs. Dobbs's face reflected doubt, but she nodded and said, "Very well, let's get on with it. What is it you wish to know?"

Being a good interviewer of people who had something to hide, Marlene was not about to reveal what she wished to know. Instead, she began by giving something. "I spoke with Harley Blaine recently," she began.

The other woman's eyes blazed. "What! Who gave you permission to do that?"

"Maggie gave me his private number. I didn't realize permission was required."

"*Decency* is what is required," Mrs. Dobbs shot back, distaste in her voice. "Harley is dying. He has cancer. I will not allow him to be disturbed in the service of some harebrained project designed to stir up unpleasant and painful memories."

"I'm sorry, Mrs. Dobbs. I didn't realize you were so opposed to Hank's attempt to clear his father's name."

"My husband does not need to have his name cleared!" Mrs. Dobbs exclaimed. Twin bars of color had appeared on those cheekbones, glowing like neon tubes.

Marlene drew a deep breath and let it out. She said calmly, "Um, look, I think we're getting off on the wrong foot here. I'm not a journalist, I'm not trying to pry into anything. I'm not getting paid for this. I'm an unemployed mom who used to be a pretty good lawyer and Maggie asked me to do her a favor on this back-

ground investigation for a book Hank is planning to write. The last thing I want is to get into a family wrangle. So, you don't want to help, fine, I'll leave this minute and I'll go back to McLean and tell Hank and Maggie you don't want to help and then the three of you can duke it out."

For a long moment Marlene met the glare of Mrs. Dobbs's steel blue eyes with her single black one and the impervious glassie. Then Mrs. Dobbs turned away and favored Marlene with a view of her strong profile, limned by the garden window. When she at last returned to speech it was with a far softer tone. "I'm sorry. I should not have spoken to you like that." A long sigh. "My only excuse is that the events surrounding the accusation of my husband are so painful, even at this long remove, that I am not quite in control of myself."

Marlene nodded sympathetically, thinking, however, that lack of control did not seem to be one of Mrs. Dobbs's big problems. Mrs. Dobbs now put on a surprising smile, showing white perfect teeth, the smile familiar from the early Dobbs films. "Would you care for some tea?" she asked.

"I'd love some."

Mrs. Dobbs rose and led Marlene, not to the door she had come through, but under an archway to the right of the desk, which led to a short hall and another exit from the study. This hall was fitted out as a little gallery, lit by bucket lights overhead, the walls covered from the wainscot to nearly the ceiling with framed pictures. Mrs. Dobbs paused to point out the more interesting ones. Most of these were of ancestors, in yellowed formal poses, bearded gentlemen and blank-faced plump ladies looking like upholstery. Selma's father the governor. Richard's father the senator. The ladies and their children were represented in posed shots taken by society photographers: Richard at various stages of childhood with his mother; Selma, the same, with brothers and sisters, retouched so as to obscure any excursion from well-bred perfection. Displayed with the photos were a Civil War general's commission for a Dobbs ancestor; a coat of arms; a family tree for the Hewletts; a certificate from the DAR; a framed display of medals on blue velvet.

Marlene examined with interest two photographs that seemed to contain no Dobbses at all. One showed Harley Blaine in western gear with a white Stetson, seated on a horse, under a rustic wooden

arch bearing the name of his Texas ranch. In the other, Blaine was posed smiling in front of an oriental-looking statue of a lion in company with two other grinning men, both younger, both with crew cuts and thin ties.

"This is Mr. Blaine," Marlene said, pointing at the group shot. "Who are the other men?"

"I haven't any idea," Mrs. Dobbs replied after a brief look. "Richard hung these here. It's one of the photos Harley sent him when he was overseas, after the war."

"He stayed in the navy?"

"The navy? Oh, no, Harley was never in the navy."

"But I saw them in the films, Mr. Dobbs and Mr. Blaine, all through the Pacific war, in Pearl Harbor, out in the Solomons. . . ."

"That was what I believe they call 'cover.' Harley was one of Bill Donovan's young men. He was in the OSS during the war. And in the CIA afterward." Mrs. Dobbs walked away down the hall. Marlene shut her gaping mouth, took a deep breath, and followed.

They went to the kitchen, a dim room with worn checkered linoleum on the floor, a long white enamel table at the center, twenty-year-old appliances, and numerous cupboards and larders painted thickly in dun paint. It was the sort of kitchen meant to be worked by a staff.

"The girl is out," said Mrs. Dobbs, as if confirming this impression. "We'll have to fend for ourselves."

They fended, and then, seated in a small stuffy parlor, they drank their tea from thin china cups with a rose pattern, and munched delicately on thin butter wafers.

The two women chatted in a civilized fashion about Washington life, the Dobbs grandchildren, Marlene's family. Mrs. Dobbs seemed anxious to use what charm she possessed to repair the initial impression she had made, not, Marlene thought, because she cared a whit for Marlene's opinion, but because she had, by that transient rudeness, departed from her own rigorous standards of polite intercourse.

Marlene brought the conversation back on track, steering it from family, to friends, to friendship in general, and then to a particular friendship. "Mr. Blaine and your husband seem to have had a particularly close relationship."

"Oh, close isn't the word. Sometimes it seemed as if they were two parts of the same person. We used to joke about it in those days, that I'd gotten two for the price of one."

"Mr. Blaine never married?"

"Oh, yes, he did, briefly, right after the war. It didn't last. He traveled a good deal, of course, and it must have been lonely for her here in Washington. A Texas girl. It was hard for her to fit in."

I'll bet, thought Marlene. Not into this little triangle. She asked, "They met at Yale? Your husband and Mr. Blaine?"

"Oh, no, much earlier—at prep school, St. Paul's. I believe they were nine or ten. Harley's parents were killed in an automobile accident in Mexico. When Richard's parents came to pick him up at the end of the term, Richard announced that Harley would be part of the family from then on. And they went along with it. Richard could be quite bull-headed when he wanted something. Harley's only relatives were a set of grandparents who weren't much interested in rearing a boy. And of course there was plenty of money. It was such a typical thing for Richard to have done."

"He was generous?"

"Oh, yes, to a fault. An open, generous, noble man. That was why it was so absurd to have accused him of spying. He could hardly keep a surprise party secret."

"But I thought he was in naval intelligence in the war," said Marlene.

"Oh, that!" replied Mrs. Dobbs dismissively. "That wasn't anything like spying. Richard was based in Tulagi at first and collected information about Japanese movements in the Coral Sea and the Solomon Sea. He had a network of coast watchers, supplied by submarines and PT boats. That's how he won his Navy Cross. One of his people had been discovered by the Japanese and he led an expedition to get the man off the island he was on. They went out in PT boats and rescued the coast watcher, and Richard stayed to the last moment with a few other men, holding off the Japanese until they could get the agent off the beach. Of course, he wasn't authorized to do any such thing, but that's the sort of man he was. He knew his duty and he did it, whatever the personal cost. Harley, of course, was a different sort of man entirely."

"You mean, you might have believed it if Mr. Blaine had been accused instead of your husband?"

"Not at all. If anything, Harley was more intensely patriotic than Richard. I meant his character. He was much . . . darker than Richard. Closed. I think he was very isolated in childhood; his parents were apparently not terribly interested in raising him, the sort of people who believe that lavish presents and the best schools are a substitute for love. I suppose it was natural for him to become a spy. After the war, Richard went to work for the secretary of the navy and Harley stayed on at CIA. Of course, we saw a great deal of him. Richard was intensely social. Harley called him one of the great politicians of his generation."

"Was he interested in actual politics?"

"Oh, my, yes! He was planning a campaign for the House in New Haven, for the 1952 election, when he was accused. Harley was to be his campaign manager. They used to sit up nights in the study, plotting. They joked that Richard would be president first, and then he'd pick Harley as his successor."

"Was that a real possibility?"

"They certainly thought it was. Joe Kennedy's money bought the presidency for his son, and between them Richard and Harley could have given the Kennedys a good run. Besides which, Richard was twice the man Jack Kennedy was. He was a real war hero, not a phony one. He wrote his own books. And he was not obsessed with bedding every woman he ever met. Yes, I think that if things had worked out, Richard Dobbs would have shown very favorably against John Kennedy. They knew each other, of course, on Tulagi. And Richard liked Jack, but you know, Richard liked everyone, but he certainly wasn't taken in. How did he put it? Bright enough and charming as the devil, but essentially corrupt and with all the character of an earthworm. And naturally, he knew the true story of what happened with that PT boat."

"What happened?" said Marlene, fascinated.

Mrs. Dobbs smiled. "Oh, it was a story he used to tell, at parties and such. I wish I could tell it the way he did! Mimicking that silly Kennedy accent. How this fine upstanding boy, this bootlegger's child, in command of the fastest, most maneuverable surface vessel in the history of naval warfare, on a clear night with visibility of over a mile, on a calm sea, managed to get himself run down by a Japanese destroyer. Well, naturally, they were all asleep, with the radio off. Failure to keep watch, I believe it's called, a court-martial offense, but of course nothing was done to him, and he did save

those sailors afterward. It made a good cocktail party story, but it would have been devastating if Richard and Jack had gone up against one another. Richard wouldn't have said a word, but Harley would have made sure everyone knew. I used to think how odd it was, and how sad. Instead of Richard and Harley, Jack and that dreadful Lyndon. I don't think the country has quite recovered."

They were silent for a moment. Mrs. Dobbs poured another round of tea. Marlene decided it was a good moment to get the conversation closer to the bone she was after.

"Speaking of Harley, do you know anything about what he did in the war, the spying part?"

Mrs. Dobbs gave her a sharp look. "How is that germane to our discussion?"

"I don't know if it is," said Marlene with a casual shrug. "You tell me. Two men whose lives have been intertwined since childhood. One of them is accused of spying, the other one is an actual spy who defends the accused. I think Mr. Blaine's character and career are important to a consideration of what happened back in 1951. But that's up to you, what you want to tell me."

After a brief pause, Mrs. Dobbs nodded and said, "Well, I don't suppose Harley would mind at this late date. He certainly was quite free in talking to Richard, and as I said, Richard was famous for not keeping a secret. Richard told me all I know about this. Harley was, as I said, recruited into the OSS right after law school and operated in the Pacific. He was a talented linguist. He spoke fluent French and he knew Japanese and Chinese, which was quite rare in those days. He spent some time in Saigon, posing as a Vichy Frenchman, spying on Japanese shipping. Then he was in the Philippines, and after the war, I think he was in Japan operating against the Soviets. I don't know why he left the Agency. Half-seriously, he used to say it was because he missed seeing us. That's really all I know."

"Then it must have been his CIA contacts that enabled him to learn about Gaiilov."

Mrs. Dobbs stiffened in surprise and her teacup clattered in its saucer. "You know about that?"

"Yes, Mr. Blaine was very forthcoming when I spoke to him. He described a prison meeting in which he laid out the Gaiilov situation for you and Mr. Dobbs, and Mr. Dobbs told him to go ahead if it wouldn't hurt the country."

"Yes, of course, and Harley assured him it wouldn't. Apparently, Harley was involved in bringing Gaiilov over to our side, so he ought to have known. Allen Dulles was insane with rage about it. He never spoke to Harley again, and I understood at one time they were quite close. Well, he's dead, and so is Richard, and so are the men who accused him, and Harley's dying. He won't let me see him, you know?"

"Who, Mr. Blaine?"

"Yes. He says he wants me to remember him as he was. When we were young and full of hope, as he puts it." Mrs. Dobbs fell silent again and Marlene saw that her eyes were brimming. "You know," she said in a strained voice, "I am suddenly quite tired. I wonder if we could continue this at some later time."

"Of course, Mrs. Dobbs. I'd like to come back, if I may, to look through any material in Mr. Dobbs's study that may be relevant."

The older woman nodded and said, "Yes, yes, as you like, although I imagine Hank took everything years ago."

Marlene rose and put her pad and pen away in her purse. "One last thing. What you just now mentioned, that all the people involved are dead. That's what makes it so hard to collect information on this project. I was wondering, do you know what happened to the Russians? Reltzin. And Gaiilov."

"Gaiilov? I have no idea. Reltzin probably lives right here in Washington."

"He does?" asked Marlene with surprise. "How do you know that?"

"Because I see him nearly every week during the concert season. He is a music lover, as am I. We have been nodding to each other for almost twenty-five years, although we have never exchanged a word. He even sent me a card when Richard died. I think Richard would have found that amusing. Harley certainly does."

"He knows you've seen Reltzin?"

"Of course. He would have told you if you'd asked him."

But Marlene had, and he hadn't.

Driving back to Virginia in the yellow VW, Marlene considered what she had learned so far and her options. It was clear that Blaine had lied to her, about being CIA, and about how he had

learned about Gaiilov, and about Reltzin being returned to the Soviet Union, and she didn't know why. He was dying, apparently. Why bother hindering the amateur investigation of an ancient case? Maybe his mind was going and he couldn't keep the old lies straight anymore. In any event, she had gone as far as she could with the accessible material and informants. Moving further would take serious investigative work, full-time work, and that, she had to admit, she could not really accomplish all by herself, and certainly not as an unpaid hobby. It was a lot easier doing investigations when you had a couple of thousand cops behind you.

"How did it go?" asked Maggie when Marlene at last arrived at the Dobbs home. "You don't seem to have any visible claw marks."

"I think it went well," said Marlene. "We had a nice conversation about the case, and about your late father-in-law. And Harley Blaine. Tell me, do you know Blaine at all?"

"Mmm, I'm not sure. He's a hard man to know. He has that perfectly opaque front that guys of that generation cultivated, charming, hail-fellow, slightly boozy, courtly manners. He used to come into town every Christmas with crates of expensive presents. Now the birthday and Christmas presents come by mail. I got the feeling he wanted to be sort of a foster dad and grandparent around here, but he didn't have the . . . I don't know, emotional energy, or whatever. We haven't seen him for a couple of years, although Hank flew out there a couple of months ago. He's very ill, I think." Then she asked, hesitantly, her voice thin and nervous, "Was she angry that I gave you his number?"

"It didn't come up," Marlene lied.

Parking her car in the Federal Gardens lot, Marlene noticed that the next bay was empty. She recalled that she had not seen the old pickup truck owned by Thug 'n' Dwarf for several days. Now that she thought about it, she hadn't seen either of the pair around since an unusually violent fight three nights ago, and she hadn't heard any country music through the party wall either. This was odd, because their dog had whined throughout the previous night. Holding Lucy's hand, she walked from the parking area to the back door of the couple's apartment and pressed her ear against the peeling paint of the door. All she could hear was a faint mewling sound and a rhythmic scratching thump. She peered

through the back window into the small kitchen, a dirtier replica of her own, except that several of the cabinet doors hung open and one of the kitchen chairs was lying on its side. She put her ear to the window. No sounds but the persistent scratch-thump-scratch-whine.

Entering her own apartment, Marlene settled the napping Lucy in her bed, then dialed the manager's office. The manager was a lazy redneck who had a reputation for shakedowns and hustling single mothers short on the rent. The phone rang fifteen times before she slammed it down. Federal Gardens was not a high-service establishment. She could, of course, hear the same lugubrious noises through her walls. The dog was obviously still there.

She bore it for ten minutes, pacing, smoking, and then with a curse she grabbed a table knife from a drawer and dashed out. It took less than a minute to pop the cheap lock on the back door of Thug 'n' Dwarf's apartment. She slipped inside.

As she had suspected, the place was abandoned. The refrigerator held only a few condiments, a moldy package of sliced bologna, and half a stick of butter. The living room was merely filthy and disordered, but the large bedroom bore the signs of serious fighting: a smashed lamp, holes in the plaster, chairs broken, and the bed torn apart. All the drawers had been pulled out of the bureau, and one of them had been flung against the wall hard enough to smash it. If Marlene had been made to guess, she would have said that the couple had engaged in an ultimate argument, Dwarf had cleared out while Thug was at work, and he had come home, observed this fact, taken out his rage on the place itself, and then made his own escape. Leaving the dog.

Who was locked in a closet in the small bedroom.

"Ah, you poor baby!" she cried when she opened the door, and then she drew back, gagging. The beast was lying in its own filth, ribs staring, its black coat matted and dull. It had obviously been half-starved for a long time and deprived of water for days at least. Marlene ran back to the kitchen, put the bologna and the butter in a bowl, filled a small pot with water, and carried both back to the dog. It lapped up the water. The food disappeared in two great gulps. Then it stood up and walked slowly on shaky legs out of the closet.

Marlene drew in her breath. The animal was huge, well over two feet high at the shoulder, with a great, sad-eyed slobbering

head. She judged it to be the result of some ill-advised mating between a St. Bernard and a black retriever.

Cautiously, Marlene patted its head. It licked her hand, coating it all over with hot dog-spit.

"Come on, Buster, let's get you cleaned up," she said, tearing the cord from the shattered lamp and tying it to the dog's chain collar. It followed her docilely next door. She found Lucy awake and curious.

"What's his name?" was her first question when she saw the dog, and then, "Why does he smell so yucky?"

"I don't know his name, dear, and he smells bad because he hasn't had a bath in a long time. That's what we're going to do now. Go run and get your baby shampoo."

Marlene tied the dog to a pipe outside the kitchen and washed it with bucket, scrub brush, and Johnson's No More Tears, and dried it with a cheap chenille bath rug she found in a closet. The dog bore this with admirable patience, lapping at puddles, but otherwise staying still. After the bath, it looked a lot better, shiny and bearing, absurdly, the scent of a clean, small child. When it shook itself, its skin flopped about in a peculiar and disconcerting manner, as if it had been sold a suit two sizes too large at the dog store. Its damp coat steamed in the chilly air, giving it the appearance of a hellhound, albeit a sweet hellhound. Big too, very big, and from the disproportionate size of the paws, planning on becoming bigger still. Marlene wondered if she was making one of her famous mistakes.

"Is he our dog now, Mommy?"

"I guess. Do you like him?"

"Uh-huh. He looks like the Peter Pan dog, but black. Could he baby-sit me when you go out?"

"Maybe. Let's go inside, it's too cold out here."

They went into the kitchen, where the dog downed another quart of water, an elderly Big Mac from the fridge, and four eggs beaten with milk. They all then adjourned to the living room, where the animal plopped himself down in front of the couch where Marlene and Lucy sat, tongue lolling and looking absurdly grateful.

"He looks like Uncle Harry," said Lucy after studying the dog for a while.

"Gosh, you're right, he does," agreed Marlene, laughing. The

dog's face—its sad, intelligent eyes and its general air of battered dependability—was the image of the detective, Harry Bello. "Lucy, you know, I'm glad you reminded me. How would you like it if I asked Uncle Harry to come down and visit?"

"Uh-huh," said Lucy distractedly. "His name is Sweetie."

"Who, the dog?"

"Uh-huh." The dog licked the child's face, throwing her into a fit of giggles. "He likes it."

"If you say so," said her mom.

Arriving at Miami International Airport a few hours after Karp and Fulton, the man who called himself Bill Caballo rented a car and drove west on the Tamiami Trail, out past where the Glades began, until he came to the enormous gun shop that is one of the landmarks of the area. There he paid $435.95 plus tax for a Remington Sportsman 78 bolt-action rifle, with sling, mounting a Tasco 40-mm 4 × scope. He also bought a cheap .22 revolver, a box of .22 long rifle cartridges, a box of 308 Winchester Super-X cartridges, and a bottle of insect repellent, paying cash for all his purchases. He also paid in cash for an hour on the range behind the shop, where he zeroed the rifle until he could put three rounds within the diameter of a half-dollar coin at two hundred yards. He fired a dozen or so rounds from the .22 also, to see if it would fire reliably, which it did. He was not concerned with its accuracy.

Leaving the gun shop, he drove further along the Trail and found a junk market, where he bought an old golf bag and a miscellany of unmatched clubs. He put his new rifle in the golf bag, and bought a meal at a nearby diner.

He then took the Trail to I-95, went north on that freeway to 922, and then took that east across the Broad Causeway, exiting at the Indian Creek Golf Course. He parked and walked around the southern edge of the golf course with the bag slung over his shoulder. He did not look very much like a golfer, but attracted no particular attention. Indian Creek is a public course and they get all kinds there.

He sat down in a mass of scrub behind a large cabbage palmetto, and smeared himself liberally with insect dope. Then he waited. Night fell. He dozed in short snatches. The sky turned gray, then became streaked with red, then the palest possible silvery blue, flecked with small clouds. He stretched and pulled his rifle out of the golf bag, wiped the scope, inserted four rounds into the magazine, and chambered one of

*them. He crawled around the side of a palmetto and lay prone in the
short grass and looked through his scope at Guido Mosca's house.*

*At around six-thirty, Guido Mosca, dressed in Bermudas and a flow-
ered shirt, with fishing rod in hand, walked barefoot out of his house
and onto his little dock. He did this every morning, although he rarely
caught a fish, and he saw no reason to interrupt his routine simply
because, in a few hours, he was scheduled to fly to Washington to testify
before the House Select Committee on Assassinations. He would have
plenty of time to get ready, he thought, which in the event was untrue,
because as soon as he reached the end of the dock he was shot once
through the heart from across the wide channel.*

FIFTEEN

"I still say," said Karp, "we should've flown back yesterday and made Mosca go with us."

Fulton, who was checking out the hang of his jacket and the tuck of his sport shirt in the motel room mirror, gave him a look. It was not the first time since their interview with the mobster that Karp had expressed such sentiments, nor the sixth either. It was starting to get on his nerves.

"Will you relax, for Chrissake!" Fulton snapped. "I should've left you in the office. Look! We're gonna go out now and get in the car, and drive somewhere and have a nice breakfast out on the beach, somewhere where we can get a decent bagel, like you're always bitching about, and then we're gonna drive out to Mr. Mosca's little house and pick him up and if his girlfriend's there we'll look at her tits for a couple minutes, and then we'll drive to the airport and be on the ten-ten flight to National."

"I don't want any breakfast," said Karp. "I want my hands on Guido Mosca. I want his head cradled on my lap. I want him up there in front of the committee, tying Paul Ashton fucking David to Bishop, and to a shooter who looks just like Lee Harvey Oswald and to Cuban shooters who didn't like Kennedy, and to Oswald himself and to whoever this Turm character is. This is *the case*, Clay. It's coming together—I can feel it."

"Can I at least get some coffee?"

"Yeah, if you can find a drive-through. And I want you to *roll* by the window," said Karp, and strode out of the room.

Fifteen minutes later they were at the house on the canal. The patio was deserted. A slight breeze ruffled the water of the pool. Fulton went to the glass door and rang the bell. After a minute, he rang again and rapped on the door with his knuckles. "Jerry's a late sleeper," he remarked.

"I hope so," said Karp, rapping on the glass himself. Fulton said, "Keep ringing. I'll check the front."

Fulton's shout brought Karp running around the side of the house. The detective was at the end of the dock, kneeling over a brightly colored mound. Karp felt his heart wrench around in his chest. He slowed his step. There was obviously no hurry anymore.

"Shot through the middle of the chest at long range," said Fulton, rising from the corpse. "Probably from those bushes across the canal." He looked at Karp and shrugged. "Okay, I was wrong. Who knew?"

"I'll take that literally. Who *did* know? The only people I told at the Washington end about coming down here to get Mosca were Crane . . . and Hank Dobbs. You tell anyone?"

"Hell, no! But you forgot one thing—Tony Bones knew all about it."

"Yeah, but why would Tony have his own guy whacked? He wants to take over South Florida when Trafficante kicks off. There's no damn reason for him to give us the go-ahead, and then give Mosca the go-ahead to talk to us, if all the time he was planning to kill him. The whole thing is too small-time. We do Tony a little favor, go easy on his kid, he does us a little favor, gets one of his guys to talk to us. It's not serious Mob business."

"Somebody Tony told, then?" offered Fulton.

"Yeah, and we're gonna have a talk with Tony about that. But what I think is, this isn't a Mob hit at all. This is a guy who likes to stand off and pop people with a rifle." Fulton thought about this for a while.

"You think the same guys, the Kennedy guys?"

"It's a possible, yeah, and it means somebody's following us. Or knows what we're doing."

Fulton gestured toward where Mosca's body lay. "Whatever, we got to call the sheriff."

"No, call Al Sangredo. Let *him* call the sheriff and explain the situation here. A little professional courtesy would go down pretty

good, and besides, the last thing I want is to get our names involved in a local investigation. Meanwhile . . ." Karp gave the house a long, significant look.

"We toss his place."

"*You* toss his place, Detective. I'm a lawyer. My place is lounging by the pool, contemplating the majesty of the Constitution, and feeling like an asshole."

Later that afternoon, Karp and Fulton were eating pastrami in Sheffler's, a large, bright, highly chilled eatery on Collins in North Miami Beach. Al Sangredo was sitting across from them, sipping on a cup of coffee brewed at about a third of the octane rating he was used to, and listening to the two of them bring him up-to-date around mouthfuls of greasy pink meat. When they were finished, Sangredo said quietly, "That's quite a story. I hope you're not holding anything back from the sheriff about this hit. I vouched for you guys and I have to live in this town."

Sangredo was a big man, six-four, two-seventy. He was a retired NYPD homicide cop who had worked with Fulton for fifteen years in Harlem, a datum recorded in his black eyes which, under an enthusiastic growth of eyebrow, were hard, suspicious, and intelligent. He had the usual tan of the region and his skin was smooth and relatively unlined for a man of fifty-seven. In a city full of "Spanish," he was distinguished by being an actual Spaniard, and he carried himself with the requisite dignity. Fulton assured him that he was not withholding anything germane to a homicide investigation, although he might have had he found anything worthwhile in his quick search of Mosca's house. Jerry Legs was, however, not the sort of mafioso who keeps careful records.

"So," Sangredo continued, "you really think it was the Kennedy people did this?"

"It's our working assumption," answered Karp. "The question is, what do we do about it. You ever run into a Cuban named Angelo Guel?" He pulled out the photograph of Guel. "He'll be older, of course."

Sangredo studied the picture and slowly shook his head. "It's not a face that sticks in my mind. You think he knows something?"

"I don't know, but I'd like to speak to any Cuban mercenary

who was standing on a street corner in New Orleans with Lee Oswald in the fall of sixty-three. Of course, there's no way of telling if he's in Miami or not. We should've asked Mosca if he knew where Guel was. Shit, *now* there's a million things I wish I'd've asked him, but I thought I'd have plenty of time to pump his brains."

"So, what do we do?" mused Sangredo. "I could try to find that girlfriend of his. She wasn't in the house, but she'd been there. She must've taken off as soon as she found the corpse."

Karp shrugged. He wasn't interested in girlfriends. "No, it's Guel we need. And this other Cuban, Carrera. And the mysterious Mr. Turm, whatever his real name is. I'm thinking this is the Sylvia Odio team, the three guys who stopped by her house in Dallas right before the assassination and told her they were going after Kennedy. Two Cubans, one named Angelo, one named Leopoldo, and an American named Leon. If Angelo was Guel—God, he even used his real name!—and Leopoldo was Carrera, then we know who Leon was, for sure. Odio IDed that Leon was Oswald to the FBI after the shooting. Mosca must've seen them in New Orleans just before they left for Dallas."

"Wait a second," said Fulton. "The problem with the Odio story was that at the time she got that visit, Oswald was on his way to Mexico—" He stopped. "Oh, shit!"

"Right," said Karp grimly. "It wasn't Oswald in Mexico at all. It was our lookalike—Caballo. He was on the bus, and he made sure that people on the bus remembered him. He's the voice on the tape the CIA sent to the FBI and then conveniently erased. He's the reason why the cameras outside the Soviet and Cuban embassies happened to go down on the day he was there, because even if he's a close match to Oswald, an actual photograph could've been analyzed to show that it really wasn't Oswald. And that, of course, explains how Oswald was identified leaving a rifle at a gun shop, cashing a big check at a little grocery store, going to a rifle range, and driving a car, even though he was other places at those times and even though he didn't know how to drive. Yeah, that was a slipup! Who would've believed that a macho American man couldn't drive a car? No, guys, this is it. This is the case. V.T. told me early on that Oswald was the key, whether he did it or not, and he was right."

Fulton had been nodding enthusiastically as Karp spoke, and his bloodhound instincts were aroused. "Okay, then the first thing we got to do is find this Odio woman and flash the pictures we got of Guel and the other people on that film, see if any of them ring a bell."

"I wouldn't do that," said Sangredo. They stared at him.

"Why the hell not?" asked Fulton.

"Because the woman's burned out. She's been telling the same story for twelve years and all it's got her is grief. She's had threats from the nutso Cubanos. Every assassination buff in the country wants to show her a picture."

"You *know* her?" asked Karp, amazed.

"Not exactly. But I know people who know her. She lives here in Miami, in what they call seclusion. My advice is, get your ducks in a row before you go see her. Find Guel and get a decent picture of him, him and this Carrera, instead of the fuzzy shit you showed me, then go see her. Because you're only going to get one shot at her and it better be right."

They all thought about this for a while. Then Karp said, "Okay, let's go for Guel. What'll it take to find him?"

Sangredo considered this in his cautious way. "Um, well, I'm one guy. I have some contacts with the sheriff and Miami PD. I could run checks."

"And we have guys in New Orleans and Dallas could do the same thing," said Fulton. "But it's going to take some time."

"Which we don't have," said Karp. "Mosca was aced right under our noses. It could happen to Guel too, if we start getting close."

Sangredo looked at him sharply. "It sounds like you're saying you guys got a leak up there."

"It's a possibility," replied Karp. "That, or we're being followed. Which is one reason why I don't want you to do what you just suggested. I don't want the cops involved." He held up a hand against the expostulations of the other two men. "No, listen! This isn't business as usual. The assassination nuts have made a lot of hay about all the people connected to the Kennedy thing who've died under mysterious circumstances over the years; I'm not saying I'm buying that whole line, but I'll go with some of it, especially after what happened this morning. So the fewer people who know we're after Guel and Carrera, the better."

"But, hell, Butch," Sangredo complained, "if I got to work alone it's going to take years to find the bastards."

"I didn't say alone," answered Karp. "My thought is we should have a talk with Tony Buonafacci."

They stared at him, stupefied. Fulton stuck a finger in his ear and screwed it around vigorously. "Hey, sorry," he said, "I must be getting deaf. I thought you just said we should bring the fucking *Mafia* in to look for this potential key witness."

"I did. No, wait! It makes sense. Tony's going to be pissed somebody whacked a made guy on his turf, one, and two, Tony doesn't particularly like Cubans and he'd be glad to finger one of them. A couple of years ago, when a bunch of Cuban gunslingers were taking potshots at me, Ray Guma sent a material witness in the case down here to Tony and she was fine. So . . ."

"Damn it, Butch," said Fulton, "that's not the same thing. We still haven't cleared up the possibility that the Mob is *involved* in this thing. We set them loose on this and even if they do find our guys they're just as likely to end up like Johnny Roselli did last summer. They cut his legs off and stuffed him into an oil drum and threw his legs in there too. He was still alive when they dumped the can in the water. You want to *work* with these assholes?"

"No, but there's Mob and Mob. Look, Tony told Mosca to spill the beans. Mosca did. Did you think he was shitting us? No, me neither. There's a possibility that Marcello in New Orleans was involved in it. Some Cubans who might've worked for Trafficante may have been involved in it. And I bet if we had the old man, Santos, on a hot grill he could tell us a lot about what really went down. But Tony's not connected to that end. He's out of the Bollano outfit in Brooklyn. Marcello's New Orleans, which is part of the Chicago outfit. There's not much love lost between New York and Chicago, especially since Chicago's got the gold mine in Vegas tied up tight. No, if Tony can slip it to Chicago in some minor, undetectable way, he's not going to lose sleep over it."

"This is incredible," said Fulton. "In all the years I worked with you, you always made it a rule not to get in bed with the Mob, and now here you're diving in and pulling up the covers."

"Oh, that," said Karp airily. "That's for a regular investigation, where you're eventually going to do some serious law. What we're doing now is some kind of political horseshit. At this stage I just

want to find out who killed Kennedy and how they did it. As for rules—no rules.''

After lunch, Karp called V.T. in Washington.

"Butch, am I glad you called!''

"Why, what's up?''

"I can't find the file. Tell me you took it with you!''

"What file, V.T.? All I have here are the stills from the Depuy film.''

"Oh, God! We've been ripped off! The file with the original Depuy film and documents and the original CIA stuff is missing. The last time I used it was the day before yesterday, and I went to add some stuff to it, and I pulled the phony jacket in the health insurance drawer where we kept it, and it was gone.''

"Who knew where we kept it?''

"Hell, *I* don't know, Butch,'' said V.T. irritably. "This isn't the KGB. People are in and out of here all day. It wouldn't take a master spy to notice that we always head for the admin files after we use that material.''

"But we have copies.''

"Yeah, sure,'' said V.T. "I had a copy of the film made, and Xeroxes of all the other stuff, one set. I've got it stashed in the—''

"No! Not over the phone. Just keep it safe, for God's sake. Without that film we've got zip.''

"Mmm, I detect new levels of paranoia blossoming. Not that I blame you. Okay, ready for some good news? I think I found PXK.''

"You did? Great, great! What is it?''

"It's a Baton Rouge trucking concern. Right area, convenient to New Orleans and its colorful fascists. It's owned by a gentleman named Patrick Xavier Kelly.

"I'm having Pete Melchior check him out, find out if he knew Depuy, and run his name by the local cops, see if there's any connection to Ferrie or that Camp Street crowd.''

"That sounds good, V.T.,'' said Karp, his mood lifting slightly. "Here's the situation down here. By the way, this is for you, me, and Bert—nobody else.'' Then he related the gist of what Mosca had revealed, and what had happened afterward. V.T. was silent throughout this narration, and afterward he made no response but

to ask when Karp would be returning; and, after having been told two or three days, he said good-bye and broke the connection, as Karp had expected. V.T. was smart enough to understand that Mosca's murder and Karp's warning meant that there was a leak at the Washington end. Then Karp called home.

Marlene was actually relieved when Karp informed her that he would be away for several days, maybe a week. She felt she needed the time to see if Sweetie was going to work out. Marlene expected a lot of her mate, but even she thought that adding a dog the size of a young bear to the household, that dog being uncontrollable, might be an excessive demand.

But Sweetie, as it turned out, proved more than controllable, and was, in fact, eager to please. Marlene got some dog-training books out of the library and bought a leash and a long line, and she and Lucy devoted an entire day to the first few chapters. We learned "no"; we learned to go on the leash without jerking Mommy off her feet; we almost learned "down"; we learned "come," which is easy, but we failed miserably at "stay," which is hard. We also learned our name is Sweetie. We got to eat a cubic foot of kibble, and rode to the store in the back of the VW hatchback, and did a good deal of face-licking and general running around. Heaven.

"Let's knock it off, honey," said Marlene to her daughter as the four o'clock sun began its descent into the trees.

"Is Sweetie trained now?" asked Lucy.

"Um, well, we made a start. We'll do some more tomorrow."

"Could we, could we train him to bite bad people, like on TV?"

"It's a possibility," said Marlene cautiously. "Do you have any bad people in mind?"

"Yes, Jeremy," said Lucy in a low and menacing voice.

"Jeremy Dobbs? But he's just a little boy. I thought you liked him."

"I hate him. He broke my pink crayon. On *purpose!*"

There followed a discussion of criminal intent and the nature of just punishment, which Marlene thought went pretty well, and they drove back from the park where they had been running the dog to their apartment. The mention of Jeremy Dobbs had raised in Marlene's mind the problem of what she was going to do with her new monster while she worked at Maggie's. Maggie had no

dog, and Marlene suspected she was a cat sort of person, and one who would not appreciate Sweetie being given the run of her lovely gardens, winter or not. Even Marlene experienced a frisson of fear when she saw Sweetie standing next to Lucy, and realized that it could, if driven by some unknowable doggy impulse, take the child's head off with a snap of its jaws. No, let's wait awhile before we spring Sweetie on old Maggs, was Marlene's thought.

Marlene started dinner and Lucy and the dog went up to Lucy's room. The animal had been quickly integrated into Lucy's fantasy play, which was rich and weird. Marlene could hear her chatting to Sweetie, as to her various dolls and toys. The dog had decided to sleep in Lucy's room, or rather in the closet thereof, the twin of the one from which Marlene had rescued it in the identical apartment next door. Marlene suspected that it had been confined there when indoors for nearly its entire life; pathetic, but there it was. Home was prison was home. Marlene had seen it often enough with criminals. Another oddity: Sweetie didn't bark, a characteristic that Marlene also attributed to its deprived puppy-hood. It made a variety of yipping and groaning noises instead. Marlene's training books said that excessive barking could be "corrected" by early discipline, which apparently Thug 'n' Dwarf (probably mostly Thug) had been excessively free with. So: the world's only wimpy hellhound, and perhaps it was for the best, all things considered. It gave her another excuse to keep Sweetie; the poor thing wouldn't last a minute in a pound pen. Dachshunds would cream it.

Marlene went into Lucy's room to announce dinner. Sweetie was lying on Lucy's bed wrapped in an old pink baby blankie, with a knitted pink doll's bonnet set absurdly on top of its massive head, and on its face there was an expression of forlorn and pathetic helplessness.

"We're playing baby," Lucy announced.

Marlene broke up.

The phone rang during dinner, and when Marlene answered it a familiar low voice said, "Tomorrow. I'm driving."

"Harry," said Marlene, "first you say, 'Hello, how are you,' then you do a little small talk, and then you say what you're going to do. Remember? We're supposed to work on our conversational skills."

"How's the kid?" said Harry Bello, refusing to be drawn.

"The kid's fine, Harry. Did you have any problem getting away on short notice?"

"I took a leave. Around four."

That concluded the conversation. Marlene had left a message at Harry's office the previous day. "Tell him I'd like to see him and that I have a situation here where I could use his help." This was the response. Harry knew "come" as well as Sweetie did. It still made Marlene sad, and a little guilty—her hold and Lucy's hold over Harry Bello—but not quite sad and guilty enough to make her not use it.

Maggie Dobbs was repotting a rare white frangipani she had grown from seed. Behind her in the conservatory she could hear Manuel working, mixing potting soil, mumbling to himself, singing snatches of tuneless song. She spent an hour or so out here most mornings, while Gloria was getting the children up and fed. Hank was long gone to the Hill, to start his usual twelve hours. It was the most peaceful and nearly the most satisfying part of her day. The plants, unlike most of the other organisms in her life, were content to merely be. Their demands were modest and easily satisfied with a slight displacement of position, a little more or less to drink, a few spoonfuls of this or that.

"There! Comfy now?" she said to the frangipani, and felt herself blush. Talking to plants, the first sign. She put the frangipani firmly back on its shelf. On the other hand they didn't talk back, didn't look at you as if you were not quite up to it, didn't roll their eyes to heaven at one of your remarks and make you feel like a dunce. She took her apron off and hung it up and as she walked down the aisle to the door a bloodred mass of begonia caught her eye and she shivered slightly, recalling the bloodied face of the monte man and the smear on the window and the waving knife. There was that too, the problem of Marlene.

She left the conservatory and went to the kitchen, poured a cup of coffee, and tried to relax into the reassuring chatter and clatter of breakfast time. It was all very well to complain about being bored and to joke about the wife-of blues, but joking and complaining were one thing; actually *leaving* the comfortable middle-class bubble in which she had spent her entire life, and entering a world in which men carried knives and waved them in your face,

spraying blood, in the company of a . . . a—Maggie Dobbs did not exactly know what Marlene was, but what it was frightened her. And yes, she was admirable, but Maggie was starting to realize that admiration and participation were quite different things.

And, of course, she had involved Marlene in the book project. She recalled Hank's reaction when she had first told him about what Marlene was doing. His face had flushed and his eyes had opened wide and his mouth had dropped open, and she had braced herself for a scolding, but somehow it hadn't happened. That was odd; as if Hank had *wanted* Marlene involved for some reason, and she thought she had seen in the moment, just before he would have started yelling at her, a calculation replace the anger in his eyes.

The phone rang. It was Marlene, calling to say she wouldn't be by today and maybe the next day too. Something had come up— a visitor from out of town. Maggie hung up the phone and felt a wave of relief. She was ashamed of it, but it was relief all the same.

Harry Bello stiffened when Lucy came into the living room, followed by Sweetie.

"A dog," he said flatly, meaning, "Unnatural mother, how can you let my precious goddaughter in the same house as this drooling monster?"

"Relax, Harry. He's a sweetheart," said Marlene, leaning over, grabbing the dog by its ears, and swinging the huge, jowly head from side to side. "Aren't you a sweetheart? Aren't you? Aren't you a lily-livered candy-ass?"

The dog licked her face ecstatically and thrashed its whiplike tail.

"See, he's harmless," said Marlene.

But Harry wasn't looking at the dog or at her; he was staring at Lucy, who was ignoring him.

"Aren't you going to say hello to Uncle Harry?" Marlene asked. "Come on, Lucy, give him a hug and a kiss."

Lucy endured an embrace and then scampered up the stairs to her own room, followed by Sweetie. Marlene took in the stricken expression on Harry's usually blank face and said, "Oh, Harry, they're like that at this age. She'll come around."

"She forgot me already," said Harry, a faint whiff of accusation in his tone.

"No, she hasn't, Harry. You'll spend some time, she'll see you, she'll get used to you again—don't worry about it." What Marlene did not voice was her understanding that Lucy didn't have to make nice to Harry because Harry was so obviously enslaved. She loved him in exactly the same way that she was coming to love Sweetie. Now she had two dogs.

Marlene made coffee and they sat at the kitchen table while Marlene spread out her notes and files on Reltzin and Gaiilov, and laid out the Dobbs project, what she had learned and what she wanted Harry to do.

"How long do you think?" she asked after Harry had sat silently shuffling bits of paper for a while.

He shrugged. Tapping a yellowed magazine photograph of Reltzin, he said, "Him? A couple of days. He goes to concerts, he's a citizen, he's got a job or a pension, a phone, electric. There's ways. The other one, the spy? Who knows? We don't have a picture? No? Then it depends. The guy wants to stay lost and he's got experts to help him, then probably never, with just me working. If he don't give a damn somebody finds him? It depends on the breaks. Maybe this Reltzin sends him a birthday card every year. We find him, we'll know better."

In fact, it took Harry Bello somewhat under forty-eight hours to find Viktor Reltzin. Marlene had made a bed for Harry on the couch, which he occupied only intermittently and for short periods. Otherwise he worked the streets and the phones. Through liberal and illegal use of his NYPD detective's shield, Harry got into the Kennedy Center's concert subscription records, and there he was. Harry then confirmed that indeed a man named Reltzin, with the right stats and face, lived in an apartment on Connecticut Avenue near Kalorama. He had an unlisted phone number, which did not prevent Harry from finding out what it was. Marlene called it.

A mild voice with a faint Slavic accent answered. Marlene had decided not to dissemble at all. If Reltzin hung up she'd figure out something else, but she thought that someone who had dwelt long in the tangled world of espionage, and who retained the grace to nod to the widow of an accused spy in public, might not be averse to some plain dealing.

And so it proved. Reltzin agreed at once to see her. Would this afternoon be convenient? It would.

Marlene dressed in a dark pink De La Renta suit and a patterned black silk shirt she had rescued from Maggie's discard pile and altered to fit. She had to run out to the mall on Route 50 to get fresh hose and a pair of black heels. Thus attired, she left Lucy with Bello and the other dog and drove into town.

Reltzin's building was one of the noble brownish piles that line the upper reaches of Connecticut Avenue south of the zoo. The man who opened the door for her was neatly dressed in a dark blue suit, the jacket buttoned over a quiet tie. The face was neat as well, the expression controlled and formally attentive. He gestured her inside. Marlene was glad she had thought to dress up; this man would not have been pleased to entertain Marlene in her usual gypsy rags.

"I have prepared tea," he said, and led her through a dark green–painted, dimly lit foyer to a large room not much less dim.

He motioned, and she sat on a heavy gray brocade sofa in front of a low mahogany table upon which tea things were laid. The windows of the room were obscured with thick maroon velvet drapes. Yellow light came from two standard lamps with fringed shades. Marlene glanced at the coffee table. There was a plate of petit fours and one of little sandwiches, made of white bread with the crusts cut off. Reltzin had gone through some trouble. She peeked at a sandwich: egg salad. It occurred to Marlene that perhaps he did not have many visitors.

She watched him as he fussed with something at a sideboard: a samovar, a tall brass one with a blue flame under it. He was not a large man, but he held himself erect. Marlene judged him to be about seventy. He had an egg-shaped head downed with sparse cropped grayish hair of the type blonds grow when old, and a blunt Russian nose. When he turned toward her, bearing a lacquered tray with two tall glasses on it, his eyes, the color of ancient blue jeans, gazed intermittently at her between the flashes from round wire spectacles.

The tea glasses were fitted with brass holders. Marlene sipped: blazing hot, bitter, smoky, strong.

"Do you like it?" asked Reltzin.

"It's fine, Mr. Reltzin," said Marlene. She took a cube of sugar from a small brass bowl and popped it into her mouth, slurping the tea past the sweet lump until it was dissolved. Reltzin smiled

at her, showing a glimpse of bad Soviet dentistry, and did the same.

"So," said Reltzin when they had slurped sufficiently and eaten a sandwich and talked a bit about beverage-drinking customs in various parts of the world, "you are writing a book about Richard Dobbs."

"Not exactly. I'm doing research for one. Your name, of course, came up."

"But I didn't know Dobbs, except by reputation, of course."

"True," said Marlene. "But you knew Jerome Weinberg. And Armand Dimitrievitch Gaiilov."

A tiny look of surprise at the mention of the latter name, a little hardness showing momentarily in the blue eyes. "Yes, Weinberg. A walk-in at the embassy. I was on duty that day and so I was designated as the contact. You understand that every Soviet embassy has standing orders on how to treat such walk-ins. Most are valueless, but occasionally we got a prize. Like Weinberg."

"Just a minute: you're saying you were a KGB officer?"

"NKVD, actually. This was in 1950. Yes, a very small NKVD officer. But Weinberg was a very big catch. He was a records clerk in the Navy Department and he had access to plans for nuclear submarines. At that time, the idea that you could build a submarine that would never have to surface, that could approach a hostile shore and fire nuclear missiles at an enemy city, this was just beginning to be discussed in military circles. So it was vital for us to understand how far the Americans had gone in both theory and practice. All of this Weinberg offered us."

"He said he came from Dobbs?"

"Most assuredly! That was what convinced us to trust him. We knew who Dobbs was, of course. An important figure."

"What proof did he have that he was working for Dobbs?" asked Marlene, scribbling notes.

"Well, proof!" answered Reltzin, with a dismissive and elegant gesture of his long-fingered hands. "He had the material, from the highest levels of naval planning, with Dobbs's initials on them. We copied them and he brought them back the same day. A good communist, Weinberg," he added reflectively. "This is why he did it."

"And he said Dobbs was a communist too?"

Reltzin smiled, "Oh, no, Weinberg considered him to be what

Lenin called a useful idiot. A man of, shall we say, somewhat foggy political beliefs. He thought the nuclear submarine program an idiocy. He thought if he gave away the secrets, the Soviet Union would of course develop its own program apace, and then, when the navy found this out, they would cancel their own program." His lifted eyebrows and rolled eyes indicated what he thought of this absurdity.

"You must understand, Miss Ciampi, that at this date the Soviet Union had just completed one of the greatest coups in the history of espionage, the capture of the secret of the atomic bomb, from the most closely guarded place in North America. Fuchs and Greenglass passed the secrets out right under the noses of your security officers. Harry Gold made regular visits to the Soviet consulate in New York. No one suspected the operation until we, the USSR that is, exploded the bomb. So, you understand, we thought we were dealing with the same hopeless sort of amateurs."

"Not quite; you got caught."

Reltzin nodded agreeably. "Yes, indeed, red-handed, so to speak." He waited for Marlene to appreciate his little joke. "It was a complete surprise, I may say. I had no indication from Weinberg or from our various sources in the U.S. government that anyone had any suspicion. A curious matter. In any case, I was captured. Ordinarily, when an embassy official is caught spying, he is declared persona non grata and shipped home. The country caught spying retaliates by expelling one of the other nation's diplomats and that is the end of the matter. In my case, however . . ."

"Yes?"

"In my case, they wanted me to testify against Dobbs. I refused, naturally. And then they said that they would let the authorities in the Soviet Union know that I had revealed damaging material, that I, in fact, had betrayed Weinberg for what we used to call imperialist gold. This, of course, was in the Stalin years. I would have been shot immediately. So, I was allowed to defect. They pumped me, I told what I knew, which was not very much. I was a very small *apparatchik*, as I have said. And they gave me this life." He gestured broadly to the apartment. "I am in the stamp business, by the way: specialty Eastern Europe and the Far East."

"You did better than Weinberg, anyhow," said Marlene.

"Oh, yes, Weinberg was given thirty years, the same as Harry

Gold. But he was a traitor. The only reason they didn't execute him was that he informed on Dobbs."

"He lied about Dobbs, you mean. To save his own neck he threw them a bigger fish."

A wintry smile. "Did he? Perhaps. I never had reason to believe that Weinberg was lying about Dobbs, but maybe you are correct. Who can tell? Weinberg was assassinated in prison two years after he began his term."

"You say, 'assassinated'?"

"Well, murdered at any rate. His throat was cut. I understand they never found the killer. Perhaps only a feeble attempt was made to find him."

"What did you think when the case against Dobbs collapsed?"

"Well, at the time, I couldn't understand it. But later things leaked out, and of course, there was the lawyer—Dobbs's lawyer, Blaine—and gradually I was able to put together what must have happened."

"Which was?"

"Oh, well, the papers were full of speculation about this mysterious Mr. X that Blaine was threatening to call as a witness that Dobbs was innocent. Of course, I knew that this had to be Gaiilov, because Gaiilov had been turned in Japan, then he doubled, and *then* he defected just as our counterintelligence people were about to grab him. Blaine was the CIA agent who turned him, there in Japan. So, of course he knew that the CIA would never let him testify in open court. Even his whereabouts were secret. Also there were many in the CIA who did not believe that Gaiilov was really a defector, so it would've been *doubly* embarrassing to the government. So to speak." He smiled again.

Amusing man, Mr. Reltzin, thought Marlene, smiling back. Hard to remember he had been a functionary in one of the most horrendous organizations in human history.

"So he wasn't exchanged either," said Marlene. "He's still in the U.S.?"

"I would think so, although I really have no idea. It's over twenty-five years now. I doubt that he is high on the KGB's list of targets. Higher than me, perhaps, but not very high. And as you see, I live comfortably, an American citizen, with a small business. I expect Gaiilov may be similarly situated. Or perhaps not."

"How do you mean?" Marlene had caught an odd tone in his last remark.

Reltzin sipped some tea and then looked away, up at the ceiling, or perhaps into the past. "He had a reputation, in the service. A high liver—women, gambling, yes, but more—he was a . . . how can I say this . . . an adventurer; spying, conspiracy, this was his life's blood. Intelligence services are wise to restrict their recruitment of such types, you understand, but each service must have some of them. Ah, *reckless*, that is the word I was looking for. Reckless. So. Perhaps he died, from this. Or he has become old and careful. I'm sorry I can't help you."

"No, you've been more than helpful, Mr. Reltzin," said Marlene.

"I am happy to," said Reltzin. "Perhaps you could in return do me a small service." He rose and went over to a bookcase and returned with a small portrait in a silver frame. A thin woman in early middle age peered out, squinting against the sun. With her was a younger woman, pretty in her dowdy clothes, and a little girl, in blond pigtails, holding her hand. "My family," said Reltzin. "They were taken, of course. I tell myself, they would have been taken anyway, if I had returned, but . . . you perhaps have contacts, with the government? They must all be dead, but, if you could, I would like to know. If you could."

"How did it go?" asked Bishop.

The man who called himself Caballo said, "Hold on," walked over and turned down the television and picked up the phone again. He said, "No problem. So, there's just Guel left here, right?"

"Right. But the situation with Guel is that he's apt to have papers."

"You're thinking a fire?"

"Yes, that would be best," said Bishop. "Make it a hot one."

SIXTEEN

Tony Bones and his little entourage were easy to spot on the sun-sodden terrace of the Bal Harbour Inn. Karp watched them for a moment from the shaded entranceway. Occupying two tables of the twenty or so arranged around the curving terrace, they wore suits in pastel fruit colors, darker shirts opened down to the chest, considerable gold showing amid the hair there, bad shaves, and sharp razor cuts. Karp himself was wearing an inappropriate dark Washington-lawyer suit and tie.

There was a churning among the population of the two tables. Men rose and left in pairs and trios, other pairs and trios arrived. One man only was stationary amid this movement. Tony Bones was dressed in a pale tan suit and a dark red open shirt, and over this he wore a long, thin hatchet face, the mouth a lipless V like a shark's, flat black eyes, same fish. A central casting Mafia don, thought Karp; with a face like that he should have gone into installing carpeting and let the guys who looked like the family grocer run the Mob.

Karp walked slowly toward the two tables. As he approached, all the button men stopped what they were doing and looked him unsmilingly over.

Then Tony spotted him. Big grin, a wave. He didn't stand, he shook Karp's hand sitting. He was very short; he didn't want his people to see him standing next to Karp. Aside from that, the gangster seemed genuinely glad to meet him. As Karp had expected; this was an odd aspect of his long-standing relationship

with the Honorable Society, in New York and, so it seemed, here in Miami. They always gave him a smile and a big hello, whether he had sent them to prison or not; maybe *especially* if he had sent them to prison. This confirmed Karp's impression that wise guys were essentially insane people.

Now Karp was being introduced to a covey of Joeys, Jimmies, Jillies, and Johnnies with indistinguishable vowel-terminating names. Tony Bones gestured him to a chair. The others drifted away.

"How's it goin', Butch? You want something? Coffee? You eat yet? Sure?"

"Yeah, I just ate, Tony. I guess you heard already."

"Yeah, yeah, hell of a thing. The girl called me in the morning. Fuckin' Colombians!"

"Why do you think it was Colombians?" asked Karp.

"Hey, Colombians, Jamaicans, Cubans, whatever. The fuck I know! I'm gonna find out who and then they're gonna wish they was still back in the fuckin' jungle."

"You're sure it wasn't an outfit?"

Tony looked insulted. "Nahh! What're you talkin', outfit? What, somebody wants to send me a message, send Santos a message, they whack *Jerry Legs*? Hey, why'nt they whack my dry cleaner, my liquor guy? It don't make no sense, follow? You're sending somebody a message, it don't make no sense to send it in Chinese, you know? They want me to fuckin *read* it. They want to whack somebody, they go for somebody with some weight on him. Him, for instance." Tony pointed out one of the Joeys.

"The other thing, it could be, maybe Jerry burned somebody. But I think, no, that wasn't his thing. He wasn't interested in business, he wasn't a hustler. You wanna know, Jerry didn't have much goin' for him upstairs, tell the truth. So why whack him, except some fuckin' jungle spic don't know any better?"

"You know this guy?" Karp slid the photo of Angelo Guel across the table. Tony looked at it carefully.

"This the one you think did Jerry? What, a Colombian, right?"

"Cuban. And I've got no reason to believe he had anything to do with the murder. In fact, I happen to think that whoever hit Jerry is going to go after this guy. Angelo Guel his name is."

"You know who he is? The shooter."

Karp passed him another eight-by-ten. "I like this guy for it. He calls himself Bill Caballo."

The capo stared at the photograph. "How come you like him for it?"

"Mostly gut feeling. This guy's turned up in a lot of places, connected to the Kennedy thing in various ways. We were talking to Jerry about stuff that might pin down the connection between Cuba, the CIA, and the assassination. It turned out he knew a lot of good stuff. He got whacked for it, so I look at who benefits from having him killed, and who among all those people has a rep as a serious shooter, and I come up with Bill here. Of course, they could've hired some kid off the street too, but I doubt it. You wouldn't."

"I wouldn't what?"

"If you wanted to kill somebody and you didn't want it traced back to you. Would you hire some kid for a couple of grand or would you get Jilly over there to do it? I mean, what's the best way of keeping it close?"

Tony nodded. "Yeah, right, I see what you're saying. Not Jilly personally, to tell the truth, but let's say I got a guy of that type." He tapped the photo of Caballo. "So, you think this scumbag is the hitter for . . . for what? The people did Kennedy?" He looked at the photograph more carefully. "Yeah! This guy looks like what's-his-name, the scumbag they framed, Oswald." He compressed his lips thoughtfully and nodded several times. Tony Bones had dropped out of school in the tenth grade but he was a full professor with tenure in the Department of Comparative Conspiracy. It gave Karp a peculiar and disturbing sense of satisfaction to find that Tony Bones was not an adherent of Warren.

"We could find this guy, if he's still in town," Tony offered.

"The only reason he'd still be in town is if Guel is in town too," said Karp. "Find Guel before he does and we have a good chance."

Tony indicated the two photographs lying on the table. "Let me keep these. I'll put the word out."

Karp wrote the phone number of his motel on the back of Guel's picture, and then hesitated, holding the glossy.

"Tony, you're gonna tell me if you find this Guel, right? And if Caballo turns up, I need to talk to him too. No Johnny Roselli on this one, okay?"

Tony smiled. The flat shark's eyes were unamused. "Roselli was a Chicago thing. Had nothing to do with any of the outfits down here. I tell you what, Butch. I find this fucker, I'll ask him did he whack Kennedy. He'll talk to me."

Fulton was waiting on Collins Avenue outside the hotel, in the Pontiac, with the AC running. When Karp got in, he asked, "How did it go?"

"Shitty," Karp snarled. "You were right, we never should've gone to see him. Crap!"

"What, he told you to get lost?"

"No, worse. He's going to look for Guel and if Caballo makes a move, he's going to grab him."

"He told you this?"

"No, but that's what's going to go down."

"So, what do we do?"

"Find him ourselves, you, me, and Al. Hell, we haven't even started. Maybe he's in the phone book. Maybe he's on late-night TV selling carpet—Crazy Angelo the Rug King. We could get lucky."

"Well," said Fulton, "we're due."

"How long do you think you'll be working on this?" asked Maggie Dobbs. "I mean, it's been a while and the . . ." She stopped, embarrassed.

They were in the Dobbs kitchen sharing a cup of coffee as usual, before Marlene went off to do research and Maggie did whatever she had planned with the children. Marlene regarded her closely. "Um, is something wrong, Maggie?"

"No, I just meant . . . well, I just wanted to know when you'll be finished."

This was so lame a request, and so obviously a cover for a deeper distress, that Marlene hardly knew how to respond. She decided to take it at face value, and answered, "Well, that depends on what you want me to do. I could write up what I've got so far, and work on developing an index to the various commentaries on the case. That should make it easy on whoever does the actual writing. I've got the beginnings of a descriptive index to the films, and I could finish that. The real problem, though, is Gaiilov." Marlene explained who Gaiilov was.

"But how do you know he's even still alive?" asked Maggie.

"I don't. But that's the only big source I haven't explored. So I'm looking for him, trying to follow up any traces he might have left." Marlene didn't mention that she had set Harry Bello on just this task. He was down at the Library of Congress now, doing searches, to see whether anyone, anywhere, had mentioned the name of Armand Dimitrievitch Gaiilov in any newspaper or magazine or phone book during the last twenty-five years. The reason Marlene didn't mention it was because it was a hopeless task, and because she did not want to spook the already desperately nervous woman with the information that she had allowed another stranger into the Dobbses' business.

"Aside from that," Marlene continued, "I plan to visit your mother-in-law again, and I guess I'd like to go out to Texas and see Harley Blaine."

"Is that necessary?"

"Yes, I think it is. You'd have to spring for the airfare and expenses, of course."

"Oh, God! This is so complicated now. When we started, I just thought . . . I don't know—organizing the things we had, the story. I didn't expect all this *investigation*. It's like having the police in the house, like we did some crime."

"Okay, I'll stop," said Marlene agreeably.

"You will?"

"Of course. It's no skin off my ass if you never find out whether sterling Dick Dobbs sold his country to the Reds or not."

"But he didn't!" cried Maggie in horror. Inanely, her glance darted around the room, as if she were checking to see if anyone had overheard this blasphemy.

"Yeah, so you say, and I believe you're right. But I talked to Viktor Reltzin the other day, and he swears he thought Jerome Weinberg *wasn't* lying. And why should he lie at this late date, a lonely old Russian gent? He's got no horse in the race: the Reds killed his whole family, so he's sure as shit not protecting a Soviet secret."

"But it's impossible!"

"No, it's only hard to believe, which is not quite the same thing. That's why we need to talk to Gaiilov. Everyone else with direct knowledge of the affair has already weighed in, pro or con, or died.

We can make a fair case for Richard's innocence, true; but a fair case isn't going to be good enough. We need fresh meat.''

Maggie wished this disturbing woman had never come into her life. She wished the great Dobbs case were still a pile of dusty papers and films into which she might dip from time to time after Hank had needled her. He really hadn't needled her that often anyway. Now she had *Marlene* needling her too. She felt an absurd urge to run back and lose herself in the aisles of her greenhouse. Suppressing it, ashamed of these thoughts, she swallowed hard and said, "I'll talk to Hank.''

The following day, Marlene awoke to the smell of coffee and the sound of domestic clatter in the kitchen. She pulled on a kimono and went to investigate. Her daughter was instructing Harry Bello on the preparation of the royal toast.

"You have to make the jelly *even*,'' said Lucy.

"Good morning,'' said Marlene. "What's going on?''

"There's coffee,'' said Harry.

"Okay, even,'' said Harry, as he finished coating the two squares of crustless toast with a millimetric layer of perfect purple. "Is that it?''

"No,'' said Lucy, "now you have to make them into *triangoos*.''

The triangoos were cut. Lucy nodded in approval and tossed one of the pieces to Sweetie.

Marlene said, "Lucy, go watch cartoons. And take the dog. And eat your breakfast yourself, understand?''

The child trotted off with the beast and soon the little apartment was filled with the sounds of cute characters killing one another.

Marlene poured herself a cup of coffee and took a welcome swallow. "This is nice of you, Harry. Did she get you up?''

"Nah. I don't sleep. I enjoy it.''

"She's a monster. *Triangoos*, my ass!'' Marlene laughed. They sat down across the battered table.

"So, Harry, any bright ideas?''

"No. The guy's gone. I couldn't even find his name, from the time when the Dobbs trial was big news. It's all this 'Mr. X' crap in the papers from back then. He's not in any phone directory. He doesn't run a business, not under Gaiilov anyway. He's got no

credit. He doesn't have a gas card. He's got no criminal record. I'm thinking they covered him."

"What, like witness protection?"

Harry nodded.

"Yeah, well," said Marlene, "that's it then. Fun while it lasted."

"So, did he?" asked Harry.

"Dobbs? Nah, what it was, I think they just squeezed this pisher Weinberg, waved the chair at him—this was just about when they toasted the Rosenbergs—and told him they'd let him cop if he gave them Mr. Big and he just pulled Dobbs's name out of a hat. The guy just doesn't say 'spy' to me. I mean, why the hell should he? He had money up the ying-yang, a wife, a kid, a good war record. He was planning on going into politics, for crying out loud! He was golden."

"There were those guys in England. Same story."

Marlene stared at him. It always surprised her when Harry Bello proved to be other than a mobile machine for solving crimes in the greater metropolitan New York area. "You mean Burgess and McLean. And Philby. Right, but they were commies from the beginning. Way back in college."

"And he wasn't. Dobbs."

Marlene shook her head, but then realized with some surprise that she knew relatively little about Richard Dobbs's early life. Some films from college days, some anecdotes from family and friends, but nothing that gave her a picture of the man's formative years. Of course, she had focused on the events and circumstances surrounding the spy case. On the other hand . . .

"The widow," said Harry, and Marlene laughed.

"Harry, stop doing that!"

"What?"

"Reading my mind. As a matter of fact, I was going to see the Widow Dobbs anyway. I could do it today, except . . . Maggie Dobbs has been acting a little, I don't know, not exactly hostile but like she'd be just as happy if I was involved in a fatal accident. Something's scaring her."

"You."

"Me?" Marlene fluttered her eyelashes fetchingly. "Little me?"

"Yeah," said Harry. "You scare *me*, and I got a gun."

"Hmm, maybe you're right," Marlene agreed after a moment's thought. "I'm probably not the most suitable companion for a proper Washington matron. Of course, Lucy's going to miss playing with Laura—for about six minutes. They're heartless at this age, and now she has the dog too. It's going to create a jam in the short run, though. I can't exactly take her to Mrs. Dobbs. . . ."

"No problem," said Harry, which was what he always said when Marlene asked him to watch Lucy.

She dressed in her one Washington lady outfit again, with a different shirt and a scarf to oblige the tradition that it was tacky to show twice at the same place wearing the same clothes, called, was told to come over, and headed to the house on L Street.

A whey-faced redheaded young woman in a pale green uniform and apron greeted her at the door with a suspicious stare.

"I'm here to see Mrs. Dobbs."

"An' who shall I say?" said the woman in a thick brogue.

Marlene gave her name and was ushered to the study at the back. Mrs. Dobbs was seated at her husband's desk talking agitatedly on the telephone. She motioned Marlene to a chair and went on talking for a few minutes. When she put down the phone she said, "Miss Ciampi, I'm terribly sorry, but something's come up. A dear friend of mine has been taken to the hospital and I'm afraid I have to go out right away. I tried to reach you at home, but you'd already left. Would it be possible for you to come back another time?"

"Oh, gosh, Mrs. Dobbs, I really wanted to finish up this week," said Marlene. "I mean, I'd hate to overlook anything, even some little thing; it might just be the one piece that brings it all together. Would it be possible for me to just look through things around here—the office . . . ?"

Marlene could see by the curl of the woman's mouth that it was not going to be possible. Time for a lie.

"By the way, I got in touch with Viktor Reltzin," she said quickly, "and he said he thought Weinberg was lying about your husband because he had a grudge against him, something, um, from back in the past."

"What? That's ridiculous! Richard never knew that man. If he did, don't you think it would've come out at the time?"

"No, I didn't say Richard *knew* him. Reltzin just said that Weinberg had a grudge against him, from something that happened in

the past, which could mean anything. Maybe Weinberg was a waiter, or a relative of someone who thought Mr. Dobbs had wronged him. Anything. But, see, it's a new lead, actually our only new lead, so I just thought it might be worth looking through old material with that in mind. It could be anything, a photo, or a souvenir, something to connect the two men and give us more leads. Otherwise . . . " She let the word hang.

"Otherwise, what?"

Marlene shrugged. "There's no point in going on. Hank doesn't have a viable book, in my opinion. All we have is the old assertions, which amount to 'Richard Dobbs was a nice guy and Weinberg lied.' Not prime time. Hank'll be pretty disappointed."

She watched Mrs. Dobbs's face working, as if from far away, as the older woman balanced the violation of her privacy against the chance of hurting her son yet again. Why am I doing this? Marlene wondered. It wasn't a case. It wasn't even a real job. A habit, maybe. An itch that made her want to get to the bottom of secrets, even if she had to lie to and browbeat a dignified old lady at a vulnerable moment, when she was concerned about a sick friend. She thought briefly about what Harry had said, about being scary. It might be true, although right now she didn't feel frightening as much as simply nasty. Which didn't mean that she was about to stop.

"Oh, I suppose it's all right," Mrs. Dobbs said with a sigh. "Although I can't imagine what there might still be in this house that's of relevance. Hank cleaned out the desk and the files in this office long ago. All that's here now is mine. There's the attic, I suppose. You can poke around up there—there are some photo albums and some of Richard's old books and other, I suppose you could call it junk, but I've never been able to get up the energy to throw it all away. It's in cartons, and on some old bookshelves up there. I'm afraid you'll get awfully dirty."

"Don't worry about that. And thank you," said Marlene, without a blush.

Mrs. Dobbs rose, as did Marlene. "I really must be going. Kathleen will show you out."

She paused. "Oh, one thing. There's a high-backed wooden trunk up there that contains some of my personal things. I'd appreciate it if you wouldn't disturb it."

"Of course," Marlene said.

The attic was low ceilinged and lit by a dusty round window and a bare forty-watt bulb. Marlene found the high-backed trunk right away, a construction in blond wood and dark iron bands of the type that wealthy people used in the twenties to take their clothes to and from the resorts. Searching around in the dark corners she found a short piece of angle iron, which she used to spring the lock.

The chest was nearly empty and smelled of dust and the ghost of some light sachet. It contained a yellowed, moth-eaten V-necked sweater with a blue Y on it, several packets of letters tied with faded red ribbons, a black portfolio, a shoe box full of post-cards and photographs, and, in the very bottom, a set of leather-bound, identical diaries for the years 1930 through 1948.

Marlene sat down in the dirt and began to explore the secret life of Selma Hewlett Dobbs.

The day after he killed Mosca, Caballo drove through the quiet streets of Hialeah, squinting in the bright sun, looking for house numbers. Like much of Latin America, Hialeah was not overly concerned with precision of address. Your friends and family knew where you lived and it was no one else's business.

He spotted a likely house, a small, lime green concrete-block-stucco with a gray tile roof, barely visible behind a wall of purplish crotons. He drove past it, stopped, and walked back to check. The number was printed on a sheet of shiny tin half-buried in the croton bushes. It was the right number. The people for whom Caballo worked had kept good track of Angelo Guel.

Caballo went back to his car and drove to a gas station on Flamingo, where he bought a tin two-gallon fuel can and had it filled with gas. He put it in his trunk, next to his golf bag. Then he visited an auto parts store nearby and made a few more purchases. Next he had lunch in a Cuban restaurant, and after lunch found a movie theater and watched two features in Spanish, twice. During the second show he had a refreshing nap.

When he emerged it was past eight and dark. He drove to Guel's house and went past the low, chain-link gate and through the dark wall of the crotons. Then he walked around the house to the back.

At the rear door, he pulled from his pocket the paper bag from

the auto parts store and removed a four-inch flashlight, a roll of gaffer's tape, and a heavy pliers. He taped one of the narrow jalousie panes of the rear door, snapped the pane in two silently with the pliers, pulled out the pane, unlocked the door, stripped off the tape, and replaced the pane in its slot. Then he went in.

Guel was not at home. The thin man checked the refrigerator, which contained half a paper case of Bud and some condiments. He took a can, cracked it, and settled down to wait in the dark.

"This is bullshit," said Karp. "I'm not going to wait around this goddamn motel for Tony to decide if he's going to tell us did he find Guel or not. And just you and Al cruising around town trying to find him is hopeless."

It was the afternoon of the second day after Mosca's murder, and Karp and Fulton were indeed hanging around their government-rate motel, the Arrowhead, off Brickell in Miami proper. They were at the side of the tiny pool, sitting in uncomfortable aluminum armchairs. When it had become clear that they were stuck in Miami for some time, Karp had broken down and purchased a pair of wash-and-wear tan slacks and a couple of short-sleeved shirts. The sporty look was constrained by the thick cordovans he continued to wear on his feet. Fulton was a good deal more Miami in flip-flops, plaid Bermudas, and a Hawaiian shirt printed with a banana motif.

"What do you suggest, boss? It's police work. It requires patience, which you ain't got. I tell you what, why don't you go back to D.C. and I'll stay down here and work the streets with Al. You can wear your suit again."

Karp seemed not to hear this. He was staring at the water, lost in thought. Suddenly he sprang up and walked quickly back to their room. He returned fifteen minutes later.

"Let's go!"

"Where're we going, Butch? We told Al we'd meet him here at four."

"FBI. They have a tap on Tony's phone."

Fulton gaped in surprise. "How the fuck did you find that . . . oh, yeah, your buddy in New York. You called what's-his-name, Pillman. The Feeb."

"He's a Feeb, but he's not my buddy. He's an unindicted felon

and I have his ass in my hands and I get to squeeze it in the public interest about once a year. He set things up so we can get a feed from the phone tap. We have to see a guy named Lorrimer."

Lorrimer was a tall, clean-cut gentleman with graying brown hair who treated Karp and Fulton like a pair of piss-bums who had wandered in off Flagler Street.

"You're not going to screw up this investigation," he stated in steely tones when they arrived at his downtown office and explained what they wanted.

"Of course not," said Karp. "All we're after is any information that's conveyed to Buonafacci about a man named Angelo Guel."

"How come he's looking for Guel?" asked Lorrimer.

"Pure coincidence," Karp lied. "We got a tip that he was, is all."

"Uh-huh. And this Guel figures in the Kennedy investigation? What, as the umbrella man?" He used the tone that the FBI adopts when citizens offer accounts of being abducted by flying saucers.

Karp ignored this. "Timing is the thing. We need to get to him before Tony does. I want to be at the tap site."

After some meaningless argument—meaningless because in the FBI, New York swings a deal more weight than Miami, and both of them knew that Karp was going to get what he wanted anyway—Lorrimer made a couple of phone calls, and half an hour later Fulton and Karp were sitting in a room in a house on Sixty-third Street in North Miami Beach, across from the La Gorce Golf Course, off of which Tony Bones had his spacious home.

The observation house was vacant and unfurnished except for some camp beds and folding chairs and tables. The Feds had rented it because it afforded a good view of the front of the target dwelling and because it was convenient to the phone lines that served the gangster. In an upstairs room, several agents took turns looking through an immense tripod-mounted telescope, while in the back, another set of agents manned the tap.

"What about the phone at the Bal Harbour?" asked Karp when the agent at the tap had explained the layout.

"We got that too," the man replied. "The material from that line is fed into that machine over there. When the sun goes down, they'll break from the hotel, fart around at a couple of clubs, and get home about eleven, twelve. We got bugs on his usual tables,

and a couple trucks that follow them around and pick up the radio feed from the bugs and send them to this radio here. That gets taped too. This is Tony Central."

They spent the next day there, Fulton and Karp sleeping on the camp beds in shifts, listening to Mafia talk over the taps, growing bored and seedy. Each of them went out once to get toilet things and a change of clothes.

At eleven-thirty on the afternoon of the second day, the home phone rang and was answered by a man the tap agent identified as Joey Cuccia. The caller said, "This is Vince. Tony there?"

"No, he ain't. Vince who?"

"Vince Malafredo. Who's this, Joey?"

"Yeah. What you got, Vince?"

"Yeah, that picture? Jimmy Ace and a couple of the fellas was by couple nights ago showin' it around. I know the guy. I thought I knew him, but like, I wasn't sure, you know. Now I know. He came in the joint and placed a bet on the dogs."

"So? He got a name?"

"Yeah." A pause. "This is for a yard, right?"

"Yeah, yeah, a yard. What, you don't think we're good for it? Who's the scumbag and where can we find him?"

"Right. He calls himself Angie Cruz. Runs a bunch of those Cubano coffee stands, sandwich joints. Lives here in Hialeah." The man gave an address on Fifty-fourth Street. "It's off Flamingo Way."

Karp and Fulton were in the Pontiac forty seconds later, tearing off east on Sixty-third, Karp flapping through a street map, calling out directions.

It took them forty minutes to get to Hialeah via the Seventy-ninth Street Causeway and 823, and twenty minutes more to find the lime green house among the numberless others on the identical streets.

Karp leaped out of the car and trotted up the path and rang the bell.

"He's not home," Karp said after five minutes of ringing.

"Maybe he's at work," said Fulton. "I mean, it's the middle of the day."

"We'll wait."

"Let's get something to eat. Then we'll wait."

"Takeout," said Karp. "We'll eat in the car."

Fulton sighed. "Man, you ever done a stakeout before?"

"No. Why, is it hard?"

"With you in the car, it's gonna be a bitch," said Fulton, and stalked off down the path.

They bought a couple of Cuban sandwiches each, two six-packs of Coke and a bag of ice and a styro box to keep the ice and the Coke in, and called Al Sangredo to come and relieve them at eleven that evening.

They waited, watching the breeze shift the crotons, watching the shadows change on the street. It was not too warm, about seventy-five; they kept the windows open. Karp learned how to pee into a can.

Around two-thirty, a green Plymouth rolled down the street slowly and pulled into a space opposite Guel's house. The driver kept the motor running. This attracted the attention of the two men in the Pontiac.

"Crap, it's Tony's guys," said Karp in a pained voice.

"Nah, no way!" Fulton scoffed. "Wrong car. You ever see wise guys in a Plymouth?"

"Not touring, but who knows what they use when they whack people? What should we do?"

"Just wait," said Fulton. They waited, watching the blue exhaust from the Plymouth curl up into the air. "Uh-oh, he's getting out."

The man in the green car had turned off his engine at last and now stood on the curb, slowly looking both ways.

"It's Guel," said Fulton between his teeth when the man looked their way. He had gained some weight since his guerrilla days, and was now a tubby man, with a higher hairline and a thicker mustache. He wore heavy sunglasses, a white guayabera shirt, and rumpled gray slacks. He hadn't shaved in a while.

Karp doubted he had just returned from gainful employment. "What's he so nervous about?"

"You'd be nervous too, if the word was out on the street that a Mafia don wanted a personal interview, plus a hood you knew in the old days had just been whacked. Okay, he's decided the coast is clear, he's crossing the street. What I think we sh— Hey, Butch, what the fuck!"

Karp had flung open his door and was heading at a good clip down the street after Guel.

"Ah, excuse me, Mr. Guel?" he called out. "Could I talk to you a—"

Guel whirled, his eyes wide.

Karp stopped talking as something big and heavy struck him in the small of the back. He saw the pavement rise up at him and he threw his hands forward to protect his face. He heard several loud sounds as he crashed into the asphalt.

There was a devastating pain in his midsection, and he struggled to bring air into his lungs. His hands stung from road burn and a weight was bearing down on his back. He was strangling. Another explosion, much louder. His ears rang. There was a brown forearm braced in front of his face. Fulton.

"Clay, goddamn it . . . ," Karp choked out. He could barely hear his own voice above the ringing in his ears.

"Stay there!" Fulton ordered. Karp felt the weight leave his back. He lifted his head and saw Fulton dash, crouched, gun in hand, across the street to Guel's house, kneel behind the croton hedge, and look cautiously around it. A door slammed, sounding very far away.

Karp rose painfully to his feet, took a few deep breaths, and inspected his scraped and bleeding hands. He walked to where Fulton knelt. Fulton motioned him down with an abrupt gesture. "Christ, Butch! Didn't you see he had a gun?"

Karp shook his head.

"You gotta be blind! It was in his belt under that shirt. He could've had a fuckin' sign on him, armed and dangerous. And antsy. Didn't you see him go for it?"

Karp cleared his throat and took several deep breaths. "Hell, no! All I saw was him walking away and then he turned and then you sacked me. I guess you had to do that, right?"

"Unless you wanted another eyehole. Goddamn, Butch! Talk about dumb-ass stupid . . . " He flapped his mouth soundlessly, as if unable to find words adequate to the stupidity.

"Hey, what do I know? I'm not a cop," objected Karp weakly, flushing now with embarrassment.

"You sure the fuck ain't. And speaking of which, Counselor, neither am I anymore, and especially not in this fucking munici-

pality which we is now in. What the fuck're we supposed to do now?"

Inside the darkened house, Caballo stood flat against the kitchen wall, barely breathing, his little pistol cocked in his hand. He had been awakened from a light doze by the ringing of the doorbell some hours since. He had no idea who had rung the bell or where they were now. Obviously it was not Guel, and just as obviously somebody else was expecting Guel to return home. After the bell ringers left, he had eaten some cold beans from a can. Guel apparently liked black Cuban beans; Caballo had found a dozen or so cans in a cupboard and he had been living on them for the past three days, that and beer. He had also searched the back bedrooms and the bathroom, just to keep himself busy. He had found a tin box full of cash, which he'd taken, but nothing of significance.

When the shots outside sounded, he had placed the food and utensils under the sink and pressed his back against the kitchen wall to the left of the doorway. It was the right place to be. Behind the wall he leaned against, the living room led to the front door on one side and a Florida room opposite. The back door opened on the Florida room. The kitchen was to the right of the living room, connecting by an open archway. Another archway led from the kitchen to a short hall and two small bedrooms and a bath.

He heard the front door opening, then slamming shut. Steps. Heavy breathing. A rustling sound. Guel was looking out his front window, pushing aside the rattan blinds. Caballo tensed. More footsteps, coming closer. Guel rushed by him on the way to the bedrooms. To get his cash.

Caballo took a silent step, extended his arm, and fired twice at the back of Guel's head at a range of about four feet. The man collapsed. Caballo leaned over the prostrate Cuban and fired three more shots into the base of Guel's skull. Then he walked out through the rear door.

"What the hell was that?" asked Fulton, peering cautiously around the foliage, his pistol clutched high in both hands.

"What?" Karp was still crouched next to him, holding his hands out as if he had just done his nails, so that the blood dripping from his palms would not get all over him.

"Didn't you hear it? It sounded like shots. From in the house."

"Well, shit, Clay, we know he's got a gun."

"No, not *his* gun, another gun. Guel had a big piece, a .38 or a .357. This was like a little gun, a .22, four or five shots. Didn't you hear it?"

"No, my ears are still ringing from when you shot at him over my head." He paused and listened, trying to ignore the ringing. "Hey, I heard *that*."

"Yeah, the door; our boy just went out the back."

Karp jumped to his feet and started to walk around the hedge, but Fulton cursed, grabbed him by the belt, and yanked him back down again. "Stay here, damn it! I oughta cuff your damn ankle to the fence, and I would, if I had cuffs."

"Clay, I—"

"Just don't move, okay? If he gets by me and goes for his car, you just stay there, understand?"

Karp nodded.

Fulton, still crouched, moved in a quick rush down the concrete path to the door, flattened himself at the hinge side of the doorway, waited for a few seconds with his ear pressed to the door, and then slipped in.

Karp sat down on the pavement and worked on recovering his breath. He had a hole in his pants at the knee, where blood oozed, and his palms were beginning to sting fiercely. He pulled out a handkerchief and used it and a little spit to clean the road grit out of the scrapes on his hands and knee. Across the street an elderly Cuban woman observed him incuriously from her front step. In a solid Cuban working-class neighborhood like this, nearly everyone would be at work or school now; those that remained seemed in no hurry to report a gun battle on the street to the authorities.

At the end of the street a battered red pickup stopped and let out a man in stained work clothes. A school bus from a parochial school came down the street and dropped off three kids, who ran into houses. Another man, in khakis, a blue ball cap, and sunglasses, walked around the corner of the block, entered a tan sedan, and drove away. An elderly man came out of a house with a small dog on a lead. Then the street was quiet.

Fulton called to him from the doorway, and Karp rose stiffly to his feet and joined him.

"He's dead," said Fulton. "Our guy was waiting for him.

There's a cracked pane in the rear door with fresh tape gum on it. He broke in and waited and shot Guel when he came in. Guel's in the kitchen; took a bunch in the back of the head with a small-caliber gun. Then our boy just strolled out the back over a little fence, into the next yard and away, while we were squatting in the fucking bushes. Shit! I *hate* this, this fucking half-assed police work. We should've come in here with a couple dozen guys and a warrant and sealed off . . . what's wrong?"

Karp had gasped and was staring wildly. "Holy shit! I *saw* him. I just saw him! It was Caballo. He was wearing a blue ball cap, a skinny guy with sunglasses. He just walked around the corner and got into a car and drove away. And I was just sitting there, watching him. Christ!"

They looked at each other. There was nothing to say. After a moment, Fulton said, "Well, fuck this! I'm gonna call it in and then we can wrap up and get the hell out of this town."

"No, wait, I want to take a look around," said Karp.

Fulton started to object, but then, seeing the expression on Karp's face, sighed and said, "You're fuckin' crazy, you know that? Make sure you get his blood on your shoes and leave plenty of prints."

Karp did not get blood on his shoes. There was a good deal of it on the kitchen floor and he had to step carefully past the corpse of Angelo Guel. One look at the two bedrooms and the bathroom told him that he was not going to find anything of relevance. All three rooms had been searched by an expert: drawers turned over, closets emptied, the mattresses and pillows slit and disemboweled. There was a blue metal bank box torn open in the mess, empty. Karp poked around desultorily for a few minutes, pausing to collect some Band-Aids and antiseptic in the ruins of the bathroom, and then came back to the kitchen, cursing under his breath.

"The fucker tossed the place too," he said in response to Fulton's questioning look.

"You think there was something Guel had that he wanted?"

"Had to be. He did a real pro job on the place."

"Uh-huh, back there, but not out here. He couldn't've, or the ambush wouldn't have worked. Guel would've seen the mess and been on his guard. He didn't touch either the kitchen or the living room or the back room that I can see."

"Let's do it!" said Karp, brightening somewhat.

"No, let *me* do it," said Fulton sourly. "You sit on that couch and if I need legal advice, I'll ask."

Karp sat on the couch and practiced first aid. Fulton started searching the Florida room. Forty minutes later, Fulton came out of the kitchen with a manila envelope and tossed it on the couch next to Karp.

"Where'd you find this?"

"Taped to the back of the fridge. Nobody ever looks there. Inside the fridge, yeah, but not behind it. Or under it. It's as safe as a—"

"What's in it?"

"Look for yourself. Bankbooks and some papers in Spanish. There's a ledger there you might find interesting." Fulton had a broad grin on his face.

"Tell me."

"Well, as far back as these bankbooks go, Guel's been depositing two grand a month in cash. Guess who from."

Karp dumped the contents of the envelope out on the couch. The account book was the old-fashioned narrow black model, with greeny yellow pages ruled for double-entry bookkeeping. Karp was not a bookkeeper and his Spanish was rusty, but it was clear that listing income under columns marked "actual" (*verdadero*) and "reported to the tax man" (*informe a impuesto*) was not a generally accepted accounting practice. As far as the IRS was concerned, Guel's coffee and sandwich business was barely hanging on. But Angelo Guel was making plenty of money, much of it from a source identified in Guel's neat handwriting as PXK.

Karp shoved the material back into its envelope and stood up. "Great, this is great," he said. "V.T.'s already got a lead on it, this PXK angle."

"So what now?" asked Fulton, indicating the feloniously violated crime scene.

"What now," said Karp pleasantly, "is that I intend to walk down the block and call a cab from the nearest phone booth, pick up my stuff at the motel, and catch the first plane back to Washington. Basically, I'm fleeing, leaving you to clean up the mess here."

Fulton laughed and sat down, rubbing his eyes. "Some guy!"

he said. "He runs like a thief and dumps me in the shit, and after I just saved his life."

"Hey, what can I say?" said Karp grinning. "I'm a lawyer."

"You didn't burn the place?"

Bishop's voice was calm over the phone, but Caballo could tell he was upset. Extremely upset.

"No, like I said, some people showed up. They tried to get in and then I heard some shots fired. Then the guy, the client, came in at a run with a gun in his hand. . . ."

"All right, I understand. Let's not discuss it over the phone. We'll have to continue under the assumption that whatever material your client had is in the hands of our competitors."

"So, what should I do? You want me to go down the list?"

"No, not just yet. And I want you to stay out of Texas for as long as possible. Things in Washington will be coming to a head soon. I think I'd like you back here."

SEVENTEEN

Marlene walked in the door and was immediately hit by, "Mommy, Mommy, guess what? Sweetie bit a bad man!"

"Oh, Christ! Harry?"

"He bit him really hard and made his pants rip off!"

"Harry!"

Harry Bello strolled in from the kitchen, wiping his hands on a dish towel tucked into the front of his pants. "How'd it go?" he asked.

"What's this about the dog?" Marlene countered.

Harry shrugged. "The kid's right. We were walking in that park up the highway a couple miles. I got a ball for the dog, we're throwing it. Guy gets out of this pickup and watches us for a while. The dog comes by him, chasing the ball, he makes a grab for its collar. The dog goes crazy, does his rabies act, growling, snapping. The guy backs off, makes a run for his truck, the dog goes after him, grabs his behind, rips the seat of his pants off, shorts and all. We're just standing there, it went down so fast. The guy's in the truck, he starts yelling his old lady paid two hundred for the dog, he's gonna sue our ass. I gave him the eye for a while and he ran out of steam and took off."

"He said a lot of bad words, Mommy."

"I bet he did, honey. Harry, this guy: about six-one, two-hundred, crew cut, bent nose, looks like a bouncer in a redneck bar?"

"Yeah. You know him?"

"In a way. He used to live next door. His wife actually did buy the dog, but this bozo was always getting on her to get rid of it. I guess he found out he could get some cash for it and wanted it back. They were real mean to him anyway, and I guess old Sweetie has a long memory." She glanced at the dish towel.

"You're cooking?"

"Yeah, she was hungry."

"We're having SpaghettiOs," crowed Lucy, and she began to hop around on one toe singing the eponymous jingle.

Marlene lowered her brows at Bello. "Harry Bello, you brought *SpaghettiOs* into *my* house?"

Bello made an appeasing gesture. "She wanted."

"This gets out, I'll never be able to walk down Grand Street again."

"I got steaks for us, wine for you," said Bello.

"Oh," said Marlene, "in that case . . ."

They ate, and afterward the dog licked all the plates and crunched up the steak T-bones like potato chips.

"So, you get anything at the old lady's?" asked Harry when they were settled over coffee.

"You could say that. I read her diaries and some old letters."

Bello's left eyebrow rose a quarter of an inch, to which implied query Marlene answered with a minuscule waggle of her head: no, she didn't want me to read them, but I did anyway.

"It keeps coming back to Harley Blaine," said Marlene. "It turns out Blaine was the one who started dating Selma, back then, and then Richard Dobbs fell in love with her, and then Harley seemed to lose interest and she started going out with Richard and then she married him. Her letters to Blaine were there too; that was one of the things a gentleman did in those days, return a lady's letters when the romance was over. And his to her too; she kept them all those years, which tells you something. It was weird reading them in order; first, he's hot as a furnace, swearing eternal love, quoting poetry, and then it's like, over the course of a week, he's turned it all off; the letters start sounding like he's writing to a pen pal in Uganda. Then her letters get cold too. She writes him a note: he left a camera. He left a hat. Hope you are well. He left another camera."

"The guy had a lot of cameras."

"Yeah, well he could afford them. Then they stop writing, except for Christmas cards. She had an affair too, later on, so it wasn't the perfect American family after all. In the diaries she talks about Richard frankly as if he were another child—'the boys,' as in 'I got the boys out of the house,' meaning Richard and Hank. In forty-five or so she falls for this guy she calls 'Q' in the diary and it lasts for three, four years. Intensely romantic. No letters from Q though. The diary says she wants to leave her husband, but Q won't let her. Finally, he breaks it off. She's crushed. She stops writing diaries. Around then is when the spy stuff started, so maybe they were afraid it would come out in the investigation."

"Backward," said Bello.

"Yeah, that's what I thought too," Marlene agreed. "Usually the lover wants the married one to leave the marriage and he or she won't. The guy wasn't married, whoever he was, that's clear from the diaries. But . . . who knows? Maybe, like the man said, the very rich are different from you and me."

An inquiring look from Harry.

"What's the connection to the case? I don't know, but there's a pattern. Here's Richard in the center, the golden boy. He brings Blaine in as a kind of brother, and Selma in as a kind of wife, and their job is sort of to protect him, and keep the gold shiny. They . . . I don't know what's the right word . . . they *invested* in him, like, if Richard shone, so would they. He was the center. In fact, now that I think of it, Blaine probably sort of *gave* Selma to Dobbs. Blaine was in love, so he said, but when the golden boy expressed an interest, it was 'take her, she's yours.' Blaine's really the most interesting character in the trio. Slick. A slick liar. And not just slick; I get the feeling of snakes below the surface. That whole CIA thing with Gaiilov and before. I'd give anything to be able to go out there and talk to him face-to-face."

"Wizard of Oz."

She laughed. "Yeah, right! With the dog pulling at the curtain. My God, Oz! I almost forgot. Wait a sec!"

She got up from the kitchen table and dashed into the living room, returning with her bag. She rummaged in it briefly and then placed a small, worn Kodak-yellow box on the table. "After I went

through the diaries and put everything back the way it was, I didn't have much time to look around. The rest of the attic was mostly the usual stuff—suitcases, a wardrobe with old clothes in it, furniture. I checked out the suitcases, nothing, the wardrobe, nothing, the bookcases . . . maybe a hundred or so books, all old kids' stuff in complete sets, boys' books: Hardy Boys, Tom Swift, Rover Boys, Zane Grey, and a complete set of the Oz books. You know the big size, with those great pictures and the funny curvy writing in gold on the covers? Okay, I used to love them when I was a kid, so of course, I looked through them, not really looking for anything in particular, just looking at the pictures. If you want to know, I was feeling kind of grimy, like you do when you find something out about someone, something shameful, that you weren't supposed to know, and I thought that Oz would cheer me up. But I found this"—she tapped the little box—"in a cut-out space in *Tik-Tok, the Mechanical Man of Oz.*"

Bello handled the little box. "So what is it?"

"Well, you can't see much on eight-millimeter just by holding it up to the light, but it looks like a naughty movie."

"Porn?"

"Not exactly. Not hard-core suck-fuck anyway. It looks like one of those old-fashioned amateur jobs. A couple at the beach, they take off their clothes, they fall on the blanket and so on. I just looked at the first couple of feet or so. I wish we had a projector here." She put the film box back in her purse.

"Why'd you take it?"

"I don't know. Maybe I didn't like the idea of the Dobbs kids visiting Granny's in a couple years and finding it and bringing it home and running it after din-din one evening. Maybe I've joined up in the great goal of protecting the rep of Richard Ewing Dobbs. I think he took this film himself, by the way, and developed it too, either with actors, or with real people, as a peeping Tom. Or maybe Blaine did."

"The skeletons," said Harry.

"Yeah, I shook the closet and out they came."

Harry went off to a motel around six-thirty and Karp came home just after ten. A snowstorm had hit the lower Midwest and Karp had been unable to get a direct flight back, and had spent

four hours on standby in Atlanta, and was in no mood to do anything but sleep.

"How was Miami?" Marlene asked anyway when they were in
bed.

"Somebody killed our two witnesses and I got shot at and Clay
knocked me down and I scraped the shit out of my palms."

"On the other hand you got some sun," said Marlene, suppressing horror. "Who shot at you?"

"One of the guys who got killed. It's a long story."

"So it was a total loss?"

"No, we found some interesting stuff. It might give us a lead
to this Irishman in Louisiana who might've been involved in some
way. He was paying off this Cuban for some reason, the guy who
got killed. Of course, the evidence was illegally taken, so I'll probably go to jail, but I don't care right now. God, I'm whipped!"

"Should I rub your back?"

"That would be nice," said Karp, rolling over.

Marlene rubbed, and thought. "One thing, on this project I'm
doing for Maggie? I'd sort of like to do some of it at home and I
need something to look at eight-millimeter film with. One of those
thingies with a little screen?"

"Umm. Yeah, an editor. I could bring one home. Umm. Keep
doing that and you can have Cinerama."

Karp was awakened the next morning by a peculiar feeling;
someone was rubbing his hand with a hot washcloth and giggling.
He had incorporated this sensation into one of those odd and vivid
early-morning dreams, as one does with the sound of the alarm
clock, and then the alarm clock did go off and Karp opened his
eyes and looked into the red-rimmed eyes of the dog that was
licking his hand.

"Yaaagh!" In one motion he heaved himself into a sitting position with a pillow between his chest and the monster. Lucy stood
there in her flowered nightie, convulsed with shrill laughter. The
dog panted and deposited a string of thick saliva on the bed.

"Marlene!"

She strolled in from the bathroom, brushing her hair.

"You called?"

Karp pointed mutely at the dog.

"Oh. I guess I forgot to tell you. Butch, Sweetie. Sweetie, Butch. I'm going to make some coffee."

"Daddy, we scared you, didn't we?" asked Lucy, still giggling.

Karp was being a model modern husband at breakfast. "What kind of dog is it?" he asked calmly.

"You're not pissed off?"

"Surprised, maybe. But, being married to you, my life is full of surprises. I come home one day, and you've bought a car, even though I know we don't have a dime. Maybe you'll tell me someday how you did it, maybe not. I come home from a trip and there's a washing-machine-sized dog in the house. Hey, I'm easy. So, what kind?"

"The vet said it was a Neapolitan mastiff."

"Neapolitan, huh? This is a full-grown dog?"

"No, it's still putting on weight. It should reach one hundred sixty pounds more or less."

"You *bought* this thing?"

"No, actually, I got it from Thug 'n' Dwarf. They abandoned it, sort of."

"Uh-huh. Gosh, a big dog, a big *stolen* dog, like that, we get back to the city, we ought to start thinking seriously about getting a house. Westchester, the Island maybe. Dog like that needs a big yard."

"Nice try, buster, but no sale. That is an *urban* Neapolitan mastiff. Naples is a city. He'll adapt to loft living, all right, probably better than some other people in the family I could mention."

"Well, in that case," replied Karp equably, putting on his suit coat and preparing to make his exit, "I'll have to content myself with the pleasure of watching you, and you alone, scooping gigantic dog turds off Crosby Street each and every morning and evening."

Karp crossed the street in front of the Annex building to avoid several of the more prominent Kennedy nuts, including the man in the red hat, and slipped into the entranceway. He had noticed in himself since the events in Miami a growing sympathy for the clan. In the office, he checked his messages, looked with distaste at a large pile of unread mail, and went immediately to Bert Crane's office.

Who was in, for a change. Dispensing with pleasantries, he told Crane what had gone down in Florida and what they'd learned from Mosca. Crane was not slow in grasping the implications. "There's a leak."

"Yeah, there is. And we should be able to find it, because the only people who knew we were going down there to talk to Jerry Mosca were me; Fulton, who was with me; V.T. Newbury, who's a total clam on stuff like this; and Dobbs and you."

Crane caught the obvious implication and to his credit did not make any protestation, but sat in thought, chewing his lip.

Karp asked, "What about Flores?"

Crane shook his head vehemently. "Hell, no! Flores doesn't talk to me anymore, except to issue formal reprimands, and if he did, he'd be the last person I'd give any sensitive information to. God, Butch, I can't think of anyone around here who knew, and Lord knows Hank didn't tell anyone on the committee. I stressed that to him very—"

Crane stopped, stricken. Karp said, "Yeah, I know. We're in deep paranoia here. If we believe that the fact that two critical witnesses were killed before they could testify is not just a sad coincidence, then we have to believe in an active conspiracy that's still intact and functioning."

"And do you believe this?"

Karp nodded slowly. "I sort of have to now. Did V.T. tell you about the stuff that got stolen right out of this office? Yeah? It adds to the picture, doesn't it? And I think I saw Caballo himself, in the flesh."

"The Oswald look-alike? Where?"

"In Miami, right after Guel was killed. He was a block away and wearing dark glasses and a hat, but the more I think about it, the more I think that's the guy. And why shouldn't they use him? It's completely safe. The guy doesn't exist, except at the bottom of a pile of false identities. What're we gonna do, put out an all points bulletin to pick up Lee Oswald? They'd lock *us* up."

"So what *are* you going to do?"

"Go through the motions with everything else, the medical stuff, the forensics, redo Warren. Like I've said before, necessary but hopeless. Nothing's going to emerge from that but endlessly debatable minutiae. I think it's still essential to get Paul David under oath."

"Forget that," Crane said. "Flores won't have it."

"Oh, great! How about Santos Trafficante?"

"We can try," said Crane, "but if he declines to show, I doubt we're going to get a contempt citation out of the chairman."

"So we're running a major investigation without any real judicial clout? Is that what I'm hearing."

"For now," said Crane

"Okay, in that case, *for now*, all we can do is pursue the new leads, this Turm character and this PXK angle, in total secrecy. Clay's still down in Miami, and I'm going to get him to New Orleans in a couple of days. Also, I'm afraid I'm going to have to ask you to stress the 'total' part. Even regarding Hank."

"Surely you don't think . . ."

"I don't know what I think, Bert. There's . . . well, Marlene has been doing some research for the Dobbs family, about the father. There's a link, or was at one time, between the family and the CIA. God knows how deep it goes."

"That's absurd, Butch! Without Hank Dobbs there'd *be* no investigation."

Karp started to protest, but then sighed and was silent for a moment, collecting his thoughts. "Yeah, of course. I don't know what's happening to me. Maybe the paranoia is getting to the point where I'm not functioning anymore. And, of course, that's the whole *point* of what's happening. Whoever's doing this, orchestrating this, knows how paranoia works. They *want* to keep that atmosphere going, so that reasonable people will embrace the Warren Report just to keep from going crazy. And it's working. They know the whole pattern, so that as we expose piece after piece, they're there before us, twisting the evidence, stealing stuff, killing witnesses." He shook his head and rubbed his face. "So," he asked, "how are things going here?"

Crane seemed glad to accept the change of subject. "Worse and worse. Flores has taken leave of his senses. He sent me a letter saying he doesn't want us besmirching his name and asking for all his official stationery back."

"His stationery? His *stationery!*" Karp started to laugh and it was a while before he could bring himself under control.

Crane laughed too, but then quickly sobered. "Actually, it's not funny. He also revoked our franking privileges and told me not to

make any more fiscal commitments under his name. Since legally everything we do is under his name, it means we're essentially out of business until we can clear this up."

"God! How's the committee taking this?"

"Well, Hank's gone to the leadership and is politicking like mad. It'll come to a head over the weekend and we should have some resolution by Monday." Crane reached over to his credenza and handed a newspaper clipping to Karp. "This was the straw that broke the camel's back."

It was a front-page *New York Times* article about Crane. Karp scanned it in growing disbelief. "But this is nothing. It's all the old crap recycled into a new piece, with some more innuendo tossed in."

"Yeah, but it puts the seal on the tomb. For seventeen years, apparently, I've been causing nothing but controversy, and doing botched and questionable investigations."

"So what'll you do?"

"There's nothing I *can* do, Butch. The press has spoken. You know very well that the last thing the *Times* and the *Post* want is for anyone to take a serious crack at Warren. They'd look like fools for endorsing it before the ink was dry if we came up with a credible alternative. My mistake was not realizing that. And . . . I guess I wasn't the politician I thought I was. So . . ." He waved his hand weakly, taking in the office, and beyond it, the Kennedy investigation and the sticky webs of the national capital in which it now writhed.

"And there's nothing we can *do*?" Karp asked inanely, knowing the answer.

"Yeah, there is," said Crane. "Wait for Monday."

"Nice tan," said V.T. when Karp walked into his office.

"I don't have a tan. I have shredded palms and a sore knee." He displayed his hands.

"That's too bad," said V.T. "Perhaps next time you should choose another resort. What happened?"

Karp described briefly the events at Guel's house, and deposited the package Fulton had found there on V.T.'s desk. He waited while V.T. perused the items in it.

"Creative bookkeeping," said V.T., tapping the little ledger book. "Interesting. Do you recognize this character?"

V.T. was pointing to a foggy Xerox copy of what appeared to be a newspaper in Spanish, and the photograph of a man.

"No, what is it?"

"Well, from the style, I'd say it was cut from *Granta*, the Castro paper. It shows, and I quote, in rough translation, 'the desperate imperialist saboteur, El Soplete, captured by the Revolutionary Militia in Cienfuegos.' *El soplete* means the blowtorch. According to this, he got the handle back when he was with Batista's secret police on account of the way he liked to extract information from prisoners. A real honeybunch. It looks like the commies shot him too. Hmm. Let me check, just to make sure."

V.T. fingered through some files stacked on his desk, extracted one, and pulled out a couple of photographs, one a glossy, one a copy of a news photo.

"This glossy is a frame from the Depuy film. This one, one of our kids just dug it up from an old émigré newspaper. Same guy in all three, right? Allowing for age, that is. The scar on the cheek shows in each one, that and that nose."

"Who is it?"

"Leopoldo Carrera. The guy we like for the third of the trio that visited Sylvia Odio in Dallas. Oswald, Guel, Carrera. All dead. As is the one guy we had who could confirm it, Guido Mosca."

"Shit! But there's still Odio herself."

"Yeah," said V.T. "There is, and a big priority right now is to get her to look at pictures."

"Okay, I'll take care of it. Meanwhile, what's happening with this PXK thing?"

"Looking better. Mr. Kelly is well known in both Baton Rouge and New Orleans. A political contributor, conservative, maybe a Bircher. He knew Clay Shaw and he knew Depuy. He's a trucker, and thus not unfamiliar with the Teamsters and hence with Carlos Marcello. And . . . are you ready for this? He ran an airfreight service back in the late fifties and early sixties, and briefly employed David Ferrie as a pilot."

"So he could be the guy."

"He's certainly worth looking at in more detail," agreed V.T.

"I should go to New Orleans."

"Yes, if you want to pay for it yourself."

"Oh, crap! I forgot." Karp clenched his fists and snarled in frustration.

"Hey, lighten up," said V.T. "We'll know Monday if we're all fired or if we can run a serious investigation, either of which would be a plus."

Karp did not lighten up, either during the remainder of the day at the office, nor upon coming home. He snapped at his wife, and his child, and the dog, who did not snap in return, but whined and cringed. It was Marlene who snapped back; dinner was unpleasant.

Karp took a walk in the chill darkness after dinner and his eye fell on the yellow VW, gleaming under a streetlamp. He returned to the apartment and made some calls.

Two hours later, Lucy Karp was in the care of Harry the godfather, and Karp and Marlene were in the car headed west on U.S. 50.

"Well," said Marlene as they cleared the outer suburbs of the capital and the land grew dark and rural, "this is quite the most romantic thing you've ever done. I'm wriggling in my seat. You won't tell me where we're going?"

"No. Nobody knows where we're going except me."

She looked at his face, dimly lit by the lights of the dash: jaw tight, the muscles bunched, mouth a straight dark shadow, and there were those hard little lines he got around the eyes when he was under pressure. His hands gripped the wheel like a rally driver's.

"You're driving very well," she observed. Karp was a terrible driver, but he had only stalled once in getting under way, and although he was creeping along at fifty-five on the extreme right edge of the highway, behind a big truck, Marlene was feeling more than charitable.

"Thank you," said Karp tightly.

"You're in hell, aren't you?" she asked after a long pause.

"Yes. Yes, I am," said Karp. "And it's like it was custom designed for me, for the kind of person I am. I still can't believe I actually volunteered for it."

"It's in the nature of hell to be customized. See Dante."

"See . . . ?"

"Dante's *Inferno*. The damned are given punishments suitable to their sins. The fornicators are locked together with their beloveds for all eternity, the gluttons are stuffed with food, and so on. Poetic justice. Gilbert and Sullivan parodied it in *The Mikado*."

She sang, in a plummy alto: " 'My object all sublime, I shall achieve in time, to let the punishment fit the crime, the punishment fit the crime. And make each prisoner pent, unwillingly represent, a source of innocent merriment, of innocent merriment.' " Karp laughed, and she sang the rest of the song.

"Yeah," said Karp, "and the homicide prosecutor is forced to work on the assassination of John F. Kennedy. Nobody really wants to know who did it. He has no resources, the bad guys know what he's doing before he does. I wonder who's laughing." Then he began to tell her about the case, in more detail than he had exposed it to her before, pouring out his anger and frustration. Karp was an adherent of the belief that real men handle their own problems, and turn toward their families a face of genial competence, interspersed from time to time with fits of insensate rage or, which was more common with Karp, periods of irritable sulking. This he had learned at his daddy's knee.

Marlene, who understood this very well, received the gush of confession in near silence, only asking clarifying questions from time to time. It was curiously like interviewing a rape victim.

When he was talked out, she laid her head against his shoulder and squeezed his arm. "I'm glad you told me all that," she said.

"You don't mind?"

"I mind when you *don't* tell me, dummy!" Marlene replied cheerfully. "Who do you think gets to carry your bile when you're bravely suffering in silence?"

"Oh," said Karp.

Marlene briefly considered unloading her own discomfort with the Dobbs case, but decided that the moment was inopportune. What was sauce for the gander was not necessarily sauce for the goose, and besides, she was aware of the vast gulf between the national historical importance of what Karp was doing and the relative triviality of her own recent pursuits. She was embarrassed by it, in fact. So she said instead, "So you think it was the CIA after all."

"No, not really, not the organization. I mean what is the CIA after all? Ninety percent of it is a bunch of GS-thirteens carpooling to Rockville, and the leaders tend to be pompous assholes like Dulles. If they actually sat down and *planned* this thing it'd have been the fuckup of the century, especially since

they would've had to bring the Latin American boys into it."

"What do you mean?"

"V.T. explained it to me once. The CIA has, like . . . leagues, like in baseball, where they distribute their talent. The majors are in Europe, Berlin, Vienna, head-to-head with the Russkies, and maybe also Japan. Those are the key countries. Triple A is the Mideast, because of Israel and the oil. Class A is the rest of Asia. Latin America and Africa is where they put the no-hopes. I mean, if you had anything on the ball, would you really want to spend your career infiltrating the Socialist party in Bolivia or Uganda and fucking with some pathetic union movement in those places? Bugging the North Korean embassy in Quito? No, but along comes Castro. All of a sudden these no-hopes are playing in Yankee Stadium on national TV. The result—the Bay of Pigs. Back to the minors, boys. Okay, two things: One, if the top guys in the Agency wanted to whack the president the absolutely last people they would've picked are the guys who did that abortion, plus their track record for hitting Castro wouldn't fill anyone with confidence. In fact, from what I've been able to gather, these guys, Bishop and company, were protecting Fidel like a brother. I mean, once Fidel goes, there goes their budget. Two, this is hard to explain, but it's not a government operation, the Kennedy thing. I've been in government my whole life, and I've seen a lot of slimy deals go down, and the one characteristic they all have is stupidity and simplicity; once you pick at them, they start to unravel. People rat each other out. They leave evidence lying around. They buy yachts they can't afford. And let's face it, you want to start a conspiracy in the government, who've you got to do the job? Guys who signed up to work at a desk eight hours a day for thirty years, with no chance of layoffs and a nice pension at the end. Not your top recruits for skullduggery, right? Prime example: Watergate. Now *that's* a government conspiracy."

"So it *wasn't* the CIA? But you said before . . ."

"No, look—I think there might've been, after the Bay of Pigs, something like . . . um, what's that play where the knights kill that guy in the cathedral?"

"*Becket.* You mean like they said, 'who will rid me of this turbulent priest'?"

"Right!" Karp exclaimed, "who will rid me of this turbulent

priest. Or president, in our case. They were angry and scared, they were talking tough-guy talk. Somebody oughta shoot the bastard and save us from the commies. And the word filtered out that maybe there'd be cover available if maybe somebody *did* do Kennedy. And now, an idea pops up in somebody's mind. I can see this guy, like you can see a picture in a patch of sky through a tree, by the leaves around it, a kind of negative shape. This guy is not a CIA guy but he understands how it works. He has connections to the kind of people who can do something like this. And he's an artist. This whole thing was designed, constructed, and constructed in such a way that it would keep running, keep getting more complex and harder to figure out the more time went by. Everybody who looks at it brings something to it, because of all the pieces he put into it. You want to believe it's a lone nut, there's your certified loser. You want to believe it's a CIA conspiracy, there's the CIA assets. You want to believe it's a Mob hit, there's the Mob. You want to believe it's the commies, there's Castro and the KGB. It's brilliant! It's like being guarded by Bill Russell or batting against Nolan Ryan. Even though the guy's whipping my ass, I got to give him credit."

"So who is it? This Bishop character? Paul David."

"Nah! David's a bureaucrat. He can follow orders and not fuck up too much, but he didn't have the sense not to send a picture of a guy who looked very little like Oswald from Mexico City and he messed up with the tapes. Definitely bush-league; he didn't plan this. No way."

"But then nobody's left except this Irish guy, PXK."

"Yeah, and I hope for his sake that he's either running the show or has nothing to do with it. Otherwise, I wouldn't want to be carrying his life insurance. Uh-oh, I think we have to turn off here."

For the remainder of the trip, their attention was taken up with navigation on the dark roads, looking for landmarks, stopping to read Karp's inadequate scrawled directions. Marlene felt something tugging at her mind, something buried in what Karp had told her, but for the moment she was unable to dredge up what it was.

They arrived finally in the courtyard of a stone-built, slate-roofed eighteenth-century structure. A carriage lamp threw soft yellow light on the graveled yard.

"This is it, huh?" said Marlene. "The Old Ragg Inn? Old *Ragg*? How romantic, how evocative of sexual denial!"

"It's a mountain, Marlene," said Karp.

It was a mountain, indeed, and they saw it the next morning from the windows of their room, a dun hump looming through gray mists. The valley between the inn and the mountain was lost in an earthbound cloud.

"God! It's like fairyland," cried Marlene sitting up in bed. "It's like Brigadoon. Maybe when we go downstairs we'll find a hundred years have passed and they finally found out who killed JFK."

"Who was it?" asked Karp sleepily from beneath the thick quilt.

Marlene leaned over and whispered in his ear. "It was Jackie. She had a gun concealed in that hat. Oswald was actually her son by a concealed teenage marriage."

He made a clumsy grab for her, but she fended him off. "You maniac! Don't you ever get enough?"

"Me? Me?" protested Karp. "It wasn't me who was hooting all night long."

"*Hooting?* I don't recall ever having had my ladylike intimate murmurs described as 'hooting.' "

"Squealing, then," said Karp. "Explicit language at top volume. It's a good thing it's the off-season and there aren't any other guests on this hall. I was afraid they'd ask us to leave."

"In your dreams," sniffed Marlene and rose from the bed. "In any case, as a result of your insensate lusts, I'm covered in your effluvia, which I now intend to wash off. In the Jacuzzi."

"This is very nice," sighed Marlene some minutes later, when the two of them were entwined in the warm, churning waters. "It's so colonial."

Karp, soaping the inside of his wife's thigh with a perfumed bath bar, agreed: "Yes, our colonial forefathers . . ."

"And foremothers."

". . . and foremothers of old Virginia set up their Jacuzzis first thing, right after the slave-whipping post. The Jacuzzi was actually invented by Thomas Jefferson or Patrick Henry or one of those guys."

"Mmm, Patrick Henry. Give me lavatory or give me bath. Oh, God, don't get me started again, I'm starving; I need food, not more of *that*."

Karp obligingly shifted his ablutions to a less critical area. "Breakfast is included," he said. "I doubt there'll be bagels, but it's included."

"Good. Which reminds me: how are we affording all this luxury? Did you take a bribe?"

"No, I put it on the card."

Marlene stared at him. "The card? Would that be the MasterCard I fought with you for a month to take out and you agreed only if we both swore that it would only be used for the most extreme emergencies, like, I believe you said, a bone-marrow transplant for Lucy. *That* card?"

Karp shrugged, only slightly embarrassed. "I thought it *was* a medical emergency. Emotional deprivation can lead to serious physical problems, you know."

"You just wanted to get laid."

"No, I wanted to provide you with a more suitable venue for hooting than our shitty thin-walled apartment. A little more polish on that knee?"

The phone rang. They both froze, as if about to be discovered in an illicit act.

"Who the hell is that?" asked Marlene. "Did you tell the office where you were?"

"Are you nuts? Nobody knows we're here. I didn't know myself until I called this joint about an hour before we left. It's probably the desk, they want to know if we want one egg or two. Or else our car's in the wrong place."

Karp got out of the bath, put on one of the thick white terry cloth robes supplied by the inn, and went to answer the phone.

It was not the desk calling, but Blake Harrison, the columnist. Karp felt a pang in his vitals. He had to clear his throat heavily before responding to Harrison's greeting, after which Harrison wasted no time on small talk.

"Butch, you'll recall our conversation at Dobbs's house? Well, now's the time. Crane will be fired on Monday."

"Don't be so sure," Karp replied. "The word is the committee is fairly pissed at the way Flores has been behaving. They might not let him."

"What happens to Flores doesn't signify, for God's sake," snapped Harrison impatiently. "Flores may be finished too, but

that doesn't mean Crane can stay. Trust me on this. So, what's your answer? Are you going to take the job?"

"I'll make that decision when it's presented to me," said Karp.

"Oh, stop being a prig!" Harrison shouted. "You think they're going to put an equal-opportunity ad in the *Post*? You'll be offered the job; my advice to you is to take it. You handle it properly, it can definitely lead to big things." There was a pause. "Karp? Are you there?"

"Yes, I'm here. I was just thinking about whether I'm ready for big things. Good-bye, Mr. Harrison." Karp put down the receiver. He could hear Harrison sputtering until the moment the connection was cut.

"Not the desk, huh?" said Marlene when Karp came back to the bathroom.

"No, it was Blake Harrison."

"The newspaper guy? How did he find out you were here?"

Karp sat down on the rim of the tub. "Well, either somebody followed us here or somebody heard me making these reservations. Since I doubt whether anyone could've followed us over those mountain roads last night without us noticing, they probably either have a tap on our phone or a bug in the apartment."

"I don't want this to be happening," Marlene said, and then put her hands over her ears and sank backward until the surface of the foamy water closed over her head.

Still, they managed to have a nice weekend, in the fashion of people for whom things cannot get much worse. They drove to the national park and Marlene walked out on a rock in the South Fork of the Shenandoah and sang all six verses of "Oh, Shenandoah," with feeling. Karp walked out to join her and fell in, immersing himself to the waist. They had a couple of good meals at the inn and spent a lot of time in bed. At intervals, Marlene told Karp about the Dobbs affair, and what she had learned in the attic.

"You don't think I'm a rat for reading that stuff, do you?" she asked after she'd finished her tale.

"Semi-ratty," answered Karp. "I think it's why you're a great investigator and not that great of a prosecutor."

"What the hell is that supposed to mean?" she snapped, bridling.

"Just that if somebody lets you loose on a case, they better be

sure they want everything to come out, and forget the niceties. What you want is truth and justice, no holds barred, and you forget the rules of evidence. You even forget the law. It's going to get you in a shitload of trouble some day."

"Yeah, yeah, so you're always telling me." Marlene propped herself up on one elbow so she could look at him as he lay next to her. "I happen to be the best rape prosecutor they ever had up there."

"It's a weak league, Marlene."

She socked him a couple of times with her pillow and then asked, "So, Mr. Lawyer, Mr. Smarty-Pants, if you're not interested in truth and justice, why are you still on this bullshit Kennedy thing? You still think you're going to make a case?"

"Oh, no," said Karp blandly. "Now I'm in it for truth and justice. I'm just like you now."

Marlene laughed and snuggled closer to him. "Oh, goody. At last, something to bring us closer together, even if it's chicanery." He was silent for a while and she caught a familiar, distant expression on his face. "What're you thinking?" she asked.

"Hmm? Oh, nothing, just one of the names you mentioned—this Gaiilov. It rang some kind of bell. I'm trying to think from where."

"From me, probably. I must've mentioned the great Gaiilov hunt. Or maybe Harry did. Or I murmured it in my fevered dreams."

"Um, I don't think so. For some strange reason, I think I heard it at the office. It'll come to me later." He ran his arm under her body and pulled her close. "Speaking of which . . . ," he said.

Back at Federal Gardens on Sunday night, Karp made a quick search for bugs, and found one almost immediately, a small transmitter screwed into the mouthpiece of the telephone. He left it in place.

"Why did you leave it there?" asked Marlene when Karp had ushered her outside to the parking lot.

"Because if I take it out they'll just put in another one that's harder to find. Anyway, I think the main thing they wanted was telephone calls, and a bug like that is a lot simpler than a tap."

Marlene shuddered and moved closer to him "Yecch! It makes me feel slimy. Do you think they bugged our bedroom too?"

"I hope so," said Karp with a quick grin. "Let them know what they're missing." He hugged her and she looked up at his face and said, "This is going to be over soon, isn't it?"

"Oh, yeah," said Karp. "Real soon."

A little past nine-thirty on Monday, a hand-delivered letter arrived at Bert Crane's office. It was from Flores and it said that Crane was fired and had to be out of his office by 5:00 P.M. that afternoon.

"What's the plan?" asked Karp when Crane told him.

"Committee meeting today. Hank thinks they can get this reversed. I'd like you to attend it."

Karp did so, and in the late afternoon reported back to his boss.

"I think Flores has become unhinged," Karp concluded. "He was behaving like a kid in a sandbox when some other kid grabs his toy truck, like this committee was his personal property. He bluntly accused Morgan of trying to steal the committee from him and become chairman. He was flinging insults at Hank too. The upshot was they reversed the firing letter. After they finally adjourned, Flores talked to a bunch of press people. He called you a rattlesnake."

Crane chuckled. "That's what they call 'colorful' on the Hill. It's a synonym for deranged."

"Bert, why is he doing this? I don't get it."

Crane made a helpless gesture with his hands. "He wanted a puppy dog. They all did, except maybe Hank and some of the King assassination people. Somebody who'd go through the motions and essentially reproduce the Warren Report, or even better, say that Oswald did it, and 'probably' there were some others but we didn't know who they were. Something vague like that, enough to take off some of the heat from the critics. What they definitely did not want was a big, expensive, freewheeling investigation involving the CIA, the FBI, and the Dallas Police Force. That was my big mistake; I thought that they definitely *did*. That's why I got involved and why I got you involved." He looked sadly into Karp's eyes. "For which I apologize."

At four-thirty, Bea Sondergard burst into Karp's office without knocking. She was pale and wide-eyed. "Flores sent the cops.

They want Bert out by close of business. They say they have orders to seal his files."

Karp leaped to his feet and dashed out into the corridor, heading to the door of Crane's office. He stood in front of the door, feeling vaguely foolish, but unable to think of anything else to do. Two men in the uniform of the Capital Police, the security forces that answer to Congress, came striding purposefully down the hall.

They stopped in front of him, and one of them, a large moon-faced man of about fifty, said, "Is Mr. Crane in there?"

"Yes," said Karp.

"Well, we got orders to remove him and take charge of all government material in his possession."

"No," said Karp.

"What?"

"You can't."

"Why not?" said the cop.

"Because I won't let you. That's an illegal order anyway. The full committee rescinded Mr. Flores's order a few hours ago."

"I didn't hear nothing about that," said the guard. "The shift captain told me to come down here and remove Mr. Crane, and escort him off the premises, and that's what we're going to do."

As this took place, Bea Sondergard had been playing Paul Revere. The staff had gathered in murmuring clumps at both ends of the corridor, and several of the male members of the staff, and Bea herself, now moved to stand in the doorway with Karp.

The cop tried out a false smile and a pleading tone. "C'mon, mister, we're only trying to do our job."

"I know," said Karp. "Nothing personal, but we're not going to let you past. You can try to remove us by force, but in that case, if the order you're carrying out is in fact illegal, I will press charges of assault against you, and sue both you personally and the Capital Police for damages. And if you choose to get physical there will certainly be damages."

Karp hunched his broad shoulders and widened his legs to a fighting stance, demonstrating how the potential damages were likely to occur. There was some eyeball work between him and the cop, who was suddenly conscious that the eyes he was staring into were seven inches higher than his own. After a tense half minute, the cop said, "I'll have to check with headquarters."

He backed off a few yards and consulted his portable radio in

low tones. Then the two cops left without a backward glance. A burst of applause from the staff. Karp was clapped on the back as he walked back to his office. Bea Sondergard, grinning, said, "A famous victory!"

"Yeah," replied Karp sourly. "Like the Alamo."

The next morning, early, Karp was called into Crane's office.

"Well, I'm gone," Crane said without preamble as Karp took a seat.

"What?"

"Yeah, I just came from Morgan's office. Hank was there and a few others. The deal is, Flores will be replaced as chairman by Louis Watson, who's been chairing the King operation. It's something of a coup for the black caucus, which is how they got the leadership to go along with it. But they want a new face in my slot. They didn't actually fire me, but it was real clear that that's what they wanted. For whatever reason, they think I've shot my bolt here. And if I were to stay, the press would keep pecking at me, Flores's friends would keep doing it too, and I'd be spending all my time answering these ridiculous charges. What do you think?"

"Yeah. I think resignation is your only option at this point."

"I agree. The question is who replaces me." He looked straight at Karp, who had some difficulty in meeting the other man's gaze.

"Well," Crane resumed, "do you want it?"

"No," said Karp without an instant's thought. "I don't. If I took the job, it would be almost an endorsement of the way you've been treated. And I agree with you. Even with Flores gone, there's no real political will to run a serious investigation."

Crane nodded several times and then swiveled to look out across the railroad tracks. When he turned back to Karp he said, "Yeah, I kind of thought that's what you'd say. But, I'll tell you, Hank Dobbs, for one, is going to be real disappointed. He had his little heart set on you."

That evening Karp brought home a small film-editing machine and a large red manila folder. In the folder was a copy of all the material that had been stolen plus the Depuy film and the Guel envelope and ledger. He had decided to remove it from the office entirely and carry it with him. He knew this was dumb, but he

couldn't think of anything else to do with it. It gave him something to hold on to, like a talisman. And if they tried to take it away from him, at least he'd get a look at one of the shadowy creatures who had dogged his steps for the last six months.

"I'm at National," said Caballo.

"Good," said Bishop. "Read the papers?"

"No, what happened?"

"The investigation just collapsed as planned," said Bishop. He sounded pleased.

The thin man hoped that this would mean he could go back to Guatemala, where it was warm. "So that's it?" he ventured.

"Not quite. I think we can get a tame dog in there, and then it'll just peter out, but there's still some sensitive material lying around. It's basically a broom job. Take a cab to this address and stay there." He read off an address in Alexandria. "I'll be in touch."

Caballo copied it down on a page ripped out of the phone book.

"Uh, Bishop. In Miami, I think that big guy, Karp? I think he might've seen me. Do you think we should . . ."

"No, no," said Bishop, chuckling. "He's going to be the tame dog."

EIGHTEEN

In the morning Karp found a message waiting for him at the office telling him that Hank Dobbs wanted to see him. Karp dutifully trudged up the Hill, the red folder enclosed in a cheap government briefcase.

Dobbs greeted him warmly and led him into his private office. Dobbs seemed to have expanded since Karp had last seen him; he filled more space, his motions were more abrupt, more decisive, his eye harder. The various manipulations that had led to the downfall of Flores had added to his stature as a man to be counted in the inner workings of Congress. He had saved the leadership from embarrassment, and that was always a consideration when the plum assignments were handed out. This new status showed in his mien, more subtle than the fruit-salad ribbons on the chest of a soldier, but as readable to those in the know.

After giving Karp a brief appreciation of the politics of the committee, Dobbs began speaking of "your" staff, and "your" plans, as if offering the job of chief counsel to Karp obliquely, as if they had already agreed that Karp was already installed.

Karp interrupted. "Hank, I don't know if you're planning to formally offer me Bert's job, but just to clear the air, I want you to know that I've decided not to take it."

Dobbs stopped with his mouth open, and the color drained from his face. "What! Why not?"

Startled by the force of this reaction, Karp stumbled through a version of the explanation he had given Crane the day before.

"But that's crazy!" said Dobbs, and now color flooded into his face, making the freckles stand out like nailheads. "You *have* to take it! What do you think all this has been about?"

"I'm not sure I know what you're talking about," said Karp.

"Oh, don't play innocent, for God's sake, Butch! Crane has been doomed for months, ever since those stories broke and he put in that crazy budget, and I've been busting my hump trying to make sure that when the crash came, you'd be wired for the job." He got up from behind his desk and paced in agitation. "Jesus! I've been goddamned horse-trading with half the committee to get you positioned, and now you have the gall to tell me you won't take it?"

He stared at Karp, his blue eyes like gas flames. "What else're you going to do, huh? You have a wife and a child. Hell, I even arranged for free day care for your kid and gave your wife something to keep her busy. God, man, think! You haven't got a dime. What do you think's available to you in this town? A GS-thirteen U.S. attorney job? You know how many of those guys would commit murder for this kind of chance? Running a big investigation— it's a launching platform, it's *national recognition*: the sky's the limit here, Butch."

Dobbs began to expatiate about how high the sky was, and as he spoke, illumination struck Karp like a slow, painful dawn after a night of bad dreams. He knew this was an important moment in his life, a place of many branchings. Part of him wanted badly to take this job, to be friends with people like Hank Dobbs, and Hank Dobbs's friends, to have a nice house in McLean, or Kalorama, or Cleveland Park, to do this little job they wanted him to do and then wait around for an assistant AG slot when the administration was right, or when it wasn't, a high-visibility job on a congressional staff. He could write legislation; he could go after big-time criminals; the FBI would jump when he cracked the whip; he could even *have* the FBI some day.

The only hitch was that the part of him that wanted the job would become, should he take it, the whole of him. His father would like that. Karp would know senators. He might even know the president. He would be on television behind the podium with a cabinet agency seal on it, pointing at charts, and he would be driven around in large cars, the kind with the little reading lamp behind the rear seat, provided so that important people might not

lose even a few minutes of precious study time as they were driven to and from home during the hours of darkness.

And Marlene, what would she make of the new Karp, the wholly owned subsidiary Karp, the great success? Well, she would get used to it. There would be advantages for her too, she'd already received some and would get more, if she'd only learn how to behave. . . .

Suddenly, almost without consciously willing it, Karp found himself on his feet.

Dobbs stopped talking and looked up at him in surprise.

"No," Karp said, and again, "No. Sorry, but I can't do it." He really *was* sorry and he really *couldn't* do it.

Dobbs struggled to control himself, being enough of a politician and student of human nature to realize that shouting and bluster would not work with this one. In a meliorative tone he said, "Butch, come on—sit down, we'll talk it through. If you have problems, or questions, or concerns, I'm sure we can work them out."

Karp remained standing. He said, "Actually, Hank, I do have some questions. I'd like to know who you told that I was going to Miami and who I was going to see there."

"What? What are you talking about?"

Karp ignored this protest. "Whoever you told, he told somebody else, and two critical witnesses were killed right in front of our noses. I know the leak had to come from you because you're the only one besides Bert and my immediate staff who knew why we were going to Miami. I told you myself, dummy that I am, remember? Another question: did you know my apartment was bugged? Your buddy Blake Harrison sure did; he located me over the weekend with information he got from that bug. So he's connected to the people who want this all derailed. What is he, CIA? He was nearly as forceful as you in urging me to take this job. So I've been asking myself why two such well-established and powerful people want me to be chief counsel."

"Butch, sit down. . . ."

"I mean, it's not like I'm going to be allowed to do any real investigation—I don't think that's on anyone's agenda right now. So it can't be my legal brilliance; Bert is brilliant too, and you didn't like him too much."

"Butch, will you just sit down and listen?"

"So it must be you think I'm hungrier than Bert, hungrier and more desperate. The trouble with Bert is that he's from a Main Line family and he's got an independent income and a big law practice. Karp, on the other hand, as you just put it so well, doesn't have a dime—no, wait, I'm almost finished. So you think when you get me in there, with the salary and all the perks, and all the promises, like you just explained it to me, you figure I'll just kind of roll over and let you have the kind of whitewash you want."

Dobbs sprang to his feet as well and slammed his fist down on his desk. "God damn it," he shouted, "that's horseshit and you know it! If it wasn't for me, there wouldn't *be* a serious investigation at all."

Karp leaned across the desk and placed his face within a foot of Dobbs's. Quietly, speaking quickly in the frozen moment, he said, "Yeah, I know. That's what Bert said too. And I can't figure it out. You want a real investigation; I know you don't believe in Warren; but you're also working a game, Hank. For whatever reason, you're trying to steer the investigation in a certain direction —toward something or away from something, I don't know which. I tell you what, Hank: I'll make a deal with you. You tell me the full story, who you told and who he's really working for, and why you're doing what you're doing, and I'll take the job."

Karp had been staring into Dobbs's eyes as he said this, so he could see the fear come into them.

"My God!" said Dobbs. "You've turned into some kind of paranoid maniac."

Karp stood up and turned to go. Almost as an aside, he said, "By the way, Hank, one of my people saw your boy Charlie Ziller swipe a bunch of evidence from the office a couple of weeks ago. Who did he give it to?"

"They couldn't have—," Dobbs blurted, and then stopped short, his face blanching.

"No? Why couldn't they have? Because he did it late at night? Because he swore that no one was watching? I don't think you ever actually practiced any criminal law, did you, Hank? And for sure you were never a prosecutor. Otherwise, you would've learned that trick the first week. So, who got the package? Harrison? The CIA? It doesn't really matter because I have copies of everything."

In a strangled voice he said, "Get out!"

"Okay, but one thing, Representative Dobbs, some advice. You ought to make sure that whoever you hire to replace Bert is someone who never saw the inside of a courtroom. It'll make things a lot easier on you."

Karp walked back down the Hill through a cold, light drizzle, feeling on the one hand pretty good and on the other like a prize schmuck, not an unfamiliar combo to him.

In the office, he told Crane he'd turned down the job, leaving the other conversation out of it. Then he went to see V.T.

V.T. was on the phone. When Karp walked in he said into the receiver, "Oh, wait a sec, he just walked in." He held the receiver out to Karp. "It's Fulton in Louisiana. He wants to talk to you."

"Clay. You find out anything?"

"Yeah," said Fulton, "I found out folks in Baton Rouge don't like smart nigger cops from New York."

"Ah, shit, Clay, I'm sorry. You got into trouble, right?"

"A couple of the local redneck cops rousted me. I flashed my buzzer, but they thought I stole it. I had to do my Sidney Poitier impression."

"I'm sorry."

"Hey, it was interesting, what can I say? Pete Melchior saved my ass. Anyway, we're still looking into this P. X. Kelly guy. So far, no connections with any Cubans. We're trying to get hold of his bank records—that's what I was talking to V.T. about—to see if we can match those transfers to Guel. What's going on up there? I heard about Crane."

"Well, we're sort of on hold here, Clay. Dobbs just offered me Crane's job, and I turned it down."

"You what?"

"I turned it down. Dobbs is our leak. No, I can't get into it now, it's a long story, and besides, I'm not sure that this line isn't bugged too."

"As bad as that, huh?"

"Maybe worse. Look, meanwhile, keep working the PXK angle. There's got to be something; I can feel it. Oh, see if you can find any connection between Kelly and Henry Dobbs, or his family."

"Yeah, right. We're gonna get yanked, aren't we?"

"Probably, but let's get as much done as we can until the ax falls."

Hanging up, Karp turned to V.T. and told him what had happened at Dobbs's office. V.T. took it with his typical aplomb. "Well, well, Hank has a taste for conspiracy, just like dear old dad."

"I thought he didn't do it. That's what Marlene's been trying to prove—oh, that reminds me. Marlene mentioned a name that rang a bell and I said I'd try to track it down. Gaiilov? Did you mention it?"

"Maybe, in passing. Armand Gaiilov, he calls himself Arnie Galinski nowadays, is one of the Dallas Russians who were friendly with Lee and Marina when they came back to Texas after their Russian stay. De Morenschildt's another."

"Gaiilov knew Oswald?" said Karp, amazed.

"Yeah, sure. Half the people in Texas knew Oswald, to hear them tell it, almost as many as people who were involved in the conspiracy. What about it? What's Marlene's angle here?"

"Nothing. Just that, well, this Gaiilov was apparently the Soviet agent who saved Richard Dobbs's ass when he was accused of spying. Dobbs's lawyer, Harley Blaine, waved Gaiilov in the government's face and they dropped the charges. And you say he knew Oswald." Karp stood with his hands in his pockets staring up at the stained ceiling.

"You're seeing a connection," said V.T.

Karp looked at him. "Shit, V.T., how do I know? Everybody knows everybody else. Dobbs knows Blaine, and he's leaking stuff to somebody. Blaine was CIA, and we know that the CIA is stonewalling. Blaine knows Gaiilov and Gaiilov knew Oswald. Now, if *P. X. Kelly* knows Oswald, Blaine, or Gaiilov . . ."

"We'd all put on grins and say 'small world' in chorus."

Karp, deep in thought, strolled around the cluttered office. V.T. had brought a rickety conference table in and covered it with labeled folders. Karp asked, "What's all this stuff?"

"Oh, just an idea, speaking of small world. I'm making a central file of every name that's come up in the investigation with all the information we have on each person and cross-references to all the other files. Maybe it'll turn something up."

"Yeah, well make one for Representative Henry Dobbs too."

"I'll do that," said V.T., laughing. "Oh, as to accomplishments, look at this." He tossed Karp a black loose-leaf notebook.

Karp riffled it. "What is it?"

"It's a sort of concordance for the Depuy film. It describes each shot, giving frame numbers and naming the people in each one, those we've identified. Where we haven't ID'd them, we give them numbers. And it includes whatever info we have on them, all in one place. You might want to check it out against the film. I've seen it so many times, I've probably made some mistakes."

"Okay," said Karp, "I might do that. Maybe I'll spot P. X. Kelly behind a bush waving a handful of cash."

A week passed, and then another. Crane's resignation was on the front page for a day, and then the assassination committee seemed to drop from the national view, like a doomed DC-10 vanishing from a radar scope. Crane slipped away back to Philadelphia after a small cheerless staff dinner. Karp had one brief meeting with Louis Watson, the new chairman. Watson said he was counting on Karp to hold the staff together until a new director could be found, and Karp said that he would try to do so. They did not discuss the work of the staff or assassination theories.

It snowed six and a half inches one Thursday, which meant that the entire federal government ground to a halt, it being a well-known condition of employment in the federal bureaucracy that you never have to drive in snow. The snowfall and its attendant disasters occupied a good chunk of the *Post*'s front page, but that newspaper did reserve five or six inches on page eleven for an announcement that a man named Claude Wilkey had been selected to replace Bert Crane. Karp noted with ironic amusement that Dobbs had indeed taken his advice: Wilkey was a professor at an Ivy League law school, and as far as Karp could determine from the brief vita in the *Post*, he had never tried a case in his life.

Karp decided to use his unexpected snow holiday to review the concordance that V.T. had made of the Depuy film. He did not imagine that this evidence would ever appear in a court of law, not the way things appeared to be going, but he was a pro, and he thought that there might be a faint chance of catching something that others had missed.

He had set up the little editor on the kitchen table and was anticipating a boring but restful winter's afternoon of running through the Depuy film frame by frame and editing the concordance. This proved more difficult than he had expected. Like many (perhaps all) men whose profession requires the exercise of

abstract thought, he had little attention to spare for the concrete realities of domestic life. If he had, he would never have embarked on a project requiring concentration and careful manipulation of a notoriously cranky device in the kitchen of a tiny apartment containing an active and curious three-year-old, an extremely large dog, an intelligent woman in the final stages of a large project that also required the use of that very same machine, in the aftermath of a blizzard that confined them all to close quarters. A more sensitive man would never have started such a project under these circumstances; a more sensitive man would therefore probably not have discovered how and why John F. Kennedy was slain, a discovery that Karp ever afterward would associate with the smell of cocoa boiling over, with gray light and swirling snow.

Karp's first mistake was being charmed by his daughter's identification of the film editor as a "dolly television." He agreed that it was indeed a dolly TV (ho ho!) but that Daddy had to play with it for now. This offended Lucy's well-developed sense of justice and entitlement; the dolly TV should be in *her* room so her dollies could watch it. Explanations. Whining. Tantrum.

"Can't you . . . um . . . go someplace?" Karp pleaded to his wife, amid the wails.

"Go where?" replied Marlene. "It's the Antarctic out there. Also, I was planning to use the machine today. I didn't expect to have you stumbling around the house."

Karp threw up his hands and choked off a nasty response. "Okay, *I'll* go out with her, and you can use the machine, and then *you* can watch her and I'll work." He turned to the child. "How about that, Lucy?" he asked, summoning his final reserves of good nature. "You want to go play in the snow?"

Lucy sniffled back tears and nodded solemnly.

"Take the dog," said Marlene.

When she was alone in the house, Marlene made herself a pot of coffee, drank some, lit a cigarette, and spent ten minutes just listening to the quiet. Then she rewound the film Karp had been looking at and spooled in the film she had taken from the Dobbs attic.

The first few seconds were an establishing shot of a locale: a stretch of wide, calm water, a bay of some sort, a deserted beach,

and a large white beach cottage. It was very early in the morning. Marlene stopped the film and studied the building curiously. Then she stripped the film out of the camera and went to get a box containing several of the Dobbs films she wanted to look at again, found one, mounted it, and rolled it for a minute or so until she found a film of a family party in the summer of fifty-five and the Dobbs and Hewlett cousins playing on the beach in front of a beach cottage. She had been right; the place in the attic film was the isolated cottage belonging to Selma Dobbs's family, at Niantic on the Sound.

Replacing the attic film, Marlene rolled on. A couple emerged from the house. The woman, a trim, pretty blond in her late thirties, was wearing a two-piece suit from the postwar era, and carrying a beach blanket. The man wore trunks and carried a bottle of champagne and two stemmed glasses. They were laughing. The woman spread the blanket and they sat on it and drank champagne and kissed and laughed and watched the sun climb higher over the Sound.

There was a cut and suddenly the man and the woman were much closer. The cameraman had changed lenses and was now shooting through a big telephoto. The image was grainier, but not grainy enough to prevent Marlene from seeing that the woman was Selma Dobbs and the man was Harley Blaine.

Marlene watched, fascinated, as the wine was finished and the kissing became more passionate. They wrapped themselves in the beach blanket; bathing suits were tossed out on the beach. The blanket became a wriggling, heaving tube. The blanket fell away; they didn't miss a stroke. Marlene tried to reconcile her image of the austere dowager she had met with this abandoned creature being pounded into the sand, her back arched in ecstasy, her legs wrapped around her lover's neck. The camera panned slowly from her face, an orgasmic mask, down to Blaine's thrusting hips. Marlene felt her face grow hot, a combination of intense embarrassment and turn-on.

Another cut, a longer blackout. Bright sun again. The couple were splashing into the water, nude. They embraced and kissed in the water. Blackout again. This time it was evening and the shot was through the window of one of the cottage's bedrooms. Marlene stopped the film and thought for a moment. The bedroom was on the second floor. The cameraman must have been lying on

the peaked roof of the nearby garage. A determined photojournalist, thought Marlene; and she was almost certain that she knew who it was, based on her considerable familiarity with the man's work. For some insane reason, Richard Ewing Dobbs, that great American, had hidden in bushes and crouched on a slanted roof to take movies of his wife screwing his best friend.

Marlene had another cigarette and thought about what this discovery meant. Harley Blaine was obviously the "Q" of Selma Dobbs's diary. The reluctance of Q to countenance a breakup of the Dobbs marriage was thus explained: Blaine's loyalty to Richard Dobbs was greater than his desire for Selma. That also threw light on that odd break in the tone of Blaine's early love letters. He *had* given his girlfriend to Dobbs. Fifteen years and a long war later the former sweethearts had obviously kicked free of the traces, jumped into a hopeless affair, and become the subject of an interesting short blue movie, shot by the cuckold.

Or maybe Dobbs was in on it; maybe they knew he was filming? Maybe they took turns with the camera. Was that too outré even for the rich? Marlene felt out of her depth; the sexual perversions that had come her way over the years, although remarkably varied, had lacked the flavor of real decadence, and ran more to simple wackos like the corpse fucker, Oscar Sobell.

Marlene cranked the film rapidly backward through the viewer, having forgotten that Karp had specifically told her not to do that or the thing would jam, and sure enough the thing jammed. She peered into the film-advance mechanism. It looked like a splice had come loose and jumped the sprockets, causing the film to pile up behind it.

She was just about to try to fix it when the front door burst open and Karp and Lucy bounced in, red-faced and soaking wet. Sweetie came in too, and dashed toward the kitchen, tongue out and dripping spit, raining chunks of matted snow from its coat. Marlene saw what was going to happen and shouted, "Nooo!" The dog stood in the center of the kitchen and shook itself vigorously, coating every surface and Marlene with a good three quarts of freezing water.

"We want cocoa! We want cocoa!" chanted Karp and Lucy in chorus.

"You planned this," said Marlene, wiping her face with the dish towel.

"Me?" said Karp, giggling with his daughter.

Thirty minutes later, they had all changed clothes, toweled the dog dry, and mopped the floor. Marlene was melting chocolate on the stove, the little girl and the dog were watching TV, and Karp was at the kitchen table looking doubtfully at his editing machine. The radio was turned up loud, against the bugging.

"You screwed it up," he said.

"A splice broke."

Karp popped the hatch on the advance mechanism and pried the errant film out. "This is the porn film the old lady had in her attic? How was it? Pretty hot?"

Marlene told him about the film and its main characters and what she had surmised about its auteur.

Karp whistled. "That's quite a story, babe. What're you going to do with it?"

"God knows! This is going to destroy the Dobbses if it gets out—" She stopped, struck by a thought. "Hey, do you think . . . ?"

"Mmm, yeah, I'm following you. It could explain why Dobbs is messing with the assassination investigation."

"What, you mean somebody is blackmailing him with this stuff? But who? And why?"

"Well, the 'why' part is easy," replied Karp. He had smoothed the film down on the edit block and was about to repair the splice, a skill he had picked up in recent months.

"There's any number of people who'd like the investigation to dry up and blow away. As to who—you got me there, kid. Are you sure the camera guy was Dobbs's old man?"

"Pretty sure. It was sort of the same kind of movie he always made: quick nervous pans and arty cuts, using a telephoto for close-ups. And the film was there where only he could've put it. Why, are you thinking that maybe some . . . agency made it? The FBI or the Russians? Or a private eye?" She was stirring milk into the chocolate, making it smooth.

"I don't know," said Karp. "We'll probably never know, but it's . . . hmm, that's peculiar."

"What?"

"There's another splice real close to the one you broke, let's see, two, four, eight frames away. Why would anyone want to splice a third of a second into a home movie? You practically

wouldn't even be able to register that you saw it before it was gone."

Marlene put down her spoon and looked over his shoulder. "What's in those frames? Can you just stick it under the gizmo there?"

Karp placed a frame from the start of the spliced strip over the little window in the editor and snapped the mechanism shut.

"Just a guy in a raincoat. Looks like a cemetery." Karp tugged at the free end of the film and drew it through the viewer. The man in the film knelt swiftly and placed a bouquet on a grave and then stood up again and faced the camera. Then the film showed the window of the house in Niantic.

"Pull it back, pull it back!" cried Marlene.

"You want the guy again?" said Karp. "I want to see the hot stuff."

But he pulled the film back to show the man's face.

"Oh, my God!" said Marlene weakly. She sat down in a chair, her knees trembling. "That's Weinberg. That was a picture of him leaving a bouquet of flowers at a grave at Arlington. That's how they did it, how he signaled where he dropped the microfilmed secrets for Reltzin. And Dobbs took a picture of him doing it. That means he knew Weinberg and knew what he was doing, just like Weinberg said. Which means he really *was* a spy and a traitor. Which means Gaiilov must have lied, because Blaine told him to or because he really was a double agent. . . . Oh, God, I'm nauseous already from this." She held a hand up over her mouth and stared at her husband with wide eyes.

"You could ask Gaiilov," said Karp.

"Yeah, right, if I could find him. He's probably in Bolivia."

"No, he's in Texas. In Dallas, as a matter of fact," said Karp with a calmness he did not feel. "Calls himself Galinski."

"What! How did you . . . ?"

"I asked V.T. and he told me. I guess I just forgot until now."

"Tell me!"

"V.T. said he's a member of the Dallas Russian community. His name came up because he was one of the people who knew Lee Oswald and his wife and because he had some kind of shadowy CIA connection—we thought—just like de Morenschildt and some others."

"And he's obviously keeping an even lower profile, because Harry didn't turn him up in any of the usual checks," said Marlene. After a moment, she continued, twirling her fingers through her hair, as she did while in intense thought. "So here's Harley Blaine's pet ex-spy, who knew Oswald, who knew that Richard Dobbs was guilty and lied about it, and here we also have Richard Dobbs's son, working himself into a position of influence on the assassination committee, and pushing for a strong investigation, he *says*, but really steering the investigation away from the CIA, or why would he have arranged to have those memos and the film ripped off, and have told someone you were going to Miami to see those guys, and that must mean—" She stopped, confused. "What must it mean?"

"It means we're becoming Kennedy nuts," said Karp sourly. He tapped the film on the editor. "But for sure this is blackmail material. If somebody else has this information, Dobbs is in their pocket. The only question is who."

"You think your Irishman in New Orleans?"

"Baton Rouge. Yeah, he's looking better and better. I want to go out there and take a look at him. And then talk to Gaiilov in Dallas. And maybe Blaine too."

"I want to come," said Marlene.

He stared at her. Behind her, unwatched, the cocoa boiled over, filling the apartment with the dark, cloying odor of burned chocolate.

The man called Caballo looked out on the falling snow and felt cold. He hated snow, not only because it was cold, but because it meant he couldn't move, couldn't do what he had come to Washington to do. He hated Washington too. The public buildings all looked like prisons to him. They were full of little people making little rules for other people to follow, pretending that you could live real life according to lists of rules. Caballo knew that wasn't true. You just had to do what was necessary; you had to survive. That was why he liked Guatemala, that and the climate.

On the second day after the blizzard, Bishop called.

"There's a little hitch," he said.

"There's always a little hitch lately," replied Caballo, with uncharacteristic impatience.

"Oh? Getting antsy, are you?"

"Yeah. I want to do the job and get out of here. I'm getting a bad feeling about this operation. What was that hitch, anyway?"

"Our candidate elected not to take over the investigation. However, the man they found is just as good, maybe better. We won't have any trouble with him. But this man, Karp, is still something of a loose cannon. He has a copy of the film, and we need it back."

"We should do him, Bishop. I told you, he saw me."

"Don't touch a hair on his head!" Bishop snapped. *"That's all we need. And don't give me any smart ideas about convenient accidents. We're past all that. The lid is just about nailed down once and for all and I'm not looking forward to spending the rest of my life waiting for another investigation. Nor are you, I imagine."* He waited, but the other man said nothing. *"This is a retrieval, pure and simple. You'll wait for the apartment to be completely empty, and then you'll go in and get it. And Bill?"*

"Yeah?"

"Don't get seen again. Our friend would be extremely upset if you were seen again."

NINETEEN

Karp had to admit it, Claude Wilkey knew how to run a meeting. He was running it in the wrong direction, but at a good clip. They were sitting around the conference table in the chief counsel's office—Wilkey, Karp, V.T., several young, intense-looking men whom Wilkey had recruited, and a small, tight-faced young woman, the new administrative chief. Bea Sondergard was gone with Crane.

Wilkey was talking. He had a pleasant, light, confident voice, well suited to reasoned academic discussions. He looked like the professor he was: a bland, pale face topped by thinning brown hair, horn-rims magnifying mild blue eyes. He wore a tweed jacket with leather patches on the elbows over a knitted sweater bearing a diamond pattern, slacks, polished loafers, and a striped button-down shirt with a foulard tie. Everyone else in the room, including the woman, wore dark suits.

Wilkey's lecture was well organized and easy to understand. The staff had one purpose and one purpose only: to complete the committee hearings as quickly as possible and to write a report. The staff would be reorganized into teams, each responsible for a section of the final report; the intense-looking men would be in charge of these teams. As Wilkey described their duties, Karp realized that no one was assigned to the conduct of any field investigation.

"What about the people we have in Miami, New Orleans, and

Dallas?" Karp interrupted. "What happens with those operations?"

"I'm afraid we're closing all that down," explained Wilkey in a patient tone. "We simply don't have time for it."

"You read my report?" Karp demanded. He had, on Wilkey's request, composed a brief summary of the major new leads he had uncovered: the Depuy film, the CIA papers, the interview with Mosca, the trove of material from Guel's house, the investigation of P. X. Kelly. He had included some of the more obvious next steps.

"Yes, I did. Interesting. But really, you don't have anything I can bring before the committee, do you? Some unsolved murders, a film of uncertain provenance, suspicions . . ." He glanced at his new people as if to say, This is just what we want to avoid. "No, I want to redirect the core of this effort toward the scientific analysis of solid evidence."

"You mean like the magic bullet? That's what you call solid evidence?"

Wilkey pursed his lips. "Yes, that's what we have to work with. We're going to settle the scientific issues, the forensics, the autopsy, once and for all. That's what the Congress expects and that's what we intend to do."

Karp was about to make his old point about the chain of evidence for all the physical sequelae of the assassination being hopelessly corrupt, but thought better of it and slumped disconsolately in his chair. The meeting resumed. Wilkey was also, it appeared, going to deal with the organized crime issue "once and for all" as well. Karp listened without interest. Of course they would try to pin it on the Mob! Congress would love that—Wilkey had written a book on the Mafia, Karp now recalled—because of all the powers in America, the Mob was the only one that didn't have a lobbying office in Washington. Not an official one anyway.

The meeting broke up. It was clear to Karp that the "team leaders," all three of them Wilkey's men, were not going to report to him in any meaningful way. It was a neat and familiar bureaucratic maneuver. The graceful thing would be for him to resign, which he intended to do as soon as possible.

He walked out of Wilkey's office and through the corridors. There was a heightened purpose in the air. People were bustling about, carrying papers; the new people were cracking the whip.

Karp had no doubt that Wilkey would produce a professional report, on time and within budget.

He went out of the building for a bite to eat. The snow had melted off the roadways but lingered in slushy piles in the gutters. The temperature was moving up into the fifties and the cherry trees in front of the botanical gardens were showing the little knobs that would be blossoms in a week or two. He doubted that he would be there to see the famous display.

Two hot dogs and a root beer later, Karp walked back to the Annex and went to see V.T.

V.T. was arranging files on his long table, working off a large stack of paper that he was distributing among the various folders.

"What zeal!" said Karp. "I guess our new leader's inspired you to really start working."

"Yeah," said V.T., "old Claude has that charismatic, inspirational quality that makes you want to do a lot of busywork, puke your guts out, and quit."

"You're quitting." It was not a question.

"The resignation's being typed," said V.T. "In fairness to my successor, I'm just placing the last of this stuff in the personality files. Then I'm out of here. You?"

"Me too, I guess," Karp responded in a dull tone. "I need to call Clay and tell him the party's over."

V.T. looked up from what he was doing and sat on his desk. "Well, it's true. We gave it our best and we got whipped. Like Clay said, way back, we were way over our heads. If they had wanted a real homicide investigation . . ."

"What *did* they want?" asked Karp, idly flipping through some folders. "Remind me."

"To forget. Warren was right, in a way. Blame it on a nut, conveniently dead, and forget it. And then we can blame all the failures of the country on the loss of Camelot—that fucking war, the riots, crime, greed, every goddamn thing we don't want to take responsibility for. If only Kennedy had lived! So. Tidy up the files and go back to real life."

"We never found out who Turm was, did we?" asked Karp waving a file.

"No, we didn't. I doubt Mr. Wilkey will be overly concerned, however."

"No, but I'm sure he'd like the bastard's phony name spelled

right." He showed V.T. the file tab. "It's not T-E-R-M. It's T-U-R-M."

V.T. looked at the lettering. "Turm with a U. Are you sure?"

"Positive. Mosca saw the forged passport. He made a point of mentioning it."

V.T. turned away from him. "Turm with a U. Oh, God. Oh, shit."

"What's wrong? Why does it matter?"

V.T. slammed the file to the floor and whirled. His face was stricken, going white around the eyes and mouth. "Those *bastards*! Those fucking infantile macho *bastard* cocksuckers . . ."

"V.T., what's—"

"Turm with a U. It was like a kid's game with them, wasn't it? Secret passwords and wiseass fake names. They didn't even bother to be subtle about it, because who was going to look? And it's an impossible move, so who would catch on? And nobody did, and now it fucking doesn't matter."

"Newbury, what the fuck are you talking about?"

"Turm. It's the German for rook, the piece in chess. And, of course, there's Bishop. And Caballo is the Spanish for knight— the one with the sneaky moves. And PXK isn't some goddamn Irish trucking executive in Baton Rouge. It's chess notation, but it's a notation for an impossible move, so of course, nobody would ever get the joke. Except the bastards who thought it up." V.T. sat on the edge of his desk and hung his head, as if exhausted.

"What do you mean, chess notation?" asked Karp.

V.T. looked at him bleakly. "In chess notation P x K, with a little x in the middle, would mean 'pawn takes king.' It's never used, of course, because the king is never taken in chess. The game ends in a checkmate, when the king can't make a legal move out of check. In real life, of course, it's different. PXK isn't the name of an individual; *it's what they called the operation!* Pawn takes king. Well, we know who the king was. And the pawn, of course."

"Oswald."

"Uh-huh. Oswald. The pawn. The necessary nut. So now we have all the pieces, so to speak." V.T. laughed bitterly. "No, one's still missing. There's a queen on this board, and I doubt very much if it's Mr. Kelly of Baton Rouge." He laughed again, a laugh edged with hysteria. "It's the perfect paranoid confection. Of course there

has to be a mastermind behind all this, pulling the strings—no, that's mixing metaphors. Controlling the pieces."

He got off the desk and walked toward the door.

"Where are you going?" Karp asked.

"To see if my resignation is ready for signature. If you want me, I'll be outside the building wearing a red hat and carrying a shopping bag full of old clippings."

Karp went back to his office and sat at his desk for a few minutes before it really hit him that he had nothing to do. He called Clay Fulton in New Orleans and left a message, and then waited around for Fulton to call back. He pulled a few files from various hiding places and stuffed them in the red envelope, tattered now from being carried around with him nearly everyplace he had gone for many weeks. He spread the material from the envelope out on his desk and looked at it. For an instant he felt a thrill of panic when he realized that the Depuy film was missing and then recovered when he recalled that he had left it at home, on the kitchen table among Marlene's films. Or had he?

Frantically, he dialed his home number.

Marlene picked up on the first ring. "God, this is weird!" she exclaimed. "I was just about to call you."

"You were? In anything wrong?"

"No, I . . . I just found out something you need to know." She paused. "Maybe we shouldn't talk about it on the phone."

"Is my, is the thing I, um, left on the kitchen table . . . ?"

"Oh, yeah, it's here," said Marlene in a peculiar voice. "I've been playing with it. We'll talk when you get here."

Karp packed the red envelope and left his office, informing his secretary that he'd be working from home for the rest of the day.

"You want me to forward calls?" she asked with a knowing look; "working at home" was a well-understood Washington euphemism for looking for another job while remaining on the payroll. He nodded and left.

When Karp walked into the apartment, Marlene met him with a finger to her lips. She then turned on the radio in the kitchen to a rock station at considerable volume. Lucy was in the living room happily watching cartoons at a similar noise level.

"I was going through some of Dobbs's later films, to finish up

my notes on the case and to check whether he left any other little surprises in them."

"Did he?"

"No," she said. "But watch this!"

Marlene sat down behind the editor and rolled it. "A pleasant backyard barbecue. Nice house, pool. A bunch of Mexican-looking servants roasting a side of beef on a spit. Prosperous guys and women in western gear, drinking and laughing. It says 'Texas' doesn't it. It is. Notice how steady the shot is? The camera's on a tripod, panning back and forth. Everybody's mugging for the camera. Okay, watch this! The cameraman wants to get in the frame. There's his back, now he's turning around and posing for the group."

She stopped the film on one frame and Karp saw a largish, intelligent-looking man with an even-toothed smile and short, dark hair, wearing a western shirt and jeans.

"Harley Blaine," said Marlene. She rolled the film rapidly. It flickered like an old silent movie. The partying people jumped around like fleas, gobbling their ribs, jerking their elbows as they drank. The film ended with some sort of ceremony; a fat man got a plaque from another fat man. Marlene slowed it to normal speed. There was a blackout and then the scene showed a forest at night, tropical swamp foliage, a white, open road, and then a line of military trucks approaching.

"Jesus! It's our film!" cried Karp.

"Yep. Your film. Shot by Harley Blaine. He did his little memento of a civic party at his ranch and then he trucked on down to Louisiana to take some pictures of the counterrevolution-to-be. Which means he was up to his neck in the Cuban business too, a dozen years after he retired from the CIA."

"But how did Depuy get hold of this?"

"No problem. We know he got it from Ferrie. Ferrie was at the training exercise. He just snitched the film. Maybe Depuy paid him for it. Maybe Blaine didn't miss the film. Selma Dobbs's letters have some stuff about him misplacing cameras. It was a family joke."

"Hilarious," said Karp. "So Ferrie gets the film and shows it to Depuy. No big deal, just Ferrie boasting and Depuy fishing for a story. After the assassination, that's a whole different situation. Whoever did it found out that Ferrie has some evidence linking

Blaine and some other CIA types to Oswald and a guy who looks a lot like Oswald, via the anti-Castro stuff. It wouldn't have been difficult; Ferrie had the biggest mouth in Louisiana. So they ace him with a drug overdose and get the film. Meanwhile, Depuy's on the sauce, he's forgotten his copy of the film, or doesn't realize its significance. He dies and his wife gives all his stuff to the AP archive."

"So now we have the connection that explains why Hank Dobbs is jamming up the investigation," said Marlene. "He's working for the man who saved his father, even though Blaine has to know that Richard Dobbs was really guilty."

"You think Blaine was blackmailing Dobbs? You think he said he'd spill the beans on the old man if Dobbs didn't help him protect Blaine's old CIA buddies?"

"No, that's not it," said Marlene definitively. "Blaine saved Richard Dobbs in 1951, in the teeth of the CIA. Why would he have pulled a switch at this late date? No, the Dobbs family was the core of his life: he loved the husband and he loved the wife. That wouldn't change, even if he pulled the trigger on JFK himself. No, he didn't need blackmail at all. Hank Dobbs was covering for Blaine from sheer gratitude."

"But what the hell was he covering?" asked Karp, his brows knotting in frustration. "Blaine's not directly tied to anyone we've turned up except Gaiilov, who's peripheral to the Oswald story, as far as we know. Like you said, Blaine retired from the CIA long before JFK became president. He was on the CIA shit list, in fact, because of the Dobbs thing, and we have no evidence that he knew the one guy we've identified as being central to the whole thing."

"Who?"

"Paul David, aka Maurice Bishop."

"Oh, yeah. But wait a minute—isn't Bishop in this film?"

"Yeah, but so're a hundred other people. Because Blaine took the film doesn't mean he was in bed with Bishop. Nobody we've talked to has ever mentioned Blaine."

Something tugged at Marlene's memory. She had an extraordinary memory for faces, the product of years of going through mug books, looking at the faces of sex criminals, of hours and hours spent with victims trying to tease a face out of violence-clouded memory.

"Bishop slash David is on the film, huh? Let me see if I can pick him out."

She started to wind the film, but Karp stopped her and got out the black loose-leaf book that V.T. had assembled, consulted it, and turned to a glossy blowup of the best David/Bishop shot on the film.

Marlene looked at it and cried "Yesss! It was nagging me. I knew I'd seen that guy before, and of course, I was thinking of Blaine when I watched the film, so I was ready for the connection. This guy, ten years younger, is in a picture with Harley Blaine that's hanging in the hallway behind Richard Dobbs's study. Blaine knew Bishop, all right, from way back. His protégé, you might say."

Karp sat on his excitement and tried to argue against the most obvious conclusion. "Okay, great, Blaine knew David/Bishop way back when. He took home movies of a Bishop operation. He's still a retired guy, a lawyer, not an active spook like the rest of them."

"Okay," Marlene conceded, "then let's look at this joker you were talking about, this Kelly guy in Baton Rouge? We know *he's* connected because Guel was getting all that cash from PXK. Maybe we should check that out, if Blaine knows him too."

Karp sighed and told her about V.T.'s enlightenment concerning the meaning of PXK. He concluded the tale with, "So according to Newbury, Kelly's yet another of the ten million false trails generated by the assassination. Hell, maybe the chess names are a coincidence too. Nah, that's hard even for me to swallow, that on top of the two murders, and seeing Oswald number two in Miami. I think the killer is really it, the core of the conspiracy. And there's not a goddamn thing we can do about it."

He told her about Wilkey and the meeting that morning, about V.T. quitting.

"Well, a total disaster," Marlene said when he was finished. "What are you going to do?"

"Oh, I'll quit too, I guess. It gripes me, though. I can't make a case, but I'd just like to know who the queen was."

"Queen?"

"Yeah, that's what V.T. said. King, pawn, knight, rook, bishop. We're not sure about the rook, Turm, except that he was apparently an expert in organizing assassinations, among other things. But the guy behind it all—the master piece on the board—V.T.

called him the queen." He laughed. "It'd be funny if it turned out
to be Clay Shaw, considering."

"Yeah, but how's this for another fascinating coincidence. You
know they have this King Ranch in Texas, supposed to be the
largest ranch in the world? Well, when Harley Blaine went back to
Texas, he added pieces to his parents' old property and set himself
up as a gentleman rancher. And do you know what he called his
ranch, the old funster?"

"Don't tell me."

"Yes. The Queen Ranch."

They were silent amid the noise from the radio and the TV.
Karp reached for her hand. "Jesus, Marlene, what're we going to
do?" It was a rhetorical question, but Marlene responded with
scarcely a thought.

"Well, obviously, we have to go and see Blaine. We'll fly out
to Texas, to the old *Queen* Ranch and have a little talk. About
Dick Dobbs and John F. Kennedy."

Karp's wife had once again succeeded in amazing him. "Why
would we want to do that, Marlene?" he asked weakly. "Why
should Blaine talk to us? Because we found one of his home movies? He'll laugh in our faces."

"No he won't. He'll talk. Maybe not on a witness stand, but
he'll tell us what we want to know, which is all that matters right
now. Aren't you dying to know how he did it? Speaking of which,
he's dying himself. Maybe he's just waiting to spill his guts."

"That I doubt, considering he's been working like crazy to kill
the investigation, which he did. Not to mention killing people in
the process. So why is he going to be such a sweetheart with you
and me?"

"Because our hearts are pure and because we have a film of
him screwing Selma Dobbs and proof that Richard Dobbs was a
spy and a traitor. He's not going to want that to get out."

Karp stared at her. "Blackmail him? Are you serious?"

"Oh, silly, it won't come to blackmail," said Marlene lightly.
"It'll be very civilized. I'll send him a copy of the film and tell him
what we know about his involvement in Kennedy, and we'll go out
there and talk."

Karp held his hands to his head. "I don't believe I'm hearing
this!" he shrieked. "If we're right, this guy has already aced a couple dozen people, not to mention the president of the United

States. How about if you're wrong and he sends three guys with machine guns? Did you ever think of that?"

They locked eyes for a full minute, tense and breathing hard. At the end of this, Marlene nodded curtly once and got up from her chair. "Fine, have it your way. I'll pack."

"What? Wait a minute, Marlene. . . ."

"Why? Why wait? Just call the goddamn office and tell them you're quitting. We can be on the road tonight, running back to New York with our tails between our legs."

"Marlene . . ."

She stomped out of the room and he followed her up the stairs to their bedroom, where with violent motions she started flinging drawers open.

"Marlene, stop it!"

She turned to him, eye blazing. "Why? Hey, you were the one who wanted to find out who whacked JFK. It was no big thing for me. I was happy in New York, remember?"

"You're not being fair," he said, despising himself for saying it.

"Oh, for Chrissake, what does 'fair' have to do with it. What the problem is, is you *still* don't trust my judgment. Look—I *know* this guy. I studied him in films over thirty years. I read nearly everything he wrote. I know how his mind works. I know what the people who were most intimate with him thought about him. I read his fucking *love letters*. I'm *telling* you that this will work."

"And if it doesn't?"

She paused and her face lost some of its tension. He was going to roll on it. "If it doesn't," she said, "we'll both be dead. Which is why I'm going to call Harry Bello to come down here."

"Bello? Why? What does he have to do with it?"

"Simple. We'll tell him the whole story and leave the stuff in the envelope with him. If anything happens to us, he'll take care of Lucy, one, and two, he'll track them down and kill them all, all the goddamn chessmen, every one."

Karp let out a long breath. He shrugged. "Well, since you put it that way, how can I resist?"

"Really?" said Marlene. "Really and truly?"

"Yeah, uh-huh."

"How do you feel?" she asked challengingly.

Karp consulted his feelings, always a creaky process.

"Um, relieved, I think. Pumped. Scared shitless."

She flung her arms around him. They hugged. They kissed, with an intensity they had not experienced for some time. She drew back from him and looked into his face, smiling. She said, "Good. That's how I feel. If you didn't want to feel like that a lot, you shouldn't have married a Sicilian."

Marlene threw on her field jacket and her Yankees cap over sweatshirt and jeans and sneakers and drove her car to downtown Rosslyn, a concentration of high-rises and commercial streets across the Potomac from Washington. She stopped first at a bank and drew five hundred dollars against the MasterCard, feeling just a twinge of guilt. After consulting a Yellow Pages, she walked three blocks to a film lab.

Placing the Dobbs film on the counter, she asked how long it would take to make a copy.

The pencil-necked young technician across the counter weighed the film in his hand. "Beginning of next week?"

"No, I need it now. I mean right now."

He shook his head. "No way, lady. I got work piled up—"

"You do this yourself?"

"Yeah, me and another guy."

"Do mine at the head of the line and it's fifty in cash, under the table."

"Uh, I don't know. . . ."

"A hundred. Cash."

He considered this for six seconds. "Okay, I'll write up a ticket."

"No ticket. Let's just do it." She moved down the counter and lifted the flap.

"Hey, um . . ."

"I'm coming with you. You said you were going to do it now, right?"

"Uh, yeah, but . . ."

"I want to watch. This is a special film."

The technician was familiar with 'special films,' although this one was not as naughty as many he'd seen. Two hours later, Marlene, smelling faintly of developer, emerged from the lab and made her way to the local FedEx office. She borrowed a phone and,

charging the call to her own phone, got Harley Blaine's mailing address from a polite young voice in Texas. Then she borrowed a pen and paper from the clerk and wrote:

Dear Mr. Blaine:

The enclosed film, which no one but me and my husband (and, of course, the photographer) has seen as yet, will be of interest to you. We know about the bishop and the pawn, the knight, the rook and the queen, and what they did. I believe a conversation would be useful. Please call at your convenience. We are prepared to depart for Texas whenever you wish. Like your own, this is not a government operation.

She added her phone number and signed it, and sent it with the film copy, in the lab envelope to make clear that it was a copy, to Harley Blaine.

There was a travel agency across the street, and there she purchased two open return tickets to Dallas. She was about to return to her car when she had a thought and went into a nearby People's variety store for some additional purchases.

"Hey, there," said a friendly voice behind her. She turned, and there was a black woman in a tan cloth coat over a pale green uniform skirt. It took a second for Marlene to recognize her as the nanny from the park.

"Hi!" said Marlene. "How're you doing?"

"Just fine! I'm goin' to Carolina next week. I'm starting school."

"Dietician?"

"Nah, X ray. That food smell make me sick. How about yourself. You take my advice?"

"Yeah. Yeah, I did. I think I'm going to be working in a law office pretty soon."

"Oooh, hey—paralegal? That's good work that paralegal, 'cept you need clothes." She cast a doubtful eye over Marlene's ensemble.

"Um, yeah," said Marlene, "except this is more like quasilegal. They don't make you dress up as much."

Marlene went home and called Harry and asked him to come down, without explaining the situation. Harry said, "Tomorrow afternoon."

The following morning Karp went to the office, not at eight, as he had in the past, but around ten-thirty. The placed bustled with people who either did not meet his eye, so busy were they, or else, even worse, spoke briefly to him in sympathetic or condescending tones. Charlie Ziller was one of those who did not meet his eye. There were several call-back messages from Clay Fulton. Karp rang the New Orleans office of Pete Melchior, the retired NYPD cop turned private investigator, and found Fulton in.

"What's up, Butch? I've been hearing all kinds of weird stuff."

"It's all true. The word is, no further field investigation. Come on home."

"No, further . . . what? I was going to go to Miami and show our pictures to Odio. And this Kelly guy is looking pretty good. I got an eyewitness who saw him with Carlos Marcello a couple times back in the sixties."

"Forget Kelly. He's another dead end. V.T. figured it out. He's quitting, by the way. I guess I am too."

A long pause on the line. "That bad, huh?"

"Yeah. We got beat, old buddy. Come home."

V.T. was in his office tossing personal items into an old leather satchel. "They accepted my resignation with regret," he remarked as Karp came in. "Jim Phelps is getting out too."

"Phelps? Why him? He's a tech. I thought Wilkey wanted to up the status of the tech work."

"Yes, up, but only in the desired direction. Phelps is convinced there was hanky-panky in the autopsy photos and the X rays. Wilkey wants a second opinion. Or a third, until, apparently, he finds a techie who believes there's no problem."

V.T. looked around the gutted office. "I'm off. Oh, speaking of no problem, have you seen the prelim report from Dr. Selig and the autopsy boys?"

"No, I didn't know it was in. They don't show me stuff anymore. What did they say?"

"Briefly, all the wounds of the two men are consistent with two shots from the upper left rear. And thus the magic bullet is still magic."

"Wendt signed on to this shit?"

"He did not. A voice crying in the wilderness, however. He'll

get his day in front of the committee, but I doubt it'll do much good. All the other docs, including your old buddy Selig, were being very cautious. Nobody wants to join the nut parade." He hefted his satchel and grasped Karp's hand. "What about you? You going to stay around for the whitewash? Tom Sawyer says it's fun."

"I don't think so. Me and Marlene are going to fly down to Dallas on our own, to check something out. Marlene found some stuff. She . . . we think there's a good chance that Harley Blaine, Richard Dobbs's old lawyer, is the queen on the board."

V.T. dropped his satchel with a bang. "You're not serious!"

Karp nodded heavily and explained the nature of the evidence and what they had done about it. V.T. remained silent for a moment, thinking and chewing his lip. Then he said, "You think this is wise? Going out there, the two of you? Whatever you've got on him, this guy's got a track record of collecting evidence from recently dead people."

"I don't know, V.T. I need to close this out, in my own mind. I mean, it's completely circumstantial. There's a million ways of laughing it out of court. The witnesses who might've talked are dead and the live ones aren't talking. It's not something I can show to Wilkey; he wouldn't understand it, because he doesn't have the instinct, and because he just wants to close this down with a minimum of fuss, and this could be big-time fuss. Marlene thinks there's a chance Blaine'll tell us something. I think you have to be Sicilian to think it'll work, but there it is: we're going, if Blaine calls back."

Blaine called back at four that day. "Will you hold for Mr. Blaine?" said a polite male voice. Marlene would.

When he came on the line, Harley Blaine sounded weaker than he had some months previously, but his voice still carried the same ironic tone.

"Miss Ciampi. Well, here we are again, talking about the dear dead days of yore. Your package arrived, and I will say that I did not expect to be surprised by anything at my stage of life, but I *was* surprised. My heart must be stronger than my doctors are telling me, or it might've just gone off the rail when I saw that film. What a devil that Dick was! And we thought he couldn't keep a secret!"

"I take it then that you didn't know about the film, or the shots of Weinberg at Arlington," said Marlene.

"Mmm, why don't we reserve such conversation for our tête-à-tête. There's a Delta plane that leaves National at ten-twenty tomorrow. Do you think you could be on it? I'll have you met."

"And my husband."

"Of course, and Mr. Karp. I'll look forward to meeting you both. Until then."

He broke the connection.

"It was weird, Butch," Marlene said later, when Karp had returned home and they were seated on the ratty couch in their living room. "It was like we were doing him a favor. He wasn't even breathing hard, or no harder than he usually breathes—the guy must be on his last legs." The front bell rang.

"That must be Harry," said Marlene, rising.

"Or a Cuban gunman," said Karp.

But it was Bello. They had a nice dinner. Marlene made a Sicilian dish, veal rolls with parsley and pine nuts, and Harry had brought a bottle of Vignamaggio Chianti from the city. Harry didn't drink anymore, of course, so Marlene had most of the wine herself, and became quite merry, despite Karp's continually referring to the dinner as the Last Meal. Harry was well briefed on the investigation and the purpose of the trip. The various negative outcomes were not mentioned, not in words, although Marlene and Bello exchanged a number of looks that contained major cable traffic.

In the morning, Karp gave Harry the thick red envelope. "Hide it behind the refrigerator," he said. "They never look there."

Harry accepted the thing solemnly. "Take care of her," he said.

"Take care of Lucy," said Karp, the statement delivered in a tone that allowed interpretation: either "for tonight" or "until age eighteen."

"No problem," said Harry. Meaning, either.

In the airliner, taxiing to the runway, Marlene said, offhandedly, "He wouldn't risk bombing the plane, would he?"

"Marlene," said Karp, "you should wait until we're high in the

air before saying things like that." He slumped in his seat and tightened the safety belt another notch.

No fireball, however, marred an uneventful flight. At Dallas–Ft. Worth International, there was man in the arrival lounge with a sign that said Ciampi/Karp. He was a young blond, with an unstylish crew cut and a roughly triangular physique, his big shoulders straining against a neat tan blazer. He wore brown whipcord trousers over cowboy boots, and a western shirt with a bolo tie. On the clasp of the bolo and the breast pocket of his blazer was a seal that bore a silhouette of a chess queen in white, on a dark green field.

They followed him out of the concourse to where a white Lincoln limo waited. The man held the door while they entered the back and sank into smooth, soft leather, and then he got behind the wheel and drove off.

"It'll be about an hour, folks," the driver said. "There's drinks and things in the little refrigerator there, if you want."

They each took a cold Coke. "Guy really knows how to run an assassination," Karp whispered. "We're going out in style."

Marlene shushed him and looked out the smoked window. As they drove north on the Tollway, suburbs changed gradually into country: wire fences, rolling hills, white-faced cattle grazing in small herds. They left the freeway and proceeded down a succession of increasingly smaller roads until they came to a barred gate with a gatehouse nearby. The man inside it came out and swung the gate aside. He was dressed in the same costume as their driver, with the additional touch of a white Stetson. On the arch over the gate, Queen Ranch was picked out in carved wooden rustic lettering; between the two words was a large plaque with the chess queen emblem.

They drove down a graveled road, across a little stream on a wooden bridge, and there, on a slight rise in the terrain, was the house.

A bribe of four hundred dollars had gained Caballo admittance to the apartment formerly occupied by the couple Marlene called Thug 'n' Dwarf. The Federal Gardens manager was happy to do it, since in its currently wrecked state the apartment was unrentable, and he hadn't gotten around to arranging the repairs. The story the thin man gave

him, of having to hide out from his wife during a messy divorce, made sense to him: he'd had several himself. Cash under the table that he could conceal from his current spouse was always welcome.

Caballo waited for three days, eating cold food and sleeping a lot in the day, on the broken bed, when the man was away at work, with the stuff in his red envelope, and the woman and the child were in and out. He thought he would have to wait for the weekend. They would go out for a family excursion, and the stuff would be left behind and he could pop in and get it. He was fairly confident that he could find anything hidden in the small apartment. If not, he was perfectly prepared to burn the place down.

He listened a good deal at the party wall too, but he could hear little except the sound of the radio or the TV. He hated not knowing what was going on. This should've been a job for half a dozen men, with complete electronics, bugs in every room and on the car. Instead it was just him, more of Bishop's paranoia. During his frequent light sleeps he had fitful dreams of green jungles and red earth, clumps of frightened people, explosions and screams. Pleasant dreams, in which he was in control of the situation. He woke and washed himself, giving himself a whore's bath at the sink, using only a trickle of water to avoid making a sound. There was an old towel on the floor, smelly, but he used it anyway to dry his face and his body. He had known worse dwellings.

On the third day another man came to the apartment and the radio came on loud and stayed on until late. During the night, Caballo found a gallon jar under the sink. There was a hose attached to a spigot outside. He cut a few feet off this and slipped out to his rental car and siphoned gas, filling the jar.

The next morning Karp and his wife left, leaving the other man alone with the child. The radio stayed off, but the man and the child did not leave. Evening came; Caballo stayed alert. He had decided that if the man and the child did not leave, he would burn the place that night.

Around seven, Caballo heard their door slam, the voice of the child and the man's deeper voice telling her not to run in the parking lot, then the sound of a car starting and pulling out.

Caballo waited two minutes. He took a miniature flashlight and a big folding knife and went out the back door. He was actually glad he did not have to burn the place. Sometimes they kept stuff in the refrigerator, where it might survive even a big fire. He intended to be on the last flight to Mexico City once the material was destroyed.

In through the kitchen door; the lock was a joke. He started his search

*from the top, as he had been taught long ago. Large bedroom, the adults'
obviously. Drawers out, scattered, bureaus turned over, closets emptied,
pottery lamp smashed. Nothing. Slash mattresses and pillows. Kick
baseboards and walls. Nothing.*

*Bathroom. Nothing in the medicine cabinet, ripped from the wall, or
the hamper. Nothing in the toilet tank or under the sink.*

*Down the hall. The kid's bedroom. Fling apart the bureau. Overturn
the toy chest. Rip the mattress and the pillows again. Slash apart the
stuffed animals, break the heads of the dolls. Pull down the bookcase.
He made the colorful books fly, tearing the bindings, scattering the pages.*

*He was working fast and efficiently. No more than five minutes had
elapsed since he entered the apartment. A thin sweat lay on his brow,
but his hard breathing was more from excitement than exertion.*

*He folded his knife and put it away and flung open the door to the
closet, shining in the thin beam of his flash.*

*The smell, the hateful smell, the scent of screaming and beating and
choking and shaking. Another person, another's scent was under it somehow, that and the reek of gasoline, soap, and anger, but there it was,
definite, horrible, coming from the figure standing in the closet doorway.*

*Caballo saw the eyes in the thin beam, glowing disks. Another toy,
was his first thought, a teddy bear. Then the eyes moved and he heard
the snarling growl. He backed away a step and something enormous and
black was on him like a piece of the darkness come alive. He was on
his back beating at it with the puny flashlight, struggling to get his knife
out of his pants pocket. There was something wrong with his right hand;
he couldn't move it. Then the pain hit him and he screamed.*

*The taste of blood, forbidden, exciting. The great head heaved, teeth
met, the sharp carnassial teeth at the side of the jaw, cutting through
flesh and tendon and bone. The screams stopped. The bad scent was
gone. Sweetie played with what he had taken for a few minutes, chewing
until most of the juice and all the bad scent was gone, and then went
back into the closet and slept.*

TWENTY

Harley Blaine's house was not the house in the Depuy film. That had been a traditional ranch house with a patio. Karp and Marlene now entered a much larger, more contemporary structure, a place of sheer white walls cut with the narrow clefts of windows.

"The architect was obviously inspired by *The Guns of Navarone*," Marlene whispered as their driver ushered them into an entrance hall tiled in glazed blue Mexican ceramic. "Notice how the house is on a little rise with the trees and shrubs cut back for a couple hundred yards? And the slit windows. The joint is a fortress."

"Yeah, you expect to see Richard Widmark coming down a rope in a watch cap," Karp agreed. "Speaking of movies, what happened to the lion and the scarecrow? And why are we whispering?"

Marlene suppressed a giggle. "I think we're trying to not scream. I wonder where the dungeons are?"

They were led through several doors and found themselves again in sunlight. The house was built around a vast atrium, glass-covered and heavily planted along its borders. Its center was occupied by a large swimming pool. By this stood a hospital-style bed. On the bed lay Harley Blaine.

"Have a seat," said Blaine when they approached the bed. "Welcome to Texas. And the Queen Ranch." They sat in the two elegant sling chairs that had been placed next to a low table by the bedside. "There are refreshments on that little bar by the pool,

and I have arranged a luncheon for you all. I regret that I take my own nourishment nowadays through a tube."

He smiled, a ghastly sight. Blaine was wasted in the manner of victims of end-stage cancer, shocking to Marlene, whose image of him was based on films taken from his early youth onward to maturity. Once a good-sized man with a full head of hair, he had become a living skeleton, his head a death camp inmate's skull bearing a few wisps of dull fuzz. His eyes, however, sunken as they were, still blazed with energy, and with, Marlene thought, an unnatural, puckish glee that seemed almost obscene in so devastated a frame.

She looked at her husband, who appeared distinctly uncomfortable, his skin pale and damp-looking, his jaw tight and twitching, his hands clenching and uncoiling. It occurred to her that the last time he saw someone in this state it had been his mother lying there, and he had been fourteen.

Karp was thinking of his mother, but his discomfort arose from rage. He was considering why the eyes of this criminal, who had done so much evil, should shine so with intelligence and life, while those of his mother, who had been sweet and mild her whole life, had, at the same state in her disease, held nothing but pain and idiotic terror. In was another item in Karp's pending lawsuit against God, and it was all he could do to keep from smashing his fists into the man's face, smashing it like a rotten pumpkin.

Blaine was talking to Marlene again, in his soft, breathy voice, and Karp had to focus his attention to hear what was being said. Small talk. Their flight, the climate, the house. "It's quite an interesting house," he said, naming its features and the famous architect who had designed them. "I regret I can't show you around personally, but—"

"Yes, it's a lovely house, Mr. Blaine," Marlene broke in. "I especially admired the fields of fire."

Blaine chuckled hoarsely. "You *are* a card, ma'am. And observant too, as I have come to know. Yes, the place is defensible, no doubt. I have, or had, some business partners who were at times prone to take extreme measures in pursuit of what they considered proper redress of grievances." He paused and glanced at Karp. "But I see your husband is growing impatient. Perhaps we can turn to the purpose of your visit. This film. What are your inten-

tions regarding this unfortunate item? I trust you understand the effect that publicizing it would have on the Dobbs family."

"Yes, I do," said Marlene. "And I, we, don't have any wish to hurt them. But what I do with the film is entirely up to you, Mr. Blaine."

"Is it? That sounds suspiciously like a blackmailer's speech. What sort of behavior on my part would be satisfactory?"

"Cut the crap, Blaine!" Karp snarled. "You know damn well we came here to find out how you killed Kennedy. So let's have it—from the beginning!"

At first they thought he was having a fit. He had thrown his head back against the pillows and a high rasping noise was emanating from his open mouth. Some tears rolled down his cheeks from his tightly shut eyes. But as Marlene glanced around nervously for someone to call, Blaine's face relaxed, and it turned out that he had only been having a laugh.

"Ahh, how very New York, Mr. Karp! How very tough! Direct and to the point. Well, first of all, I should tell you that when I heard the news about the tragic end of our late president, I was on board the cruise ship *Pride of Norway* in transit between Cancún and Trinidad. Like everyone else, I remember it quite clearly. For some days it cast quite a pall on the public merrymaking, although privately many of my shipmates wept only crocodile tears. The cruise was organized here in Texas, and Mr. Kennedy was not popular among certain circles in Texas."

"But you did it," Karp persisted, "wherever you were personally on November twenty-second. You thought up this whole chess-piece plot, this PXK thing. You're the queen. Bishop was your boy, and Caballo was Bishop's boy. You were neck-deep with anti-Castro Cubans. Your money financed the whole thing, the payoffs to Angelo Guel came from you, and you had Mosca and Guel killed when we got to them."

"There are many conspiracy theories, Mr. Karp," said Blaine in a mild tone. "That would seem to be a particularly florescent one and impossible to prove."

"I know it's impossible to prove," admitted Karp. "That's why we're here blackmailing you into telling us the truth."

Blaine smiled and his eyes sparkled wetly. "Yes, truth. So hard to determine after the passage of years. So far, in many cases, from

justice. 'What is Truth, said jesting Pilate, and would not stay for an answer.' Bacon. Do you know the essay? I see that Miss Ciampi does. I've always wondered whether, if Pilate had stayed for an answer, he would have gotten anything he could've understood from Jesus."

Karp said, "Let's get out of here, Marlene. This guy just wants to blow smoke."

Marlene gathered her purse. "Well, it's been pleasant meeting you, Mr. Blaine. I'm sorry we couldn't come to an agreement."

Blaine flapped his hand, waving them back to their seats. "Sit down, sit down. I'm sick and I tend to ramble." His voice grew sharper. "All right, my direct New York friends, let's horse-trade. You want a full accounting of how John F. Kennedy was killed, in return for which you will undertake to destroy the original of the film you most assuredly have in your possession. Obviously, I will never myself be a witness before any panel or court. I am, in several ways, beyond the reach of the law. In any case, we are not at a deposition, are we? You are not yourselves here in any legal guise, unless during my recent absence from the bar the threat of blackmail has been added to the armamentarium of congressional inquiry. Our status is thus that of . . . I won't say friends . . . acquaintances, doing one another reciprocal favors. I satisfy your curiosity; you relieve a family I cherish from the threat of embarrassment. Agreed?"

Marlene assented immediately. It took Karp longer. At last, he nodded his head, feeling miserable, as his urge to know triumphed over whatever trace of responsibility to the House committee remained in him.

"Well, then," Blaine began, "you might trace my involvement way back to the year 1947. The CIA was a new agency, full of piss and vinegar. It was formed, you'll recall, in the wake of the worst intelligence catastrophe in U.S. history, the penetration of the Manhattan Project by Soviet agents. That the Soviets could, with relative ease, break into the most secret project of all, was on everyone's mind. Counterintelligence on domestic soil was supposed to be the province of the FBI, but we considered them a bunch of clowns, chasing parlor pinks and harmless socialists under the command of a megalomanic fraud. Putting J. Edgar Hoover up against Lavrenty Beria and his men—it was preposterous! And, of course, we feared even worse penetrations. What if they had a mole

in the heart of our political process itself? Such a person, in public office, could do far worse damage than a mere cipher clerk or some such, the sort of people the FBI seemed competent to tackle. So we set up an . . . informal study group, let's say, to discuss the issue. I was a member, and my task was to design a program for the elimination by extreme measures of a prominent American politician known to be in the service of the Soviets: assassination, to be blunt. This was all theoretical, mind; we were just playing safe.

"I therefore studied assassinations with great vigor, and came to the conclusion that in the domestic context, there were only three major approaches: one, the feigned accident; two, the sacrificial *attentat* at close range; and three, the attack at long range, with the assassin escaping. There are problems with all of these. As I'm sure you know, with recent advances in forensic techniques, it is nearly impossible to successfully feign an accident, especially if the victim is important enough to warrant an exhaustive investigation. And the FBI, despite their shortcomings in other areas, are superb in this narrow field. For the sacrificial attack, one needs a madman. Madmen are easy to come by, but difficult to point at the desired target. We tried some . . . experiments. They were unsuccessful, both with natural and induced mania. The third method has many advantages, both in terms of control, and as a way of sending a message to our adversaries that we are onto their plot. But it shares the disadvantage of the first method. It is hard to get away with it. As I pondered this problem, it occurred to me that a melding, so to speak, of the second two methods might offer a solution. That is, if one committed the actual assassination with a trained professional, and was afterward able to blame it on a madman, one might have the best of both. The work would be efficiently done, and the hue and cry and the subsequent investigation would be truncated by the existence of a plausible dupe. I wrote a paper on this, which was quite well received. That was the origin of PXK. It was quite irregular and so secret that it did not bear a standard code name. As far as the CIA proper is concerned, no such project ever existed.

"To understand the next phase, you have to know that every intelligence agency is plagued by volunteers—individuals who wish to become spies. Virtually all of them are useless for real intelligence work, unstable, maniacal, lazy, or criminal types for the most part, but some of them can be used as pigeons, that is, as false

members of a spy network who can distract the attention of counterintelligence operatives, and can be betrayed to them with misleading or damaging information in their heads. Lists are kept of such potential pigeons at foreign CIA stations; I began to keep such a list of American citizens for PXK."

"Oswald," said Karp.

"Indeed, Oswald was precisely the type, but of course, I was long gone from the CIA by the time Oswald entered its purview, during his time as a marine in Japan, in 1958. Nevertheless, PXK was still alive. Lists were still maintained, and a marine spouting Marxist propaganda at a top-secret radar base could not have escaped the attention of those who maintained them. Bureaucracy, even invisible bureaucracy, has considerable inertia. The man you know as Maurice Bishop found Oswald's name and looked him up in Texas in 1962, and cultivated him, using some of our old assets in the White Russian community."

"Okay, we know you knew Bishop from way back," Marlene said. "How did he suddenly surface with reference to Oswald and PXK?"

"Oh, Bishop was quite ready to kill Kennedy from the moment the Bay of Pigs invasion was betrayed. He simply didn't know how to carry it off. He came to me and I told him about the PXK plan and how to find out who was on the current list. There were several potential candidates, but Oswald was by far the best: the infantile Marxism, the megalomania, the propensity for violence, the Soviet defection, even the family link to organized crime. He was perfect. The final joy was when Bishop met Oswald and realized that the man bore a close resemblance to . . . I believe you know him as William Caballo. It was obvious that we had the germ of a perfect PXK operation.

"The next step was to get Oswald deep into the Cuban exile orbit. He was told that he was being prepared to assassinate Fidel Castro, then we switched him to Kennedy. In fact, he did not care at all whom he was going to shoot. He was in it for the thrill. At last he was being taken seriously by important people and embarking on large undertakings. He was told, of course, to maintain his leftist connections, which he did to the extent he was capable of performing any assigned task. The story Bishop gave him was that as a good leftist, it would be easy for him to get close to

Castro, as if even the most incompetent Communist counterintelligence apparat would have taken more than three minutes to see through him. And the Cubans, as poor Bishop learned, are far from incompetent.

"Bishop assembled the other members of the team and gave them the operational names by which you know them. A romantic, Bishop, like so many of the people who entered the CIA just after the war. Of course, PXK gave him the chess theme, so I suppose I am responsible for that bit of fun. The assassination was planned and the necessary arrangements were made, and then everything fell apart. A complete failure."

"What!" Marlene and Karp spoke in unison.

"I mean, of course, the first attempt. In Miami, 1961. Oswald had wandered off somewhere, and missed the pickup. Bishop was in a rare state. He wanted to scratch Oswald and start afresh with somebody else, but I dissuaded him. I recall telling him that we would never again find somebody with so many of the characteristics we wanted in a lone, deranged assassin. Except the ability to fire a rifle accurately, of course, which we did not in this case require. I suggested Dallas as the next venue. This was in June of sixty-three, just after the Dallas speech was scheduled."

"But Oswald only got his job in the book depository in October," said Karp.

"That's right. The book depository wasn't part of the original plan. We were exploring ways to work the thing at the airport, or the Trade Mart where he was giving the speech. I had the group up here for a couple of weeks in late August, early September, to work out alternate plans. It was quite professional, with little models of the various buildings and escape routes. Oswald was very impressed. He stayed on for some special training, we called it, in which drinking and willing ladies figured prominently. During that period, Caballo went to Mexico City. We cut Oswald loose on October third, and he went back to Dallas. He wanted money, which we refused to give him. He had to fit into his background we said, he had to get a regular job. He didn't like that much, but we knew that with serious money in his pocket, he might decide to do anything—go to China, or Australia, or God knows what. As I said, an extremely unstable young man. During the next month, of course, Caballo was also in Dallas, being Oswald, shoot-

ing his rifle, for example, buying ammunition for it, making himself memorable, as he had on the bus trip and at the Communist embassies in Mexico.''

"Oswald gave his rifle to Caballo?" asked Karp in disbelief.

"Of course not. Ah, a clarification. Caballo and Oswald had no contact, of course. Bishop kept them strictly apart at the guerrilla operations and during training. It was Turm and Bishop who acted as intermediaries throughout all of this. Turm got the rifle; he admired the weapon and said he wanted to have it checked out by a gunsmith. Oswald was ridiculously proud of that piece of junk. It also gave us the premise for the real assassination weapons.''

"Real . . . ?"

"Yes. Caballo procured four mint M1938 Mannlicher-Carcano rifles from the same series as Oswald's own. He cut the barrels down, tuned them up nearly to match standards, and fitted them with folding stocks and high-quality optics. The finished weapons were works of art, a little over twenty inches long and concealable under a jacket when they were folded.''

"But the ballistics still wouldn't match Oswald's rifle," Karp objected. He realized he was treating Blaine like just another Kennedy nut with a theory.

Blaine seemed to realize this and gave him a long, humorous stare. "No, but they'd be close, perhaps close enough for government work, as the saying goes, and of course the ammunition was exactly the same as Oswald's. In any case, while this was going on, Oswald got the job in the book depository, in mid-October I think, and shortly after that, the White House added plans for a motorcade to the trip. Bishop, through his sources, was able to get preliminary plans for the route, and when we saw where they intended to go, everything fell into place. The other plans were immediately abandoned and we settled on a shooting from the book depository. Perhaps that was foolish, but I balanced the possibility of something going amiss in a more spontaneous plan against the overwhelming advantage of having the shooting done from Oswald's place of work.

"In the morning, Oswald dutifully brought his silly rifle in his homemade paper sack. The plan called for him to shoot from the second-floor window, from which he had an easier escape route. Just after he arrived, however, Carrera walked in and told him that

the plan had been canceled, that the FBI had become suspicious of him, and that he was to hide his rifle on the sixth floor behind some cartons, lie low, and await orders."

"He *bought* that?"

"Oh, yes. He was already nervous from his earlier contretemps with Agent Hosty. It was plausible."

"Not to mention that he was basically a paranoid maniac to begin with," added Marlene.

"How true," said Blaine. "In any case he did as he was told. Carrera stayed on the second floor and went to the window."

"Nobody noticed him?" asked Karp.

"Another Latino man in work clothes in a book warehouse? This was not the Federal Reserve, Mr. Karp; people were coming in and out with deliveries all the time. Caballo came in about eleven and went to the sixth floor. He talked to no one, but several of Oswald's coworkers saw him and accepted him as Oswald. He removed Oswald's rifle from its bag and arranged the bag and rifle artistically in the places where they were to be found by the police. He placed three spent cartridges from Oswald's rifle, brass that he'd secured at the firing range, on the floor."

"Why three?" asked Karp.

Blaine shrugged. "I have no idea. He was improvising by then. Perhaps he and Carrera agreed that they would only need three shots. Now to the event: the motorcade arrived and made the turn onto Elm Street. Carrera fired first, striking Kennedy in the upper back. Kennedy moved in reaction to that shot, and that threw Caballo's aim off and he hit Governor Connally instead. A few seconds after that, he fired again and hit Kennedy in the back of the head. Carrera folded his weapon, stuck it under his jacket, and walked out the back. He went one street over, where Guel was waiting for him in a station wagon. Caballo picked up his own spent cases and walked down the stairs and out the back too, with the weapon under his jacket. Unfortunately he was seen doing it, which made for some confusion afterward, since Oswald was at that time having his famous Coke in the second-floor lunchroom. Of course, as soon as Oswald learned that the president—not Castro—had really been shot, he realized that something was desperately wrong. He simply left and went home, without even trying to take his rifle. Naturally, Bishop, who had excellent connections

with the Dallas Police Force, was able to leak Oswald's description and address to them. Unfortunately, they dispatched Officer Tippet."

"Why unfortunately," Marlene asked.

"I mean unfortunately for Tippet. Tippet and Oswald knew each other. They were rather birds of a feather, in fact: tough-talking real men with guns. They used to meet at Jack Ruby's place. Oswald had armed himself and was wandering aimlessly. He now must have understood that all his delusions had come to nothing; he was simply being set up as a fall guy for the assassination. When Tippet approached him, Oswald panicked and killed him."

"So Tippet wasn't sent to assassinate Oswald?" asked Karp.

"Not by us, at any rate. No, we had Ruby set up to do that from the beginning. I thought an assassin assassin, so to speak, with organized-crime connections, was a nice touch. The last little item was that Turm went up to Parkland and dropped the magic bullet on a stretcher lying in the hallway. That was, of course, one of the errors; he should have used a banged-up slug; he had plenty, from his target practice with Oswald's rifle. The other error was the shot from the second floor. A proper autopsy would have recognized that this shot was angled upward and could not possibly have come from the sixth floor."

"What about the autopsy?" Karp asked. "Did you fiddle with that too?"

"No, in fact, we simply trusted to the incompetence and confusion of the federal government, a never-failing friend. The Secret Service, the FBI, and of course, our own CIA had all been very derelict, which helped prove my theory. Once a plausible patsy was presented to them, moreover, one who had all the kaleidoscopic qualities of Lee Harvey Oswald, every responsible party would join in the effort to enhance evidence pointing to Oswald and suppress any which did not or which pointed back at the agency in question. And so it proved; as you should know, it is proving so yet."

Blaine relaxed back onto his pillow and closed his eyes. He looked utterly spent. Karp and Marlene waited for him to resume, but instead a dark woman in a nurse's uniform strode out onto the terrace, nodded at the two of them, smiled at Blaine, and said, "It's time, Mr. Blaine." She knelt and released the brakes on the bed, and switched on a motor. Blaine said, "I'm sorry I am unable

to continue for the moment. I have to get my oil changed. Perhaps this would be a good time for you to have lunch."

The mechanized bed rolled off, guided by the nurse. A Mexican in a white coat brought out a tray with an assortment of sandwiches and fruit and set it down on the little table.

They ate without much appetite, speaking little, as if the place were listening, as if Blaine were still there.

An hour passed. The nurse rolled Blaine back to the terrace. He asked how their lunch had been and whether they wanted anything. The treatment he had received seemed to have exhausted him even more. He was speaking very slowly now, with long pauses between thoughts.

"Where were we? Ruby, of course, did his part the following day. He had cancer, you know, and we took care of his family. By that time, the group had scattered. The Dallas police and the FBI combined to make a botch of the evidence. The seed was planted for a thousand conspiracies, of which our little impromptu would appear as just one. I must say, however, that you came as close as anyone to ferreting us out. Bishop was quite beside himself when he learned you had the film and were on to Mr. Mosca."

Karp ignored the implied compliment. "What about the grassy knoll shot?" he demanded. "Who did that?"

"That? If there ever was such a shot, I'm as much in the dark about it as you. Have you ever seen a bullfight? No? Well, on occasion, people in the stands become so overwhelmed by the event that they leap out into the arena and try to work the bull themselves. They call them *espontáneos*. That's what the Grassy Knoll shot was, I believe, an *espontáneo*, one of the many citizens of Dallas who wanted Kennedy dead. Perhaps it was another conspiracy; we certainly didn't have any fake Secret Service men about. Or perhaps it was an *actual* lone nut." He uttered a hacking chuckle. "Ironic, when you come to think of it. All that trouble, my precious PXK operation, the clever plans, and all we had to do was sit back and watch some idiot Birchers with a deer rifle do the job. In fact, if I were still hale, I could take you on a round of bars and barbecue joints in south Dallas and find half a dozen men who'd confess to being the trigger man on the grassy knoll. It's a wonder that anyone in Dealey Plaza survived the day."

Karp asked a few more questions, which Blaine answered with declining strength, about the murders committed as part of the

cover-up. Blaine acknowledged them, but did not seem to know the details. He assumed they had been ordered by Bishop and carried out by Caballo.

"What about Gaiilov?" Marlene asked.

"Ah, yes. Very sad, and very coincidental. Do you know that just this morning poor Armand took his own life by means of a shotgun blast to the head?"

"Caballo again," said Karp.

"Mmm, I rather doubt it. Armand liked the high life. He was a tire salesman and failing at it. Perhaps it was a genuine suicide. So many people die from violence in this country that our occasional additions to the toll are hardly noticed. Some coincidences really are coincidences, you know."

As he listened, Karp found it oddly difficult to retain his interest: the crime of the century, one of the great mysteries of the ages, and it was starting to bore him. It was like being in a French chef's kitchen without the possibility of getting a meal, or like sex without orgasm: why bother?

There was a pause, a silence, broken only by Blaine's labored breathing. Then Marlene said, "Why? Why did you do it? I understand why Bishop and the Cubans did it, but what about you? Why did *you* want him dead?"

Blaine seemed to recover himself slightly. "Oh, that. He had to be eliminated, my dear. He was a Communist."

"Oh, come on! Kennedy was, if anything, a right-of-center Democrat, probably to the right of Johnson if it comes to that."

"Oh, no, I mean he was an *actual* Communist. A covert agent of the Soviet Union."

"Wha-a-a-t!" Marlene cried.

"Yes, it was hard for me to believe too, at first. Gaiilov gave me the story in the late forties. He'd been one of Beria's aides and the old monster boasted about it one night during the war. It didn't mean much then—who could've imagined that this frail little degenerate playboy would become president of the United States some day? But Armand remembered it, and when his own people were after him, and I saved his life, he told me. They'd recruited Kennedy in Prague, in 1939. His father had sent him on a so-called fact-finding tour of Eastern Europe. Pissed the State Department boys off no end. The NKVD leaped at the chance to

compromise the son of one of America's most prominent rightists. They set a honey trap, not the hardest thing to do with JFK, and once he was in the hotel room, they drugged him and set up the cameras. An orgy scene, and not just with girls either. Once he got over his fright, he sort of warmed to the idea. It was a way of getting back at Dad, don't you know. He hated the old bastard, as who wouldn't? The Sovs let him sleep for a long time, of course. They had no idea he would become so prominent so quickly. He may even have imagined that with the war and all, the destruction, they might have forgotten. But when he was safely in the White House, they rang his bell. The Cuban sellout was the first payment. The Reds got a permanent base in the New World and the elimination of a bunch of missiles based in Turkey. And it was just the beginning."

"So you're saying it was simple patriotism!" said Marlene. "Why didn't you go to the authorities, for God's sake, way back then, if you knew?"

"Ah, but way back then, you'll recall, I had made myself persona non grata with the authorities, because of Dick and the trial. And I had compromised Gaiilov totally. No one would've believed him. And, of course, the Prague film we did not have."

"But Dick Dobbs was a spy and a traitor," said Marlene. "For all practical purposes, what you did for him released a vastly more damaging agent, assuming for a minute that I believe your Kennedy story. This is patriotism?"

A look of intense pain passed over Blaine's face, pain that was patently not of the body, pain against which morphine was impotent. "Yes. Quite correct. Of course I did stop what he was doing."

"Ah, right," Marlene exclaimed. "*You* must have turned the FBI onto Reltzin. He always wondered about that."

"Yes, I did that. And then I broke their case against Dick. All I can say in justification is to quote Mr. Forster: 'If I had to choose between betraying my friend and betraying my country, I hope I should have the guts to betray my country.' " A long breath, a winning smile. "But, as you see, I made it right in the end."

They didn't speak at all during the ride back to the airport, not because the driver might have overheard, but because their minds

had been thrown off track, and until they had done some thinking they lacked the ground for a meaningful conversation about what Harley Blaine had revealed. Marlene helped herself to several vodka tonics, but when she asked Karp whether he wanted a drink he shook his head and turned away, staring out at the darkening Texas sky.

In the airport lounge, Marlene finally broke the silence. "There are flaws, aren't there? In what he told us."

"Flaws? *Flaws!*" Karp expostulated. "Marlene, there are holes in that fucking story I could drive a tank through. JFK was a Communist spy? Give me a break! The guy's a fucking maniac, an assassination buff, except instead of saying *they* did it, he's saying *we* did it. Hey, you know what? This shit is enough to make anyone convert to the church of Warren. It's so simple. One nut, three shots, case closed. But then you start thinking about the flaws in Warren and add on all the coincidences and the bitty little connections and before you know it you're back at the Queen Ranch. Or in with the Mob, if that's your fancy."

"But all the evidence leads to Blaine," Marlene persisted. "He knew about all the stuff you found, the chessmen . . . and it fits him, the clever lonely boy who never changed, who never got the girl. . . ."

"Marlene, cut the Psychology 101 crap! Do you honestly believe that John Kennedy was a conscious agent of the Soviet Union?"

For twenty seconds, Marlene tried hard to make herself believe it, if only for the poetic symmetry of the idea. Then she cursed and rolled her eye, and said, "No, hell, that's too weird even for me. The interesting question is whether Harley Blaine believes it."

"Why is that the interesting question?"

"Because this guy is the most fascinating character in the case. Him and Dobbs. Look, in 1950 they were on top of the world. Dobbs could've done what JFK did—House, Senate, Presidency. He was just as attractive, nearly as rich, had a better war record, and a lot more brains. Instead, he decided to screw it all up, and JFK walked off with the prize. And the fact that he was decent to Dobbs after the fall probably just added salt to the wound, from Blaine's perspective. That's one part of it. The other part is the

crazy triangle with Selma—I don't even want to get into that. So, late fifties—he lost his career, lost his hopes for his friend, lost his great love. What does he have left? Control, manipulation. He convinces himself that this spy gossip is true, about JFK. Hell, people have convinced themselves of crazier stuff. And think how satisfying it must have been when he heard it from Gaiilov! A new focus for his life. And Harley just happens to be sitting on a plan for a fail-safe hit on a president. How can he not try it out, and on such a deserving target? The Bay of Pigs fiasco gave him the troops he needed—and the rest . . ."

"Is history. Yeah, and so what!" said Karp, and then, more vehemently, "I hate this. I hate what we just did, I can't tell you how much. And I can see you sort of like it. Your clever plan worked, we got the whole story, assuming it wasn't yet another level of Chinese box, or something a crazy old guy made up out of his head." He slumped and looked away from her across the concourse. "And it's something between us."

"What? You wanted, we wanted to know the story."

"No! Knowing the story is nothing. The *process* is what counts. The ritual, the oaths, the witnesses, the . . . I don't know, the *seeing* that justice is done. We're never going to have that, and that bastard knew that when he set this whole thing up. He's a lawyer, maybe a great lawyer. Maybe only a really great lawyer could have arranged it so that whatever anybody ever learned about JFK, whatever the suspicions, there could never be closure, there could never be a *case*. The wound could never heal. That's his real crime, Mr. Blaine. Christ! Even if we had a tape of what he just told us, what could we do with it?"

"We do have a tape," said Marlene. She reached into her bag and pulled out a small Sony microrecorder. "A hundred and ten eighty-nine at People's."

Karp sighed. "That's just what I mean. It's just another story. It's got no evidentiary context. If I played that thing to Wilkey, he'd laugh me out of his office. Shit, if somebody played it for *me*, I'd do the same. A sick old guy claiming JFK was KGB? Get out of here!"

"It'd be funny, though, if it were true," said Marlene. "Dick Dobbs and Jack Kennedy, birds of a feather, sort of like Burgess and McLean, gentlemen traitors."

Karp welcomed the chance to leave the subject of the assassination. Lately it had started to produce nausea and headache whenever he tried to roll it around in his mind, and he was now fighting a particularly strong attack. He asked, "And so why do you think old Dick did it?"

"Oh, that! Well, maybe he had a crackpot notion that the U.S. shouldn't get too far ahead of the Sovs in nuclear sub design. A lot of the old atom scientists felt that way, especially during the war. But the main reason, the *psychological* reason, you should excuse the expression, I think, was to spit in the world's eye, and maybe in the eye of his best friend, who he'd just found out was fucking his wife. Everybody thought Dick Dobbs was perfect and he couldn't stand it, so he became a traitor. Perfection's an unbearable burden, when you think about it."

"Oh, it's not so heavy," said Karp. "I do all right with it."

She laughed and punched his arm, then leaned against his shoulder and said, "And then there's Hank Dobbs, betraying his trust, his oath too, to protect his father's friend."

"Corruption of blood," said Karp.

"Say what?"

"Corruption of blood. It's in the Constitution. In cases of treason, corruption of blood means any kind of civil disability imposed on a family of a traitor. The Constitution says it can only last as long as the life of the person convicted of treason—after that his family is just like everyone else."

"How little they knew," said Marlene.

Driving home from National Airport, Marlene asked, "Feeling better?"

"Yeah, I guess," said Karp, eyes on the road. "I'm resigned to leaving it to the judgment of history. What if we took all our stuff and just buried it in some library? Just a mass of anonymous evidence, everything we learned."

"Misfile it, you mean? Like under, say, millet production in Hunan 1947 to 1959?"

"Yeah. Somebody will find it someday. I mean, if I give it to Wilkey, it'll just get ripped off and destroyed. I don't want that to happen. And for some reason, I don't want to write a book about it, or give it to an assassination buff.

"Is that dumb? I mean, why bury it?"

"No, I don't think it's dumb at all," said Marlene. "I think it means you still have hope for a better age to come. It's sweet."

At the apartment, a worried Harry Bello met them at the door. "We got hit," he said without preamble. "They trashed the bedrooms and the bathroom upstairs."

"Did they . . . ?" Karp began.

"Nah, I had it with me. Me and the kid went out to get Dairy Queen."

"Where is . . . ?" asked Marlene.

"I got her sleeping in front of the TV. I didn't want her to go upstairs. All her toys are wrecked and there's a lot of blood."

"That's why your friend didn't mind talking," said Karp. "He figured by the time we got back, all our evidence would be gone."

Marlene didn't listen. "Blood?" she cried, digging her nails into her cheeks. "*Mama mia*, they killed the dog!"

"Other way around," said Bello. "Come here, I'll show you." In the kitchen, he indicated where he was nearly finished mopping up a trail of drying, still gluey blood that led from the stairs to the kitchen door. "And this." He went to the refrigerator and brought out a package wrapped in a paper towel. "The dog's fine. It's back in the closet. I found this there."

It was half of a human right hand, the thumb and the first two fingers, badly mangled but all too recognizable. Marlene felt her gorge rise and she turned away. Karp had a similar feeling in his gut but forced himself to examine the specimen. "The top of the index finger's missing," he observed. "Did you look . . . ?"

Harry shook his head, opened his mouth, and pointed to it.

Karp collapsed into a kitchen chair. After a moment, he found himself chuckling. "Well, what do you know? Marlene, if this guy was Caballo, your dog ate the actual trigger finger. Is this a historic moment, or what?"

Marlene stumbled to a cabinet, pulled out a flat pint of Smirnoff, got a glass and some ice, and poured herself a shot. She sat at the table and drank it down. "Correct me if I'm wrong," she said, "but I recall that this is not the first time that we have had human body parts deposited in our actual domicile, is it? Are we doing something wrong?"

"That's too fat a target for me to even swing at," said Karp. "I would modify the 'we' part, however."

Marlene stuck out her tongue at him.

Harry asked, "What should I do with this?"

"I don't know," said Marlene, "we must know somebody who needs a hand." She sputtered and sprayed vodka and ice over the table. There followed half a minute of uncontrollable hysterical laughter; even Harry contributed a few throaty guffaws.

Still laughing, Marlene went to the refrigerator and pulled out a large olive jar. She dumped the olives onto the dish and held the jar out to Harry. He put the hand in it, and Marlene covered the thing with Smirnoff.

"Anyone want an olive?" she asked brightly.

They packed their scant possessions and spent the night in a Holiday Inn in Rosslyn. Sweetie stayed in the car.

"We're going to lose our security deposit," said Karp as they settled in to bed. "And the bill for this and the airfare is going to wipe out our credit. Too bad about Lucy's bone marrow transplant."

"No problem," said Marlene, "I have my special rosary with the plastic beads full of water from Lourdes."

"Oh, right," said Karp, "how could I forget? Seriously, though, what are we actually the fuck going to do?"

"I don't know, go back to the city. Get jobs. Live in our rapidly appreciating loft."

"Oh, God! Interviews!" Karp moaned. "Dewey, Ripoff, and Howe. Are we going to be able to stand it?"

"I always liked Cheating, Poore, Widdowes, and Leffing," said Marlene.

"Hell, you don't have to worry, your good buddy Bloom will take you back."

Oh, shit, thought Marlene. It was like the moment when you're lying on your back after an overindulgence and you know that whatever you do you are going to end up on your knees with your head over the toilet. Marlene sighed and said, "Um, not really." And it all came out.

Karp considered this for a long moment and then said, "You popped him good, huh?"

"Yeah. I think he lost a couple of caps."

"Well, that solves one problem anyway."

"How do you mean?"

"I mean he's gone. I'll take him out. I'll find a way. He'll go. I might let him keep his law license, I don't know. But it'll mean we can both go back to work for the DA."

"You're not pissed?"

"No," said Karp in surprise. "Why should I be pissed? You didn't try to rape him, he tried to rape you."

Marlene felt the most wonderful relaxation seeping into her body; she felt little demons flying in panic out of her fingertips. She started to giggle. "Oh, dear, we can go back to working our asses off among the scum of the earth. What joy! I've never been so happy."

She stretched languorously and rolled over. "But you know what I'd really *like* to do, though. I'd like us to live in a classy midtown hotel, with lots of art deco furniture, and solve high-tone crimes that don't involve severed body parts. Nick and Nora Charles never had to cope with body parts that I can recall."

"Dear, Nick and Nora were childless, wealthy alcoholics, none of which we are. And they were fictional."

"But they had a dog," said Marlene sleepily. "We have a dog. It's a start."

"It's not a start. If you recall, Asta was a cute little thing that Nora could scoop up at a run when she jumped into a cab to chase the bad guy down Fifth Avenue. Your dog is the *size* of a taxicab. It's not the same thing. Marlene?"

"Sleep," said Marlene.

The next day, before they checked out, Karp dressed carefully in a blue suit and went down to the Annex Building to quit, asking Marlene to pick him up at Georgetown University at around noon. He took his raincoat. A front was coming through and the sky was dark and blustery, and rain was falling when he left the metro at Federal Center Southwest.

Wilkey, he learned, was up on the Hill. Karp found a vacant typewriter, hunt-and-pecked out a brief letter of resignation, and left it on Wilkey's desk. Before leaving, he added to his list of recent crimes against the United States by stealing a case box from

the supply room. He transferred the material from the tattered red envelope into the case box and left without a backward look.

Karp stuck the phone message slip back in the box. He read over what he had written and tossed the stack of legal bond into the box too. The other material followed. Carrying his raincoat and the case, he went back into the library archives, row upon row of dusty boxes stacked on steel shelves. He selected a particularly disused-looking section at random and put the case into one of the boxes.

Marlene was waiting for him in her yellow car, just beyond the ornate iron gates. It had stopped raining, or rather the rain had turned into a thick drizzling mist.

"Where to, chief?" asked Marlene.

"Daddy, are we going back to New York?" Lucy asked from the backseat.

"Yeah, baby, but first I want to stop somewhere."

Karp got behind the wheel and drove across the Key Bridge to Arlington. He took the turnoff to the cemetery. "I've never been. I thought we'd pay our respects on the way home."

He parked in the lot. The mist was thicker in the low land by the river. Lucy was delighted with it and trotted up ahead until she was lost from view and then ran back giggling. "Don't get too far, Lucy!" Marlene called out.

They stood in front of Kennedy's grave, with its yellow flame, for a minute or so, in private thought. Then Karp asked, "What about Maggie Dobbs?"

"I was by there while you were in the library. We had tea. I handed over all the material and my notes, except for the film. I think she was glad to see my back, poor lady. But it's her life."

"You told her he didn't do it."

"Yeah. I mean, what the hell! Why should the dead plague the living?" She addressed the grave: "Including you."

"What did you do with it? The film."

"I have it right here." She patted her bag. "You know, the place is deserted. If Lucy wasn't running around, we could rip off a quick one right here. On the grave."

Karp laughed. "Yeah, right. Being him, he'd probably look down and laugh."

"Up and laugh. If Sister Mary Agnes at St. Joe's wasn't just jiving

us about mortal sin and the sanctity of the sacrament of marriage, where he is, he'd have to be looking up."

She stepped forward and took the roll of film out of her bag. She stripped it in long loops off the spool and held an end over the eternal flame. It caught immediately, and the old celluloid stock started burning fiercely. She threw the flaming coils onto the pathway and they watched it, silently, as it turned to indecipherable ashes.

· A NOTE ON THE TYPE ·

The typeface used in this book is a version of Plantin, designed in 1913 by Frank Hinman Pierpoint (1860–1937). Although he was an American, Pierpoint spent most of his life working in England for the Monotype company, which he helped found. The font was named after Christophe Plantin (1514?–1589), a French bookbinder who turned to printing and by midcentury had established himself in Antwerp as the founder of a publishing dynasty—like Pierpoint, one who "made good" away from home. Plantin was not, however, a designer of type, nor was the modern font strictly speaking a revival (Pierpoint was unenthusiastic about Stanley Morison's revivals at Monotype in the 1920s). Plantin was based on what is now known to be Robert Granjon's Gros Cicero font, created for but never used by Plantin, which Pierpoint found in the Plantin-Moretus Museum. Later, its full-bodied but compact quality attracted Morison to Plantin as the model for Times Roman.